PENDLE
COTTAGE

Alan Reynolds

Fisher King Publishing

Dedicated to my family and friends, and to all
those who have supported me in my writing –
your encouragement has been inspirational.
Much love.

A huge thanks to Rick Armstrong for his
unstinting support, guidance, and friendship,
also to Samantha Richardson and Rachel Topping
at Fisher King Publishing.

My thanks also to my very talented niece, Karen Paxton
for her superb cover art work and to Jane Wheater
for editorial and proof-reading support.

Also by Alan Reynolds

Spirits are merely a phenomena that rationalises situations presently beyond our comprehension.

Chapter One

"Dad, are we nearly there yet?" The enquiry was delivered as a plea.

"Hmm, well we're a bit closer than we were ten minutes ago when you last asked, Zack."

"But, I'm hungry." He wasn't letting go.

Jo Drake looked across at her husband. "I think we should take a break, Liam. We've been on the road nearly four hours."

The family Volvo was comfortable with the air-conditioning control set at 'full'. Saturday at the end of July and, despite the early start from their London home, the traffic was busy, the motorway, stop/start in places.

"Yes, ok, keep an eye out for a service station or something."

"How many miles is it, do you think?"

"To the cottage? According to the Sat Nav, about another hundred or so. It depends on the roads; there're no motorways in Cornwall. Should be a couple of hours if we don't keep stopping."

About ten minutes later, Jo spotted a sign. "Oh, look, there, services, half a mile."

Moments later, Liam Drake was guiding the Volvo into the large car park. It was busy, with most spaces taken.

"That family seem to be leaving, I'll ask them," said Jo and lowered the window.

"Excuse me, are you leaving?" she called.

The driver indicated with a thumbs up and Liam waited while the man's over-weight partner climbed into the passenger seat; she seemed stressed. Three raucous children made themselves comfortable in the back.

With the manoeuvre completed, Liam gave a polite wave to the driver and drove into the vacant parking spot.

"Did you see that woman's face? Obviously wasn't enjoying <u>her</u> holiday."

"Yes, but with three teenagers, I think I'd be pretty stressed too," said Liam.

"That's true. Come on Zack, Far, make sure you put your games away. You don't want to get them pinched."

Ten-year-old Zack and his eight-year-old sibling, Farrah, had been playing computer games since they had left home.

The family exited the car. Liam, early forties – young for a top barrister, was dressed comfortably for the drive; jeans, short-sleeved shirt, trainers. Nearly six-foot, with well-groomed fair hair, he walked alongside his wife, Jo, a physiotherapist, while the two children skipped towards the entrance.

A coach party was just leaving, creating a bottleneck which took a few moments to clear. It was a typical trunk road service station with an array of shops close to the entrance and a filling station with petrol at exorbitant prices.

"Right, first stop, toilet. Do you want to go, Zack?" said Liam.

"Yeah," said the lad and followed his dad to the gents, while Jo escorted Farrah to the ladies.

Having completed the toilet, the family reconvened and made their way to the cafeteria.

"Find a seat; I'll get the drinks," said Liam.

"Can I have a chocolate brownie?" asked Zack.

Liam looked at Jo who frowned, then nodded. "Go on, why not? I'll have one too; we're on holiday."

The family eventually settled on a four-seater table to enjoy their refreshments.

"Hey, these are really scrummy... Good choice, Zack,"

said Jo and turned to her son. "You've got chocolate all 'round your mouth; you'll get it everywhere. Wait, let me get a tissue."

She rummaged through her rucksack and handed Zack a Wet-Wipe.

"Have you got the folder with you?" asked Liam.

Jo was back in the rucksack and handed him a foolscap plastic folder containing various documents.

Liam started to look through.

"Just want to check when we can collect the keys."

"From two o'clock, I think it said," advised Jo.

Liam checked his watch. "Well it's two now. It'll be nearer four when we get there, I reckon."

He looked at the photo of the cottage. "I hope it lives up to the billing in the brochure. It said a new let."

"You can always sue them under the Trades Description Act," said Jo.

"Ha, I've got enough cases on the go without taking on any more. Which reminds me."

Liam took out his mobile phone and checked his messages.

"I thought we were going to dispense with phones for three weeks."

"Sorry, force of habit," replied Liam, but continued scrolling through his emails anyway.

"You said Sunita was handling your cases?" said Jo.

"Yes, she is, but I did say to contact me if she had any problems."

"Oh, great! So you'll be back and forward to your Chambers every five minutes."

Liam turned off his phone. "No, no, no, just in emergencies."

Jo frowned.

"Promise," said Liam. "Right, if you're ready, let's go on holiday. Next stop, Polgissy."

"Ha, you hope," said Jo. "You watch, there'll be tailbacks as soon as we get to the hotspots."

"Well, not necessarily, the brochure did say it was quiet, for those wanting to unwind. It was one of the reasons we chose it if you remember."

"Hmm, we'll see," reposted Jo.

"You're such a sceptic."

"No, just realistic. If something seems too good to be true, then it usually is."

Liam smiled. "Come on guys, let's get this show back on the road."

The family exited the Services and headed for the car. The sun was now making its presence felt. It was a glorious summer's day, the end of July, and the excitement of a holiday put everyone in a good mood.

They made themselves comfortable and buckled up.

"Just check the Sat Nav," said Liam and the dashboard screen lit up with a map, the predicted mileage and journey time. "Hm, no reports of any jams. We may be lucky."

Jo turned and addressed the children. "Anybody want water?"

"No, thanks," said Zack. Farrah shook her head, eyes firmly concentrating on her games console.

With about fifty miles to go, Liam was virtually on autopilot. The Sat-Nav with its digitalised voice was providing occasional updates; the radio was playing in the background. Thoughts of work and the recent court case was still on his mind; it would take a few days before he could switch off.

As a major trunk road, it was a dual carriageway. The

verges were lush and verdant. Woods, farmland passed by; the scenery was spectacular. Jo was admiring the views, relaxing in the warmth of the sun as it streamed through the windows.

BANG!

From nowhere, something hit the windscreen and bounced into the road. Blood was smeared down the glass.

"God, that made me jump," said Jo. "What was it?"

"A crow, I think. A dead crow now," said Liam, and started the washer to remove the mess on the windscreen.

"Dad, what was that?" said Farrah drowsily, from the back seat.

"Just a bird, Far."

"Oh, that's a shame."

The incident had certainly woken up Liam; he was shaking.

"Isn't it bad luck to kill a crow?" asked Jo.

"Well it is for the crow," replied Liam and chuckled. "I think that old wives' tale referred to a magpie."

It was nearly two hours later; the Volvo was on a minor road, being directed by the comforting voice of the navigation system. There seemed to be little traffic.

"How much further?" asked Jo. "I could do with the loo."

"And me," shouted Zack.

"Me too," added Farrah.

"Yes, ok, I could do with stopping too. According to the Sat Nav, it should only be five minutes. Look, there's the turning, 'Polgissy two miles'." Liam pointed to an old road sign, one of the white ones with black script; it was leaning down slightly.

"Well, that was a good spot," said Jo.

"Yes, I'm not sure why the Sat Nav didn't pick it up."

Liam indicated left and made the turn.

They were immediately surrounded by an impenetrable forest of trees, thick with foliage.

"Good grief, this is a bit narrow," said Liam.

The carriageway was only wide enough for one car. There were passing points every hundred yards or so where the verge had been worn to accommodate two vehicles. The trees seemed to be enveloping them.

"Yes, I can see why the brochure said it was off the beaten track; no one's found it yet," said Jo and started to laugh.

Liam's attention was suddenly drawn to the dashboard. "That's strange..."

"What's the matter?" asked Jo.

"The Sat Nav's gone blank. Look, there's no map."

Jo stared at the dashboard screen. "Yes, you're right."

"It's probably why it didn't pick up the turning. I wonder if there's a Volvo garage about. I can get it checked out."

"You're kidding, I bet the nearest one's Plymouth or Penzance," said Jo.

"Hmm, yes, you're probably right. I'll check the website later and see."

Jo turned around. "Are you two ok?"

"I don't like all these trees," said Farrah. "They're scary."

"Don't worry, Far, we'll be out of them soon," said Liam. "Look, it's brighter ahead."

"It's like we're in a tunnel," said Jo. "Feels weird."

Moments later they were out of the trees.

"There, that wasn't so bad, was it?" said Liam. "What the...? Where's this come from?"

"Fog? In July? Now that is_ weird," said Jo, leaning forward and looking up at the sky.

"I can hardly see a thing. It must be the hills."

The car was moving at little more than walking pace.

"What's that?" asked Liam, pointing to a shape, just visible on the left-hand roadside through the white murk. It was an object covered in creeping ivy. Jo dropped down the window to take a closer look.

"It's the village sign, Polgissy."

"Hmm, well it looks like we've arrived."

"Someone needs to clean the ivy off that sign; it's hardly readable."

"Look, the fog's clearing. Wait, what's that?" said Liam.

Liam slowed the car again. The high verge had dropped for about three feet and was festooned with ribbon, flowers, candles and cuddly toys; there was a metal container with a lit candle inside.

"Oh, it's one of those roadside shrines. I don't know why people do that; it's just too morbid for words," said Jo. "Look there're teddy bears as well as flowers; must be a child, how sad."

"Can you turn off that game, Zack? Your Dad's trying to concentrate," said Jo.

"It is off."

Jo turned around and could see the game console on the seat.

"What's that noise?" said Jo.

"It sounds like children playing," said Farrah.

"I can't hear anything," said Liam and pressed the accelerator.

Jo dropped down the window. "It's stopped now."

"I think you were imagining things."

"I did hear something. So did Far, didn't you Poppet?" Jo turned to her daughter.

"Yes, Mom, children's voices."

"Hmm, it's a mystery, probably ghosts," said Liam, and chuckled.

Jo had moved on and was looking at the sky. "I can't believe how the weather's changed; there's hardly a cloud."

The road had widened, but not by much, and, after some wasteland, the first cottage appeared on the right-hand side. The dwelling was stone-built, one would say of typical Cornish design; a two-up, two-down cottage. It had been whitewashed and, having left the fog behind, it shimmered in the sun. It marked the start of a very steep downwards hill.

"Look, guys, there's the sea," shouted Jo.

Before them, the ocean stretched out into the horizon, azure blue, shimmering in the sun. There was a modest harbour with a few small fishing boats bobbing at their anchorage inside, then a short piece of sand before the sea wall and the road. Flocks of seagulls peppered the sky and foreshore; many lined up on the breakwater taking a breather from their scavenging.

The village was surrounded by hills and steep cliffs as if protecting it from outside forces. Telegraph poles were the only blot on the landscape. Wires seemed to criss-cross the village in all directions.

The children unbuckled their seatbelts, leaned forward and peered over the front seats.

"Hey, that looks so pretty," said Farah.

"Can't wait to swim in that," said Zack.

The downhill road continued. Liam's foot was firmly on the brake to prevent it careering forward. It was flanked by more cottages of a similar design to the first, and went on for about a quarter of a mile before they reached the bottom, at which point the road turned sharp right and ran parallel to the sea wall. There were double yellow lines. Liam noticed them.

"Ha, not quite the land that time forgot. I see the council have made their presence felt. We need to park somewhere and find out where we need to collect the keys."

"Look, there's a pub," said Jo, and pointed to the line of sea-front properties on the right. It stood out from the rest of the cottages.

"They should have parking, hopefully," added Liam.

"Yes, and a loo," said Jo. "There, between the pub and the next house, there's a sign. It says, 'car park'."

"Got it," said Liam and turned cautiously into the narrow drive to avoid scraping the car's wing mirrors.

It opened into a small car park, with room for about ten vehicles. Liam pulled into one of the many vacant spots. The only other car was a ten-year-old Skoda which looked like it had seen better days.

"Doesn't look very busy," commented Jo, seeing the empty spaces.

"No, you're right," said Liam, as he got out of the car. "Come on guys, let's go and explore."

He stretched his back before picking up his wallet from the glove-box.

The family got out of the Volvo and Liam aimed the fob at the car. The indicators flashed to confirm locking. They turned left out of the car park, and walked the short distance to the pub entrance.

"Can we go and see the sea?" said Zack, excitedly, looking across at the small harbour to the right.

"Yes, later, let's get a drink first and something to eat. We can use the loos, too."

"Oh, that's quaint," said Jo, looking up at the swinging sign above the door. "'The Crab Pot', how unusual."

The sign looked worn and very old with a painting of a crab pot, confirming its name.

The narrow doorway was low and Liam instinctively ducked as he walked in; although he might just have managed it without the stoop. Inside, the pub was dark after the bright sunshine and it took a moment to adjust their eyes. There were no other customers.

"What would you like to drink?" whispered Liam, still stretching his back. There was no reason to whisper, but for some reason, it seemed appropriate.

"Oh, I think a G and T is in order after that journey."

"What about you, Zack?"

"A Coke, please."

"And me," said Farrah.

"I'll get the drinks, find a seat," said Liam and went to the bar.

The bar counter was lit with small ceiling spotlights which cast downward shadows. A man entered the serving area from a back room. Liam squinted to make eye contact. The man's face was lined with significant bags under his eyes, as if he hadn't slept for a week. Thin wisps of white hair protruded from underneath a flat cap. He was dressed in dungarees and a white shirt, resembling a fisherman. He approached Liam.

"Yes, m'dear, what can I get you?" The dialect was soft, and typically Cornish.

"Two Cokes, a G and T, and half a lager," responded Liam.

Liam looked around the pub; it seemed like someone's front room. There were a few, maybe ten, wooden tables with cast-iron legs and matching chairs on a stone floor. Wooden beams ran along the ceiling, signs of a bygone age. The walls still retained tobacco stains from a time when the pub would be filled with smoke from cigarettes and corncob pipes.

The counter was also wooden, a stained hardwood, which glistened from years of polish. Two long towel mats protected it from spills.

The landlord dispensed the drinks and lined them up on the counter.

"Do you do food at all?" asked Liam.

"I can do you a sandwich or two; we don't do no 'ot food."

"Is there a restaurant around here?"

"What in Polgissy? Sorry."

"Not even a fish and chip shop?"

"Not much call for one of them. We don't get many visitors, being a bit cut-off, like."

"What about shops? There must be one of those."

"Aye, at the end of the road by the hawn, Mrs Trevelyan's, but you'll need to look sharp; she closes at five."

Liam checked his watch, twenty-to. He had no idea of the meaning of the word 'hawn' but said nothing, not wishing to appear stupid.

"Right thanks."

"Do you want a tray for the drinks?"

"Oh, yes please."

The landlord reached under the counter and pulled out a circular metal tray, decorated in the emblem of the owning brewery. Liam paid for the drinks. "Where are the loos?"

"Toilets're just through there," replied the landlord, pointing to a door the far side of the bar.

Liam returned to the family. A red-coloured, padded bench seat ran along the far wall, and Jo and the children had made themselves comfortable on a table in the corner. There was a small window, the size of a porthole, with a view of the road and harbour beyond. Zack was kneeling on the bench, looking through.

"The loos are over there," said Liam, pointing to the door indicated by the landlord. "I don't know what you want to do for food; they only do sandwiches here. He says there's a shop up the road but they close at five."

"Well, we'll need something more substantial than sandwiches, I'm starving."

"Look, I'll go and see what they've got; you can look after the kids," said Liam.

"No, it's ok; I know what we need. I don't suppose there'll be any food in the cottage. I'll do an essentials shop; milk, butter, bread, cereals, and see if they have any ready meals, something quick. I don't want to be cooking all night. It's a good job we bought the tea and coffee."

"Yes, ok, you better get going."

"I'll just pop to the ladies."

"Ok, I'll look after the stuff," said Liam.

Jo got up and was quickly joined by the children and headed for the toilets.

A few minutes later, she collected her rucksack from the bench-seat and headed for the exit. Liam took a sip of his beer and turned to Zack.

"So, what do you think?"

"It's a bit dead," he replied.

"No, you wait there'll be loads to do, you'll see."

"Do you want some crisps?"

"Oh, yeah, thanks," said Zack.

"Yes, please, Dad," said Farrah.

Liam went back to the bar via the gents. The landlord had retired to the back room and returned seeing there was custom.

"Yes, m'dear."

"Three packets of crisps, please."

"Any particular flavour? We got all sorts now."

"Just plain, please."

The landlord returned to the back room and produced the

snacks. Liam paid.

"You don't know where I can find Mrs Thornton, do you? I need to collect some keys."

"You're staying here then?" His voice had an inflection of surprise.

"Well, yes, that's the general idea. I need to pick up the keys from a Mrs Thornton it said in the letter, only my Sat Nav's on the blink."

"Aye, they don't work 'round 'ere; no signal, you see... no internet, neither."

"What do you mean?"

"Well, it's like this; we got no signal down 'ere.; it's the hills. We've been onto Council but they don't do nothin'. Low priority, they said, too expensive."

"The squire next to the old rectory's got internet. 'Ad to pay for it, mind. 'Ad to dig a trench, they did, all the way to the main road, took weeks."

"Oh, I see." Liam's face was etched with disappointment and was thinking through the implications. He had hopes of keeping in touch with his Chambers, despite his promise to Jo.

"So, where you stayin' then, only we don't have no hotels here?"

"Er, my wife's got the details. I can't remember, off hand. Hmm, let me think. Yes, Pendle Cottage, could it be that? Is that right?"

"Pendle Cottage? Are you certain?"

"Yes, I think so. As I said, my wife's got the folder with all the details in it."

The landlord, deep in thought, picked up a glass and started wiping it with a cloth.

"Oi didn't know they was renting it out, but I knows someone's been doing it up. Been up for sale since January.

Not been able to sell it, I expect. Mind you, I'm not surprised."

"Why's that?"

"The murder."

"Murder!?"

"Aye, back in January it were, terrible goings on. About the same time as the Morgan girls were killed."

"A murder, you said? But that's dreadful."

"Aye, that it were."

"So, what happened? If you can tell me."

"Folk 'round 'ere don't like to talk about it much. It were in the newspapers, though. We had people from Plymouth, even Exeter, all over, down here, journalists an' that. Oi 'ad to order in more ale." His voice tailed off.

"Oh, I'm sorry. What about, the girls? You mentioned something about the girls."

"Oh, aye, that was only a couple of days later, it was. Mrs Morgan over at Fairland Cottage; she were a writer, 'ad twin girls, her did. Beautiful they was, just six-year-old - Meli and Clementine. So 'appy they was. Hit by a car; bowled over like nine pins."

The landlord looked down, clearly upset.

"Where was this?" said Liam, ignoring the man's distress.

The landlord looked up; his eyes were bloodshot. "Just as you comes in from the top road. There's flowers an' things up there."

"Oh, yes, we saw them when we came in. That's so sad"

While Liam was finding out more about the village, courtesy of the landlord, Jo walked along the row of cottages towards the shop. Several of the houses had their front doors open allowing passers-by to look inside. It seemed most belonged to fishermen, judging by the crab and lobster pots visible.

Jo reached the shop; it wasn't quite what she was expecting, visualising a typical convenience store. It was a converted cottage with the downstairs transformed into a shop. A faded 'Bero flour' advertisement on the side of the building, probably dating from the nineteen-forties, was the only indication of a retail establishment.

The front door was open, with an umbrella-holder containing about twenty fishing nets wedged against it to stop it from closing. Immediately in front of her was a carousel containing faded picture postcards of the surrounding countryside and Cornish scenes. Jo took a quick glance; there seemed to be no cards featuring Polgissy. She was intending to send one back to her mother. There were also no buckets and spades one would normally associate with a seaside store, but there was a small stock of fishing equipment, Jo noticed.

With limited natural lighting, just the one side window, the interior was quite gloomy and not particularly conducive for a retail experience. To the left, below the window, were a series of wooden pallets containing fresh vegetables, then a freezer cabinet. A wide variety of tinned food was displayed on the right-hand side, including soups, baked beans, spaghetti and so on. The serving counter was immediately in front of Jo, with an array of chocolate bars and other confectionery, placed strategically in front of it to encourage impulse buying.

The figure behind the counter had been sitting on an old stool and stood up with difficulty when she detected a customer.

"Wasson, m'dear, can I help you?" Jo had been scouring the merchandise and the greeting startled her.

"Oh, hi, yes, I need something for dinner. Do you stock any ready-meals?"

"Only frozen, I'm afraid, m'dear. Should be some in the freezer cabinet, next to the ice creams."

"Thanks," said Jo, and started rummaging through the produce. The range was not great but there were three shepherds' pies at the bottom which looked like they had been in there for a while judging by the 'snow' sticking to them. Jo was in danger of falling in head first but managed to retain her balance and extricated herself from the freezer clutching the items. She also took a tub of ice cream, then approached the counter.

"I need some bread, milk, and, er, breakfast cereals."

"Right you are m'dear. I keeps the milk in the fridge; won't be a minute. How many pints?"

"Four, if you have them."

"Aye, should have. The cereals are in the corner." She pointed to the appropriate section.

Jo scanned the selection, no muesli, just Corn Flakes, Puffed Wheat, and a few other traditional brands. She picked up a packet of Sugar Puffs and started to read the ingredients; salt and sugar content were both red. She tutted and picked up a packet of Shredded Wheat; not great but it would do.

"There's some porridge at the back," came a voice from the counter.

"Oh, thank you, yes." Jo replaced the Shredded Wheat, picked up a box of porridge, and took it to the counter.

Jo could see the woman more clearly; she looked like she was in her late-seventies and moved in a laboured fashion, as if every action was painful. She was dressed in a blue overall, which would be fashionable in the nineteen-sixty's. Her demeanour was not typical of someone running a shop; her expression was dour, straightforward to the point of rudeness.

"Will that be all?"

"Oh, sorry, bread, yes, mustn't forget that, and butter. We'll need some toast to keep us going in the morning."

"Aye, butter's in the fridge." The woman seemed annoyed she had to make another journey to the refrigerator. She returned with a loaf of bread and the butter.

"Do you have any sliced?" asked Jo.

"Sorry, all gone; this is the last of it till Monday. We don't get delivery on a Sunday."

"Oh, ok that will have to do."

"Will that be all?"

The giant clock behind the counter, which looked like it may have come from a railway station, clicked over to five o'clock.

"Yes, thanks. Do you have a carrier bag, please?"

"Aye, I have somewhere; need to charge you for it, though. It's the Government, not me."

"Yes, that's ok, no problem."

The woman started putting the produce in a large plastic carrier bag.

"Staying local are we?" she said as she started to key the amounts into the till.

"Yes, Pendle Cottage. Do you know it?"

She stopped abruptly.

"Pendle Cottage? Are you sure?" Her face was one of concern.

"Yes, wait, I've got the brochure somewhere." Jo rummaged in her rucksack and pulled out the document. "There, Pendle Cottage."

The woman stopped loading the carrier bag and stared at the photograph on the front. "Hmm, they should have pulled it down; some folks 'round 'ere reckon the place is cursed."

"Why would you say that?"

"Oh, no reason." She noticed Jo was holding a debit card.

"I'll just get the machine."

The transaction was completed and the woman handed Jo the bulging carrier bag.

"Mind how you go," said the woman and followed Jo to the front door.

Jo had stepped onto the street and turned to say something to the woman, but the door slammed shut. She could see the woman changing the hanging sign from 'open' to 'closed'.

Jo was in deep thought as she walked back to the pub. To her right, on the other side of the road, lobster pots had been stacked on the sea wall. She couldn't remember seeing them earlier.

She entered the pub and squinted until her eyes once again became accustomed to the gloomy interior. She saw the family in the corner.

"Hi," said Liam as Jo approached. "How did you get on?"

"Not bad; at least we won't starve. Actually, we better get going. There's some frozen stuff in the bag; it'll start melting."

"Yes, we're ready. The landlord's given me directions to Mrs. Thornton's; it's not far."

The family approached the exit just as the landlord came out of the back room.

"Thanks," shouted Liam and waved.

"Mind 'owye goes," said the landlord.

The family left the pub to be greeted again by bright sunshine.

"So, where's this place then?" said Jo as they turned right. She was holding the carrier bag in her arms and not by the handles.

"Just along here. Do you want to dump the shopping?" said Liam.

"No, it'll be stifling in the car; I'll manage," said Jo.

They followed the pavement towards the grocery store. Liam was looking along the row of cottages.

"He said there was an alleyway just before the shop. A nip, he called it."

They walked a few more yards. "Yes, here it is."

"Do you know, I never noticed that. I must've walked right past it," said Jo.

"Well, it's not that obvious, why would you? Second cottage on the right, he said."

The family turned up the narrow path; it was just wide enough for a car. Ruts in the compacted ground suggested it had been used for that purpose. It was predominantly grass and weeds.

On the right-hand side there was a row of three terraced cottages. There, 'Brook Cottage', that's it. Wait here; I'll go and see what's happening."

There was a small crazy-paved footpath leading to the front door. Liam noticed a net curtain twitch and the front door opened before he reached it.

"Hello, you must be Mr Drake."

Liam did a double take. She was much younger than he was expecting, probably the same age as himself, attractive, with long dark hair, and dressed in skinny jeans and a tee shirt.

"Oh, yes, and family," said Liam pointing to Jo and the kids at the top of the path. He chuckled. The woman waved.

"I'm April Thornton, pleased to meet you. Do you want to come in and have a cup of tea? You would be very welcome after that long drive."

"That's very kind of you, but I think we need to get settled in. We've got some shopping that needs to go in the fridge."

"Yes, ok, just a minute." The woman went back inside

and returned with the keys and a piece of paper.

"There're the keys and some information. Oh, yes, while I remember, you'll need some change; the electricity's on a meter, under the sink. Pound coins."

"Oh, thanks for the warning, I'll stock up."

"The sheets are fresh on this morning, and I've put some basics in the pantry; you'll see. If there's anything you need, just let me know. Unfortunately, there's no mobile phone signal in the village, but there's a phone box just on the corner; it's close to the cottage. My number's on that slip of paper."

"That's very kind. Where do we go?"

"Oh, yes, of course. It's along here till you get to the shop, then turn right." She indicated with hand signals. "It's up a bit of a hill, then about two hundred yards, there's a turning to the left which leads to the church, you'll see it; take that turn. Then just after the church the road bends to the right; you'll see the phone box I mentioned, on the corner of a cul-de-sac; the cottage is right in front of you. You can't miss it."

"That's very kind, thanks; I'm sure we'll find it."

The family left the cottage and headed back to the car. A few minutes later, Liam was driving along the road next to the sea wall. The tide appeared to be on the turn. They passed the shop and immediately turned right, as instructed, up the steep hill. The road was not much more than a car's width wide with cottages on either side. Pebble-dashed concrete walls separated their small frontages from the street.

After a short distance, they reached the church turning and made a left; the small ancient spire was in view. There was a patch of ground adjacent to the church wall, presumably for cars. The road passed by to the right and then the telephone kiosk appeared.

"There, that must be it," said Liam, pointing to the object, and turned right into a cul-de-sac.

In front of them was a thatched dwelling, set back from the road.

With a chimney stack on one end, it appeared larger than the other cottages in the village. The windows were traditional but looked as if they had been recently painted. There was a patch of lawn at the front, encased by a three-feet high trellis fence. It all looked neat and tidy.

"Well, we've arrived," said Liam, as he parked up outside.

"It looks like it backs onto the trees," said Jo. "There's not much daylight at the rear."

"Hmm, I see what you mean," said Liam surveying the landscape. "Let's get our things inside, and we can have a look around."

There was a small gate which opened onto a paved footpath to the front door, less than fifteen yards away.

"Dad," said Farrah, in one of her pleading voices. She was also looking at the house. "I don't like it here; it's spooky."

"No, Far, it'll be fine when you get used to it; you'll see."

Liam grabbed one of the large suitcases from the back of the Volvo and led the way down the path. He took out the keys from his pocket. The front door was old and latch-opening but a more substantial lock had been added later together with a letterbox.

Liam opened the door and went inside; the family followed, each carrying some luggage.

The door opened directly onto a large lounge. A mix of smells greeted them, furniture polish and a hint of paint. There was something else, too, not particularly pleasant.

"It's a bit stuffy in here, I'll open a few windows when we've got settled," said Jo.

The 'lounge' was tastefully furnished, and decorated in

a neutral magnolia colour. The centre-piece was a brown, patterned three-piece suite with matching cushions. There was a dining table, big enough for four people and accompanying chairs, and a bureau in the corner. An electric fire dominated the right-hand wall in what looked like the original fireplace. The chimney had been blocked off but the brick flue was still visible rising up through the ceiling.

Zack looked around the room, his expression, one of horror. "Where's the TV?"

"Hmm," said Liam. "It doesn't look like there is one."

"What? But I thought all houses had TV's."

"Not in Cornwall, it seems. But, hey, maybe that's a good thing; we do spend too much time watching it. We can make our own entertainment."

Zack was not for appeasing. "But what are we supposed to do?"

"Oh, I'm sure there'll be lots to do," said Liam, positively. "Come on let's take a look upstairs."

"I need to put this shopping away before it spoils," said Jo.

"Yes, ok, let's check the kitchen first."

There was a door at the back of the room in the left-hand corner, which Jo opened. Again, it was spotlessly clean, not particularly big, but with most of the usual appliances including an electric cooker, sink, and drainer. There was a microwave on top of the worktop.

"Oh, there's no washing machine. Looks like we're going to need to find a launderette," she exclaimed, with a hint of complaint.

After the sink, there was a side door with frosted glass panels which opened to the back garden. The fridge was next to another door which Jo opened.

"Oh look, a pantry, how quaint," Jo observed.

She opened the refrigerator door. "Oh, no, it's not working, the electricity's off."

"Yes, it will be. Wait, let's put some money in the meter."

Liam opened the cupboard under the sink and, sure enough, the electricity meter was situated just to the right of the downpipe. He took out three pound coins from his pocket and fed them into the slot. Immediately the kitchen light came on and the fridge burst into life.

"I don't think it will take too long to start cooling. It's not a bad size; there's plenty of room for your shopping," said Liam, and moved out of the way so Jo could get to it.

Jo started to unpack the carrier bag and placed the perishable contents in the fridge, then went back to the pantry to investigated further. "Oh, that's good; there's some bread, and vegetables. There's some tinned stuff, too. How thoughtful."

"Come on, guys, let's check upstairs," said Liam, leaving Jo to look after the kitchen.

There was a door at the other side of the lounge. Liam opened it and to the left, a flight of stairs.

He manoeuvred the suitcase to the bottom, then started lugging it to the first floor. The wooden staircase was steep and covered with a carpet tile on each step. They creaked and groaned under the weight as Liam progressed slowly upwards.

He reached the landing. There was a large bedroom to the left which overlooked the front of the house and two smaller rooms to the right. Beyond the master bedroom was another door which turned out to be the bathroom. Liam took a quick peek, then turned to Zack and Farrah who were still stood at the top of the stairs.

"Hey, kids, choose your rooms, but no fighting, eh?"

Zack made a beeline for the first door. "I'll have this one;

Far can have the other."

There appeared to be no disagreements and Farrah took her bag with her bits and pieces next door.

Liam had a quick check of the main bedroom. It was as advertised in the photo in the brochure, a large double bed, dressing table, and wardrobes. The walls were plain, nondescript, and the smell of paint more obvious. He went to the window and opened it. He could see the church spire and more trees, and, shimmering in the distance to the left, the sea.

He left the suitcase next to the bed and went into Zack's room.

There was a single bed and tall boy; the décor matched the master bedroom. Zack was looking out of the window.

"So what do you think?"

"Yeah, it's cool. What's that?"

Liam joined him. There was an overgrown garden with an ancient sycamore tree against the boundary wall at the end of a crazy-paved path about a hundred yards from the cottage. Immediately to the left was what looked like an outbuilding of some sort. The other side of the dry-stone wall was a small cemetery. It was surrounded by trees.

"I don't know; I can't make it out. We'll go and take a look when we've unpacked."

Just then Farrah came into the room, sobbing.

"Whatever's wrong, Far?" said Liam.

"I don't want that room; There's somebody in there."

Chapter Two

Liam went to her and put a consoling arm around her shoulders. "Hey, come on, stop crying, what makes you say that?"

"I heard somebody talking," Farrah was shaking.

"No, you must be imagining things. Come on, let's go and look."

"No! I don't want to go in there."

"It's ok, I'll come with you."

Liam walked the short distance to Farrah's room; she was right behind him, still shaking, followed by Zack. Liam entered the room and looked around.

It was very similar to Zack's room except, instead of a tallboy, there was a built-in wardrobe set back into the wall on the left-hand side. The single bed was quite a substantial affair, contained in an old brass bedstead, probably fifty years old; it was positioned against the opposite wall.

Liam opened the wardrobe doors and looked inside. It was empty, except for a few metal coat hangers, the sort you would get from a dry cleaner. As he looked more closely, he noticed, like the other rooms, it had been painted with a pale yellow, but there appeared to be drawings underneath the paint, a child's handiwork, by the look of it.

"Look, Far, there's no-one here; I think you were imagining things. You're probably tired from the journey."

Farrah slowly entered the room and looked in the wardrobe, then at the bed. Liam made a point of looking underneath it. "There's nothing here, Far, no bogie-men or ghosts; I promise."

She was calmer now.

Liam again put a consoling arm around her. "Come on,

let's unpack your things; we can make it look like home."

Farrah put her small rucksack on the bed and opened it. Slowly she took out her soft toys and computer games.

"Is there a plug for my game?" asked a tear-stained Farrah, handing Liam her games console.

"Well, there should be." Liam checked the skirting board. "Yes, there. Wait, I'll plug it in for you."

After a few minutes, Farrah had her various soft toys lined up on her pillow and her game console in operation. Her initial apprehension seemed to have dissipated.

"If you guys are ok, I'll just check on your Mom."

With Zack also now playing computer games and not answering, Liam took this as affirmation and returned downstairs to the living room. Jo came in from the kitchen. "So, are they settled?"

"Hmm, I think so. Far was complaining about hearing voices in her bedroom, but she seems ok now. I think she was just worn out from the journey. I'll go and finish emptying the car. How's the kitchen?"

"It seems ok. There's an electric oven which is going to take some getting used to, but other than that, I'm sure we'll manage. There's plenty of pots and a decent frying pan. I'll just pop upstairs and check on the kids."

Liam returned to the car and collected the remainder of the luggage. He locked up and was about to return to the cottage when he spotted something at the bottom of the windscreen. It was a black feather which had become stuck in the mechanism. It was covered in blood washed into the run-off gutter from the windscreen wipers. He pulled it out and dropped it on the ground. From nowhere a gust of wind caught it. Liam watched as it floated aimlessly into the air.

He suddenly felt a pang of guilt at the demise of the crow.

Liam picked up the two suitcases and carried them back to the cottage just as Jo returned to the living room.

"How are they?" asked Liam.

"They seem fine. Far's still complaining that it's spooky, but she's on her games console now and I couldn't get much of a word out of her. Zack's ok, wants to go fishing tomorrow. What do you think?"

"I don't see why not. I didn't bring any gear or anything."

"I'm sure I saw some fishing lines at the shop; we can ask. Not sure where else, without going further afield."

"Yes, you could be right. Do you need anything doing?"

"No, thanks, I've put the shepherd pies in the oven. Should be ready in half an hour. I'll add a few baked beans; there are some tins in the pantry."

"In which case, I'm going to have a look around. I could do with stretching my legs."

"Yes, ok, what about the unpacking?"

"We can finish it after dinner; it won't take long."

Liam walked through the kitchen; Jo followed to check on the dinner. The side door which led to the back garden had an old-fashioned ball handle and it took a firm pull to open it.

Liam turned to Jo. "I don't think this door's been used much; the frame's warped." Jo looked outside.

"Looks a bit overgrown; could do with a tidy up."

"Yes, you're not kidding. I'm going to take a look around; won't be long."

Liam was at the side of the cottage. He looked up and could see the eaves. There was a swallows nest in the apex of the roof where the two sides of the thatch met. Below it, the white-washed wall was covered in bird droppings. The thatch looked discoloured, with moss visible. From nowhere, the mother bird arrived and entered the nest. There was a lot of chick-squawking, then she left again for more insects. Liam watched with interest; he'd seen nothing like this in London.

He was keen to check out the outbuilding he'd seen from Zack's window and headed up the footpath towards the giant sycamore tree at the end of the garden. Either side of the paving, the garden was overgrown with weeds of all kinds. There were signs that the garden had been planted, with several tops of potatoes visible, their familiar pale-yellow flowers lording above the weeds.

He reached the tree. To the right there was an old chicken pen which he'd not noticed from the window. The ground had been cleared of much of the vegetation, presumably from former residents, but there were no birds present now.

He turned left. The narrow footpath was not defined in any way by paving, just worn through use. The grass was starting to encroach. Before the outbuilding, there was a brick pen with a small enclosure; it was a pigsty, Liam recognised. He peered inside. There were crusts of decaying dung in the dirt. He could see old straw laying on the ground inside the pen itself. But there was something else, discarded police tape, the blue sort that they use for cordoning off areas. Liam suddenly remembered the murder; his curiosity was driving him forward.

He moved on to the outbuilding itself. It wasn't that big, about the size of a large garden shed, like any you would find in suburban London, but brick-built. There was a rotten wooden door with a black, metal latch. The door didn't reach the floor or the top of the frame, and several knot-holes were visible. Liam lifted the latch and slowly pulled it open.

The smell hit him straight away.

Two large wooden boxes were against the wall in front of him; one was higher than the other, with circular holes cut out of the top of each. Liam realised straight away that this was the original outside privy. The large hole was for the adult, the smaller for children. To the left, hanging on corroded hooks screwed into the wall, were several rusting gardening implements, including a pitchfork, a rake, a garden fork, an axe, and an old, curved shovel. All were brown and appeared unused for some time.

Liam walked further inside. The door was on a long spring and, without warning, bang! It slammed shut behind him. Liam jumped.

Then, from nowhere, he felt a cold blast of air; it made him shiver. Liam was wearing a tee shirt and jeans and unconsciously rubbed his arms. He looked around trying to fathom what was happening.

He turned to leave when, suddenly, he experienced a strange sensation; it was as if the ground was moving under his feet. He looked down. The ground was in motion, undulating, rippling, rolling. An earthquake, Liam quickly diagnosed, must be. The whole building was pulsing; it began to shake. He instinctively reached for the wall to steady himself; it was like touching a block of ice. The rake fell to the ground.

Then, just as quickly, it stopped.

Liam was trembling. He blinked, screwed his eyes. It was just his imagination; it had to be.

He saw the rake on the floor, picked it up, and returned it to its position. Out of curiosity, he touched the bare brick wall. It was, just normal. He looked at his fingers and touched it again to make sure.

The door was right behind him. He turned again and pressed down on the latch with his thumb. It wouldn't move; it was stuck, welded tight. He pressed harder, increasing the pressure; he felt a surge of panic. Then... a click; the latch released.

He flicked it up and down several times; it was fine. He frowned, unable to make sense of it. He pushed open the door and hastily left the outbuilding. The door slammed shut behind him. He thought he heard a muffled scream from within, but decided not investigate further.

He inhaled to clear his head of the smell and tried to take in what had happened. He was an intelligent man, a barrister with his own Chambers, for goodness sake; there had to be a logical explanation. His whole body was shaking, perspiration glistened his brow.

He put his hands on his knees and spent a few moments composing himself and decided to continue along the dirt footpath for a few yards to the thick hedge which marked the boundary of the property. It was difficult to see what was on the other side.

To the right was a drystone wall about four feet high, which ran the length of the garden. He peered over the top. It was the cemetery he'd seen from the window.

It was surrounded on all sides by deciduous trees, mostly beech, oak, and sycamore, their luxuriant cover like giant hands, providing a protective shield on the graves below. The headstones were mostly ancient, covered in lichen and weather-worn. He could just make out the faded writing on the nearest one; 'Mary Dooley; wife of George Dooley; died this day of our Lord, November 14th, 1778, aged 19 years'.

He continued scanning the lines of gravestones from his vantage point. There appeared to be a newer grave on the third row. Soft toys and flowers had been placed in front of the headstone, wet and soggy from rainstorms. It was too far away to read the inscription.

Liam was deep in thought, still unnerved by his earlier experience. He looked up at the impenetrable greenery encasing the graveyard and took more deep breaths. He suddenly detected a change; it had gone very gloomy. The thin sunbeams, which had lit up the gravestones like mini spotlights, had disappeared. The atmosphere had turned humid, heavy; breathing became laboured, an effort. Then a sound, the unmistakeable pit-pat, pit-pat of falling rain unable to breach the canopy.

Liam took one last look at the cemetery, then walked back past the privy towards the cottage. He left the protection of the sycamore tree and looked up. The blue sky had been replaced by heavy billowing cumulus clouds, rolling in from the sea. A gust of wind started the tall weeds swaying this way and that blowing 'fairy' seeds in all directions. Liam quickened his stride. He felt the first blobs of rain; then it was like some terrestrial being emptying a large watering can across the village. Liam made a dash and arrived at the kitchen door just as the first clap of thunder echoed across the bay.

Liam pushed open the door into the kitchen which was now bathed in a bright light. Jo was stirring the beans on the hob, and looked up from the saucepan.

"Good grief, I don't know where that came from; it seemed to change in seconds," said Liam, shaking his arms and head to dispel the water.

"Yes, you're all wet; you need to change," replied Jo.

"It's ok, it'll soon dry. Have you heard anything from the kids? I thought they might have come downstairs, with the thunder."

"No, they're still in their rooms; they'll have their headphones on I expect. How did you get on in the garden?"

"Hmm, well, I don't think we should let the kids up there; that outbuilding's not safe. It looks like it was the old privy."

"Really?"

"Yes, stinks to high heaven."

"Urgh, I think I'll give it a miss."

Liam looked at Jo with a serious expression. "Actually, there's something I need to mention; something the landlord at the pub told me."

Jo closed the oven door to give him full attention. "Go on."

"Well, according to him, this place has been on the market since January. There was a murder, apparently."

"Murder!"

"Yes."

Jo looked at Liam incredulously. "Well now that's certainly something that wasn't in the brochure!"

"Yes, and you know that shrine we saw on the way in?"

"Yes, what about it?"

"It seems a couple of young girls were hit by a car and killed, about the same time; that's what he said."

"Oh no, how awful."

"Yes, sisters. Some journalist, apparently, knocked them over; he'd been sent across to cover the murder."

"But what happened, the murder, I mean?"

"Well, I asked him that, and he said, 'folk 'round 'ere don't like to tark about it'." Liam was trying his best Cornish accent. "Anyway, I didn't like to press, but I'll ask that Mrs Thornton when we see her next; she seemed sensible enough."

"How terrible. I'll say this; it's a good job we didn't know about that before we arrived. I don't think we'd have booked it. I mean, it wasn't particularly cheap," said Jo.

"No, that's true, but we're here now; so I think we need to make the best of it."

"Hmm, yes, I guess. Actually, now you've come to

mention it, the woman at the shop said something strange; something about the cottage being cursed. I didn't take much notice of it at the time. She didn't say anything about a murder, though. What about outside? Did you find anything? A body perhaps!" Jo smiled.

Liam decided not to say anything about his experience in the outside privy. He didn't want to cause any alarm. He still didn't know what to make of it.

"Ha, ha, funny you should say that; there's a graveyard at the bottom of the garden."

"Really?"

"Yes, the other side of the wall. I thought I could see a new grave. I might go and investigate further tomorrow."

"Sounds a bit morbid."

"No, not really, just interested. I think, while we're here, we should learn a bit about the local history."

The rain outside was still pouring, interspersed with lightning. Farrah appeared at the kitchen door, sobbing bitterly. "I want to go home, Mom; I hate it here."

Jo went to her and put her arms around her. "Don't worry, Poppet, it's just a storm; it'll soon blow over."

Zack appeared. "What time's dinner; I'm starving."

Liam looked at Jo and started laughing. "You and Far can help me lay the table and it'll be ready in a couple of minutes. Come on, Poppet, there's nothing to be frightened of; it'll be gone soon."

As if to defy that prophecy, a huge clap of thunder rattled the windows of the cottage. Farrah held onto her mother and wouldn't let go.

"Go on, go and help Zack. The knives and forks are in that drawer."

Jo leaned across and pulled it open. She looked down and leapt back as an enormous garden spider scurried over the cutlery and down the back of the drawer.

"Oh, shit, that made me jump," said Jo, breathing heavily.

"Don't swear, Mom. You said it was wrong to swear," said Farrah.

"Yes, Poppet, sorry, it just made me jump."

Liam had also seen it. "Don't worry, it's only a spider; it won't hurt you."

He started removing the necessary utensils and passing them to the kids.

A few minutes later, the family were enjoying their first meal at the cottage. The room was suddenly bathed in sunshine; it was as if someone had pulled back curtains.

"Look, the storm's gone," said Liam.

"So it has," said Jo. "They certainly have weird weather down here."

"I don't like it here, Mom. I want to go home." Farrah put down her knife and fork and started to cry.

Jo put her arm around her. "Come on Poppet, don't cry. I know, let's go to the beach tomorrow while Zack and your dad go fishing; how does that sound?"

She looked up at Jo. "Whatever."

Jo looked at Liam, looking for support. "Come on Far; we'll have a great time, you'll see. It just takes a little while to get used to new things. In a couple of days this place will seem like home. Come on, you and Zack can help me wash up for your Mom and then we can go for a walk. How does that sound?"

Farrah didn't seem totally placated.

After a few minutes, the family had cleared away the empty plates.

"I've bought some ice-cream, Zack, for you and Far; it's in the fridge. Do you want to get it, while your dad and me wash the dishes?"

Zack opened the refrigerator and removed the carton.

"What no dishwasher?" said Liam, as he brought in the remaining plates,

"That'll be you," said Jo and started to laugh.

By half-past eight, both children were in bed. Farrah didn't fancy the walk suggestion and had gone back on her games console in her room.

Jo and Liam were relaxing enjoying a glass of wine. Jo was reading a chick-lit; Liam, one of the broadsheets he had bought from the service station.

Liam put down his newspaper and looked outside. He felt restless, still trying to rationalise what had happened in the outbuilding.

"It'll be dark soon; I think I'll go for a walk."

Jo looked up from her book and took off her reading glasses. "You seem on edge, dear, can't you relax?"

"No, you're right; it always takes me a couple of days to unwind on holiday. I think a bit of exercise will help me sleep."

"I can think of a more pleasurable exercise if you're up for it."

"Hmm, yes, now that sounds like a good idea. I won't be long."

Liam placed his newspaper on the table and headed for the door.

"Mind how you go. Take the front door key; I'll go and have a shower."

Liam picked up the set of keys from the table and held them up to Jo in confirmation.

Moments later, he was walking down the garden path, skipping the puddles and water-filled potholes, left by the recent rain, then through the gate, and down the short road to the junction with the telephone kiosk on the corner. The small church was in front of him.

Despite the storm, the air was still humid, the surrounding trees vivid green and heavy with water. The slightest breeze caused a cascade of droplets to fall to the ground.

He crossed the road and approached the church boundary wall. Like the one at end of the cottage garden, it was of dry-stone construction, about the same height, and of similar age, judging by the dark, weathered colour, and more lichen. In the middle of the wall there was a stone archway containing a small lynchgate with a paved path beyond, leading to the church door.

Something was drawing him to it. He walked up to the entrance and into the lynchgate, the small shelter which, in years gone by, would have held the shrouds of the deceased as they waited for burial, protecting them from rain, and body snatchers.

He continued along the pathway into the churchyard. He looked up at the spire, silhouetted against the darkening skies. It was small by most standards, but in keeping with the size of the church.

There were a few chest-tombs and headstones dotted around, most of which were unkempt and bent at strange angles. From the weathered inscriptions, he could see they were also extremely old.

He walked up to the church door, turned the large drop-handle, and pushed.

He entered the small vestibule into the narthex and stood for a moment. He looked around at the gloomy interior. The stained-glass windows depicted fishing vessels, crab pots, and sailors. The fading light cast shadows, illuminating countless dust particles.

"Can I help you?"

Liam almost jumped out of his skin.

He turned to see a clergyman, white-haired with bushy eyebrows and ear-hair, complete with dog-collar.

"Jeezus; you made me jump!"

"My apologies, we don't get many folk in, after hours, I mean. James Slaughter, Vicar of St Edwen's." His voice was definitely West Country, but his accent not as marked as the locals.

"Oh, er, Liam Drake, pleased to meet you, sorry for the, er, expletive."

The vicar smiled and they shook hands. Liam reacted to the touch; the clergyman's hands were freezing.

"Sorry, I've been in the crypt; it's very cold down there. Were you looking for private prayer, only I was just about to lock up?"

"Oh, no, no, thanks. I've been for a walk and thought I would have a look at the church."

"In which case, I'll walk you to the door. You're not from 'round here." The intonation expected confirmation.

While Liam was in discourse with the vicar, Jo was in the bathroom, opposite Farrah's room. She had checked on the kids and they were both still asleep. The bathroom was small, but, like most of the cottage, had been given a makeover. The shower cubicle was adequate for one person and looked new; then there was a wash basin, a cupboard and toilet. Not quite the en-suite from their London home, but quite acceptable.

She had taken a bath towel from the suitcase and started running the hot water. She put her hand under the stream; it was cold.

"Shit!" she exclaimed. She walked down to the airing cupboard and opened the door. There was an immersion heater on top of the water boiler. She flicked a switch and a red light appeared indicating power.

She was faced with a decision, wait for half an hour for some hot water, or put up with a cold shower. She decided to chance it and removed her clothes. She washed her face in the sink with her usual soap and dried. She placed the towel outside the shower to step out on, entered the cubicle, and turned on the water. She took a sharp intake of breath as the cold water, like needles, attacked her skin.

Suddenly a black shape fell on her shoulder. Her whole body convulsed with shock. It was another spider, even larger than the one in the kitchen. She managed to stifle a scream which would have awakened the children.

She instantly brushed it off and watched as it swashed around in the water at the bottom of the shower tray, looking for an escape route. Jo was dodging it with her feet like some frenetic fandango dancer. It was too big to go down the outlet pipe which was covered by a circular chrome grill about two inches across. Jo bent down and managed to pull the cover from its housing, and watched as the spider was unceremoniously swept down the drain by the flowing water. Jo replaced the grill and composed herself. The water was still cold and she quickly finished washing.

She wrapped a towel around her. Then suddenly... nothing. The lights had gone out.

"Oh, shit, the electricity," she said aloud.

She waited a couple of moments for her eyes to get accustomed to the ambience. There was a just a hint of natural daylight as the dusk was fading into night. She gingerly made her way along the corridor and down the stairs one at a time. They creaked at every step.

In the growing gloom of the living room, she hunted for her handbag. It was beside the settee.

She rummaged inside, located her purse and felt around. "Come on, come on." She found a pound coin, then another. She headed to the kitchen, opened the cupboard under the sink, and fed the coins in to the meter. The lights came on immediately. There was a low hum from the refrigerator.

Liam, meanwhile, followed the priest to the door and stepped out into the darkening night. The vicar turned, produced an enormous key, and pushed it into the lock, then gave it a twist. He looked at Liam.

"You know, there was a time when we could keep the church unlocked, but not these days. We get vagrants in the summer trying to use the church as a hotel."

"Hmm, yes, I can imagine. In answer to your question, we arrived this afternoon from London. We're staying at Pendle Cottage, just across the road."

The vicar was striding quickly towards the lynchgate, but suddenly stopped in his tracks. He turned to Liam.

"Did you say Pendle Cottage?"

"Yes, we've rented it for three weeks."

His face was etched with concern. "Oh dear, I counselled Mrs Thornton against allowing anyone into the property so soon after... Still, what's done is done."

"Sorry, what do you mean?"

"Oh, nothing, nothing. Anyway must be away; enjoy your stay."

"But wait..."

Too late, the vicar was walking briskly in the opposite direction. Liam thought about chasing after him but decided against it, and started heading back to the cottage. He took one last look over his shoulder towards the church; the vicar had gone.

It was almost dark, the light inside the cottage appeared

welcoming as he strode down the footpath. He fiddled in his pocket for the keys. As he retrieved them, was it his imagination.? They appeared to leap from his fingers and drop onto the doorstep.

"Shit!" he exclaimed.

He leant down to pick them up, and as he did so, he caught his foot on the step and fell forward striking his head a heavy blow on the door.

He sat dazed for a moment and rubbed his forehead. It was sticky to the touch and a lump was already forming. He could hear Jo calling from the other side of the door. "Are you alright, Liam."

Liam retrieved the keys and managed to get the front door opened.

"What was that noise? Are you ok?"

Liam went inside and closed the door. "You're bleeding," said Jo, looking at his face. "What happened?"

"I don't know, I caught my foot on the doorstep and fell into the door."

Jo was wearing a dressing gown and a towel wrapped around her head.

"Here, let me clean that up for you; I'll just boil a kettle. It's a good job I remembered the medical kit."

A few minutes later, Jo was bathing Liam's forehead. She examined it closely. "Nothing serious; I'll put a plaster on it. Looks as if you'll have a bit of a bruise tomorrow. So, where did you go?"

"Over to the church. I met the vicar; he was just closing up."

"What made you go to the church? You normally avoid those places like the plague. What is it you call them? Dens of iniquity?"

"Yes, I think I did say that. I was referring to all the

hypocrisy that goes on, you know, all those child-abuse cases... Ouch!"

Liam winced as Jo applied the plaster. "There, all done."

She stood back and admired her handiwork. "I think you should go to bed. It's been a long day."

"Yes, you can say that again," said Liam.

"By the way, I put some more money in the electricity meter. Would you believe it ran out while I was in the shower? Luckily, I had some change in my purse."

"Oh, that's good. We must remember to get some more tomorrow; we don't want to be stuck in the dark."

"Why don't you have a shower? The water should be warmish now. Mine was freezing!"

"Yes, good idea."

Liam got up cautiously from the chair; his head was still a bit woozy. "I'll just check round."

Twenty minutes later, Liam joined Jo in bed. Jo had turned on the bedside table-lights; giving the room a cosy feel.

Jo was reading and put down the book, as Liam got into bed. She put her arm around him.

"How is your head?"

"It's fine, now, thanks."

"I think we should christen the bed. What do you think?"

"Now that sounds like a good idea."

The alarm clock in the master bedroom was on Liam's side of the bed. The luminous radium dial gave off a pale-green light, three twenty-six. The air was humid again, the skylight window open but offering limited respite to the temperature.

In Farrah's room, she was still fast asleep cuddling her favourite soft toy, a grey elephant she had named Jumbo on

Liam's suggestion. She was a big Disney fan.

The room was cooler, much cooler. The window was shut, and Farrah was hunkered down under the covers to keep warm. She wouldn't have been aware of her movements; it was a natural response to the fall in temperature.

"Hello, little girl, do you want to play?"

Farrah tossed and turned over. Jumbo fell off the bed and was now lying forlorn on the floor.

"Hello, little girl, do you want to play? Please, I'm so lonely."

Farrah stirred, her eyes opened.

"Hello, little girl, my name's Lily; what's yours?"

Farrah was in a trance state. She sat up in bed, her eyes, distant and unfocussed. Her lips moved, her voice quiet, almost a whisper.

"I'm Farrah."

"Hello, Farrah, I'm Lily. Do you want to play? Please don't be afraid; I won't hurt you."

Farrah was still sat upright. "I don't mind."

"What do you like to play?"

"I play with my computer games."

"My Mom won't let me have one of those; she says they are bad for you."

"I think they are ok."

"Are you staying here long?"

"No, I don't think so."

"Oh, that's a shame. We can be friends."

"Yes, we can be friends."

"Yes, yes. What is your elephant called?"

"He's called Jumbo."

"He's fallen on the floor. Do you want me to pick him up for you?"

"Yes please."

Farrah hadn't moved and was still transfixed.

"Oh, dear, it's not possible, but I'm sure he'll be ok. I better go back; I'll be missed. Will you be here tomorrow?"

"I expect so."

"Oh, I do hope so; it's been so lonely on my own."

A slight breeze wafted around the room, no more than a wisp. The room temperature gradually returned to normal. Farrah's eyes flickered and she lay back down.

Liam and Jo were dead to the world; the luminous dial said eight o'clock. Suddenly, the sound of a single bell echoed across the vicinity, a rhythmic one and two, and three and four; not the normal peel of bells you would expect for a Sunday service.

Liam opened his eyes. "Good grief, where did that racket come from?"

Jo stirred. "I'll give you three guesses."

"Well, it sounds more like a funeral to me. Do you want a cup of tea? I won't be able to sleep till it stops."

"Yeah, thanks, good idea. Just popping to the loo. How's your head, by the way?"

"Oh, it's fine thanks; no pain, just a bruise."

"Well, I'll put a new plaster on before we go out."

Just then Farrah came out of her room clutching Jumbo.

"Mom, can I play with Lily?"

"Who's Lily, Poppet?"

"She's my friend; she said she's lonely."

Jo looked puzzled, but decided not to make a big thing of it.

"Well, I think we're going out this morning. Remember, we were going to the beach, while your Dad and Zack go fishing?"

"Oh, yeah."

Farrah went back to her room; Jo went into the bathroom, deep in thought. She was back in bed when Liam brought up two mugs.

"Oo, just what the doctor ordered." Jo took one of the mugs from Liam while he got back into bed.

Liam had closed the door.

"Far just asked me if she can play with Lily."

Liam took a sip of tea.

"Who's Lily?"

"She said she was her friend and was lonely."

"It's probably one of those computer games."

"Oh, yes, I hadn't thought about that."

"Are you still going fishing today?"

"I don't know, it depends on Zack."

"I think it would do you both good; you were very restless last night."

"Yes, sorry about that." He picked up his mug and started to drink. "Actually, I had some really strange dreams."

"Oh yeah? What sort of dreams?" Jo took a sip of her tea and looked at Liam and smiled.

"Ha, not those sort, no, they were weird. I can't remember all of them, but I do recall one. I was in the graveyard, you know, the one over the back wall, and I could hear voices."

"What kind of voices?"

"Kids, it sounded like; I couldn't see them. I could just hear voices."

"What were they saying?"

"I don't remember; it was like they were warning me."

"Warning you?" Jo stopped drinking and looked at Liam.

"Well, that's what it seemed like; something about not disturbing them. I have to say it was quite unnerving; it woke me up."

Liam thought for a moment about the incident at the

outhouse the previous evening; then quickly put it out of his mind.

"Hmm, it was probably the journey yesterday; you definitely need a break."

"Yes, you're right."

Just then a pleading call from outside the bedroom door. "Mom, when's breakfast?"

"Just getting up, Zack. Go and get your shower," replied Jo.

Chapter Three

By ten-thirty, the family were heading out for their morning in the village. Liam was sporting a large sticking plaster on his forehead which had already been the butt of jokes. The lump had gone down, but the bruise was now a yellowy-purple colour. He stopped at the junction with the telephone kiosk on the corner and looked across at the church. There were a few cars parked outside the boundary wall.

"Looks like a service is on," said Liam.

"Hmm, yes. At least that dreadful noise has stopped," said Jo.

They turned left and down the steep hill into the village. Jo was admiring the cottages as they went by, all nicely maintained and looking their finest on this sunny morning. Five minutes later, they had reached the sea front. Liam decided to park in the pub car park as they had agreed to meet there for lunch.

Liam slowly negotiated the entrance. The battered Skoda, which was there the previous day, was the only other car in the parking bays.

"Make sure you've got everything?" said Liam as the family got out. He locked up.

Jo was carrying a large holdall containing towels, swimming costumes, and bottles of sunscreen. "Shall we meet here at, what, about twelve-thirty? Does that give you enough time?"

Liam checked his watch and smiled. "Oh, definitely."

The family walked out of the car park and reached the street. Liam surveyed the scene.

"Have you noticed anything?"

"Not particularly," replied Jo.

"Exactly. It's a Sunday morning, high season, the weather's good, where are all the visitors?"

"Hey, you're right; I hadn't noticed, how strange. Well, at least we should have the beach to ourselves."

The family looked like holidaymakers. Jo, her hair tied back, was sporting sunglasses, a tee shirt with the words 'Gym-world' emblazoned across the front, shorts and flip-flops; while Liam, also in shorts and a tee shirt, was wearing trainers.

Jo and Farrah walked over the road towards the jetty and the steps down to the foreshore. The weather was still warm with a cloudless sky, but there was a gentle breeze, making it a very pleasant day. The pair reached the top of the steps and looked at the small patch of dry sand below, littered with dried seaweed and other flotsam and jetsam. Jo put her hand over her eyes to shield them from the sun and scanned the area as a mariner might do. The tide was out and what little sea that was left in the harbour, was in large puddles. Several of the small boats were aground on the wet sand; their chains draped with sea-weed like green curtains. Their anchors lay redundant.

"Well, I don't think we can do much swimming till the tide comes in. We can have a look for shells. What do you think, Poppet?" said Jo.

"Yeah, ok," replied Farrah.

"What about your friend, Lily? Were you able to play with her?"

"No, she's gone back, I think."

"Where to?"

"I don't know. Where she came from, I suppose."

"Maybe you'll see her later."

"Yes, I hope so, she seemed nice. I don't like people being lonely."

"That's sweet of you, Poppet."

Meanwhile Liam and Zack had arrived at the shop and were examining the rather limited supplies of fishing gear.

"Hey, Zack, there're some hand-lines here. We can fish off the harbour wall. What do you think?"

"Sure, cool," said Zack. Liam took two hand-lines up to the counter where the elderly proprietor was sat. She got up slowly when she saw Liam and Zack approach.

"Wasson, m'dear, can I help you?" She looked at Zack. "And you, me 'ansom, what's your name?"

"Zack."

"Zack, eh? That's an unusual name. I knows a Jack, not a Zack."

She looked at Liam and stared for a moment at his bruised forehead. "You bin in the wars, m'dear?"

"What? Oh, that? No, no, not looking where I was going, just tripped."

"You need to be careful, m'dear, trips can be nasty. Is it you stayin' up at Pendle Cottage, then?"

"Yes, how did you know?"

"We don't get many visitors here, There was a lady in yesterday sayin' she were stayin' there."

"Yes, that was my wife."

"Ah, I see, 'andsome woman, she were. Just these was it?"

Liam handed over cash and thanked her. She picked up the two items, squinted at the price on the sticky labels and keyed it into an ancient-looking cash register. Every movement appeared laboured. She handed Liam some change and the merchandise. "Do you want a bag for these, m'dear?"

"No, no, that's fine thanks; we're just going to use them.

You don't know if there's anywhere that sells bait, by any chance?"

"Yes, m'dear. If you turns right and keeps going over the road, past the hawn, then past the Harbourmaster's office, you'll see a few folk about checking pots and that. They'll sell yer some squid or the like if you asks."

"Thanks, that's very kind."

Liam turned to leave.

"Now you mind 'ow you go, m'dear, 'specially on that jetty. It can be a dangerous place for those of a mind not to be careful."

Liam looked at the woman over his shoulder and smiled. "Yes, thank you, we'll be careful." He ushered Zack towards the door.

They got outside; Liam was carrying the fishing gear. Zack looked at him.

"Dad... what's a hawn?"

"I have no idea, Zack, but if we keep our eyes open, maybe we'll see one."

Liam and Zack walked along the road as directed by the shopkeeper.

They passed the concrete jetty that led down to the beach, constructed to launch boats. Then after the harbour wall, the road continued in front of them for about two hundred yards to a dead end with sweeping cliffs towering upward. Signs were displayed, 'Beware of Rock Falls', with an illustration of a slope and falling rocks.

Immediately to the right, a line of ten or so cottages almost reaching the dead end. There were two small pick-up trucks parked in front of the nearest and another car further on. Behind them, the land rose sharply and was covered in trees. In front, the foreshore was littered with huge boulders; any beach that was visible was pebbled. The sea shimmered in the distance, waiting for its return on the incoming tide.

The first dwelling showed evidence of recent attention with new windows and a lick of paint. A notice above the door said, 'Harbourmaster's Office', as the lady in the store had mentioned.

In front of the cottages, on the other side of the road, the sea wall was littered with crab and lobster pots being attended by two men, seemingly checking for holes.

Liam crossed the road and approached the first man.

"Sorry to disturb you, the lady in the shop said you might be able to provide us with some bait. We want to try our luck off the jetty."

"Aye, I can let yer have a bit of squid. The fish like it; mind you, so do the cankers. You'll catch loads of them but they ain't no good to eat. You'll need to watch your fingers an'all; they can be quite vicious, the bigger ones."

"Oh, right, yes, thanks for the advice," said Liam. "Er... cankers?"

"Ha, ha, you out-of-towners." He gave a toothy grin. "Crabs, harbour crabs, cankers." Liam looked suitably foolish at not understanding the word.

The man crossed the road and went into one of the adjacent cottages. He returned a few minutes later carrying something wrapped in an old newspaper; he handed it to Liam.

"What do I owe you?"

"Nothin', it's old; I wuz only going to chuck it out."

"Oh, that's very kind."

The man went back to his pots and sat down on a wooden, three-legged stool. He looked up at Liam.

"So where're you thinking of fishing?"

"I don't know; we've not been here before."

"Well, if you're going to be fishing off the hawn, don't go

climbing on it; it's very slippery on top. We lost a young lad last summer. Dreadful, it wuz."

"Sorry... hawn?"

"Aye, the harbour, over yonder." The fisherman pointed at the harbour wall.

"Ah, I understand now; it's not a word I've come across."

"Hmm. Just visitin', are we?"

"Yes, we've booked a cottage for three weeks."

"A cottage? I didn't know no-one wuz rentin' out cottages."

"Yes, Pendle Cottage, up by the church."

The man had been examining one of the pots, but stopped abruptly and looked at Liam, his face one of concern.

"Aye, I knows Pendle Cottage, right enough. Mind you take care up there."

"Yes, of course, er, any particular reason?"

"Just what folk say, pay no mind."

"Oh, right, well, thanks again, Mr?"

"Just Jack," said the man.

"Jack," said Liam.

By twelve-thirty, Jo and Farrah were waiting outside the pub as arranged. They could see Liam and Zack in the distance walking towards them.

"Doesn't look like they've caught anything. I don't think we'll be having fish for dinner," said Jo to Farrah and started laughing.

"How did you get on?" she enquired as Liam got closer.

"Hmm, plenty of... what do they call them, Zack?"

"Cankers."

"Yes, that's right, cankers."

"Cankers?" said Jo.

"Yes, crabs to you and me, no fish though. Seemed like

they were waiting, the crabs. You could see them on the bottom. We managed to get some bait from one of the old fishermen, the other side of the harbour, squid, very smelly."

"It was gross," added Zack.

"As soon as the line went in, the crabs just made a mad dash for it. They were even fighting each other. The fish didn't get a look in," continued Liam, enthusiastically.

"Well, I hope you've got rid of it; it'll stink the place out," said Jo.

"Yes, we threw it in; the cankers can fight over what was left," said Liam and laughed.

"Well, it's probably just as well you didn't catch any fish; I wouldn't know where to start gutting them. Did you enjoy it, Zack?" asked Jo.

"Yes, it was good fun," he replied. "I'm hungry, can we get something to eat?"

"Yes, let's go in," said Liam. "How was the swimming?"

"Hmm, the tide was out; there wasn't any water," said Jo.

"Ah, yes, that does provide a problem. So what did you do?"

"Just looked for shells. Show your Dad what you found, Poppet."

Farrah was clutching a small plastic bag that had previously contained wet-wipes and opened it.

"Hey, you've got some really good ones there. Come on, let's go in and we can have a closer look."

Liam opened the pub door and the family entered. Again, it was much darker inside and the lights of the bar shone brightly in the gloom. There were two men in the far corner, dressed in fishermen's clothing, including dark-blue, woollen sweaters, which seemed incongruous in the clement weather.

They were in conversation but stopped and watched the

family as they located a table, then carried on talking in a conspiratorial whisper.

"What would you like?" said Liam, as the family made themselves comfortable.

He took the orders and went to the bar.

The landlord had been wiping a glass and stopped as Liam approached.

"Hello m'dear, still 'ere, I see. I thought that were your car in the car park; I remembered it from yesterday. What can I get for yas?"

Liam ordered the drinks. "Can we get some sandwiches?"

"Aye, m'dear, what would you like?"

"What have you got?"

"Well, I can do you a ploughman's, or some 'am, and I've got some fresh crab, just come in this mornin'. Aswen's just been dressin' 'em. My wife, she does all the cookin' and that."

"Let me check with the guys." Liam carried the drinks to the table and relayed the choices.

Liam returned to the bar and ordered the sandwiches and a ploughman's lunch for himself; the landlord left the counter and went into the kitchen.

"Oh, and four packets of crisps, plain please."

"Aye, right you are, won't be long. What you been up to then?" He was staring at Liam's forehead,

"What? Oh, that. Nothing, just tripped."

"Aye? Well, you take care. There've been strange things 'appenin' up there."

"Strange things? What do you mean?"

"Oh, nothin', just what folk 'round 'ere says, that's all."

Liam wanted to explore further but decided to let it drop. "You mentioned yesterday about the murder."

The landlord looked at Liam with a stern expression.

"Oh, aye, I did. I should have said naught. Folks 'round 'ere don't like to talk about it."

"Oh, yes, of course, sorry." Liam paid for the drinks and food and returned to the table with the crisps.

Liam walked back to the table. "He's bringing them over," he announced to the family. "What do you fancy doing this afternoon?"

"Well, I need to get back and sort a few bits out," said Jo.

"I'll see if Lily wants to play," said Farrah. Liam looked at Jo and raised his eyebrows.

"Yes, I'm sure she'll enjoy that, Poppet" said Jo. "Actually, come to think about it, we could do with finding a supermarket first and stocking up; we don't have much in. I don't suppose the shop will be open."

"No, it closes at one o'clock on Sundays, I noticed. There's a sign on the door. I could do with filling up with petrol too; it's getting low."

"Where's the nearest?"

"Hmm, I'll ask the landlord when he comes over. St Austell, I expect."

A few minutes later, the landlord and his wife appeared from a side door carrying two plates each, containing the food. A portion of chips and a few lettuce leaves were also included.

They distributed the plates around the table. "Any sarces or such?" asked the man.

Jo looked at Liam. "Ah, sauces... No, not for me thanks," said Liam.

"I'm fine," said Jo.

The landlord turned and was about to walk away when Liam called him. "Oh, sorry, do you know where the nearest supermarket is?"

The landlord cast a disapproving look at his wife before

replying.

"Hmm, let me see. Well, there's one in St Aussell, I think. Mind you, Aswen, here, uses the shop 'ere mostly. It's 'andy, like, ain't it? Not keen on supermarkets."

The woman nodded. "Aye, that it is," she replied.

Liam looked at the woman. In her sixties he guessed, with a friendly, smiley face and a ruddy complexion.

"How far's that?" asked Liam. "St Austell, only my Satnav's not working."

"Don't rightly knows. Last time I went, it were about half an hour, maybe a bit more, if I remembers right. Didn't like the place, too many people about. You couldn't breathe."

"Oh, right, thank you," said Liam.

The pair left and went back through the door. It closed sharply behind them.

"Well, I don't know what to make of that," said Liam.

"How strange. I mean, how do they manage? There's no mobile signal, no internet, and the only store sells beans and not a lot else," said Jo.

"No, I agree, but we need to get going if we're going to get to the supermarket before it closes. I assume it will be four o'clock on a Sunday."

The family finished their lunch and headed back to the car. Liam opened the boot and stowed the bags and handlines. He got in the driver's seat, reversed out of the parking spot, before cautiously negotiating the narrow entrance.

The sun was still blazing down and the car was warm, despite having been parked in the shade of the pub. Liam opened all the windows, turned left and headed along the sea-front. It looked like the tide was on the turn.

"It's so pretty here," said Jo, scanning the vista. "What do you think, Poppet?"

"Yes... How long will we be?"

"I don't know," said Jo. "Not too long, I wouldn't think." She sensed Farrah was not keen on the journey. "We can find a few treats, how does that sound?"

"Yeah, whatever," said Farrah and looked out of the window.

After a couple of minutes, they arrived at the end of the promenade. A rocky promontory reached out at least half a mile towards the sea, preventing any further expansion to the village. The road turned left at almost ninety degrees and the steep narrow incline faced them.

"Look at the cottages, don't they look pretty? I don't think I've seen so many hollyhocks," said Jo. "Goodness, this is steep."

After about half a mile of steady climb, they reached the end of the cottages. Then Jo spotted the shrine on the right-hand side. "Those poor children," she commented as they passed it.

"What on earth?" said Liam, ignoring her remark.

The car was suddenly engulfed in a white blanket. "It's that fog again!"

It was a white-out with visibility no more than a couple of yards. Liam slowed the car to a walking pace, then everything seemed to stop. He engaged the gear stick in 'parking' mode.

"What's the matter?" asked Jo.

Liam was pressing the start button. The engine made no response.

"I don't know; it just died."

He tried again... nothing. There was a look of concern.

"Well, we can't stay here. Anyone coming from the main road's going to hit us head on in this stuff," exclaimed Liam.

"Can you reverse?" asked Jo.

"I'll need someone to watch for me; I can't see a thing. I think everyone should get out just in case."

The family exited the car and Jo went to the driver's window. Liam lowered it.

"It looks clear. Can you roll back?" said Jo.

"I should be able to with this slope."

Liam put the Volvo into 'neutral' and slowly allowed the car to roll backwards, using his brake to control the speed. Jo was guiding.

Moments later, they were out of the blanket of fog and passing the shrine. The car was able to maintain its backward momentum, but it was taking all Liam's concentration to keep it steady. Jo was walking alongside. He removed his seat belt which was cutting into his shoulder.

"Across the road, by the first cottage, can you park it on there?" shouted Jo and pointing.

There was a plot of bare ground next to the cottage which looked as though it had been used as a parking space in the past. There was a line of tall thistles against the white-washed brick wall which marked the boundary of the property.

Liam was still looking over his shoulder and could see the cottage about fifty yards away on the right-hand side. Suddenly the car started gathering pace. He pushed his foot harder on the brake pedal to stem its momentum but it seemed to have no effect. He pushed down harder; his foot was on the floor, but the Volvo was still gaining speed. He was beginning to panic the gradient loomed behind him.

Jo was now running and having trouble keeping up with it. "Slow down, Liam, slow down," she screamed.

"I can't stop it! I can't stop it!" he yelled back.

Liam could see the steep hill stretching down to the sea front in the distance and made a decision. He yanked the steering wheel down, directing the car backwards into the space next to the cottage at over twenty miles an hour. It was not enough to tip the heavy car and somehow it missed the brick wall but, with no means of stopping, it careered through a low chain-wire fence and into an adjoining field. Luckily, the fence served as a brake, slowing down the runaway Volvo. It bounced up and down, sending Liam flying before coming to a halt in the tall grass.

Jo ran to the car and opened the door. "Liam, Liam, are you ok?"

He slowly eased himself out of the car.

"I... I... I think so." He stood and stretched his back, checking the rest of his body. The sticking plaster had gone from his forehead.

"What happened?"

"I don't know; the brakes wouldn't work." He looked around the car. "Jeezus, have you seen that?"

Liam walked towards the end of the grass about twenty yards away. He slowly peered over the edge. It was a cliff with a sheer drop to the bottom, which was covered in boulders and scrub. It seemed like an abandoned quarry.

Jo went to join him. "No! Stay back, it might give way," shouted Liam.

"What is it?"

"A cliff. It must be nearly a hundred foot drop to the bottom. A few more yards and I could have been over the edge. Where're the kids?"

Jo turned and looked back. "I can't see them... Zack, Farrah, are you there?" she called.

Jo left Liam, who was back examining the car, and walked to the road. She peered up the hill. Suddenly, she noticed the white wall of fog; it seemed to be moving, disappearing into the trees. She could see Zack and Farrah at the shrine and breathed a sigh of relief. She called again.

"Zack... Farrah..."

They turned and started walking down the hill towards her. "What have you been doing? Didn't you see the car?"

"No," said Zack. "Where is it?"

Jo pointed to the field. The top of the Volvo was just visible. Liam was walking towards them.

"What's it doing in that field?" asked Zack.

"There was a problem with the brakes. What have you been doing?"

"We were talking to the little girls," said Farrah.

"What little girls?" said Jo.

"The ones by all the flowers and teddies, Meli and Clementine."

"You were talking to them, Far. I couldn't hear anything," said Zack. "You were hearing things, I think."

"But I did hear them, Mom," said Farrah.

"Yes, Poppet, but we need to sort out the car."

Liam joined them.

"What are we going to do?" asked Jo.

"Hmm, well, I need to call the breakdown company. I'll see if the people here will let me use their phone."

Liam was shaken but gradually recovered from his ordeal. First priority was to sort out the car.

There was a small brick-built boundary wall about three foot tall separating the waste ground from the first cottage.

He walked around it and up the short path to the front door. He searched for a bell, but being unable to locate one he rapped with his knuckle. He thought he could hear movement from inside, then the door opened very slowly. There was a gap of maybe two inches and Liam could see the side of a face.

"Who is it? What do you want?"

"My name's Liam, we've had an accident. The car's

run off the road; it's in the field next to your house. I was wondering if I could use your phone to call someone."

The door opened a fraction wider. Liam could see the full face of an elderly woman, certainly in her eighties, maybe older.

"We don't have a car. What do you say's wrong with it?"

"No, my car. It's in the field next door."

"What's it doing there?"

"I drove it in there."

"Why do you want to go an' do that for? It's very dangerous; you could've gone over the cliff. And you wouldn't be the first neither."

"No, I had problems with the brakes."

"Well, you need to get them fixed, 'specially with all the hills 'round 'ere."

"Yes, I intend to, but I need to call out a breakdown truck."

"Well, you won't get one of those 'round 'ere. There's a garage in St Aussell; they might have one. Why don't you call them?"

"Yes, but I need to use your phone, if you don't mind. I'll pay for the call. Can I come in?"

"Well, you best 'ad." She noticed Jo and the children at the front gate. "Is that your family?"

"Yes, it is."

"Well, they don't want to be stood out there. We gets fog, you know, just before the trees, very dangerous. Comes and goes it does ever since that nice family got killed. One minute it's there, next it's gone. Not seen nothin' like it; folks 'round 'ere reckon it's evil spirits, but I ain't so sure. You better get 'em in; it's not safe to be walking about."

Liam gestured to the family to join him, and the lady opened the door wider to accommodate.

The room was dark and gloomy. There was an old settee, probably dating from the fifties, judging by the style; the brown-patterned upholstery was worn from years of use. There were two matching armchairs, a small dining table, and a standard lamp which was lit, providing some illumination. There was a sideboard that took up most of one wall with several black and white pictures on top. The only form of heating seemed to be an ancient two-bar electric fire against the opposite wall. The old woman stood behind the settee to allow the visitors to sit.

"Sit down, sit down," she ordered. "I can make you a cup of tea if you like. Phone's over there on the sideboard." The old woman pointed.

Liam looked at Jo. "We don't want to be any trouble."

"It's no trouble." She looked at Zack. "My you're a 'ansom fellow; what's your name?"

"Zack," he replied.

"And you, my little beauty, what's your name?" She placed her hand, withered with age, on Farrah's head.

"Farrah," she replied, nervously.

"That's a nice name; not 'eard that one afore."

"Do you want a cup of tea?" Liam looked at Jo.

"Can I help you? Sorry I don't know your name," said Jo.

"Hmm, it comes and goes you know, the fog. Would you like a cup of tea?"

"Yes, let me help you."

"Yes, if you wouldn't mind, and what's your name?" said the woman.

"Jo."

"It can't be; that's a boy's name."

"Oh, yes, it's short for Josephine."

"Ah, I see. I don't know why people shortens their name. Josephine, now that's a fine name; French, I think. Would you like a cup of tea?"

"Yes, please. Let me help you. Do you want to show me where the kitchen is?"

"It's over there."

At the far end of the room was a window that overlooked the back garden. The curtains were almost drawn which was one of the reasons the room was so dark. To the right was a door.

The old woman pulled one of the curtains to one side and peered through. "Nice day today. Didn't like the storm last night. The trees were complaining, make no mistake; you should have 'eard 'em. They don't like the lightning, you know; worried they might get burned down, I reckon."

"Shall we make the tea?" said Jo, and walked behind the old woman into the kitchen. Her steps were more a shuffle.

There was a stained, square white sink with a drainer and worktop, and an electric cooker with rings, which looked as though it too could be fifty years old. There was a picture window behind the sink which looked over the field. Jo could see there was a big gap where the cliff dropped before rising again to the tree line on the other side of a small valley. She could see the cottages in the distance, including the top of Pendle Cottage.

"Do you have a fridge?" asked Jo.

"No, never 'ad no cause, like, pantry's always cold enough."

"It's just there." She pointed at a door at the end of the kitchen. "Cups and saucers are in the cupboard."

There was a set of cupboards opposite the sink containing the kitchen utensils. Jo went into the pantry. She couldn't believe it; it was like walking into a refrigerator. Her arms quickly resembled goose flesh. She saw three pint bottles of milk lined up and chose one.

"You were right about the pantry; it is cold in there."

"Aye, never needed one of them refrigerator things. I've got some sugar somewhere," added the woman.

"We don't take sugar, but thank you," said Jo.

Meanwhile, in the sitting room, Liam had got his wallet and was searching for the card with the breakdown company's details on it. Farrah and Zack were just seated on the settee, seemingly locked in thought.

The telephone was an old magnolia G.P.O. rotary 1970s-style, complete with a curly cord. Liam located the card, placed it on the sideboard, and dialled the number. As usual, a number of options were offered to direct the call to the right department. Liam was at a loss; there were no buttons to press.

Luckily, there was another, emergency number. He tried again and this time, after a few minutes, his call was answered; he was speaking to a real person.

"Oh, hello, yes, can you help me, please? My car's broken down and run off the road. My name? Yes, Liam Drake." He provided his membership number.

"Are you with the vehicle now, Mr Drake?" asked the helpful adviser.

"Close to it, I'm in someone's house using their phone."

"Have you got the post code so I can locate your position?"

"Just a moment." Liam put the phone down on the sideboard and went into the kitchen where the tea-making activity was in full swing.

"Excuse me, do you know your post code?"

The lady looked at Liam. "Don't know us got one of those."

"Have you got any letters or bills from the council, perhaps?"

"Let me 'ave a look." She shuffled into the sitting room and opened one of the drawers in the sideboard.

"I got these," she said, lifting out several unopened envelopes with an elastic band wrapped around them.

"Let me look," said Liam. He took the letters, and started to read the address.

"Ada Wilkins. Is that you?"

"Yes, although I used to be Dorkins. They changed it you see when I got married. Mind you, that were a while ago now. It was my 'usband's name; Archie, they called 'im. Dead now he is, morun ten year it'll be."

"Chine Cottage, Polgissy. Ah yes, here it is, just a minute."

Liam went back to the phone. "Sorry about that, I have it here. Are you there? Oh, good." Liam read the postcode from the letter. There was a clicking of keys, then a pause.

"Sorry, Mr Drake, that's not on our system," said the adviser.

"What does that mean?"

"Hmm, well I can't get anyone out without a postcode; they won't be able to find you."

"Well, how did you manage before Sat-navs?"

"I don't know, I wasn't working here then."

"Well, you can't just leave us stranded," said Liam who was beginning to get angry.

"Just a moment, let me ask my supervisor." The line was suddenly emanating awful tinny music.

After several more minutes of inane pop music and messages suggesting using the website for 'a more complete service', a new voice appeared.

"Hello, Mr Drake, Jordan Masters, I'm one of the supervisors, I understand you haven't got a post code."

"Well, I have but apparently it's not on your system."

"Can you read it out again just to make sure." Liam

complied and there was another clicking of a keyboard.

"No, you're right, now that is unusual. Do you have an address?" Liam read out the address; there was another delay.

"Cornwall, you say? Hmm, unfortunately all our drivers are out. It's been busy with the holiday weekend. We won't be able to get to you today, I'm sorry. Do you have somewhere to stay?"

"Yes, we're on holiday here."

"Hmm, well what I suggest is that one of our drivers will call you between ten and twelve tomorrow morning and you can give him directions. Where's the nearest town?"

"St Austell, I think."

"Ok, that's great. What's your mobile number?"

"It's no good; there's no signal here."

"Oh, what about a landline?"

"There's not one in the cottage. Wait, just a moment."

Liam put his hand over the mouthpiece and called. "Jo, have you got Mrs Thornton's telephone number?"

Jo came in from the kitchen and went to her handbag. She rummaged around and then pulled out the slip of paper with the details.

"Hello, are you there? I have a number where you should be able to contact us. It's a Mrs Thornton." Liam read out the number and confirmed.

"Right, so your driver will call Mrs Thornton between ten and twelve tomorrow and she can give him directions. Great, thanks for your help." Liam replaced the receiver.

"So what's happening?" said Jo.

"They can't get anyone to us today; all the drivers are out, but sometime tomorrow morning. I had to give them Mrs Thornton's number. I'll ring her now and let her know."

"I hope she's in," said Jo.

"'Ere you are m'dears," said the old woman shuffling in from the kitchen carrying a tray.

Chapter Four

Jo took the tray from the old woman and put it down on the table, while Mrs Wilkins made herself comfortable in one of the armchairs. Jo started pouring the teas.

"Cups and saucers, and a tea pot," remarked Liam. "Now, that is a treat."

"Aye, always like my cups and saucers," said Mrs Wilkins.

"So, how long have you lived here?" asked Jo, as she took her first sip.

"Can't rightly remember. It was Archie's mother's house, a long while since."

"Can I use your telephone again, make another call?"

"Aye, you help yourself, m'dear; I don't have much call for it."

Liam got up and dialled Mrs Thornton's number. It rang for probably thirty seconds and Liam was about to give up when the call was picked up.

"Is that Mrs Thornton?"

"Yes, who's this?" It was answered abruptly as if the recipient was being disturbed.

"Oh, am I glad to hear you. It's Liam Drake from Pendle Cottage; we've had an accident."

There was a pause. The demeanour changed to one of concern. "Oh, an accident, I'm sorry to hear that. Is everyone alright?"

"Yes, we're fine thanks but the car's died."

"Oh, that's terrible. Where are you?"

"We're at Chine Cottage."

"What...? Mrs Wilkins place?"

"Yes."

"Oh dear, stay there; I'll come and collect you right away."

"That's very kind of you, thank you."

"About twenty minutes; I'll be as quick as I can."

"No problem, thanks again." Liam hung up.

"That was Mrs Thornton; she's coming to pick us up," he announced.

"Oh, that's nice of her. She didn't have to; we could have walked," said Jo.

"She didn't give me an option. Said she would be here in about twenty minutes."

Liam sat back down and picked up his tea cup.

"Do you want another cup? I can make some fresh," said Mrs Wilkins.

"No, I'm fine thanks."

"How do you manage here on your own?" asked Jo.

"What do you mean?" She looked at Jo with an expression of surprise.

"Well, do you get Social Services popping in to help?"

"No, no, nothin' like that; the Squire comes by and sees to everything. Looks after me like I was his mother, he do."

"Really? Well, that's good. What about the pandemic, the lockdown? How did you cope with that?"

"Oh, that. We never bothered 'ere. No one caught nothin' as far as I knows; never had none of them injections neither. The Squire reckons it was the Government trying to scare people; that's what he said. Would you like another cup of tea?"

"No, I'm fine, thanks," said Jo. She looked at Farrah. "What about you, Poppet?"

"No, thanks. Can I use the toilet?"

"Of course, m'dear. It's upstairs. Your mum can take you; me legs don't take too kindly to stairs these days. Just through there, you'll see," said the old woman, pointing to the kitchen door.

Jo got up and escorted Farrah. The stairs were through the door that led to the kitchen, on the right.

The toilet was at the top of the creaking staircase, and while Farrah was relieving herself, Jo went into the adjacent bedroom and looked through the window. The view was spectacular. To the left she could see the village and the harbour below. To the right, the Volvo; she suddenly realised how close it was to the edge of the cliff, beyond that, the trees. The earlier fog seemed to have cleared completely.

She looked around the bedroom; very modest with just a bed and a dressing table; it seemed it had not been decorated for many years. Jo felt a sadness as she noticed an old black and white picture of a man in uniform on the bedside cabinet.

Jo and Farrah returned to the sitting room where Liam was in conversation with the old woman. She looked up. "Did you find it alright, m'dear?"

"Yes, thank you," Jo replied. She finished the remainder of her tea and placed the empty cup on the tray.

She looked at the old woman. "Do you mind me asking? Were you here at the time of the accident, the little girls?"

Mrs Wilkins was holding her cup in two hands to avoid spilling any tea; her hands started to shake.

"Aye, we're not supposed to talk about it."

"Why's that?" asked Jo.

"It upsets 'em."

"Who does it upset?"

"Them that can't speak."

Just then a Kia 4x4 pulled up outside and Liam could see Mrs. Thornton getting out.

"Oh, that's our lift," said Liam.

Jo and the children stood up.

"Thank you so much Mrs Wilkins for your hospitality, you have been very kind. Can I help with the washing up?" said Jo.

"No, no, no, I can manage. You get yourself away."

She struggled out of her chair and Jo gave her a hug. The old lady smelled of moth-balls. "Can we pop by again while we're here?"

"Aye, I don't see why not. I don't go out much these days," said the old woman and shuffled towards the front door following the family.

Mrs Thornton was stood by the driver's door as the children got in the back. Jo turned and waved to the old lady.

"Oh, I just remembered, we need to get the bags out of the car, Liam; have you got the keys?"

Liam rummaged in his pocket and gave Jo the fob.

She walked across the barren patch of ground next to the cottage and through the gap in the chain-link fence made by the out-of-control car. She aimed the fob at the stricken Volvo and the hazard lights indicated reception. The car was facing her and she walked around to the back.

As she was about to open the boot door of the Estate, she felt a presence, then voices, playful, children's voices. They seemed to be coming from the other side of the cliff edge, just a few yards behind her. She shivered and looked towards the trees; the fog seemed to be rolling at the edges. Jo made a grab for the bags; she would leave the fishing gear, and locked up. Suddenly a dark shape ran across her feet from under the car and into the long grass; a snake, not a large snake, and not venomous, disturbed from its resting place. Jo screamed and walked quickly back to the Kia.

Liam had heard the scream and got out as Jo walked towards him. "Are you ok?"

"Yes, I'm fine. I just saw a snake; it really made me jump."

"A snake? Goodness, you've gone quite pale."

Mrs Thornton heard the conversation. "Oh, that's probably a grass snake; there are quite a few around here. They're quite harmless, they won't bite or anything."

Jo handed the bags to Liam and got in the back with the children.

"Are you alright, mom?" said Farrah.

"Yes, I'm fine, Poppet."

She breathed in deeply and decided to say nothing about the voices.

Liam turned to the driver. "We're so grateful, Mrs Thornton, for coming to pick us up. We were quite happy to walk."

"It's no problem; I wasn't busy. Sunday's tend to drag... It's April, by the way." Liam was confused.

"My name," clarified Mrs Thornton, and laughed.

"Oh, yes, right, April."

The Kia pulled forward and Liam pointed to the Volvo. The wire fence had been pushed down by the impact and lay on the ground. There were tyre tracks through the long grass and the front of the car was visible about thirty feet into the field. "That's where the car ended up."

"Goodness, you were so lucky; it really is close to the edge of the cliff."

"Yes, I didn't see it till I got out. I'll pay for the damage to the fence, by the way; if you know who owns it."

"I think it's the Council; I wouldn't worry about it," said April. "So, what happened?"

"Well, we were going to the supermarket in St Austell to stock up. When we got to the top of the hill, by that shrine up there, we hit a bank of fog and the car just died on me."

"Fog? So, you were leaving the village?"

"Yes, as I said, we were going over to St Austell."

"I see."

Liam was looking up the road which was completely clear. "It's strange, the fog seems to have gone now."

"Yes it has. So, what did you do?" said Mrs Thornton as she made a three-point turn.

"Well, the car was stuck in the middle of the road which was incredibly dangerous given the lack of visibility, so I decided to roll it back and park somewhere safer. One minute I was slowly rolling backwards; the next thing I knew, the brakes had gone and I was careering down the hill. I managed to steer it into the field, otherwise I could have ended up in the sea. I had no idea about the cliff."

"Hmm, yes, it's very dangerous; there's a problem with erosion, you know. We've had geologists here to look at it and they say it's only a matter of time. We could lose some of the cottages."

"That's terrible," said Liam.

"Yes, it is. We've tried persuading Mrs Wilkins to move; but she insists on staying."

"Yes, it must be difficult," said Liam.

"So, what's going to happen?" asked April,

She was dressed casually in jeans, slip-on shoes, and an attractive sleeveless top; her makeup was fresh.

"Well, the breakdown people can't get out until tomorrow morning. They said they would ring with a time. I hope you don't mind, I gave them your number; there's no mobile phone signal here."

"No, that's fine. I can take you up to meet them if you like."

"That's very good of you, thank you."

April glanced right at the cottage as she started back

down the hill.

She quickly looked across at Liam. "Did Mrs Wilkins say anything?"

"About what?"

"Hmm, well she's suffering from dementia, you know, and she can ramble a bit. She has a notion that the trees speak to her, spirits and all that. Mind, I've not spoke to her for a while but Christopher has."

"Christopher?"

"Yes, Christopher Deakin, people call him 'the Squire'; I have no idea why. He lives next to the old rectory."

"Ah, yes, the landlord at the pub mentioned him; the one with the internet."

"Yes, that's him." April turned her head slightly to direct her comments to the back of the car. "So, are you alright for food? Only, it's too late to go to St Austell?"

"Well, I've only got bread and some beans in until I can get to the shop," replied Jo.

"Oh, we can't have that; we'll call in the house. I've got a few things in the freezer. I get a delivery from the supermarket once a month."

"Oh, so you don't use the shop in the village?"

"Goodness no, she never has anything in. I don't know how she manages to make any money."

"But going back to Mrs Wilkins, surely she can't look after herself?" said Jo.

"Well, as I said, Christopher pops in fairly regularly. She's got no family that we know of."

"It must be dreadfully lonely for her," said Jo, as they reached the sea front and turned right.

"She has a next-door neighbour that pops in occasionally. Mind you, he's nearly as bad as she is."

The car passed the pub and turned right up the narrow

'nip'. "I've got a parking spot at the top." April explained, and drove slowly up the hill. After the row of cottages there was a patch of waste ground and she parked up.

Geographically, they were the other side of the valley and they could just see the tops of the cottages in the distance where the car had broken down. The dark granite cliff face rose sharply from the valley floor. To the left, the trees that would stretch back all the way to the main road.

They left the car and walked down to April's cottage.

"While we're here, I'll just pop to the pub to get some pound coins for the electricity," said Liam, as the rest of the family followed April into the cottage.

A few minutes later, the family were reunited and back in April's car.

Jo was holding her purse. She took out a twenty pound note and passed it to April.

"Please take this; it will cover the food, and your petrol."

"Oh, you didn't have to, but thanks." She took the money and started the car.

April looked across at Liam. "Did you manage to get the change?"

"Yes, it should last us a few days, I hope."

The car pulled away. "I was saying to Jo, earlier, how on earth do you survive here? It should be packed out with tourists. The pub was empty," said Liam.

"Oh, we manage. The fishing's important; that's what brings in the money. Clem had his own boat until he retired, so he's not short."

"Clem?"

"The landlord at the pub," April clarified.

They left the seafront and after five minutes pulled up outside the cottage.

"Would you like to come in for a drink, April, if you're

not busy? It's the least we can do," said Jo. "We'd love to hear more about the village, wouldn't we, dear?"

"Sure," replied Liam.

"No, I'm not busy," replied April.

"You can stay for dinner if you like; there'll be enough for all of us."

"No, it's fine thanks, but I'll join you for a drink."

They exited the car and April locked up. For some reason, Liam felt wary as he approached the front door and got out his keys, but there was no repetition of the tripping incident.

"I'm going to play on my computer game," said Zack and headed upstairs to his room.

"I'm going to see if Lily's there. I can play with her," said Farrah, and followed her brother.

Jo went to the kitchen to put the produce she had chosen from April's freezer into the fridge, then returned to the sitting room holding a bottle of red wine and three glasses.

"I don't know about you but I could murder a drink," said Jo. "Are you ok with red?" she added, looking at April.

April seemed distracted. "Oh, oh, yes, that would be lovely, thank you; it's been a while since I've had any alcohol."

Jo poured out the drinks and picked up her glass. "Cheers." April and Liam responded.

"And thanks for all you have done for us today. We're very grateful," said Liam.

April still seemed distant. "Oh, it's fine, don't mention it... Can I ask you something? Did your daughter say she was going to play with Lily?"

"Yes," said Jo. "Between you and me, I think she's got a make-believe friend; you know what girls can be like, and she does have a vivid imagination."

"Yes, of course," said April. "It's just that, well, the little girl who lived here, the one who was killed, her name was Lily."

"The murder, you mean? Really? How strange," said Jo and looked at Liam.

"Yes, you heard about that?"

"Oh, only that there had been a murder here, in January. The landlord at the pub mentioned it; but he wouldn't go into detail," said Liam.

"No, no, the villagers won't talk about it; it's a superstition thing," said April.

"Well, I must admit, I don't think we'd have booked the cottage if we had known about it," said Jo.

"Yes, I can appreciate that. It was the solicitor's idea, actually," said April. "We tried putting it on the market but had no interest, so they suggested advertising it as a holiday let."

"Hmm, I'm not surprised you didn't get any buyers," said Jo. "So, what happened, the murder?"

"It was tragic, the police wouldn't go into too much detail; we had to get most of the information from the newspapers. The village was crawling with police; we had forensic people down here from Plymouth for at least a week. Then, there were the reporters and news crews. It was one of them that killed the twins."

"Oh, yes, the shrine by the village sign. We heard about that."

"Yes, dreadful, dreadful. Some of the villagers seem to think there's some kind of curse, or some such nonsense." She took another sip of her drink.

"So, the murder, what happened, can you tell us?"

April took a long drink of wine. "Well, from what it said in the newspapers, the whole family were beaten to death. The Waltons, lovely people, George, Lizzy, and little Lily, it was desperately sad. Who on earth would want to do that, I have no idea. The police were here for ages but they've never caught anyone. They turned the place inside out. It was a hell of a mess after they left. I had to have it completely redecorated."

"So, you own it, the cottage?"

"Yes, we bought it as an investment, my late husband and I, not long after we moved here."

"Late husband?" said Liam.

"Yes, he was killed in a diving accident in 2016. We'd just finished renovating the cottage and he went out with one of his friends to the wreck." April looked down at her wine, the hurt still visible.

"The wreck?" said Liam.

"Yes, there's a Spanish Galleon, part of the Armada, about three miles off the coast; it's a popular diving spot. Unfortunately, Stuart's gear got caught up, according to the Coroner, a tragic accident."

Liam looked at Jo.

"Oh, I'm so sorry," said Liam.

"It's ok, thanks. It was going to be our big project, Pendle Cottage. Stuart and I spent months renovating it - plumbing, wiring, the lot. It hadn't been touched in fifty years."

"Out of interest, where does the name come from?" asked Jo.

"I don't honestly know; we did try to look it up. We thought it might have something to do with the witch trials in Lancashire in the seventeenth century, but it's always been known as Pendle Cottage as far as I know," replied April.

Jo looked at Liam.

"So, what happened next, after you'd finished?" asked Liam.

"We managed to let it to a couple in London as a second

home, but of course, with the pandemic, they weren't able to visit, so they gave notice. It was empty for a while, and then the Waltons got in touch through the agents; said it was just what they were looking for. They arrived just after the end of lockdown, about a year or so ago it would be. Moved here from Plymouth. George was an illustrator; he used to use one of the bedrooms as a studio. Lizzie worked at the school in St Austell where Lily went to. I used to see them quite regularly, lovely family. Got really involved with the community. We have a meeting once a month at the village hall; they always used to come."

"That's terrible; and the twins, what happened there?" asked Jo.

"Oh, that was so awful." She took another drink of her wine. "They had been out for a walk with Ashley, their mother. They were at the top of the bank, not far from Mrs Wilkins place, and this car came out of the fog and just went into them. Killed instantly, according to the post mortem. Ashley was a close friend of mine. We use to go shopping over in St Austell, even Plymouth during the school holidays."

"What's happened to her?"

"She's got a sister in Reading and went to stay with her; she's not been back since. Her cottage is a couple of doors up from mine, the end one. I've tried contacting her, but she's not answered my calls."

"Oh, that's so tragic. What happened about the driver?"

"It was one of the journalists, sent over to cover the murder, driving too fast. He said he hit some fog as he was coming into the village. The police arrested him, but while he was out on bail, he was killed on the motorway a couple of days later. Apparently, his car broke down and was hit by a lorry. That's what it said in the papers."

"My goodness; how tragic."

"Yes, it was; although I don't think anyone round here were shedding any tears."

"No, I can understand that. So, what do you do?"

"I'm a freelance writer," said April. "I write for several of the nationals, mostly the weekend supplements."

"Really? How on earth do you manage, without the internet, I mean?" said Liam.

"I use Christopher's when I want to email."

"The squire?"

"Ha, yes. I usually pop over on Thursdays to send the copy for the weekend editions, but if they want anything separately, then he lets me know. He picks up my emails. I can use my laptop at home, just no internet."

"So, how long have you lived here?"

"We bought Swallow Cottage in 2012, that's my place, and we used it as a second home for a couple of years, but we decided to get off the merry-go-round. We were both had demanding jobs. Stuart was a Commodities Broker in the City; I worked as journalist for one of the dailies. We sold our place in Pimlico and moved here permanently in 2014."

"It must have been a hell of a transformation?" said Liam.

"Yes, it was, but it was what we both wanted. It was a much better quality of life. Stuart managed to get a job on one of the boats, and I continued with my writing freelancing. I don't think we were ever happier."

"What about the locals?" asked Liam. "You hear things about close-knit communities not being particularly welcoming."

"Ha, it took a while, but once Stuart started working and mixing with the villagers, it was fine. He was a regular down the Crab."

"The crab?"

"Oh, sorry, the pub. They always called it 'the Crab', the

fishermen."

"Ah, yes," said Liam.

"Mind you, they are a superstitious lot," continued April.

"Would you like a top up?" asked Jo, noticing April's glass was empty.

"I shouldn't, but go on. It's been ages since I've had some good company."

Jo finished pouring the rest of the wine in equal measures.

April took a sip. "You were saying about the villagers being superstitious," said Liam.

Jo and Liam were listening intently. "Oh, yes, ha. Do you know one, of the fishermen suggested Stuart was killed by a Bucca."

Liam looked at Jo. "A Bucca?" said Liam.

"Yes, it's a sea spirit; that's how Jack explained it."

"Jack...? Oh, I think I met him today. Gave us some bait. Zack and I went fishing this morning."

"Yes, he's got one of the cottages on Low Harbour. He reckons that Stuart had upset a Bucca by diving on the wreck. It still has bones of dead sailors onboard, apparently. Do you know if the fishermen catch a Conger Eel, they throw it back immediately? According to the folklore here, the Bucca can take the shape of an eel. They even throwback one fish from every catch to appease them."

"That's amazing in this day and age," said Liam.

"It is, but it's quite quaint really. Adds to the charm of the village, I think."

"So, what do you think? Do you believe in these evil spirits?" asked Liam.

April looked at him with a serious expression. "Let's just say that not everything that happens has an explanation."

"Hmm, that's true," said Liam, pensively. His thoughts suddenly went back to the incident in the old privy.

"Actually, the woman at the shop said that this place is cursed," said Jo.

"Hmm, yes, that will be Mrs Trevelyan. She said the same to us not long after we bought it." April was now looking pensive and took a sip of wine. She looked at Liam and Jo. "If you ever want to know anything about the folklore around here, you should ask her; she's an authority on anything to do with Polgissy. I don't think she's ever left the village in her life. Her Dad used to run the store till he died, and he was in his nineties."

"So, do you think it's cursed, the cottage?" asked Jo.

"Goodness, no, we had a great time renovating the place, and we found lots of interesting things. There were some old papers hidden under the floorboards in one of the bedrooms dating back to the sixteenth century."

"Oh, really, how fascinating," said Jo.

"Yes, we took them over to the museum in Truro. I don't know what they did with them. The writing wasn't in English. Stuart thought it might be Spanish. The archivist had an idea that the papers might be from one of the crew of the wrecked galleon and was hiding here, but I don't think they've managed to translate them yet. Actually, you've reminded me, I must give them a call and see if they have found anything. I haven't spoken to them in ages."

April finished her wine. "Oh, there is one superstition that involves the churchyard you might be interested in."

"Go on," said Liam. She leaned closer and spoke in a whisper.

"Well, according to local folklore, you can hear the sound of a ship's bell tolling four and eight bells at midnight on the night of the full moon. There's a grave of a sea captain in the churchyard who, legend has it, refused to leave his sinking ship until all his sailors were safe; Captain Dewar was his name. He went down with the ship and his body was washed up on the foreshore a few days later. According to the story, a Bucca returned the body in recognition of his bravery. That's one of Jack's; Stuart told it me. I'll never forget it. Several of the villagers say they've heard the bell, but what on earth they were doing in the graveyard at midnight, heaven only knows."

April looked at her watch.

"Actually, I better get going. Thanks for the wine. I'll call round tomorrow after I've heard from the breakdown people."

Jo and Liam stood up and gave April a cheek kiss. "No, thank you for driving us about, and for your stories. It's been fascinating."

April left the cottage and Farrah came down the stairs.

"Hello, Poppet, did you manage to play with you friend?"

"No, I think she was busy. What's for dinner? I'm hungry."

"You're as bad as your brother. You can give me a hand if you like. How do you fancy lamb casserole?"

"That sounds good," said Liam, hearing the conversation.

"Yes, April gave me some lamb chops; I thought I would cook them with some vegetables in a casserole. There's some gravy cubes in the pantry; I'll see what else I can find. Do you think there are any herbs in the garden?"

"I don't know, we can have a look. Do you want to come and help me, Far?" said Liam.

"Sure," replied Farrah.

While Jo started preparing the meal, Liam opened the back door. He felt uneasy as he left the kitchen. The sky was no longer blue, but filled with billowing clouds. Farrah was right beside him as he walked slowly up the path.

"Oh, look, Far, swallows. They're nesting in the eaves. Can you see?"

They both watched as the mother bird swooped into the small mud nest followed by a considerable amount of chirping, and away she went again.

"Hey, that's cool," said Farrah.

They left the lee of the cottage and Liam started scanning the array of weeds and assorted wild flowers.

"What do herbs look like, Dad? I've only seen them in the jars Mom gets from the supermarket."

"Hmm, good question. They're green mostly," said Liam.

"What about these?" Farrah made a grab for a bunch of stinging nettles.

"No! Don't touch those," shouted Liam. She pulled her hand away just in time.

"They're stinging nettles; they can really hurt. Come and look what I've found." Liam was further up the footpath and pointed to a neat row of carrot tops.

Farrah walked to his side and looked down. "What are they?"

"Carrots, look, there are lots of them. I just need something to dig them up with."

He remembered the tools in the privy. "Wait here, I won't be a moment."

"Where are you going?"

"There's a spade in the shed over there."

"No, you shouldn't go in there."

Liam stopped. "Why do you say that?"

"I don't know, but I don't think they will be pleased."

"Who?"

"I don't know. I heard them say. Can we go back? I'm cold."

"Yes, ok, just give me a minute; I'll see if I can pull them up."

Liam wrapped his hand around the first plant and gave it a tug. Gradually the resistance gave way and a bright orange/red vegetable about six inches long appeared.

"Hey, look at that. Mum'll be pleased. Let's get a few more then we'll go in. Do you want to help?"

Farrah walked over and pulled on one of the plants. The ground was still fairly soft from the previous evening's storm, and the carrot appeared.

"Well done, just a couple more. Oh, and I think there's some thyme over there, and some parsley. Wait, it looks like it was a herb garden."

Liam walked towards the small plot on the edge of the garden, just below the boundary hedge.

"Hey, look what I've found." Liam was holding a child's plastic spade.

Farrah dropped her carrots and went over to Liam.

"Don't touch that; it's Lily's."

"Lily's"

"Yes."

"How do you know that?"

Farrah took the spade from Liam and placed it back on the ground next to the thyme bush.

"I don't know. Can we go in now?"

"Yes, ok let's just take a couple of sprigs of this and our carrots."

They walked back to the kitchen and presented their finds to Jo who was at the sink peeling potatoes.

"Look what we found," said Liam, proudly. "Show your Mum."

Farrah lifted up the fresh carrots.

"Hey, that's great," said Jo.

"And I found some thyme, too. There's a small herb

garden over by the hedge; there's plenty more carrots and some potatoes. I think they must have been keen gardeners, the Waltons."

"Yes, it's so sad, and here we are benefiting from all their work."

"Well, they will only rot, so, I'm sure they won't mind."

"Lily says it's ok," said Farrah.

Jo looked at Liam.

"What do you mean?" asked Jo, her expression one of concern.

"She won't mind, that's all," said Farrah. "I'm going to my room."

She put the carrots down on the worktop and headed into the sitting room. Jo looked at Liam.

"What was all that about?"

"I don't know, but I found a child's spade by the herb garden. Farrah said it belonged to Lily. She was quite insistent I left it alone."

"Hmm, it's a worry, but I don't think we should make a big thing about it; she could be just making it up. You know what a vivid imagination she has. Her teacher even comment on it. She was saying some of the stories she writes for school show a very creative mind; those were her words."

"No, I agree. Hmm, something smells nice."

"That will be the onions. I found a net of them hanging up at the back of the pantry. I've no idea how long they've been there, but they were ok."

By seven-thirty, the family had eaten and the chores done. Zack and Farrah were back in their rooms playing computer games. Both Liam and Jo were reading. The room was bathed in some early evening brightness as the clouds rolled back to allow the sun a last hurrah.

Liam was having difficulty concentrating on his book; the words on the page seemed to be dancing in lines mocking his ability of making sense of them. He was thinking about Farrah and her comments in the garden and whether to say anything to Jo. For the moment, he decided to keep it to himself. As Jo had said, it was probably her imagination.

He put the book down and stood up, then lifted the empty wine bottle. "Is there anymore wine left?"

Jo looked up from her book. "There should be another bottle in the pantry; you'll see it, on the floor."

Liam got up from the settee, went through the kitchen, and opened the pantry door. The drop in temperature was quite marked and he shivered as he reached for the bottle on the floor. It was not a large room, about double the size of the broom cupboard in their London home.

He picked up the bottle and, for no particular reason, started scanning the three shelves at the back. There were several cans of food; beans, spaghetti, peas, sweetcorn, mixed vegetables, and six cans of soup in different varieties. There was a layer of dust and dead insects across the top of them. He picked up one of the cans and checked the 'sell-by' date, then put it back.

To the left, there was a grimy window with a small circular metal dot-grill to let in fresh air. Then something caught his eye. "What on earth!?"

Chapter Five

He returned to the sitting room. "Jo, come and have a look at this."

Jo sighed at being interrupted.

"It won't take a moment," said Liam.

The pair walked through the kitchen into the pantry. "Have you seen the tins of food?"

"Yes, I meant to thank April; it was very generous of her."

"Hmm, well I don't think it was her generosity; they've been here a while. Have a look at the sell-buy dates."

Jo picked up a can of soup; a dead blue-bottle dropped to the floor. "Hey, you're right; it's next month."

"Yes, and these cans would last for probably twelve months, maybe longer."

"There are a couple of jars of jam too. It looks like one of them's been opened."

Jo undid the lid and looked inside.

"Urgh, well that will have to be chucked; it's covered with fur. Reminds me of the culture trays at Uni. April probably got them from the shop; goodness knows how old the stock is there."

"Hmm, possibly but that doesn't account for all the dust."

"No, that's true."

"Or the fur."

"Hmm."

"I think they belonged to the Waltons."

"Really?"

"Yes, it's the only explanation. But that's not what I wanted to show you. Have a look up there, above the window, the lintel."

"What am I looking at?"

"Those markings."

"Oh, yes, I'd not noticed them."

"Well, there's no reason why you would."

"It looks like two diamonds, interlocked in a circle. What do they mean?"

"I'm not sure, but I know in some old houses they used symbols to ward off evil spirits and witches."

"Hmm. Maybe one of the past owners was a Mason."

"No, no, these are definitely not Masonic. Wait, I'll get my phone and take a photo and next time we can get an Internet connection; I can try and look it up."

They both left the pantry, Jo clutching the bottle of wine. Liam returned with his phone and took several pictures of the markings.

Two forty-two was displayed on the luminous dial of the alarm clock on Liam and Jo's bedside cabinet. In Farrah's bedroom, the temperature had dropped significantly and she was tucked under the covers.

"Hello Farrah, can you come out to play?"

Farrah stirred. The voice was familiar.

"Please play with me; I'm so lonely."

Farrah's eyes opened, a blank stare. She rolled onto her back then slowly raised herself into a sitting position without using her arms.

"Hello Lily. Yes, I can play. Have you seen the shells I found on the beach today? They are so pretty. They are on the table."

"Yes, I can see them; I wish I could hold them."

"You can; I don't mind."

The bag of shells was on the dressing table. A gust of cold air swirled around the bedroom, disturbing Farrah's hair. She stared straight ahead, unmoved. The bag of shells rustled, then inched forward then stopped, more rustling, then again. It reached the end of the dressing table. Gravity took hold and they fell to the floor; the contents scattered across the carpet.

"Oh, yes, they are pretty. I will take one for my garden."

"Yes, you can take what you like. I saw your garden today; your spade is quite safe. I left it where it was."

"I used to like helping my Daddy, but I don't know where he is now. I've been looking everywhere for him."

"I hope you find him."

"Thank you, Farrah, you are a kind person. You must be careful here; there are some bad people. They might try to hurt you."

"Yes, I will."

"Oh, I need to go, they are calling me. I will play again when I'm allowed."

Farrah was still sat upright; the room had return to normal temperature. She blinked her eyes, then slowly lowered herself back to her pillow and hunkered down under the covers.

She was awake by quarter-to-eight; and was about to get out of bed, when she noticed the shells scattered across the floor. She stepped out carefully trying to avoid treading on them in her bare feet. There were one or two still in the wet-wipe bag. She started picking up the spilt shells and returned them to their container then replaced it back on the dressing table.

Farrah walked out of her bedroom and called. "Mom, what time's breakfast?"

By eight-thirty the family were eating. Liam had finished a bowl of porridge and was tucking into some toast. He had endured a restless night. He looked at Jo.

"Do you know, I had the weirdest of dreams again last night about a Spanish Sea Captain. I can even remember his name... Cortes."

"Oh, that narrows it down a bit; I thought they were all called Cortes," said Jo and started to laugh. "I've told you about eating cheese before you go to bed; you know it doesn't agree with you."

"I didn't have any cheese. Mind you, three glasses of wine; that probably did it."

"Yes, that's true." Jo helped herself to another slice of toast. "We do need to go to the supermarket today. Do you think you'll get a replacement car while ours is being fixed?"

"Well, we should do. I'll make enquiries with the driver when he comes."

Just after eleven o'clock, April's Kia pulled up outside the cottage.

"April's here," shouted Liam. Jo was in the kitchen, the children in their bedrooms.

Liam went to the front door and invited April in before she had the chance to knock.

"Hi April, how are you? We won't be a minute, just rounding everybody up."

"That's ok, the breakdown firm have just been on the phone; the driver should be here in half an hour."

"Hello, April, how are you," said Jo, as she came in from the kitchen,

"Fine thanks," April acknowledged. "Nice morning."

"The breakdown truck's on its way. We need to get going; I don't want to miss him," called Liam.

Five minutes later, the family were in the Kia and heading to the abandoned Volvo.

April parked in the spot adjacent to Mrs Wilkins' cottage.

"He's not here yet," said Jo. "I think I'll call on Mrs Wilkins and see how she is."

"Can I come?" said Farrah.

"And me," said Zack.

"Yes, but behave yourselves," said Jo.

"I'll stay and wait for the truck," said Liam.

"I'll keep you company," said April.

Jo walked around the boundary wall and up the footpath to Mrs Wilkins' front door. She knocked and waited. There was a sound of movement from inside and the door opened. The old woman's eyes squinted in the sunshine.

"Hello, m'dears, how are you?" She stared at the callers. "Come in, would you like a cup of tea? I don't get many visitors but you're the second in two days. I had a lovely family call yesterday. Their car 'ad broke down."

"Yes, thanks, Mrs Wilkins."

They followed the old woman inside; the door closed behind them. Liam and April went to the stricken Volvo.

The fence was still lay on the floor. "You better not come too far; we don't want the cliff to give way."

"It's granite; it should be fine," said April, and walked behind Liam who started examining the bodywork. He rubbed his hand down the exterior.

"Hmm, one or two scratches, but it could have been much worse."

"Yes," said April.

"Thank goodness that fog's gone," said Liam scanning the trees along to the road.

"It comes and goes. The locals say it's evil spirits."

"What...? Do you mean, like poltergeists?"

"Something like that," replied April. "Do you know

anything about the spirit world?"

"No, not a thing, but I did see the film when I was a kid."

"Film?"

"Yes, Poltergeist."

"Ah, I see."

"Scared me to death."

Just then the throaty roar of a truck could be heard in the distance,

"Oh, that sounds like our man," said Liam, and walked back towards the roadside.

Moments later, the truck appeared, complete with rotating flashing yellow light. The words 'Brotherton's Autos, St Austell' were emblazoned on the side in red paint.

Liam walked into the road and started waving. The truck drew to a halt on the grass verge next to the Kia.

The driver jumped down from the cab clutching an iPad.

"Hello, Jim Brotherton, Brotherton's Autos, I understand you've 'ad a problem; your breakdown insurance people have been in touch. Mr Drake is it?" He spoke in that lovely Cornish brogue.

"Yes, thanks so much for coming; there was no-one available yesterday they told us."

"Aye, that's true enough. I was out till ten last night."

"Well, it's handy being local, you must know the area. They couldn't find the postcode on their system."

"Aye? Is that right...? Mind you, this is the first time I've been down here; never had cause. The wife's been once. She said the place was dead."

"Yes, I can understand that," interjected April and smiled.

"So, what seems to be the problem?" said Jim.

"It's over here." Liam led the man to the Volvo, explaining the circumstances.

"Can you open the bonnet? I'll just get my monitor."

Jim returned to his truck and returned with an impressive looking piece of kit with wires running from it.

"How old is it?"

"I've only had it six months. This was the first long drive. I don't think I've done two thousand miles."

"Hmm, I see, well, these Volvos have got diagnostics built in. I'll just check. Can you switch it on?"

"I'll try, but it was completely dead yesterday."

Liam sat in the driver's seat and pressed the ignition button while the mechanic watched. The dash board lit up.

"What the...?"

"Well, that looks promising. Let me check it over," said the mechanic.

Jim spent a few minutes checking the onboard computer. "Well, everything looks normal according to the readings. You mentioned the brakes?"

"Yes, they had completely gone. I had my foot on the floor."

"Press them now."

"That's strange, they feel normal, but... I can't make it out."

"Just try moving forward next to the truck, for me," said Jim.

He got out and watched while Liam moved the Volvo slowly forward. It bounced over the long tufts of grass and the flattened fence. Liam applied the brakes and the car immediately stopped dead.

April was looking on with interest. "Oh dear," she said to herself.

Liam parked next to the truck and got out. "I don't understand it. I just don't understand it."

"Well, I've checked all the diagnostics and everything reads normal," said Jim. "I can't find anything wrong. The brake indicators are fine. I think you're good to go."

"Well, thanks Jim, I'm sorry to get you out on a wild goose chase."

"It's no problem; I get paid either way," he said and chuckled. "Can you sign this for me?"

He handed Liam the iPad. "It's a touchpad. Just in that space; you can use your finger."

Liam complied and returned the device.

"Thank you, much appreciated," said Liam.

Jim started up the truck and turned around in the road. Clouds of diesel fumes spewed from the exhaust pipe as he accelerated away. Then he was gone, the sound gradually fading into the distance.

Liam just looked at April. "I just don't understand, I really don't."

"Well, everything seems fine. What are you going to do?"

"Well, I need to get some petrol and Jo needs to get some more supplies in, so I think we'll head off to the supermarket."

"Would you like me to come with you? I know the way and where to park."

"Yes, that would be great, thanks. I'll just go and get the family."

A few minutes later, Jo and the two kids were waving to Mrs Wilkins and walking up the path.

"So there was nothing wrong with it?" said Jo, with a hint of surprise in her voice.

"No, he checked everything and all the readings were normal; that's what he said. How was Mrs Wilkins?" asked Liam.

"Oh, she seemed ok, but something was bothering her about the forest. Kept looking out of the window, something about the fog being angry. That's what it sounded like. It was difficult to follow what she was saying; she was mumbling a lot. I said we would call around again. I'd like to keep an eye on her while we're here."

"Oh, you don't need to do that," said April, who had taken an interest in the exchanges. "Christopher calls round regularly to make sure she's ok and if she needs anything."

"Oh, that's good. I'm not sure she should be left on her own."

They walked towards the Volvo.

"So, what do you want to do?" asked Jo.

"I said we would head over to St Austell. April's asked if she could come," said Liam.

Jo looked at April who had been stood next to Liam. "Yes, of course."

"Thanks, I'll just get my things and lock up."

April went to the Kia and collected her handbag then joined the children who were buckling up in the back of the Volvo.

Despite the mechanic's assurance, Liam was uneasy as he started the Volvo. He cautiously increased the pressure on the accelerator and immediately checked the dials. There were no warning lights.

"Don't worry, you'll be fine now," said April.

Liam pondered the remark as he eased the car onto the tarmac and headed up the road. They passed the shrine. Liam couldn't resist taking a glance. He checked the dashboard again; everything looked normal. He applied the brakes and the car immediately responded, sending those in the back forwards in their seat belts.

"Sorry about that, just testing the brakes."

The road was completely clear, not a sign of fog, although the trees were making it very dark. The headlights had automatically reacted to the luminosity and were lighting the way. Then, Liam saw something ahead.

"What's that?" he said and slowed down.

"It's the breakdown truck; looks like an accident," said Jo.

The back end of the truck was just off the road; it's crane hanging loose on its side. The front was in a hollow resting at a forty-five degree angle. Steam was coming from the radiator.

Liam got out of the Volvo and rushed to the scene. As he reached the front of the truck, he looked through the driver's window, then recoiled in horror at the sight in front of him.

There was a large elm tree. The trunk was broken about half way up and forlornly hanging down, its canopy spread across the ground. There were scorch marks in the bark, possibly due to a lightning strike. Below the break, a number of decaying branches pointed in all directions. Most were small, but there were a couple over ten feet long around the base.

One of them had pierced the truck's windscreen like a pike, going straight through the driver's face, and out through the back of his head. There was blood and bits of brain matter everywhere.

Liam turned away and vomited in the bushes. He looked one more time to see if there was any signs of life, but he knew it was hopeless.

Jo and April were out of the car and coming to help, the children peering through the window trying to get a better view.

"No, no, go back, there's nothing we can do. We need the police and ambulance."

Jo took her phone out from her handbag. "I've got a signal," she shouted, and punched in the three nines.

The call was answered straight away. "Yes, we need an

ambulance, and police." She turned to April. "Where are we?"

"High Lane, Polgissy," replied April,

Jo relayed the address. "Please hurry," she exclaimed.

"How's the driver?" asked April.

Liam had joined them. "He's dead. I can't believe it. We were only chatting to him a few minutes ago."

He placed his hands on his knees and started breathing deeply. As he looked up, he noticed something white, swirling away from them in the distance.

"Look, there. It's... the fog."

"Don't worry, it's going away; we're quite safe," said April.

"We better wait in the car," said Liam, and the three got inside and closed the doors.

"Are you ok, Liam? You're as white as a sheet," said Jo.

"I don't know; I feel really weird. It's a sight I never want to see again."

"I think it might be shock," said Jo. "You need to ask the ambulance crew to check you over when they get here."

"I'll be ok."

It was half an hour before they heard the siren in the distance. Liam got out of the car to meet them. No other car had passed during that time. The flashing blue light came into view. Liam stood in the middle of the road and started waving. The ambulance slowed and parked in front of the Volvo. Two paramedics climbed out and walked towards Liam.

"Hi... Pete Conway, senior paramedic. What have we got?" asked the first, a man in his mid-forties in a green uniform. His name was emblazoned on his breast-pocket.

"I don't know," said Liam. "We just came up the road

from Polgissy and saw that truck in the ditch." He pointed to the stricken vehicle. "The driver's dead."

"Right, let's have a look, and you are?"

"Liam, Liam Drake."

They were quickly joined by a fresh-faced woman in her early twenties.

"This is Alice Caldwell, my partner."

Liam led the two medics to the front of the truck.

"I better warn you, it's not a pretty sight."

Pete reached the cab and stared at the carnage. "Jeezus... You better stay back Alice; I'll deal with this."

He opened the cab door and checked the driver's pulse, but was only able to confirm Liam's diagnosis.

He noticed a mobile phone on the floor and picked it up. "The police might want this. Did you call them?"

"Yes, although I don't know how long they'll be."

"I'll give them another shout from the ambulance and chase them up."

"I'll do it," said Alice, and she climbed into the cab and picked up the walkie-talkie.

Pete and Liam were outside the ambulance.

"In all my years on ambulances, I've never seen anything like that before. I mean, what were the chances of him hitting that branch, and at that angle? It must be like, a million to one."

"Yes, I can't understand it. It was my car he'd come to repair. We'd broken down yesterday just outside the village. If we hadn't called the breakdown people; he'd still be alive."

"The fickle hand of fate," said the medic. "We get called out all the time, but you never get used to it. I've seen some awful tragedies, particularly high speed collisions; they're the worst. The dual carriageway towards Plymouth is notorious. We must get a shout at least once a week... Are you alright? You look very pale; I can check you over if you like."

"No, I'll be ok; it's been a bit of a shock, that's all."

"Well, if you feel no better in a couple of hours, get yourself over to A and E; they'll have a quick look at you, see you're ok."

"Thanks, I'll be fine."

The medic suddenly stopped, distracted by movement in the forest. Liam noticed his interested.

"What's that?" he said, pointing into the trees.

"Where?" asked Liam.

"There, over yonder. It looks like fog. Never seen fog this time of year."

Liam followed his direction and could see the swirling mass. It seemed to be moving towards them.

Just then, April got out of the Volvo and joined Liam and the paramedic.

"What's happening?"

"Just waiting for the police. Look, the fog's back again."

April looked at the white cloud. It was swirling around the trees in the distance as if it was dancing.

"Strangest fog, I've ever seen," said the paramedic. "Look it's moving away again. Not seen nothin' like that afore."

"Five minutes," shouted a voice from the cab.

Twenty minutes later, the area was filled with emergency vehicles. A fire engine had also been called to release the unfortunate mechanic.

After providing a statement to the police officer in charge, Liam was allowed to leave and they continued on their way.

"Turn right at the junction," said April as the reached the main road.

After the solitude of Polgissy, St Austell was a welcome change, particularly for the children.

They parked in a multi-story car park not far from the Parish Church.

"I don't know about you, but I could do with something to eat," said Jo, as they exited the car.

"Can we go for a MacDonald's?" said Zack.

"Yes, yes, yes, can we?" echoed Farrah.

"How about you, April, my shout?" said Liam.

"Yes, why not? That would be lovely. I don't think I've ever had one. I've always wanted to try but never had the opportunity."

It was a warm, sunny day and the town was packed with tourists. Jo was dressed in a tee shirt, beige-coloured jeans and trainers. April was wearing a floral-print, knee-length summer dress with white sandals.

Having noticed the restaurant on the way to the car park, it was only a short walk to the fast-food outlet; it was heaving.

"I don't know if we're going to get a seat," said Liam, looking at the queue.

It was a ten-minute wait, but eventually the group were seated and Liam took the orders. Inside, it was rowdy and packed with youngsters. Zack and Farrah had their own table, with the three adults a short distance away.

April looked at the menu, unfazed by the mayhem around them. "What do you recommend?"

"I usually have a Big Mac when I take the kids," said Jo.

"Yes, I've heard a lot about them," said April.

"I'm not feeling very hungry," said Liam, staring at the menu.

"Yes, you're still very pale. I hope you're not sickening for anything," said Jo.

"No, no, I'm fine. I just keep seeing that poor mechanic in his cab. He didn't deserve to die like that."

"Yes, poor man," said April, and started scanning the restaurant. "My goodness, it's so popular."

"It's always like this; the one at home's the same," said Jo.

Liam had gone to get the food accompanied by Farrah. Zack was already on his phone, making the most of the in-house Wi-Fi.

"Where is home, exactly?" asked April.

"Barnes," replied Jo.

"Oh, it's lovely there. So what do you do?"

"I'm a physiotherapist."

"And Liam?"

"He's a barrister."

"A barrister, how interesting."

"Yes, he's just finished a big murder trial at the Old Bailey. He was in need of a break. Well, we both were, really."

She was sat next to Jo and leaned closer to be heard over the mayhem. "Out of curiosity, why did you choose the cottage? It might help with a future marketing campaign," said April and laughed.

"Oh, it was fairly random, actually. We only booked it a couple of weeks ago, a last minute thing; most of the popular places were full, but we quite liked the idea of somewhere off the beaten track."

"Have you been to Cornwall before?"

"A long time ago, when I was at Uni. A group of us went to Newquay. What a holiday that was. The less said about that the better," she said and laughed.

Liam returned to the table with a tray loaded with burgers, fries, and chicken pieces, together with a selection of sauces and three plastic containers of coffee. Farrah was holding two similar containers filled with Cola and gave one to Zack.

"Goodness, how on earth will they manage to drink a whole one of those?" said April, looking at the children sucking on straws.

"Ha, they'll probably leave half of it. I don't know why they serve such large measures. It's full of sugar."

Liam distributed the orders and sat down opposite the two women. He looked pensive and withdrawn.

"Jo was telling me you're a lawyer," said April, helping herself to a few fries.

"Eh... oh, sorry, yes."

"That sounds really exciting. I used to cover court cases occasionally when I worked for the Telegraph."

"You worked for the Telegraph?" said Jo.

"For a couple of years, then I joined The Mail until we moved here."

"Are you alright, Liam?" asked Jo.

"Yes, I'm ok, just a bit tired; I didn't sleep so well last night."

Jo turned to April. "He's been having nightmares. Tell April about the Spanish sea captain."

He smiled for a moment. "Ha, I don't remember much now."

"But you remember his name."

"Ah, yes, Cortes," said Liam and took a bite from his burger.

April almost choked and started coughing. "Are you alright?" asked Jo.

"Yes, yes, thanks." She took a drink of coffee and composed herself.

"You did say Cortes?" asked April.

"Yes, it was quite vivid."

April had a quizzical expression. "You remember I told

you about the old papers I took to the museum?"

"Yes," said Liam.

"There was a name on one of them... Cortes, Francisco Cortes. Stuart thought it might be a will, but as I said, it was all in Spanish. Beautiful handwriting, whoever did write it was clearly intelligent, and artistic."

"What a coincidence," said Jo, who was halfway through her burger. "What do you think of the food?"

"Very good, although I don't think I could make a habit of it," said April.

"No, you'd be the size of a house," said Jo and chuckled.

Liam had gone quiet again and was struggling to finish his food. He looked across at the children who were chatting away to each other, clearly enjoying their outing.

He picked up his phone. "Can you excuse me a moment? I'm just going check my emails while I've got a reception."

Jo looked at him disapprovingly, but he ignored the critical gaze and got up from his seat. He walked towards the exit door. The decibel level had got even higher.

"Look where you're going!" he snapped at a young lad about Zack's age, who had barged into him at the exit. His mother was following and gave Liam a withering look.

A few minutes later, he returned to the table.

"Anything urgent?" enquired Jo.

"No, nothing that won't wait."

He sat back down and started fiddling with his phone. Jo observed the hordes of children, then turned to April.

"Can I ask you a question?"

"Of course," replied April. Her burger was only half eaten and most of her fries were still in their container; it was clear she had finished eating.

"Where are all the children in the village?"

"Hmm, good question. Actually, there aren't any, not

of school age anyway. Those that had children are, what's the term? Empty nesting, yes that's it. There's no work in the village, so they leave. Plymouth, Exeter, Bristol. That's where the jobs are. One or two are in London. The average age of the village now is probably over seventy."

"What does that say about the sustainability of the village?" said Jo. Liam was still concentrating on his phone.

"It's a good point and it's something we've raised at our village meetings. There's no easy answer. The fishing industry's virtually dead; just a couple of boats now, and I'm sure when Jack, and Matt Davies retire, that will be then end of that. It's very hard trying to make a living these days. Tourism would be the obvious answer, but the residents are dead against B & B's and holiday lets. I've had one or two comments already since you arrived about outsiders. For some reason they see it as a threat... like the Internet. Some think it's the devil incarnate."

"Hmm, they might have a point," said Jo and smiled.

"I think it's an age thing; people are just resistant to change," said April.

Liam looked up from his phone. "Has everybody finished? We should get the shopping out of the way and get back."

"Yes," said Jo, and called to Zack and Farrah, who were chatting with two other children on an adjacent table.

An hour later, the group were heading back to the village. Liam had filled the car with petrol and drawn some cash out from the automatic dispenser at the garage, while Jo, April, and the children did the shopping in the huge 'superstore', as it was branded. There were several plastic carrier bags in the boot.

They reached the sign to the village on the main road and Liam turned left. The atmosphere quickly changed. The trees surrounded them like a shroud, cutting out the sunlight. The Volvo's headlights illuminated the road once more. The map on the dashboard screen had disappeared.

"Looks like the fog's lifted," said Liam.

"Yes, it should be clear now," said April.

Liam slowed as they reached the scene of the accident. The fire engine and ambulance had gone, but there was still a police car and a large recovery vehicle which was in the process of removing the beleaguered truck from its resting place. Two officers were supervising.

One of them held his hand up for Liam to stop, and they watched while the breakdown wagon was pulled out of the ditch. Liam could see the hole in the windscreen where the branch had penetrated, almost a perfect circle. The blood-splattered cab was also visible. He shivered.

Eventually, the manoeuvre was completed and the officer waved Liam through. A few minutes later, they were out of the trees and passing the shrine. Liam felt a sense of relief.

The harbour and sea stretched out before them. It was a fine late afternoon and there was no sign of the fog. Liam pulled up outside Mrs Wilkins' cottage.

April got out and said her farewells to Jo and the children. Liam was at the back of the car opening the boot to allow April to reach in and collect her shopping. As she turned, her hand brushed Liam's; there was a shock of static electricity which made him jump.

April looked at him in the eyes. "Sorry," she said then lowered her gaze.

There was a brief pause. "Have you got everything?" said Liam, breaking the moment.

"Yes, thanks, and for letting me join you; I've enjoyed it."

"Anytime," said Liam.

April walked to her car and opened the boot to stow the shopping. She waved to Jo and the children as the Volvo pulled away and headed down the steep incline into the village. Liam was taking no chances maintaining a speed of no more than twenty miles an hour; the brakes did their job.

A few minutes later, they were outside their cottage and unloading the carrier bags.

"What do you fancy for dinner tonight? After a MacDonald's, I didn't think you would want anything too heavy," asked Jo.

"No, you're right. I don't mind; I'm not very hungry. A sandwich or something will be fine," replied Liam as he took one of the bags into the kitchen.

"I thought we could have a curry tomorrow night; I've bought one of their ready meals" said Jo. "I don't know what it's like, but the picture on the front looks appetising. There's some onion bhajis and samosas too, and some Basmati rice. They'll keep in the fridge."

"Sounds good," replied Liam. "Actually, I think I'll go and have a lie down; I feel shattered."

"Yes, you still look pale. Would you like a cup of tea?"

"Later, thanks."

Just then Farrah joined them in the kitchen. "Mom, can I go and play in Lily's garden?"

Chapter Six

"What do you mean, Poppet?" said Jo, and put her hand on Farrah's shoulder like a concerned mother.

"In the garden, by the carrots."

"Yes, come on, Far, I'll come with you," said Liam. He looked at Jo and whispered out of Farrah's earshot. "I don't want her out there on her own."

Jo gave him a quizzical look. "Do you want anything from the garden?" said Liam in his normal voice.

"I don't think so, unless there's any salad stuff."

"I'll have a look around, see what I can find," said Liam, and yanked the kitchen door open. "I'm sure that's getting worse. It needs planing down. I wonder if April's got any tools."

"Why don't you ask her next time you see her?" said Jo, and watched as Liam and Farrah went into the garden,

"Look, Dad, the birds are back," said Farrah, pointing to the swallows nest. They watched as the parent birds took it in turn to feed their hungry offspring.

"I'm going to Lily's garden," said Farrah, and skipped merrily up the path before crossing the carrot bed.

As she arrived at the small plot, the plastic spade was still there but it was surrounded by a ring of shells, mostly cockle and periwinkle.

"Look, Lily's been playing," said Farrah as Liam joined her. He looked at the display.

"Well, someone has," said Liam.

"I'll just have a look and see if I can find any lettuce."

"I'll stay here," said Farrah.

Liam went back to the footpath and crossed to the other side of the garden below the chicken pen. Among the weeds and wild flowers, he could see a row of lettuces. Behind them, a line of canes with tomato plants, some with their white flowers, others with fruit but still green. Then he spotted a row of spring onions. He pulled up one of the lettuces and three spring onions and walked back to Farrah. As he approached her, she seemed to be talking. She turned around hearing Liam approach.

"Go away, Lily doesn't want to play with you."

"Yes, ok, but we need to go in. Look what I found."

Farrah got up turned towards the herb garden. "I've got to go now," Liam heard her say.

She walked towards Liam.

"Who was that?" asked Liam.

"It was Lily, but she will only play with me."

"Oh, ok," said Liam. "Here, look at these onions."

"Cool," said Farrah and walked back to the kitchen. She looked up at the swallows for a moment before entering the cottage.

Liam followed and was keen to show Jo what he had found.

"Look at the size of these spring onions; they're the size of golf balls."

He put the produce from the garden on the draining board as Jo came out of the pantry.

"Hey, they look great; did you find anything else?"

"There's some tomatoes but they're not ready yet; another week I think. They must have been really keen gardeners, the Waltons."

"Yes, I think it's so sad. I almost feel guilty taking all their hard work."

"Lily says it's ok," said Farrah who had returned from the pantry with a can of diet coke.

"What do you mean, Poppet?" said Jo.

"Lily, she says she doesn't mind us having their food. She doesn't need it."

Jo looked at Liam. "How do you know this, Poppet?" said Jo.

"She tells me things; she's a very kind person."

"I'm sure she is, Poppet."

"Can we have something to eat, Mom?" Jo looked at Liam.

"Yes, give me a few minutes; I'll make a sandwich."

Just then Zack came into the kitchen. "I'm bored, can we do something?"

Liam thought for a moment. "I know, what about a boat trip?"

"Hey, yeah that's cool," said Zack. "Can we go tomorrow?"

Liam looked at Jo. "I don't see why not; what do you think?"

"It's alright by me; I can look after Far. I'm sure we'll find something to do while you're out."

Farrah looked at her father with a concerned expression. "Lily says you shouldn't go on the boat; it's dangerous."

"Why would she say that, Poppet?" asked Jo.

"I don't know. She said it's dangerous."

"When did she tell you this?"

"Just now, I heard her."

"I think you're hearing things; you're making it up. I never heard anything," exclaimed Zack.

"Well, she doesn't speak to you, does she?" countered Farrah.

"Well, I want to go on a boat," He turned and looked at Liam. "Dad, you promised."

Jo looked at Liam.

"Let me speak to April and see what's available. They

might not be doing any trips, but I'm sure she'll know. I can pop down in few minutes before dinner."

"Whatever," said Zack and stomped back upstairs, clearly not appeased.

"Lily won't be pleased," said Farrah.

Jo put her hand on Farrah's shoulder. "I'm sure she won't mind, Poppet. You can play with her while the men are away."

"She might not be here. She doesn't always come."

"Well, we can look for some more shells, or go for a swim, if we can find some water. We can go the other side of the harbour and see what's down there. What do you think?"

"Oh, all right," said Farrah and she too headed upstairs.

"I think we need to chat about Farrah," said Jo in a whisper.

"Hmm, yes, she does seem to be obsessed by this girl. I'll pop down and see April and find out about the boats. I won't be long. We can talk about it when they're in bed."

"Yes, ok, I'll start preparing the salad. Did you see any salad cream in the pantry?"

"No, I can't say I did."

"Not to worry; I'll get some from the store tomorrow."

Liam left the cottage and started up the Volvo. Before moving off, he checked all the onboard diagnostics and the brakes; everything seemed normal. He still couldn't make out what had happened; it would remain a mystery.

He pulled away to the junction and headed down the hill into the village. At the bottom he turned left and passed the store, then turned into the 'nip'. He decided to park next to April's Kia on the patch of ground at the end of the cul-de-sac.

He turned off the ignition and got out of the car. It was

a bright early evening, a gentle on-shore breeze brought with it the smell of the sea, fresh and invigorating. He was starting to recover from his earlier trauma.

The village was bathed in sunshine. He looked across to the cliff and could see the top of the cottages where the car had broken down. He blinked and looked again, to make sure he was not imagining it. The bank of fog was on the move again. He could see it leaving the trees and move very slowly past the spot where the Volvo had ended up on the cliff top. It was as though it was an entity with its own momentum.

Suddenly, it had encircled Mrs Wilkins' cottage. Liam watched as to seemed to rise and fall. The tops of the trees were clearly visible. Then after a couple of minutes, it slowly moved back into the trees before disappearing altogether.

Liam had a final look before walking down to April's cottage.

He knocked on the door with his knuckles and moments later the door opened.

"Liam, what a lovely surprise. Come in, to what do I owe this pleasure?"

"I'm sorry to call unannounced."

"Don't mention it; it's lovely to see you. I was just going to make a cup of tea; would you like one?"

"Oh, yes, ok, thanks."

Liam sat on the settee and looked around the room. It reflected April's personality, tastefully decorated and furnished, and tidy; everything looked organised. There was an impressive shelving on the left-hand wall filled with books. Liam went over and started looking at the titles. Everything from classics to modern thrillers and autobiographies.

April returned with the teas and noticed his interest. "Do you read, Liam?"

"When I get the time. I've bought a couple of paperbacks down with me but not opened them yet."

April sat down on the settee and put down the mugs on the adjacent coffee table.

"What do you enjoy?"

"Oh, nothing too deep; thrillers, I guess, mainly, oh, and John Grisham, of course."

"Ah, yes, the lawyer."

"Yes, he's a great storyteller."

Liam looked at her; she was wearing the same print-dress, her hair down and tied at the back with a scarf. There was something Bohemian about her, well-suited to village life.

"I hope you don't mind the intrusion, but I was thinking of taking Zack on a boat trip, just around the bay, nothing too far and wondered if there was anything around here."

"Well, there're no pleasure cruises, but I'm pretty sure Jack will take you out if he's not working, helps his cashflow. Do you want me to give him a ring and see?"

"Oh, I don't want to put you to any trouble."

"It's no trouble."

April got up and walked to the sideboard. There was a modern telephone in a cradle. She picked it up and keyed in some numbers.

"Hello, Jack? It's April Thornton, Swallow Cottage; I've got Liam with me. Yes, the one staying at the cottage. Wants to take his son out on a boat, just a short trip. I wondered if you would be free tomorrow. You will? Excellent... Just a minute."

April turned towards Liam. "What time?"

"Oh, about eleven/twelve something like that."

April confirmed the arrangement. "Eleven-thirty, yes, I'll tell him, thanks Jack."

She turned to Liam. "Yes, that'll be fine. He says to meet

him outside the Harbourmaster's Office at eleven-thirty. He'll take you out for a couple of hours."

"Did he say how much?"

"No, I didn't think to ask, but I don't think it will be too expensive."

"Oh, that's great, Zack's been complaining about being bored."

"Yes, there's not much to do for kids around here. So, how are you feeling after today's trauma?"

"Hmm, a bit better, thanks. I keep seeing that poor man in his cab. It's a sight that won't go away."

"No, I can imagine. Can I ask a question? How long have you been a barrister?"

"Just over ten years."

"I bet you've seen some juicy cases in that time."

"Ha, yes, that's for sure."

"So are you defence or prosecution?"

"Mostly prosecution. I enjoy seeing criminals being banged to rights. For all its faults, we do have a good justice system in this country."

"Yes, I guess, I hadn't really thought about it. I think we take it for granted."

"Hmm, true." Liam took a long sip of his tea. "I've just seen something really strange."

"Oh, what was that?"

"That fog," Liam looked down for a moment, recounting the incident. "It appeared again. It seemed to come out of the trees, move over the cottages at the top and then, after a couple of minutes, it moved back again. It was really strange, as though it was, I know this sounds weird, a deliberate movement."

"No, it's not weird; it does look like that, but it's the air circulation up there. The cliffs and the trees create unusual weather patterns apparently."

"It seems very strange. I should have taken a photo. I could have sent it to one of the meteorology sites and got some more information."

"No, I would be careful about taking pictures." Her tone was assertive.

"Oh, any particular reason?"

"I think the people here value their privacy. We'd get all the nutters here wanting to take a look."

"Ah, yes, I hadn't thought of that."

Liam finished his tea and put the empty mug on the coffee table. April went to take it from him and accidentally caught his hand. She quickly apologised. "Oh, sorry."

Liam took little notice.

"Anyway, I better go, Jo's preparing some dinner. There are quite a lot of vegetables in the garden, did you know?"

"No, I've not been in the garden for some time. That will be George, I expect. He was a keen gardener, kept it immaculate."

"We've been using some; I hope you don't mind. It's a shame to let them go to waste."

"No, no, of course not, help yourself."

"Thanks."

Liam got up from the settee and April went to see him to the door. She opened it, leant forward and gave Liam a cheek kiss.

"Call round anytime if you need anything. It's always nice to have company."

"Thanks," replied Liam.

He and turned and walked up the path and up the 'nip' to collect his car, with a lot on his mind. As he reached it, he took another look across the valley. The sky was completely clear, no sign of fog.

Liam returned to the cottage and the children were seated at the table as Jo was serving salad and potatoes.

"That was good timing; I was just dishing up. How did you get on?"

"Well, it seems like we're in luck. The guy who sold us the bait will take us out; he's not working tomorrow. Eleven-thirty, what do you think, Zack?"

"Hey, that's cool. Will we be able to do any fishing?"

"I don't know. We can take the lines with us and see," said Liam.

After dinner, the kids were back in their rooms and Liam was helping Jo with the washing up.

"What should we do about Farrah?" said Liam, as he started wiping a plate with a tea towel.

"I don't know; it's been on my mind too. I don't think we should make a big deal of it. It's clearly real to her and it's not doing any harm."

"Humour her, you mean?" said Liam.

"No, not really, that's a bit patronising; no, I mean we listen to what she says and take it seriously. Mind you, it's a bizarre coincidence the girl who was killed here was called Lily. Now that, I do find weird, but honestly, I don't see what else we can do; I don't want to create any tension with her."

"No, I agree. I think you're right."

Liam and Jo finished the dishes. "I think I'm going to have a look around the garden again; I'll see what else is there. Do you want any vegetables?"

"Well, I've got some lamb left over we can have tomorrow, so if there's any mint we can make some mint sauce. The curry can wait another day."

"Yes, ok, I'll have a look."

Liam yanked open the kitchen door and left the cottage. The swallows were still in a feeding frenzy with the parent birds providing food on almost a conveyor-belt regularity. It was a pleasant summer evening, the sun still providing a degree of warmth.

He walked up the garden and across to the chicken pen to the right of the sycamore tree. There was more police tape in the corner, blown by the wind and sodden by rain. Liam saw it but it wouldn't register; he had a lot on his mind. He could still see the image of the luckless breakdown truck driver. It seemed to be seared into his brain.

Then something brought him down to earth, a sound. It resembled the intermittent noise you get when trying to tune in a radio when first one station, then another appears. There it was again. Liam was suddenly on alert, the adrenaline levels high. It seemed to be coming from the other side of the wall.

There was no way of looking from this side of the garden; he couldn't get close enough to the wall for nettles. He would need to go past the privy. He hesitated, but curiosity got the better of him. He was used to problem solving. There it was again.

He walked across to the sycamore tree and took a deep breath. Then went past the pigsty and reached the privy. He looked at the door and couldn't believe his eyes. It was rattling. The black metal latch appeared to be moving up and down, click, click; click, click; click, click. He had no explanation, but he remembered Farrah's warning. He ignored it and continued to the boundary hedge where the drystone wall was accessible. He looked over the top into the graveyard. The noise seemed to have gone.

Halfway down the wall, one of the stones protruded at ninety degrees providing a step. It was worn smooth, obviously used for this purpose. He placed his right leg on it and hoisted himself to the top.

It was a six foot drop to the grass of the graveyard floor and there was another protruding stone halfway up the wall. He used it to support his foot, and dropped down to the ground. He stopped and looked around. It seemed very quiet; the graveyard was deserted. There was a yellow/orange-chipping path running around the perimeter and in between the five rows of gravestones.

With the shade of the trees deflecting any sunlight, the temperature had dropped considerably, and his arms had goose-bumps. He walked along the first line of headstones looking at the inscriptions, and was amazed at the age of many of them. He was almost at the end of the row when he was drawn to a small headstone, no more than two feet tall. It was thicker than the other gravestones. There was a carving of a skull on either side of the top. There were various engravings in the stone, including a sextant, which Liam worked out probably indicated a sailor. There was writing in Latin - 'momento mori'. There were other depictions all worn by the centuries, cherubs, angels, then a name and a date.

Liam looked at it, then shuddered. 'Cortes 1625'. It was very feint, but just about readable, carved into the stone by a skilled mason. Could it be the same one referred to in April's letters? He took out his phone and accessed the camera, photographing the front and back of the headstone.

He was about to walk on, when the noise returned. It seemed to be coming from the other side of the boundary wall, towards the trees. He looked for a moment trying to pin-point it, and sensed a movement in the distance. He couldn't make it out at first, but it seemed to be getting closer. Suddenly the fog appeared - white, shroud-like. It had come from nowhere, but was just beyond the far wall. It rose to traverse it, but then dropped back down as if there was something stopping it.

Liam could feel his pulse racing. He looked along the footpath. It would be at least hundred yards to the sycamore tree. He turned and quickened his stride, reached the tree, and looked back. The fog was still behind the far boundary wall. The trees beyond that were not visible.

He walked to his climb point in the corner and placed his right foot on the stepping stone. He tried pulling himself up, but his foot slipped on the smooth surface. His elbows took the force of his stumble on the jagged stones.

"Shit!" he exclaimed, as pain shot down his arms.

His heart rate was off the scale. He took one last look. The presence was still there. He tried again, this time with more upward momentum. The extra effort propelled him onto the boundary wall. He stopped to get his breath and took a last look across the graveyard. The fog had gone.

He looked at his elbows; they had been skinned and were bleeding.

He walked quickly past the old privy and reached the footpath to the cottage; then remembered the mint. He crossed the carrot patch to the herb garden and noticed the spade and the surrounding shells, quite artistic; he made a mental note to compliment Farrah. There was a bush of mint with large leaves and Liam picked a couple of sprigs before heading back to the cottage.

Jo came into the kitchen, hearing Liam's return.

"Did you find some mint?"

"Yes. It's on the draining board."

"What have you done? You're bleeding," said Jo, seeing Liam's elbows.

"Oh, it's nothing, just a graze."

"Let me get some plasters; I'll clean it off for you. There's some antiseptic in the medical chest."

Jo returned from the pantry with some cotton wool, antiseptic, and a couple of plasters, before starting to administer the first aid.

"This might sting a bit."

"Ouch!!" shouted Liam as she applied the antiseptic.

She looked up and smiled. "I did warn you."

Repairs completed, Jo returned the antiseptic back to the medical chest in the pantry.

"How did you managed to do that?" said Jo, as she came back into the kitchen.

"Hmm, climbing over the wall to the graveyard."

"You're getting a bit old for climbing walls, don't you think?"

"Ha, you could be right, but you'll never guess. I found an interesting headstone. Here, have a look."

Liam opened his phone and showed Jo the picture, expanding it so she could read the inscription.

"What does 'momento mori' mean?"

"If my Latin's right, 'remember death'."

"That's a bit morbid. I wonder why someone would have that on their tombstone."

"Who knows, but that's not it. Have a look at the date and name."

Jo squinted. "It looks like... Oh my god, Cortes. What's that? 1625?"

"Yes, must be the year he died. I must tell April, see if she knows about it."

Liam decided not to say anything about the fog; mainly because he couldn't think of a rational explanation.

Tuesday morning, it was just turned eight o'clock. Liam had endured a restless night as the sight of the truck driver haunted him. Jo had made some tea and they were both sat in bed drinking tea.

"You were very restless last night; did you not sleep well?"

"Hmm, not really, sorry if I disturbed you. I kept thinking about that poor truck driver; I don't think I will ever forget that sight as long as I live."

"I'm sure it will go, just the shock. Are you still going out on the boat today?"

"Yes, I think it will do Zack good, a bit of fresh air away from his phone."

"Yes, you're right there. I'm not sure what I'll do with Far; I'll ask her when she gets up."

"How's your head?"

"Oh, it's much better, thanks, forgot all about it."

"Yes, the bruise has almost gone."

"And the elbows?"

He looked at the dressings; there were traces of blood on them.

"They're fine. I'll change the plasters after breakfast."

Just then, Liam heard a knock on the front door.

"I wonder who that is," said Liam, putting his mug down on the bedside table.

Liam got out of bed and went downstairs in just his boxer shorts. There was another knock before he could reach the door.

"Oh, hello, April, please excuse the attire, we were still in bed," said Liam in greeting.

April did a double-take. "Oh, please don't apologise; it's my fault for calling so early. The thing is... Ada Wilkins is dead."

"What?"

Liam stood for a moment, in shock.

"You better come in and tell us more. Would you like a cup of tea?"

"Yes, please, that would be lovely. I haven't had one yet this morning."

April followed Liam into the lounge just as Jo entered the room from the stairs, wearing a dressing gown.

"Ada Wilkins is dead," said Liam.

"What? Oh, no, when was this?" said Jo.

April looked at her. "I don't know exactly. Christopher called round to see her about half an hour ago to pick up her shopping list and found her at the bottom of the stairs and rang me. I thought you would want to know."

"Yes, thanks, I can't believe it; that's dreadful, and so sad."

"Can you make the tea, dear? I'll just go and get dressed," said Liam.

April followed Jo into the kitchen. "So, do we know what happened?" said Jo as she filled up the kettle.

"Not at the moment, Christopher's still waiting for the ambulance and police, but I don't think there's any suggestion of foul play."

Just then, Farrah walked into the kitchen in her pyjamas. "Hello, Poppet, do you want a drink?"

"Yes, please... who's died?"

"Poor Mrs Wilkins, you remember, from the cottage."

"Oh, yes, that's sad. Lily said they are angry."

"Who are, Poppet?"

"I don't know; she didn't say."

"When did she say this?"

"I can't remember," said Farrah. Jo looked at April.

"Do you speak to Lily very often?" asked April.

"Quite often, when she's not busy," replied Farrah.

"Do you see her?"

"No, but she speaks to me."

Jo started pouring the boiling water into the teapot, when suddenly the kettle seemed to move in her hand. Boiling water started to spill onto her wrist and hand and she seemed powerless to stop it.

"Shit!!" she shouted.

"What have you done?" asked April with concern. Jo was holding her wrist; it was bright red.

"Quick, run some cold water on it. What happened?"

"I don't know; it was as though someone had taken control of the kettle and just poured the water down my arm." April started running the cold water tap.

"Here, put your arm under there for a moment; it should take the sting out of it. Have you got any antiseptic ointment?"

"Yes, somewhere, I brought our medical chest. It's in the pantry on the floor."

April went into the pantry and found the green canvas rucksack with a red cross on it.

"Is this it?"

"Yes, there should be some antiseptic cream in there."

April rummaged around and pulled out a tube of ointment. "Yes that's it."

"Dry your arm; I'll put some on for you."

Jo gently pat-dried her wrist and top of her hand which had taken the full force of the boiling water. It was starting to blister.

April slowly applied the cream.

"Are you alright, Mom?" said Farrah.

"Yes, Poppet, it was just silly Mummy not looking what

she was doing."

"Lily says we need to be careful; there are evil people around."

April was listening. "Did she say anything else?"

Farrah looked as if she was in a trance. "No, she had to go."

Just then, Liam joined them in the kitchen and saw April applying some cream to Jo's hand.

"What's happened? Are you alright?"

"Yes, just spilled some hot water on my hand, not looking what I was doing."

"Are you sure you're alright?" he repeated.

"Yes, just stings a bit, the ointment will ease it."

"You need to put a bandage on it if you go out," said April.

"Yes, I will. There's some in the bag."

"Any more news on Mrs Wilkins?" asked Liam.

"No, I've not been back home. I'll ring Christopher when I get in," said April.

"Yes, of course, I keep forgetting you don't have mobile phones here."

"No, Christopher rang me from Mrs Wilkins phone."

"Actually, I'm glad you called, I was in the graveyard last night and came across this."

He took his phone out of his pocket and accessed the pictures. He found the image and showed it to April.

"What is it?" Liam expanded the image.

"See the inscription."

"My goodness, yes, Cortes, 1625. How strange. I've not been in the graveyard for years. What were you doing in there?"

"Just curious, wanted to have a look round."

"What were you hoping to find?"

"I honestly don't know; as I said, I was just curious."

April noticed Liam's arms.

"What have you done to your elbows?"

"Oh, that. Just tripped and grazed them, nothing serious." Liam checked his abrasions in turn. He had removed the plasters before his shower and his elbows looked sore.

"That's good; you need to be careful." April added, looking concerned. "Actually, you've reminded me, I must give the museum a call. I'll mention the tombstone; I'm sure they'll be interested."

Zack joined the gathering in the kitchen. "What's for breakfast, Mom? I'm starving."

"Don't worry, we'll get something in a moment; we're just talking to April."

"It's ok, I'll let you get on... I'll let you know if I hear anything more about Mrs Wilkins. Are you still going on your boat trip, Liam?" said April.

"Yes, about eleven-thirty."

April looked at Jo. "What about you and Farrah?"

"I don't know yet; we've not made any arrangements."

"Well, I'm not busy today. Why don't you pop in when Liam goes down to the boat? I can take you out somewhere."

"Yes, thanks, that would be nice."

By eleven-fifteen the family were ready. Jo had bandaged her wrist, but her hand was still painful.

Liam decided to park the car at the top of the nip next to April's Kia; it was only a short walk to the harbour. He locked up with Zack carrying the hand-lines. As they reached April's cottage, she came out to meet them.

"Hi, I just thought you would like to know the latest on Mrs. Wilkins."

"Yes, thanks," said Liam and stopped, leaving Jo and Farrah to continue towards the cottage.

"Well, Christopher says there's going to be a post mortem, but according to the police, they reckon she died yesterday evening, around seven, sometime."

"Oh, ok," said Liam. "Thanks for the update. We'll call when we get back, about two-ish I expect."

"Stay safe," said April.

Jo kissed Liam, and he and Zack continued to the main road.

"What do you think we can catch?" said Zack excitedly, as they turned right and headed towards the Harbourmaster's office.

"I don't know. We can ask Jack but there should be some mackerel."

"What do they look like?" asked Zack.

"Hmm, I don't know; like fish I think."

April opened the door to the cottage and escorted Jo and Farrah inside.

"So what do you fancy doing? We can go across to St Austell again if you like. It might not be so busy after the weekend tourists have gone."

"Yes, that would be lovely. What do you think, Poppet?"

"Sure," she said but started staring ahead blankly. Jo noticed.

"Are you alright, Poppet?"

"Eh ?"

"You seemed to be day-dreaming."

"Lily says Dad and Zack shouldn't go fishing."

Jo looked at April.

"Why should she say that?" said Jo. "I'm sure they'll be alright."

"Yes," agreed April. "Don't worry, Farrah, your dad and Zack are in safe hands. Jack has been fishing these waters around here for at least fifty years. He knows every inch of the area."

"Lily says they are in danger."

Jo looked at April. "What should we do? I don't want to spoil their trip; Zack's been really looking forward to it."

"No, it'll be fine. As I said, they couldn't be in safer hands around here. He'll probably bore them to death with his stories; that will be the main danger." April chuckled.

Farrah was far from happy.

"Come on, let's go into town; maybe we can have another MacDonald's," said April.

"Oh, I don't know if I can face another," said Jo.

"Don't worry there are plenty of eating places that cater for kids," said April.

With Farrah still sulking at her warning not being taken seriously, they left the cottage and walked up the nip to April's car. In the distance, they could see the reflection of flashing blue lights over the top of the cliff towards Mrs Wilkins cottage.

Meanwhile, Liam and Zack had reached the Harbourmaster's office where Jack, the fisherman, was waiting.

"Hello m'dears," he said as they approached.

"Hello Jack. Do you remember us from Sunday? You kindly gave us some bait."

"Aye, of course. Did you catch anythin'?"

"No, plenty of... what do you call them? Cankers."

"Oh, aye, you'll catch plenty of them, alright," he said and laughed. "Mrs Thornton says you want a boat. Where do you want to go? "

"Well, Zack would like to do some fishing, if that's ok. Say a couple of hours."

"Aye, fair enough. It's sixty pounds for an hour. Is that alright?"

"Yes, that's fine. I can pay cash."

"Aye, that you will. I don't use them fancy machines or nothin'."

Liam started to count out the notes from his wallet.

"That's kind, sir. I'll put some bait in for you. Boat's at the end of the harbour; tide's not in until later. I'll just go and register with the Harbourmaster."

Jack entered the office, leaving Liam and Zack waiting outside. The harbour wall was immediately opposite. In the distance Liam could see two fishing smacks moored at anchor. The empty crab pots were stacked in piles waiting for their next outing. Liam looked at them; they resembled pet transporters, the containers used to take dogs or cats to the vets.

Just then, Jack re-appeared. "Right, m'dears, follow me; let's see if we can catch a few fish."

Chapter Seven

They crossed the road following the sailor who was striding at a pace that Liam and Zack were finding difficulty in maintaining; Zack was almost running. Here was someone used to being in a hurry. He looked every inch a mariner with his deck shoes, fisherman's cardigan, and trousers, stained from fish slime.

The harbour wall and docking area curved in a half crescent. The roadway along it was about a car's width, with capstans at various intervals. At the end of the harbour there was a large iron, trellis construction, resembling a miniature Eifel Tower, rising twenty feet above the dock, with a revolving light on top. The roadway followed the curve. They eventually reached Jack's boat, close to the end of the harbour. The name 'Spirit of the Sea' was stencilled on the stern in black letters, together with the port of registration – 'Polgissy'. It bobbed up and down gently in the water.

By fishing boat standards, it was a small vessel, less than thirty feet, of wooden construction with a blue hull which had been sculptured so the prow was probably three feet higher than the stern. There was a small, white-painted wheelhouse with a pinky/orange top in the middle. Half a dozen orange rubber globes, resembling 'Space Hoppers', were placed along the side of the boat, together with a couple of old truck tyres, to protect it from damage when docking. Behind the wheelhouse, there was a small winching device and other equipment used for hauling in the crab pots. There were two circular life belts attached to the back of the wheelhouse and another on the top. Two masts protruded from the top of the wheelhouse, one for the radio, the second for the GPS system; not that Jack would need any navigation aids.

Jack stepped on board the stern of the boat and helped Zack then Liam.

"Make yourselves comfortable in the wheelhouse; there should be enough room for you," said the sailor, and went to the bow to remove the for'ard rope from the capstan. He walked past the wheelhouse and repeated the exercise with the stern cable. The boat bobbed free from its tethers and Jack returned to the wheelhouse and started the engine. Slowly, The Spirit of The Sea eased away from its mooring and out of the harbour.

The engine made a gentle put, put, sound as it slowly headed into open waters. Zack and Liam were stood alongside, thoroughly enjoying the experience. Jack was steering the boat using a traditional, large wooden ship's wheel.

"You may want to put a life jacket on. They're in the corner," said Jack.

Liam picked them up and gave one to Zack. Once secured, the pair were looking back at the village behind them, and from the sea, it looked even more remote, boxed in by the headland on one side, and cliffs on the other. Liam could see the road leading out of the village quite clearly in the distance and a police vehicle parked at the top outside Mrs Wilkin's house.

"You heard about poor Mrs Wilkins?" said Liam, making conversation.

"Aye," said Jack. "Sad it was, but I suppose it was 'er time. Mind you, folks round 'ere reckon she'd been upsetting 'em."

"Who?" asked Liam. Zack was listening to the conversation.

"Them that you don't want to be upsetting, like that Walton family, and that Mrs Thornton's husband a few years back."

"Who? Stuart?"

"Aye, I warned him about the Spanish wreck a week afore. I told 'im bodies of sailors were still on board. The Buccas protect it, the wreck. But 'im and his fancy crowd from Falmouth knew better."

"Buccas?"

"Aye."

Liam didn't ask him to expand. "Do you know what happened?"

"Aye, they chartered a boat out of Falmouth, 'im and three others, to go diving on the wreck. As I said, I warned 'im, I did, but he just laughed said it were all superstitious nonsense; but mark my words, you don't mess with the spirits. He were inside the wreck and he got his tank caught, by all accounts, but by the time they managed to free 'im, he were dead. That's what I 'eard." Jack was looking straight ahead and made no eye contact.

"What about the Waltons? You mentioned the Waltons."

"Aye, that I did. Only what folks round 'ere were saying, that's all." Jack looked at their position with an expert's eye, probably about a mile out. The coastal communities further to the south were visible. To the north it was just cliffs and rocks.

"I reckon 'ere would be as good a place as any, if you wanted to do some fishing. It's not deep and there's a sandy bottom, good for flat fish."

Jack was clearly not going to discuss the Waltons further.

"Thanks, you mentioned some bait."

"Oh, aye, that I did; it's in that old newspaper there."

Jack switched off engine and dropped the anchor. Liam handed one of the hand-lines to Zack. "You go one side; I'll go the other," he said, and walked to the back of the boat next to the winching equipment.

Liam put the old newspaper down in the bottom of the boat and they started baiting their hooks, while Jack started opening a flask of coffee, something that Liam had forgotten. Jack noticed Liam looking. "Help yourselves to coffee; there're some mugs here when you're ready."

"Thanks," Liam acknowledged.

Liam and Zack dropped their lines over the side and waited. Liam decided to take up Jack's offer of a coffee and went back to the wheelhouse while Zack continued fishing.

After about twenty minutes and a change of bait, Zack suddenly felt a pull on the line. "I think I've got one on," he shouted.

Liam was alongside him and slowly pulled the line in. "It's heavy," Zack shouted excitedly.

Jack joined them from the wheelhouse. "Looks like you got a nice one there, m'lad," he said as he reached them.

Between them, they managed to pull the fish to the surface.

"That's a nice looking plaice you've got there, young Zack. Be careful, take your time, he ain't going nowhere."

They eventually managed to lift the fish onto the bottom of the boat where it thrashed around for a short while until Jack dispatched it with a sharp blow to the head using a small, heavy, metal 'priest'.

"You'll be wanting that for your dinner tonight," said Jack, as he presented Zack with the dead fish wrapped in a bin liner. Zack was beside himself with joy.

Jack looked upwards; he would be the first to sense a change in the weather. The wind had veered to the South West.

"That's strange," he said to Liam. "Nothin' in the forecast. We need to be headin' back; weather's on the change."

Within moments, the once docile sea was starting to swell, nothing alarming, but nevertheless enough to cause the boat to bob vigorously in the water.

"Best get in the wheelhouse," said Jack. "Safer there."

He raised the anchor and started the engine; or at least pressed the starter button. He tried again.

"What's the problem?" said Liam, seeing Jack's anxious expression.

"Engine's not working; all the systems are out."

Liam immediately thought back to the Volvo.

"What about the radio?"

Jack picked up the mouthpiece. "Fishing boat, Spirit of the Seas to Coastguard, come in."

There was a static crackled. "Fishing boat, Spirit of the Seas to Coastguard, come in," he repeated. "Is there anyone there?"

More static. He tried turning the tuner to different frequencies, just static.

"Tide's taking us out to sea," said Jack, his face etched with concern. "I'll drop the anchor and see if I can find out what's wrong."

Spray was starting to hit the window of the wheelhouse as the swell increased.

Jack left the wheelhouse and walked up to the front of the boat. Liam watched him through the window; he seemed to be muttering something to himself. He dropped the anchor, then touched the front of the boat. Then went to the stern and repeated the same procedure, before returning to the wheelhouse.

He was climbing up the short flight of wooden steps, and as he reached the top, his right foot slipped on the wet surface. His momentum carried him forward, falling head first into the wheelhouse and crashing into one of the spokes of the ship's wheel.

"Jack, Jack, are you ok?" shouted Liam. There was a large gash on the skipper's forehead and blood was dripping down the side of his face. Liam managed to get him into a sitting position. Zack watched anxiously. "Is Jack going to be ok?"

"Yes, Zack, I think so; he's hit his head. Can you see if you can find a first-aid box anywhere?"

The swell was making it hard to stand up but Zack was opening the various cupboards in the wheelhouse. "Yes, it's here," he exclaimed and passed it to his father.

Jack was falling in and out of consciousness and was mumbling incoherently. Liam could hear the word 'Bucca'. He opened the medical box, and took out some bandages and dabbed the bleeding. "Can you hold that there, Zack?" said Liam. "Apply some pressure; we need to stop it bleeding."

Liam looked at the dials in front of him and saw the ignition switch. He turned it on, still nothing. At least with the anchor down they would not drift further out to sea. He went through the cupboards again. Old maps and charts, a sexton, various other sailing paraphernalia he didn't recognise. Then he spotted something that just might help.

"Look, Zack, a flare gun." It resembled a large starting pistol, with an orange barrel, and was stowed safely in a spring clip together with four cartridges.

He released it from its container.

"Do you know how to use it, Dad?" asked Jack.

"I don't, only what I've seen on TV. I think you pull this down." He pushed down the barrel revealing the chamber. "Then the cartridge goes in here." He pushed in the cartridge and clicked back the barrel.

"Ok, let's give it a try."

Liam went to the door of the wheelhouse. Jack was

unconscious and lay on the floor underneath the wheel. Zack was still holding the bandage to his head.

Liam held the flare gun and pointed it upwards, well away from his face. He pulled the trigger and immediately a whoosh of red smoke shot into the air followed by a starburst, then more red smoke drifted slowly to the sea.

"We'll fire another in three minutes," said Liam and went back to Jack. "How is he?"

"I don't know; he keeps mumbling."

"How's his head? Is it still bleeding?"

Zack removed the bandage which was now completely red. Blood streamed from the wound. "Hmm, that answers that question. Get another bandage and keep the pressure on. We need to try to stop the bleeding. I'll fire another flare."

Outside, thankfully, the weather hadn't deteriorated. The sea was still choppy, but well within the boat's tolerance.

Liam put in another cartridge, steadied himself, then fired the flare gun. The flare would be quite visible from the shore; he was sure that someone would see it.

Three minutes later, he fired the third. "We'll keep the last one in case we see a boat," said Liam.

He tried the engine again, but it was still dead.

Liam was keeping a sharp look out. Visibility was still reasonably good and the swell still hadn't got any worse, but Liam was concerned in case it did. He went outside the wheelhouse holding the flare gun and scanned the shoreline in the distance. Then he saw it, feint but unmistakeable.

"Zack, there's a boat's coming. I think it's a lifeboat."

Liam fired off the last remaining cartridge and watched as the red flare whooshed upwards then exploded into a falling red curtain. He watched as the boat got closer.

"He's seen us, Zack. How's Jack?"

"Still the same."

Liam looked at the man's rugged face, thin wisps of hair, and stubbly chin covered in blood. He continued to mumble.

It took another seven minutes before the lifeboat was close enough to call. Liam had been on the stern waving.

"What's the problem?" shouted the coxswain.

"We've got no power and the captain's hit his head; he's unconscious."

"Right stay there; we'll come aboard." The lifeboat pulled alongside and one of the crew stepped onto the boat.

"My name's Damian, can you tell me what's happened?"

Liam described the course of events.

"So you're out of Polgissy?"

"Yes."

"If we can get you going, do you think you can get there under your own steam?"

"No, I've never driven a boat in my life," said Liam.

"Right, first thing we need to do is get the skipper to a hospital. The air ambulance is on its way should be here in five minutes. I'll get one of my crew to check the boat and, if the worst comes to the worst, we'll tow you in."

A few minutes later the low drone of a helicopter could be heard, and in a matter of moments, it was hovering over the boat. A winchman was lowered.

"Right, we've got the skipper stable. They'll winch him onto the helicopter and take him to Falmouth."

Liam and Zack watched as Jack was hoisted safely into the helicopter. It swung away towards the coast and quickly disappeared into the distance.

"Right, let's have a look." The lifeboat coxswain turned the ignition switch. The wheelhouse was suddenly brimming with lights.

"Well, that looks ok. I'll raise the anchor and see if we can move."

Moments later, the Spirit of the Sea was chugging back to Polgissy under its own power with the lifeboat following behind.

"I just don't understand it. Jack's been fishing these waters for over fifty years. The boat was definitely without power. He checked everything," said Liam to the coxswain.

"Hmm, there'll be some explanation, but it seems to be ok, now; it handles well enough. Good boats these."

The lifeboat followed the fishing smack into the harbour and waited while the coxswain docked and secured it.

"Right, good luck. Can you let the Harbourmaster know? The skipper will be in Falmouth if you can get a message to his family."

"Thanks, Damian, you're a life-saver, literally."

"That's what we're here for."

The coxswain jumped back onboard the lifeboat, and Liam and Zack watched it leave the harbour at speed.

"We'd better call in and see the Harbourmaster. Oh, don't forget your fish," said Liam.

Zack picked up the bin-liner containing the plaice. He was also carrying the hand-lines.

They walked down the dock to the Harbourmaster's office and Liam went inside. He gave the official the details of what had happened, and handed in the ignition key.

"I'll let his wife know," said the man.

"Let's go and find your Mum, I don't know about you but I'm starving," said Liam with his arm around Zack.

They arrived at April's cottage and knocked on the door. "I hope they're back," said Liam, as an afterthought.

April opened the door and her eyes lit up seeing Liam stood there.

"Oh, thank goodness; we were getting quite worried.

Come in, would you like something to eat?"

"Yes, please, thanks."

Liam and Zack walked in and sat down.

"Are you alright Liam?" asked Jo. Farrah ran to her father and put her arms around his neck.

"I'm glad you're safe, Dad."

"Yes, we're fine, Far. Come and see what we've got. Zack show your Mum and Far your catch."

Zack opened the bin-liner and revealed the plaice; there was a distinct 'fishy' smell.

"Oo, it stinks," said Farrah.

"Hey, that's a beauty, but I don't know what we're going to do with it; I've never gutted a fish before," said Jo.

"Don't worry, I can do that for you," said April and peeked at the dead fish. "Wow, that is a nice one, must be four or five pounds. Enough for the family, I think."

Liam looked at the pair. "Actually, the trip wasn't as successful as we would've hoped," said Liam. "The boat broke down, and Jack slipped and hurt his head. We had to be rescued by the lifeboat. That's why we're a bit late. They took Jack to Falmouth by helicopter."

"What!?" said Jo.

"Lily said not to go," said Farrah. Liam looked at Jo.

"Don't worry Far, we're ok, thanks."

Liam gave more details about what had happened. "It was quite weird; one minute everything was fine; the next, the weather had changed and Jack couldn't start the engine. It was completely dead, just like the Volvo. He went to check something on the boat and as he came back to the wheelhouse, he slipped, and banged into the ship's wheel. Gave his head a hell of a crack."

"How is he?" asked April.

"I think he'll be ok; he's got a nasty gash on his forehead

and probably concussion. He'll be in hospital by now. I called in to see Harbourmaster to let him know; he was going to speak to his wife."

"Hmm, let's hope so. They live in one of the cottages on Low Harbour. I must call round tomorrow and see how he is. Let me go and make you both a sandwich and you can tell us more," said April and went into the kitchen.

Liam noticed the bandage on Jo's hand. "How's the hand?"

She held it up and looked at it. "Oh, it'll be fine, just a bit sore."

"So where did you go then?"

Farrah interrupted. "We went to this really cool place; it had an aquarium, and tropical plants and things."

"Yes, it had a really lovely coffee shop too; you'd have liked it," added Jo. "Not far from St Austell."

"Well, we can go again if you like," said Liam.

April came in from the kitchen carrying a plate of sandwiches. She put it on the coffee table in front of the settee.

"I'll just get the plates and teas, help yourselves."

"I'll give you a hand," said Jo, and followed April into the kitchen.

Liam and Zack piled into the sandwiches.

Jo and April returned with the mugs and plates.

"Goodness, you look like you were hungry," said April watching Liam and Zack getting through their sandwiches.

"Yes we've not eaten anything since breakfast."

"How's your head?" asked April as she sat down.

Liam had to think for a moment. "Oh, that, it's fine thanks, forgotten all about it."

"And your elbows?"

"Yes, all good thanks... Jo said you went to a tropical garden centre," said Liam trying to clear his mouth from uneaten sandwich.

"Yes, it was lovely; you must visit it while you're here," said April.

"Yes, Far was saying how good it was." Liam picked up another sandwich and took a large bite.

Liam looked at April. "Did you manage to find out any more about your Spanish sailor, Cortes? You said you were going to speak to the museum."

"Oh, yes, thanks for reminding me. I did, I spoke to them earlier. They've managed to get it translated. One of the professors at Exeter University specialises in old Spanish. He drove over to Truro to see the documents. He was amazed at the condition they were in. I don't think they'd been touched since he wrote them. He said they were of national historical importance."

"Wow, that's impressive. Do you have copies? I would love to read it."

"They're going to email the translation tomorrow. I'll get Christopher to print off two copies."

"Oh, that's great, thanks. Talking of historical things, I wanted to ask you, have you noticed the apotropaic symbols in the cottage?" said Liam.

"You mean signs to ward off evil spirits, that sort of thing? "

"Yes."

"I can't say I have."

"There's some in the lintel in the pantry window."

"Really? I must admit, it's something I'd not noticed."

"I was wondering if they were connected with the Spanish sailor in some way."

"I don't know. It's possible, I suppose. The translations

may throw some light on it."

"Let's hope so. By the way, I noticed there's a loft in the cottage. Would you mind if I take a look?"

"Yes, there is. No, of course not. What are you hoping to find?"

"I don't know, maybe some answers. There are a lot of things happening around here which I can't explain and that doesn't sit comfortable with me. I have an inquisitive nature, comes with being a barrister."

"He's always been like this. He can be quite obsessive," confirmed Jo, as she sat listening to the conversation and drinking her tea. "I've just thought, why don't you come to dinner tonight? You can show me how to gut the fish. There should be enough to go round. I was going to do some lamb but it'll keep in the fridge for another day."

April pondered for a moment. "Yes, ok, that would be nice. I'd love to, thank you."

"What time is it now?" Jo looked at her watch. "Four-ten," she said, answering her own question. "Shall we say sixish?"'

"Yes, that should be fine; give me a chance to tidy round," replied April.

A few minutes later, the family headed back to the car. Farrah was holding her Dad's hand. "Dad, Lily says not to go in the roof; it's dangerous."

Liam looked at Jo then back to Farrah.

"Tell her not to worry; I won't disturb anything. I'm just seeing if I can find some answers."

"Ok," said Farrah and got into the back of the car.

They arrived back at the cottage.

"You're quiet dear," said Jo as they got out of the car.

"Yes, I was just thinking about Jack, and that poor truck driver yesterday. So much for a peaceful holiday."

"Yes, it's been certainly more eventful than I was expecting; that's for sure. I said that killing that crow was bad luck." Jo smiled.

"That's superstitious nonsense," retorted Liam.

"I know, I was just teasing."

He took out his keys and opened the door. The room smelt musty and stale.

"It smells funny in here," said Jo. "I'll open a few windows."

"Here's the fish, Mom, where do you want it?"

"Pop it in the kitchen, Zack. I'll see to it."

Jo turned to Liam. "I could do with a few potatoes and carrots. Do you think you can get some for me from the garden."

"Yes, I'll just go and change and freshen up."

"What are you guys going to do?" said Jo, looking at the children.

"I'm going to play on my Gameboy," said Zack.

"I'm going to see if Lily wants to play," said Farrah.

A few minutes later Liam returned, dressed in jeans and tee shirt. He walked into the kitchen.

"So, what vegetables do you need?"

"Are there any potatoes? We don't have many left."

"Yes, I think so and there're plenty of carrots. I think there were a few cabbages as well."

"Oh, that will be great. There's a trug in the pantry; why don't you use that?"

Liam opened the pantry door. The wicker trug was on the floor underneath the last shelf of tins. He pulled it out and another large spider ran across the floor having been disturbed from its hiding place. It made him jump. He stood up and took another look at the lintel above the window; the marks scraped by a sharp object. He was stood two inches away examining every line in minute detail.

"What do you mean? What are you trying to say?" he said under his breath.

"Are you alright, dear?" asked Jo, as he came out from the pantry.

"Oh, er, yes. I was just muttering to myself."

He tugged at the door and it opened. "Must do something about that," he said as he left the kitchen.

He walked up the path and reached the vegetable patch. He could see the tops of the potatoes and walked over to the plants. He pulled at the first, but most of the top came away in his hand leaving some of the vegetables in the ground. He needed a spade.

He looked across at the old privy; it seemed to be challenging him.

"Sod it," he said to himself and strode across the garden to the front door. He put his hand on the latch and pressed it down and pulled on the door. It opened. All the gardening utensils were scattered on the floor, except for an old axe which was still hanging from the shed wall, secured by two nails like a cradle.

He bent down to pick up the shovel and fork when, suddenly, he felt the presence again. A cold draft wafted around the shed.

Without warning, the axe, tethered to the wall for a millennium, started moving. Liam was on the floor recovering the rest of the tools and looked up. The axe rattled in its tethers. He was transfixed. Suddenly, it became dislodged from its resting place and fell. Liam was like a rabbit caught in the headlights but managed to snap out of his inertia at the last moment. He looked at the axe which was now embedded blade first into the floor.

Liam left it where it was.

He picked up the fork and shovel, then reached for the latch. This time, there was no resistance and he quickly made his exit. He walked to the vegetable patch without looking back, carrying the gardening utensils. He stopped at the row of potatoes, put his hands on his knees, and breathed deeply.

He quickly composed himself and started digging up three more potato plants, probably five or six pounds worth, some carrots, and a good sized cabbage. He put them in his trug and headed back to the kitchen, leaving the spade and fork in the ground.

He looked up at the swallows, still busy with their feeding duties.

He opened the kitchen door and presented the trug to Jo. "Oh, they look great. You can't beat home-grown vegetables."

She looked at Liam. "Are you alright? You've gone quite pale."

"Yes, I'm fine thanks. Do you want a cup of tea?"

"It's ok, I'll make it. The immersion heater's on. Go and have a quick shower; it'll freshen you up. The water should be warm."

"Yes, good idea."

Just a couple of minutes after six, the sound of April's Kia echoed around the cul-de-sac. Liam was seated on the settee, feeling invigorated by his shower, but had yet to make sense of the incident in the privy. He got up and looked through the window. "April's here," he shouted. Jo was in the kitchen.

Liam got to the door before April had chance to knock

and was immediately presented with a bottle of red wine.

"Oh, that's very kind of you," said Liam.

"I know it should be white, but I didn't have any in."

"Don't worry, it's much appreciated. Come in, Jo's in the kitchen."

Liam looked at April; she was wearing smart, bottom-hugging jeans, and a peasant top which looked like a throwback form the sixties; a black bra was clearly visible though the material. Her shoulder-length auburn hair shone in the light. As she walked into the sitting room, Liam could smell her perfume in her wake.

Jo came out of the kitchen and Liam handed her the bottle of red. "From April."

"Oh, thanks very much. Are you still ok to give me a hand with the fish? The vegetables are cooking. I thought I could make a cheese sauce but I'm not an expert on fish."

"Yes, of course, I've bought one of my knives; I don't think the ones in the drawer here will be sharp enough. Parsley sauce is good with fish. Do you have any?"

"There's parsley in the herb garden. I can get some," said Liam.

April produced a box from her handbag with a picture of a kitchen knife on the front and placed it on the draining board.

"Oh, that's very thoughtful of you, thanks. The fish is in the fridge," said Jo.

Liam tugged open the kitchen door and walked over to the herb garden. Given his recent experience, a trip into the garden was feeling stressful and he hastened his stride. He picked a couple of large sprigs of parsley and returned to the kitchen as quickly as he could.

"Will that be enough?" he said as he placed the herbs on the draining board.

"Oh, yes, that's just right," said April and smiled.

"Where are the kids?" asked Liam.

"Both in their rooms. Far's talking about playing with Lily."

April interjected. "Look, please don't think I'm intruding, but does Farrah have lots of these... experiences?"

"Only since she's been here. She's convinced she's able to chat to this Lily. We're just going along with it; it's not doing any harm."

"No, no, you're right. It's just, hmm, how can I put this...? Only special people can communicate with spirits."

Both Liam and Jo looked at each other.

"You mean like mediums and that?" said Liam.

"Yes, exactly."

"Well, I don't know what we can do. I'm worried that if we make a big deal about it, it'll start to affect her mental health," said Jo.

"No, that's quite a possibility, but you're right to take it seriously. I think you're doing exactly the right thing," said April. "So, where's this fish, then?"

"I'll just get it," said Jo and went to the fridge.

"I think I'll go and take a look in the loft and see if there's anything in there."

"What exactly are you looking for?" asked April.

"I don't know if I'm honest."

"Well, I don't think there'll be anything of interest. I'm pretty sure the police forensic people would have given it a good going over during the investigation."

"Hmm, good point," said Liam. " But I would like to satisfy my curiosity."

Liam left the kitchen, picked up one of the dining chairs from the lounge, and walked up the stairs.

The entrance to the loft was via a square panel in the ceiling at the end of the corridor, just outside Farrah's bedroom. Her door was shut. Liam placed the chair under the opening and stood on it. He pushed the panel with his hands and was able to manoeuvre it from the hole. Liam held onto the sides of the opening, placed his right foot on the chair back and pushed himself up through. He was hit by a stale, pungent, musty smell, similar to that which afflicted the lounge that afternoon. He stopped for a moment and sat with his feet dangling below. It was pitch black.

He took his phone out of his pocket and turned on the torch feature. He started scanning the inside of the loft. There were three wooden gables, one at each end and one in the middle which held the pitch membrane in place which supported the thatch. The floor beams had been covered by sheets of Conti board, which must have been a fairly recent addition.

He slowly stood up, his head almost touching the eaves.

The light from the torch formed strange shapes and shadows as he swung round. At he far end he could see some children's toys, and he slowly edged his way towards them, testing each step; there was no way of knowing if the flooring would withstand his weight. Halfway along, he could see the water tank and the pipes that lead down to the shower.

He reached the middle gable. The wood was incredibly old and gnarled. There were lots of markings on them but none that would resemble anything meaningful. He reached the toys and bent down. Some dolls, a toy truck, the sort you would have to help a child to walk, a pram. Liam picked up one of the dolls and started to examine it.

Suddenly, there was a drop in temperature and a slight breeze, as if someone had opened a door on a cold windy morning. Then a presence.

He dropped the doll, and he stood in a stoop, mesmerised, as the apparition took shape. It was a girl, around Farrah's age, dressed in a smock, like someone from the Victorian era.

"Hello, have you see my Daddy?"

Chapter Eight

The voice was high-pitched, a child's voice. The apparition had no substance; he could see the water tank through her body, but at the same time, it took on a real shape.

"No, I haven't. What's your name?" asked Liam.

"Lily," said the girl. *"Have you come to hurt me like the other man?"*

"No, Lily, I am Farrah's Daddy; I would never hurt you."

"I like Farrah; she's my friend."

"Yes, she's a friendly girl. What other man do you mean?"

"The one who hurt my Mummy and Daddy, and me."

"Can you tell me about him?"

"Not really. Can you help me find my Daddy?"

"I don't know where to look."

"I think he must be near; I can smell him sometimes." Her head swivelled around a hundred and eighty degrees, then back again, like an owl. Liam recoiled almost falling over, unable to take in the sight. Her plaintive voice echoed. *"I have to go now."*

"Lily! Lily!" said Liam in a shout-whisper.

The apparition had gone. Liam couldn't believe what he had just seen, or what he thought he'd seen. His hands were sweating and trembling, his heart rate off the scale. The question was what he should do about it.

He decided to give up any further investigations in the loft for the moment and edged slowly toward his exit point. He jumped as a cobweb wrapped itself around his face, sticky, clingy; he wiped it away with his hand. Liam reached the centre gable and ducked under it.

Then another noise.

He could hear scurrying coming from behind him. He

turned and swung his phone-torch in the direction of the
noise. The scurrying stopped. There was a dark shape about
halfway between him and the toys at the back wall. It turned
and made a bee-line for the edge of the roof and disappeared.
It looked like a rodent of some kind.

Liam reached the opening and the welcoming sight of
daylight. He lowered himself onto the chair and replaced the
wooden cover into position. He composed himself, picked
up the chair, then went downstairs. He left the chair at the
dining table and went into the kitchen to be greeted by
wonderful cooking aromas.

Jo and April were sharing the cooker with all four rings
in operation.

"Mmm, something smells good," said Liam, trying to act
nonchalantly as if nothing had happened. They couldn't see
his hands shaking.

Jo looked up from stirring a saucepan. "Did you find
anything?"

"No, there're some kiddies' toys up there but nothing else
that I could see. Although, you may have squirrels, April."

April turned around. "Hmm, I'm not surprised; it's all the
trees. Wait, what have you got in your hair?"

She stopped stirring her cooking and wiped her hand
across Liam's face. "Ha, you're covered in cobwebs."

April removed the offending items and dropped them
into a pedal bin.

"Thanks," said Liam.

"Are you alright? You look very pale," said April.

"Yes. I'm fine thanks," replied Liam.

The family and April sat down to fresh plaice fillets with
potatoes, carrots, cabbage, and parsley sauce. The red wine
was distributed, with the children drinking Coke.

Zack and Farrah were answering questions about their school work from April when Zack raised a question with Liam. "Dad, what did Jack mean about Buccas?"

"Buccas?" Liam looked in surprise.

"Yes, Jack said something about people upsetting them."

April answered. "You'll find that fishermen are terribly superstitious. Buccas are what they call sea spirits; some people believe they protect the ocean. Fishermen try to make sure they don't upset them."

"You mean like your husband?"

"Zack, don't be disrespectful," said Liam, and gave Zack a disapproving look.

"It's alright Liam. No, Zack, Stuart was just unlucky, that's all. It was an accident. Certainly, nothing to do with sea spirits."

"Oh, ok," said Zack.

Liam looked at April. "Thanks for explaining. I'm sorry if Zack was speaking out of turn."

"Please, no need to apologise. It's good to be inquisitive at that age."

The meal was finished, and by eight-thirty, the kids were in the bedroom and Liam, Jo, and April were chatting over a glass of wine.

"Are you still going to see the Squire tomorrow?" asked Liam.

"Yes, he's printing out the translations of the Cortes documents. I can't wait to read them," replied April.

"Do you think he would mind me using his internet connection?"

"No, not at all, I can introduce you to him if you like. I'm sure he won't mind."

"What time are you seeing him?"

"I don't know. I said I would be there about nine-thirty/ ten o'clock. It was nothing firm."

Liam turned to Jo. "You don't mind, do you?" Jo's expression indicated that she did mind.

"What do you need the Internet for?"

"I wanted to download my emails and do a bit of research."

"What sort of research?"

Liam was slightly on the back foot. "Just some things about the village."

Just then Farrah came down stairs in her pyjamas and entered the lounge. "Dad," she said in that voice she used when she wanted a treat. The word 'dad' became two syllables.

"Yes, Far."

"Did you speak to Lily?"

"Why do you ask?"

"Oh, nothing. Can I have a drink of water?" She rubbed her eyes.

Jo interrupted. "Sure, Poppet, I'll get you a drink. Go back to bed, I'll bring you up a glass in a second."

Farrah turned and went back upstairs while Jo went to get the water.

"I can help you with your research," said April as Jo was in the kitchen. "Just tell me what you want to know."

"Thank you," said Liam.

Jo took up Farrah's drink; she was in bed under the covers. Farrah opened her eyes then sat up, took the glass from Jo. "Have you seen Lily?" she asked.

"No, Poppet."

"You would like her; she's very nice."

"I'm sure she is Poppet."

Jo returned to the lounge and looked at Liam. "Why did Far ask whether you'd seen Lily?" she asked as she sat down.

"I don't know," said Liam.

"Only, she's just asked me the same question. Do you think we need to say anything to her? It does seem to be dominating her world at the moment."

April interrupted. "I wouldn't... Sorry, I'm not trying to teach you how to raise your children; it's just, well, she might find the scrutiny upsetting."

Liam was trying to decide whether to say anything about his experience in the loft, but decided not to, not for the moment. He still couldn't equate what had happened.

"Yes, I agree; let's keep an eye on it," said Liam. He took another sip of wine. "I was thinking about tomorrow." He looked at Jo. "Why don't you take the kids to the beach in the morning? You can take the car. I'm sure there are some nice beaches nearby, and we can meet up at the pub for lunch."

April joined in. "Oh there are several. Polperrin Beach is closest; the sand is excellent. It's just off the main road, only about four miles away. It gets quite busy there at weekends, but it should be ok tomorrow."

Jo thought for a moment. "Yes, ok."

"I can meet you about one o'clock; that will give me plenty of time. How does that sound?" said Liam.

April agreed to pick up Liam at nine-thirty to visit the Squire and took her leave.

Later, the lounge was quiet. Liam was trying to do the cryptic crossword in the newspaper but finding it hard to concentrate.

" 'Gegs!' What sort of clue is that?" he said in frustration.

Jo looked up from her chic-lit.

"How many letters?"

"Nine and four."

Jo thought for a moment. "How do you spell 'Gegs'?"

"G.E.G.S." replied Liam.

"Scrambled Eggs," replied Jo, triumphantly.

"Oh, very good. I don't think I'd have ever got that."

Jo looked up. "What do you think about Farrah and this Lily? I didn't want to say anything in front of April."

"Hmm, it's a difficult one, but I don't think we should say anything. As April said, it may upset her even more. Let's just keep an eye on it. She seems to be sleeping ok and she's not said anything about nightmares."

"Do you think we should leave?" asked Jo.

"Leave? You mean, as in, go home?"

"Yes."

"I don't know; I hadn't thought about it. Do you think we should?"

"Well, we can't put the children in any danger."

"I don't think they are in any danger, but I do want to do some digging and see if I can make sense of it all."

"What sort of digging?"

"I don't know, but I would like to find out more about what happened to the Waltons."

"Ha, you can't stop working, can you?"

"Oh, no, no, it's not work; call it problem solving."

The following morning, the children were excited about going to a 'proper' beach, as Jo had sold it. There was no more mention of Lily, and Liam didn't want to raise the topic. They packed up the beach things and loaded them into the back of the Volvo.

Liam checked the car. Everything seemed to be in order, and handed the keys over to Jo.

"I'll see you at the pub at one o'clock," said Liam and

watched as the car pulled away.

A few minutes later, Liam heard the Kia pull up outside the cottage. He picked up his keys, phone, and wallet, and locked up. April was waiting for him by the gate, wearing her long printed dress with white sandals. Her hair seemed to shine in the morning sunshine.

"Good morning," said Liam. "Lovely day."

"Hi, yes it is. Do you want to walk? It's only five minutes away."

"Yes, fine, lead the way."

She locked up the car and the pair walked to the junction, crossed the road, and headed towards the church.

"Have you heard any more about Jack?" asked Liam, as they reached the boundary wall to the church yard.

"Yes, he's fine, concussion, apparently; they're letting him out today. Christopher's going to pick him up this afternoon."

"That's very decent of him."

"Jack's done a lot of work for Christopher over the years."

"I see. What about poor Mrs Wilkins?"

"There's a post-mortem today, but there's no indication of any foul play, according to Christopher."

They continued walking past the church where a cinder path, the width of a lorry, ran beyond the car park, behind the cottages of the adjacent road. They came to a large house.

"That's the rectory," explained April. "Where Reverend Slaughter lives. Christopher's house is the next one."

"Wow, that's impressive," said Liam observing a large Georgian building set back in sumptuous gardens.

They walked for another hundred yards or so when they reached a ten foot high brick wall with razor wire on top. Although made from the same stone as the majority of the surrounding properties, it seemed out of keeping with the rest of the village. There was no doubt the wall had been designed to keep people out. There were cameras on the corner and further down at the entrance.

"Wow," said Liam. "This is some serious security."

"Yes, Christopher does seem obsessive about it for some reason."

"What does he do for work?"

"I honestly don't know; trading he said when I asked him. Bitcoin, I think. I'm not really up on it."

About fifty yards along the wall, they came to the entrance. Liam looked in amazement. A high wrought-iron gate with a coat of arms in the design. There were two ornamental lights on each of the pillars supporting the gate.

Next to the main entrance, there was a smaller, elaborately-designed gate just about wide enough for a person to pass through, with an intercom recessed in the wall to the right. April pressed the button. A security camera moved with a slight whirr.

"Come in, April," said an assertive voice from the speaker.

There was a click as the lock disengaged. April pushed open the heavy gate and the pair walked through.

"Wow," said Liam. "Business must be good."

Before them, the drive swept upwards with immaculate lawns either side, bordered by luxuriant plants - roses, rhododendrons, daisies of various kinds, all adding colour to the grounds. Due to the incline, just the top of the house was visible from the front gate.

April walked alongside Liam up the long drive.

"This is magnificent," said Liam.

"You wait till you see the house... Actually, there was a lot of controversy when it was built. The villagers were up in arms about it."

"Really? Why was that?"

"According to legend, it's built over a plague pit."

"A plague pit?"

"Yes, apparently, the village was nearly wiped out in the fifteen hundreds by the Black Death. There are no records to substantiate this, but the story goes that a traveller arrived from London suffering from it and spread it to the rest of the village. Those that died were buried in a mass grave."

"And this was here?" said Liam.

"So the story goes. Christopher told me it was just scrubland when bought the plot. Apparently, planning permission got delayed after one or two protests from the villagers. There was going to be an enquiry to find out if there was any evidence of the plague pits, but a lack of funding became an issue, so the building went ahead. Between you and me, I think money changed hands. Christopher intimated as such. How did he put it? Oiled the wheels of bureaucracy."

"Ha, yes, that wouldn't surprise me," replied Liam. "What do you think, about the plague pits?"

"It's the kind of thing that could have happened, and I've always wanted to do some research to see if I could find anything, but I just haven't had the time."

The tarmac driveway snaked to the left and passed a three-car garage. A yellow Porsche 911 was parked outside.

The drive went right and, immediately in front of them, the magnificent house glinted in the morning sunshine. As they got closer, Liam's jaw dropped; it was something from the pages of a design magazine, totally unique.

The property was on two floors and appeared to be constructed mostly of glass, supported by large hardwood beams, giving it a geometric, box-like feel. The interior was clearly visible from the outside. The blinds on the first floor had been raised and Liam could see a bedroom, and next to that, what looked like a study, with book shelves and computer equipment. It would overlook the grounds and sea beyond. The pair continued up the drive into an open area at the side of the house, half-covered with a matching wooden veranda.

The entrance was a box-like construction which looked like it had been tagged onto the side of the house, with a picture widow and a glass door.

"Wow, this is something else," said Liam as they approached the veranda.

"Ha, you've not seen the half of it," replied April.

Opposite the entrance, to the right, there was a covered outdoor area with plastic grass and a half-sized swimming pool, surrounded by marble paving. In front of that, more marble with a five-seater settee facing outwards, and accompanying coffee table.

Then, the view - the drive and gardens, the village, and beyond that, the harbour and sea; it was breath-taking.

The shape of a man appeared at the glass door and pulled it open.

"April, so lovely to see you."

"Hello Christopher, can I introduce Liam Drake? He's come to borrow your Internet." April laughed.

"Pleased to meet you, Christopher, and thanks so much for allowing me access to the outside world." This time Liam laughed.

"My pleasure. Would you like a coffee? I thought we could have it on the patio, make the most of this lovely weather."

"Yes, please," said April and Liam, almost in unison.

He walked back inside and then led the pair to the outside

social area in front of the swimming pool.

"Please take a seat; Molly will bring the coffees shortly."

He spoke in a deep resonant timbre, his voice not regionally distinguishable. His accent leaning towards Thames Valley, not 'posh' exactly, but a voice that would sit comfortably on BBC Radio 4.

Liam was trying to weigh up the man. Almost six foot tall, fit looking, and, one would say, distinguished, down to the mauve shirt and matching beige jeans and loafers. Mid/late-forties, probably, his dark hair was showing signs of receding, definitely a candidate for one of the hair-replacement organisations. A trimmed beard completed the look; the similarity with the usual vision of an English squire could not be more removed. There was an intimidating presence about him.

"It's a magnificent house, Christopher, I have to say. How long have you lived here?" said Liam.

"Thank you, about ten years. As soon as I could run my business from just about anywhere, I could see no reason to be surrounded by houses and traffic, so I moved here."

"What line of business is it? If you don't mind me asking."

"I'm a trader... crypto-currencies."

"Bitcoin?"

"No, that one's plateaued. There are newer ones that have emerged which I'm trading in which provide far better returns. Is it something <u>you</u> might be interested in?"

"No, not really, it's an area I know nothing about."

"Well, if you change your mind, please let me know; I'd be happy to explain more. It's very straightforward once you know what you're doing."

"I'll bear it in mind," said Liam, his body-language indicating the topic was closed.

Just then, an elderly lady in a pinafore walked towards

them carrying a tray with three mugs and a cafetière. She placed the tray on one of the glass coffee tables in front of the guests and went back into the house, returning with another tray containing a small jug of cream and an assortment of biscuits on a plate.

"Help yourself to cream and biscuits," said Deakin. April and Liam did just that.

Deakin raised his mug to his lips and took the first sip of coffee.

"And you're a barrister, I understand from April?" he said, continuing his inquisition.

"Yes, I have my chambers in the City."

"No wonder you wanted to get away. Do you specialise?"

"Mostly criminal work, I've been in the Old Bailey for the last six weeks."

"Ah, the Rainsford Case?"

"Yes, you're well informed. How did you know?"

"It's the only case on at the Old Bailey. Prosecution or Defence?"

"Prosecution."

"Hmm, congratulations I think is in order, well done." said Christopher and took another sip of his coffee. "Quite a result."

"Thank you, yes it was."

"Can someone let me into the secret?" said April, who had been listening intently.

"Marty Rainsford, him and how many was it?" said Deakin.

"Seven," confirmed Liam.

"Yes, that's right, an organised crime syndicate, allegedly. Twenty-five years each, if I recall. Do you think they'll appeal?"

"Almost certainly, they usually do, and there was nothing

'allegedly' about it. It was a unanimous verdict," replied Liam.

"Yes, yes, of course," back-tracked Deakin.

Liam changed the subject. "I understand you're collecting Jack this afternoon from the hospital. I'm so glad he wasn't badly hurt."

"Yes, oh, of course, you were on the boat."

"Yes, with my son. I hired Jack to take us out fishing."

"What happened, exactly?"

"Well, the weather changed and Jack suggested we headed back but he couldn't get the engine started. I mean, I'm no expert, but the engine looked totally dead. He was convinced it was something to do with the sea-spirits."

"Ha, yes, that sounds like Jack. They're an incredibly superstitious lot the fishermen round here."

Liam continued. "He went outside to check on something and as he was coming back into the wheelhouse he seemed to slip on the top step and hurtled into the ship's wheel. Blood everywhere. Luckily, I found the flare gun and alerted the lifeboat. That was it, really."

"Well, that was quick thinking of you. I'm sure Jack will be very appreciative of your help."

"It was nothing; I'm just glad he's ok." Liam took a sip of coffee. "I was sad to hear about poor Mrs Wilkins. She was very kind to us when our car broke down."

"Yes, indeed, the police were saying they have no idea what happened, but they're not treating it as suspicious. I think she just fell down the stairs, but I don't think we will ever know what really went on," said Deakin.

They finished their coffees and Molly collected the empty mugs.

"I've got a spare study you can use, Liam. Did you bring

a laptop?"

"No, just my phone. I just need to download my emails."

"Of course, no problem. If you follow me, I'll give you the broadband password and leave you to it. April and I have one or two admin matters to discuss, the village council," he clarified, raising his eyebrows. He turned to April. "Oh, and I've printed out that email you wanted. Seems very intriguing."

The Squire led Liam and April through the glass door into an incredible lounge. Liam caught his breath; ornamental lights, a four-seater leather settee with matching armchairs, a TV which would not have looked out of place at a local cinema, exquisite rugs and furniture, and the pièce de resistance an enormous bookcase which took the whole of the back wall, the height of taste. Liam stopped himself from saying 'wow'.

Through the lounge into a corridor and at the end of which another room, set out as a fully-functional office. It looked out at the back of the property with an extensive lawn, and in the distance, the boundary wall with the forest beyond. In many respects, it resembled a luxury prison.

"Help yourself if you want to use one of the computers; there's some spare pen-drives in the drawer if you need to save anything."

"Thanks Christopher, that's very kind."

"My pleasure; I'll leave you to it. The password's on the desk."

He closed the door and Liam watched as Christopher and April returned to the lounge. In a matter of moments, Liam was downloading his emails. It was a strange feeling; he hadn't realised how much he had missed contact with the outside world.

Most of the emails were from his clerk, nothing urgent,

just the daily updates he had requested. It was good to see his phone with a signal again; it eased the sense of isolation.

He spent a few minutes replying to requests for information and then made a note of the password. He thought it might be possible to access the internet from outside the house without having to disturb Christopher if he needed it again in the future.

Liam looked around the room. There was some serious computer equipment and monitors as well as the usual office paraphernalia.

He had intended to do some research but in all honesty, he didn't know where to start. He would leave it for now and speak to April. She seemed to know what was going on.

Having completed his tasks, he left the room and walked back along the corridor to the lounge where April and Christopher were still in conversation.

"Oh, hi, Liam. Did you get everything you wanted?" said Deakin.

"Yes, thanks, I'm very grateful."

"Have you finished, Liam? I've got something to show you." said April excitedly.

"Yes, all done."

"Great, Christopher was saying he needs to go shortly to get to Falmouth. I thought we can leave him to get on."

"Yes, I'm in your hands," said Liam prompting a smile from April.

They bade farewell and expressed their gratitude. Christopher showed them out to the door. Liam looked across to the garages and noticed a young man in his late-twenties, cleaning the Porsche.

Christopher saw Liam's interest. "That's Nathan; does all my odd jobs, so useful around the house. I couldn't manage without him."

Christopher closed the door. Liam and April walked down the drive towards the gate. Liam nodded at the car-cleaner as they walked past. The greeting was ignored.

"Take no notice of Nathan; I think he's a bit simple," whispered April as they reached the gate. "Actually there're rumours in the village he's Christopher's lover, but I think that's probably malicious." She paused for a moment. "Having said that, I've not seen Christopher with a woman since I've been here, which, given all his money, is a bit unusual, so it is possible, I suppose."

Liam looked back at the magnificent house; he couldn't wait to tell Jo. The security lock clicked, allowing them to leave, and Liam pushed the gate open.

"Come on then, tell me what it is you want to show me? You seem quite excited," said Liam as they walked past the church.

"Oh, I am. I can't wait to show you. Why don't you come back to the cottage? There are some other things I think you may be interested in."

"Yes, ok," said Liam.

They reached the Kia and got in. Liam noticed April was holding a folder.

"Is that what I think it is?".

"Yes, it's the translation."

A few minutes later, they had reached April's cottage. "Would you like a beer?" asked April as they walked into her lounge.

"It's a bit early."

"You're on holiday."

"Ha, yes, so I am. Go on then."

Liam sat down on the settee while April went into the kitchen. She returned with two glasses of beer.

"It should be cold; the bottles have been in the fridge."

"I'm sure it will be fine," said Liam and accepted the offered glass.

April sat down next to Liam. She had the folder next to her and opened it.

"I can't wait for you to read it; it's so exciting," said April, handing him one of the two letters.

There was a preamble, thanking April for submitting the documents. Liam started to read. "Of National historical importance," said Liam. "Wow."

He read the translation out loud.

"To whosoever it might concern

Be it known that I, Francisco López de Grijalva Cortes of Cordoba, Espagnole, lately residing in the hamlet of Polgissy, Cornwall, captain of His majesty King Philip's ship Tobago Valencera, wish it to be known that on 18th September 1588 in a storm off the County of Cornwall, my ship foundered with the loss of all hands. My deliverance was due to the kindness and bravery of the people of the said Polgissy, who found me clinging to a wine barrel and brought me to shore. Instead of handing me to the authorities to be tried and hanged, they treated me with great compassion, as though I was one of their own, for which I will be eternally grateful. It was here I met my wife Mary and we raised our two children in the cottage that bears the name 'Pendle Cottage'. In acknowledgement of this generosity, I hereby declare that it is my dying wish to be buried here so that my spirit will remain in Polgissy for time immemorial and will protect it from whosoever might cause it harm.

I sign this deed.

14th October 1625."

"That's amazing," said Liam. "That must have been shortly before he died, the date on the tombstone."

"Yes, I'm sure it is. The University said they're going

to send one of the research students down to look at the gravestone."

"Did they say when?"

"Later this week, apparently."

"If we can find out when, we can tell them about the other things."

"Other things?" said April as she took another sip of beer.

"Ah, yes, I didn't know whether to say anything or not; I didn't want you to think I was going crazy. I've not said anything to Jo; she would want us to leave."

April was looking at Liam intensely. "No you're not going crazy; there are many things we can't explain."

Liam continued. "Well, you know that Farrah has been getting messages from Lily?"

"Yes, go on."

"Well, last night I had a vision as well."

"What?"

"Yes, when I was in the loft. I didn't say anything at the time as I wanted to try to rationalise what it was I saw, and frankly, I can't."

Liam described the apparition and the brief conversation.

"She actually said a man hurt them?"

"Yes, I tried to get more information but she said she had to go, and it just vanished. There have been other strange things, too." Liam explained about the incidents in the privy and the graveyard.

"I don't frighten easily, but I have to say, it scared me."

"I don't think there's anything you should be concerned about and don't worry, you're not going crazy, but thank you for sharing that. I need to share some things with you too. Do you know what a Pellar is?"

Liam looked at her. "No, I can't recall that name."

"It's Cornish, it translates roughly as a white witch."

"A white witch? You mean, like Narnia?"

April laughed.

"Well, sort of, my mother was a distant relative of Tamsin Blight. She was a famous pellar in the eighteen hundreds. People used to travel miles just to see her. She was, I guess, what you would call a sooth-sayer, or fortune teller in today's world. Women would visit her to find out what kind of man they might marry, that sort of thing." April smiled. "But they can also communicate with the spirit world."

"So, you are saying you are a white witch?"

"Yes, I am, but I'm also sensitive to spiritual activity, although I've never actually communicated with one directly. I have though felt a presence at Pendle Cottage since the Walton murder. It's why I was interested in your experiences and that of your daughter."

"Talking about the Waltons, do you have any more information about them? I would love to understand what happened."

"Yes, I have a lot of newspaper cuttings I kept at the time. It was a huge deal in the village; it upset the whole community for several weeks. Then of course we had the twins' tragedy straight after. A lot of folk here were talking about evil spirits on the basis there seemed no other rational explanation at the time."

"And you don't subscribe to that?"

"No, I don't, and not all spirits are evil. Your Lily, for instance, just seems lost; she won't do harm to people. It's why I don't think you have anything to fear regarding your daughter."

"Thanks, yes, that make sense. So, can you cast spells?"

"Ha, ha, not in the magical sense, no. White witches are benevolent; they can't prescribe evil deeds."

"So, how does this manifest itself? Do you get... what do

they call them? Visitations?"

"It's a good question. Mostly I get a premonitions, a feeling if you like. I had one before Stuart went on his dive. I tried to warn him, but he thought it was all nonsense."

"Yes, Jack told me he had said something to Stuart, too."

"Yes, unfortunately, Jack can be a bit over the top with his prophesies, which is why Stuart wouldn't take any notice."

April looked down in sadness. Liam put his arm around her by way of comfort.

"Thanks, I'll be ok."

April got up from the settee. "Would you like a cup of tea? I've no more beer, I'm sorry."

"Yes, thanks."

She walked to one of the cupboards and rummaged around. Then returned to Liam holding an A4 folder.

"Those are the newspaper clippings I mentioned. You can keep them for the time being. I'm not sure how helpful they'll be but it will give you some background. I'll just go and make the tea."

April returned a few minutes later carrying two mugs and held one to him. Liam had been browsing the headlines. 'Horror killing in peaceful village', raged one. 'Slaughter in paradise', said another.

"Thanks." Liam took the mug and closed the folder. "You knew the Waltons reasonably well; can you think why anyone would want to kill them?"

She sat down next to Liam. "That's the thing, the police asked me the same question and, quite frankly, I can't. They were a lovely family."

"Did you socialise with them at all?"

"Not socialise exactly, I didn't go round for drinks or anything. They tended to keep themselves to themselves. They did enjoy walking, though. George liked to go into the forest and take photos of the wildlife. I remember him showing me some of his pictures; they were excellent. The family used to come to our monthly meetings; although I can't remember them contributing. They rarely said anything; I remember Christopher commenting on it."

"Do you know anything about George's clients? Who he worked for?"

"No, not really. Mostly periodicals and occasionally dailies, he told me."

"Did George leave the village much do you know?"

"Hmm, well, he spent most of his time in his studio, but he did have the odd business meeting in Plymouth, and also London. I know, because I occasionally picked Lily up from school if Lizzie had a parent's evening or school meeting. She would stay with me until one of them picked her up."

"What was she like, Lily?"

"A delightful girl, so well mannered; she was never a problem. It was sad because she had no-one of her own age in the village; all her friends were at school, so she spent a lot of time in adult company."

"What about before they came here? Do you know anything about their background?"

"Not really, moved here from Plymouth, that's all I know. George was an excellent artist. Come to think of it, I don't know what they did with the paintings; there were lots in his studio. I wonder what happened to them."

"The people who cleared the cottage after the police had finished, I would imagine."

"Yes, it was a specialist firm the police recommended. I have to say, they did an amazing job. I can't imagine what it must have been like. The newspapers painted a really gory picture. I have no idea where the hacks got their information."

"Ha, that will be the police. One of the journalists

probably slipped them an incentive."

"Really? Money you mean?"

"Oh yes, it's not unheard of."

"That's dreadful."

"Hmm. What about other family members?"

"I don't think there was anyone else; I never heard them discuss relatives. What are you hoping to find?"

"I honestly don't know. In my line of work I have to do a lot of investigating. Not like the police, of course, but I do have to make sure that the evidence will convict the criminal and I do have a good eye for detail. Sometimes we can see things in a slightly different way. But there's something else. Since that... apparition, shall we call it? I feel a need to see justice prevail. I have this thing about criminals not getting away with it."

"Well, if I can help in any way, just ask. I would love to find out what really happened."

"Thank you." Liam opened the folder again and flicked through more clippings. "It looks dreadful."

April was looking across at the photos. "It was; I try to block it out, and none of the villagers will talk about it."

"Yes, I was aware of that when I spoke to the pub landlord. You mentioned something about sensing spirits after the murders."

"Yes, I had to visit the cottage after the clean up to check around; that's when I first noticed it."

"What did it feel like?"

"It's hard to explain, there was a very strong feeling of... presence. That's the only way I can describe it, as if I wasn't alone in the cottage."

Liam looked at April. "I see, well thanks for sharing."

He finished his tea and checked his watch. "Actually, I better go and meet the family. Thanks for your time this morning."

"Not at all, as I said, anytime." She leaned forward and kissed his cheek.

Chapter Nine

Just before one o'clock, Liam walked down to the pub to meet the family, carrying the folder of newspaper cuttings, with a lot on his mind. He felt an overwhelming sense of injustice, heightened since the 'visit' of Lily.

Three hours earlier, Jo and the two children had arrived at Polperrin Beach. As she drove the Volvo down the hill into the village, it was impossible to escape the comparison with Polgissy. The approach road was two-laned and littered with Bed and Breakfast establishments. The only similarity was the gradient to the seafront, although it was nothing like as steep. The promenade was lined with gift shops and cafés, the pavements busy with holiday makers window shopping or topping up with provisions. There was even a mini-supermarket.

Zack and Farrah were looking out of the window, excited at what they saw.

"Look, Mom. Look, Mom," shouted Farrah from the back seat.

Shorts and sunhats with the occasional bikini seemed to be the dress code of choice. The weather was glorious with the temperature now almost reaching eighty degrees, adding to the seaside experience.

"Hey Mom, this is cool," said Zack, as they scanned the surroundings He was in the passenger seat at the front, as befitting the eldest sibling.

"Yes, but we need to make sure you put your sunscreen on," said Jo.

There was parking all the way down the promenade on both sides of the road which meant there was only room for one car to pass at a time. Jo was checking for a space.

"There's one," shouted Zack, pointing about thirty yards in front of them.

Jo slowly parallel parked creating a delay in waiting traffic. "Oh," she said, looking at a notice. "It's a meter. I hope I've got some change."

Farrah passed Jo her handbag from the back seat.

"Lily says we shouldn't go into the sea," she announced.

"Tell Lily not to worry; we will be very careful," said Jo, extracting two pound coins from her purse. "Remind me to get some more change when we get to the pub for the electricity," she added.

There was no reply.

The family exited the Volvo. The two children waited by the car as Jo fed the necessary coins into the parking machine and extracted the ticket.

"That gives us three hours; that will be enough," she said, as she peeled back the adhesive strip and stuck it to the windscreen.

Jo went to the boot and took out the holdall containing the beach stuff.

"Come on then, let's have a look at the sea."

They walked along the promenade to a set of stone steps that led down to the sand. They were shiny, worn smooth by probably a hundred years of excited holiday makers. There was a definite dip in the middle which had taken the brunt of the footfall.

The children led the way. They took off their shoes as they reached the golden sand and Zack danced around excitedly.

The beach, as April had said, was a good size, probably a quarter of a mile long, and not encased by a harbour. There were a few boats bobbing around, mainly of the speed variety, nothing to suggest any fishing activity. This was a village purely dependent on the holiday season.

It was busy with families dotted about at regular intervals. Occasionally, unoccupied towels lay on the sand with stones stopping them from blowing away, the owners presumably in the water, or at the shops.

The sea looked inviting, the waves merely lapping the shoreline; this was not a surfer's paradise. Even so, there were many families in the water. Lilos of all descriptions were being paddled; balls and frisbees were being thrown, mostly between teenage lads. Jo spotted a hut with the word 'Lifeguard' in large letters, about a hundred yards further down the beach.

"How about here?" said Jo, dropping down the holdall. There was no-one else in the immediate vicinity.

She started getting the towels out and placing them on the sand. "Come on you two, come and get changed."

Jo passed their swimming costumes and held up a towel so they could undress in privacy. Zack was about to charge towards the sea.

"Wait Zack, you need your sunscreen," shouted Jo.

Zack moaned. "Oh, Mom," but complied.

Jo started rubbing the cream into his shoulders and back.

"Now you, Poppet." Farrah was given the same treatment.

"I don't want to go in the water," said Farrah. "Lily says it's dangerous."

"You don't have to if you don't want to, Poppet, but I'll be keeping a careful watch."

Jo started changing into a bikini under a strategically placed towel; then applied some sunscreen. Her arm was still red from the scalding, but much less painful. She made sure it was well protected from the warm sun. She was quite tall and her regular exercise routine, together with her weekly lengths in the local swimming pool, ensured she had stayed fit and slim. She was comfortable in a swimsuit. She tied back her shoulder-length auburn hair off her face with a hairband and was now beach ready.

"Oh, this is more like it," she said to no one in particular.

Zack was already in the sea. Farrah stood by the water's edge watching anxiously.

Jo finished applying the sun cream, lay down on the towel, and closed her eyes. She could feel the warmth of the sun permeating her body. It reminded her of some of the Mediterranean holidays she and Liam used to enjoy before the children came along. The whole ambience was relaxing and within five minutes she was asleep.

She had no idea how long she had been napping, but was woken by Farrah, shaking her frantically.

"Mom, Mom, wake up; I can't see Zack."

Jo was quickly awake and ran down to the shoreline and scanned the swimmers.

"Where was he? Can you remember?" exclaimed Jo, anxiously.

"Over there," said Farrah pointing out to sea.

"Go and get the lifeguard; I'll see if I can find him."

Farrah ran across to the hut while Jo dived in. She was a strong swimmer and was soon at the depth where it was not possible to stand. There were only a few swimmers out this far.

She trod water and shouted. "Zack! Zack!"

She turned around three-sixty degrees, scanning every inch of water. Just then a jet-ski approached and slowed. The blond-haired lifeguard was wearing a red lifejacket over his bronzed, well-sculpted torso.

"Are you ok?" he shouted.

"I can't find my son?"

"What's his name?"

"Zack."

"Ok, I'll do a quick sweep; try not to worry. You should get back to shore; it's quite deep here," he shouted to be heard over the engine.

"I need to find my son."

"Yes, but I don't want to be looking for two people; the currents here are quite difficult."

Jo turned and started swimming back to the shore. Farrah was standing with her feet just in the sea.

Jo reached her depth and stood up. There were dozens of people about, seemingly oblivious to Zack's plight.`

She could see the jet-ski criss-crossing the bay. Then it stopped. Jo continued walking backwards to the shore, anxiously maintaining eye contact on the lifeguard, the sea lapping around her waist. Just then, the jet-ski turned and started heading towards shore. Jo could see two people on board.

Jo joined Farrah and watched as the lifeguard got closer.

"It's Zack," shouted Farrah.

"Oh, thank goodness," said Jo and put her hand to her mouth.

Moments later, the jet-ski reached Jo and Farrah. The 'hunk' got off and helped Zack who immediately ran to Jo and flung his arms around her.

"He'll be ok," said the lifeguard. "But another five minutes, it could have been a different story."

"Thank you, thank you," said Jo; the sense of relief, palpable.

She watched as the lifeguard started up his chariot and roared back along the beach, parking outside the hut.

"What happened?" asked Jo with her arm around her son.

"I'm sorry, Mom. I'm really sorry. One minute I was swimming, the next, it felt like someone was pushing me out to sea. You don't think it was a Bucca, do you?"

"No, dear, I don't. As long as you're ok."

"Yes, I'm ok now. Can we get an ice cream?"

"Yes, come on, I'll get some clothes on. Let's get off this beach."

"Mom, Lily said not to go into the sea."

"Yes, she did, Poppet."

Jo changed back into her day clothes, her hair still wet and streaked down the side of her face. She took a dry towel from the holdall, removed the hairband, and started rubbing it dry. The children were still in their swimming costumes.

They walked up the steps to the promenade and across the road to an ice cream cabin. Jo ordered three cones. "Come on let's sit over there," she said pointing to the sea wall.

"Are you sure you're ok, Zack," said Jo.

"Sure, Mom, don't worry."

"But why did you go out that far? I said to stay close."

Zack was licking his cone frantically to avoid melted ice cream dripping onto the pavement.

"I was Mom, honest; I was waiting for you. I was playing ball with some people."

"What people?"

Zack looked across the beach. "I don't know; they must have gone now. He said his name was George. He was with a lady and a girl. They were playing catch and I joined in. The man threw the ball over my head and I was swimming to fetch it. Then I felt the current suddenly take me out and my feet couldn't touch the bottom. I was trying to swim back to shore but it kept pushing me further and further out. I was really scared. I was getting so tired. Then I spotted the jet-ski and started waving."

Jo looked at him. "And you're ok.? You're sure?"

"Yes, I'm ok. When are we going to meet Dad?"

Jo checked her watch. "We'll go now. You can change in

the car."

They finished their ice creams and walked the short distance to the Volvo.

It was ten-past one as Jo pulled into the pub car park back in Polgissy The weather was similar to the neighbouring village and the car was hot.

Jo picked up her handbag from the back seat and the three left the car and walked around the corner to the pub entrance.

It was dark as they entered, and Jo stopped for a moment to allow her eyes to adjust. Liam was sitting in the corner with a glass of beer, going through the newspaper clippings in April's folder.

He stopped and looked up as the family approached.

"Hi, guys, had a good time?"

Jo's expression suggested otherwise.

"What's wrong? What happened?"

"Can you get the drinks and sandwiches? I'll tell you all about it."

"Yes, ok. You're all alright though?"

"Yes, we're fine," said Jo and took the next seat to Liam's.

They decided on their food and Liam went to the bar to order. He was warmly welcomed by the landlord. "Mornin' m'dear; nice day."

While Liam was ordering the drinks and food, Jo was curious about the folder and opened it. The newspaper cuttings with their gory headlines were displayed. Jo started to look through them. She was holding the folder in her hands out of the gaze of the children, when a number of the clippings slid onto the floor. Jo quickly closed the folder and bent down to retrieve the spilled items.

"You've missed one," said Zack and he crawled under

the table.

He picked up the cutting. It was a reproduced family photograph; the ones they frequently use in newspapers, often with the caption – 'in happier times'.

Zack sat back and looked at it. Jo went to retrieve it from him.

"Wait, that's them," said Zack. His eyes were close to the photo examining it carefully.

"What do you mean, 'them'?" said Jo, taking the newspaper article from him and putting it back in the folder.

"That's George and the other two I was playing catch with, in the sea."

"I don't think so," said Jo. "These people are dead."

"It was them, Mom, I'm positive."

Liam returned carrying a tray of drinks. "They'll bring the sandwiches over shortly. So, come on then; what happened?"

Liam distributed the drinks and crisps, and sat down.

Jo looked down. "Zack got carried out to sea and had to be rescued by the lifeguard."

"What? How did that happen?"

Zack interjected. "I was playing catch with a family and I was just getting the ball when the current just took me out. It was so strong."

"What about the family? Didn't they try to help?"

"I couldn't see them; I kept shouting."

Jo looked down. "It was my fault, I fell asleep. It was Far who spotted something was wrong."

"So how were you rescued?"

Jo continued. "I swam out to look for Zack, but I couldn't see him. Luckily, the lifeguards have jet-skis; he saw me and came over. He told me to go back because of the currents. Then he went off and did a search and found him."

"You don't think it's the Buccas, Dad?"

"No, Zack, that's all superstition."

"Hmm, well there's something else." said Jo. "When we sat down at the table, I was reading some of those newspaper cuttings in that folder. One or two of them fell on the floor, including..." Jo opened the folder. "This one."

"Tell your Dad what you told me, Zack."

Zack took the picture. "That's them, I'm sure of it."

"Them?" enquired Liam.

"The family in the sea. He said his name was George."

"George?"

"What does it mean, Liam?" asked Jo. "We looked along the beach and there was no sign of them."

"I don't know; I really don't, but there must be some explanation. Zack must have been mistaken."

"I wasn't Dad. I'm sure it was the people in the picture," interrupted Zack who was listening to the conversation.

"Then it's a mystery. Still, you're alright; that's the main thing."

Liam looked at Jo. He didn't want to make a big deal of it and worry Zack.

Just then, the landlord approached with the sandwiches. "Aswen's done a few chips for you; they won't be a minute."

"That's very kind of you."

"I hears you was on the boat with Jack yesserday?"

"Yes, that's right. I'm glad he's ok."

"Aye, Squire's fetching 'im back, so I 'eard."

"Yes, this afternoon apparently."

"They're saying it were a Bucca."

"Who was saying?" asked Liam.

"Oh, just folk."

"No, it was nothing like that. The engine cut out and Jack slipped and banged his head; that was all there was to it."

"Ah, that would account for it," said the landlord.

Just then, the landlord's wife appeared with a bowl of chips and placed them on the table.

"Mornin' m'dears. Lovely day," she said, as she presented the food."

"Yes, it is, thanks," said Liam.

"What have you been up to?" she asked.

"Well, we went to Polperrin this morning," said Jo.

"Polperrin? Hmm, not keen on that place, too busy for my liking. You get all sorts there," said Aswen. "Do you want any ketchup?"

"Have you got tomato, please?" asked Zack.

"Aye, should 'ave."

Aswen returned to the kitchen and returned with a bottle of ketchup. The pair returned to their duties chatting animatedly to each other.

Jo took a sip of her beer. "So, how did you get on this morning?"

"Now that was something else. This guy's house, Christopher, you should see it; it's out of this world. All glass and wood, spectacular. He's got this enormous wall going all the way 'round. Security cameras everywhere. Between you and me, it looks like a luxury prison."

"Sounds amazing."

"Yes, it is. I'll take you next time I go." He took a sip of beer. "Actually, April was saying that according to stories, the house was built over a mass grave, something to do with the plague, way back."

"Really? I don't think I'd like living there."

"No, me neither." He took another sip of beer. "What do you fancy doing this afternoon?"

"Well, I could do with going to the supermarket again to get some bits and pieces. What about you?"

"I think I'll stay here and work my way through these cuttings if you don't mind. Why don't you see if April wants to go?"

"Yes, ok, I can call round on the way, see if she's free."

Later that afternoon, April was finalising her latest article ready for Thursday's deadline, when Jo knocked on her cottage door. She went to answer it.

Her eyes widened. "Hi Jo, this is an unexpected pleasure."

"Yes, I was going across to the supermarket, wondered if you wanted anything. You can join us if you like. Liam's staying in the cottage to continue his investigations, whatever that means."

"Yes, I'd love to. Perfect timing, I've just finished an article for Thursday. Give me five minutes and I'll be with you."

"Yes, ok, I'll be in the car. We're just outside."

Jo returned to the car and ushered Zack into the back, causing a sulk. "April's coming with us; adults should sit in the front."

"Whatever," said Zack with his arms folded.

"Lily said we need to mind the fog," said Farrah, as Jo got into the car and buckled up.

Jo turned around. "Why's that, Poppet?"

"She says it's evil."

"Tell her we'll be careful."

Jo was deep in thought as April opened the door, making her jump.

"Oh, sorry, I was miles away," said Jo, as April got in.

"It's good to daydream, so they say," she said and smiled. She turned around. "How are you both?"

"Ok," said Zack.

"Zack nearly drowned," said Farrah, with a hint of drama.

"Really?" said April.

Jo turned the car around and headed along the sea front.

"That's a bit of an exaggeration," said Jo. "He got caught by the current and the lifeguard had to get him back."

"Oh, that's terrible," said April. "Are you ok?"

"Yeah, sure," said Zack.

"There was something strange though," said Jo. "I didn't know whether to mention it."

"Go on," said April.

"Zack said he was playing catch-ball with a family in the sea. Hmm, you won't believe this. He said it was the Waltons. He saw a photo of them among the newspaper cuttings you gave Liam."

"It was them," shouted Zack from the back. "He said his name was George."

"What does it mean?" said Jo.

"It's nothing to worry about." She continued in a whisper. "Probably auto-suggestion."

"You mean he made it up?"

"It's a possibility, so he wouldn't get into trouble. Wasn't someone watching him?"

"Hmm, no. That was my fault. I should have been, but I fell asleep. Luckily, Far was keeping an eye on him."

"Did she see them?"

"Actually, come to mention it, she hasn't said anything. She just kept saying that Lily told her not to go into the water."

"Why are you whispering?" shouted Farrah as they headed up the steep hill out of the village.

"Sorry, Poppet, just grown-up talk. Tell April what Lily said about the fog."

"She said it was evil."

"Oh dear," said April.

"You're not taking it seriously are you?" asked Jo.

"Well, there's a lot about the spiritual world we don't understand. Let's just say, I keep an open mind."

They reached the outskirts of the village and the shrine. April looked across at it.

"Lily says they are looking for their Mom."

"Who are, Poppet?"

"The girls who were knocked down."

Jo looked across at April.

Liam, meanwhile, was at the table in the lounge, reading the newspaper cuttings. He had a note book beside him and was making comments. As it happened, there wasn't anything new. The three family members had been 'bludgeoned to death', according to several headlines. The police had found no clues, motive, or the murder weapon. There was a little about their background which confirmed April's account. George Walton was an illustrator from Plymouth, his wife Lizzy, a teaching assistant, and their daughter, Lily. 'A nice family', all of the cuttings said the same, nothing that warranted a violent death.

Liam drew on his years of dealing with dangerous criminals. He had met a few that would definitely have had no compunction in meting out this level of brutality. It had all the hallmarks of psychopathic behaviour, a topic he had studied, both from a professional and intellectual perspective.

Psychopaths are not usually random killers. They are narcissistic, often with an anti-social personality. They lack empathy and remorse for their actions. Liam pondered this; there must be a motive of some sort. He decided to make a cup of tea to help him think.

When he returned to the table, the folder of cuttings was

on the floor. There was a chill in the air as if someone had left a window open on a winter's day. It was high summer.

Liam bent down and collected the cuttings together and put them on the table on top of the open folder, then started to sort them back into date order again. He was about to pick up one of the clippings, when it suddenly flew from the pile and back on the floor. Liam felt a strange sensation; like the one when he saw the vision in the loft.

He looked around. "Who's there?" he shouted. There was no reply.

Liam knelt on the floor retrieving the errant clipping. As he put it back on the table, he started to read it. There was a headline. 'Village in mourning over slaughtered family.' Then a picture he recognised. It was the Squire.

Liam read the narrative under the photograph. *'Christopher Deakin, a resident of Polgissy for almost ten years, gave his reaction to the killings. "I don't know who would want to kill them; they were a lovely family and well-liked in the community. This is such a peaceful place; our prayers go to their family and friends."'*

Liam read the article again. The room returned to its normal temperature. He needed to speak to April.

Jo, April, and the children were returning from the supermarket in St Austell, loaded with provisions. They reached the junction from the main road and turned left along the narrow road into the trees.

"April, I don't like the trees," said Farrah from the back seat.

April turned in her seat. "There's nothing to be frightened of."

"Lily says the evil ones live in the trees." April looked across at Jo.

"What did she tell you?" asked April.

"She just said the evil ones live in the trees."

"What does that mean?" asked Jo, looking across at April. "I remember Mrs Wilkins saying something about upsetting the trees."

"Hmm, yes, she was often going on about them, mind you, trees have had mystic properties since ancient times, particularly oak, ash, hawthorn, also elderberry. There are quite a few oak in the forest, and around the village. There's a very old one in the corner of the graveyard. Mrs Wilkins used to talk to them, bless her. She would say they would whisper back to her."

"You used to see her a lot?" said Jo.

"I visited her a few times when Christopher was away on one of his business trips."

"Oh, yes, Liam was telling me about his house."

"Hmm, now that is a sight to behold. Mind you, it didn't go down well with the villagers when he had it built apparently. There was an issue with planning consent, one or two objections."

"Oh, yes, Liam mentioned something about graves."

"The plague pit, yes; it's only a legend, mind. There's no evidence that I know of, and, of course, with the house now built, I guess we'll never know. To be fair, Christopher has invested a great deal in the village and he's very active in the community. He seems to have won over the villagers. They all look up to him; it's why they call him the Squire. I think he enjoys all the attention, and being called 'Squire'."

Farrah was trying to follow the conversation from the back seat. "Lily says the fog hides in the trees," she interjected.

Jo looked at April. "What does that mean?"

"Hmm, it's all superstition. We don't normally get too much of it in the summer. I do admit that has been unusual, but November it's often quite bad and can last for days. Come to think of it, it was very foggy when the Waltons died. I remember thinking about it at the time. The locals still believe it was the work of the spirits."

Jo looked left and right, heavily laden trees stretched in both directions' The headlights had activated automatically, illuminating the way.

"I'm scared, Mom," said Zack.

"There's nothing to worry about, only a couple more minutes," Jo replied, although she too was also feeling slightly uneasy.

Suddenly, as if a blanket had been thrown around them, they were engulfed.

"It's the fog," shouted Farrah.

"Don't worry, there's nothing to worry about," said April. "We'll be out of it in a second or two."

Jo was driving at walking pace.

"Lookout!!" shouted Farrah who was looking through the window from the backseat.

Jo slammed on the brakes. About two feet in front of them was the rear of a large delivery van. Everyone was thrown forward by the momentum. Jo flicked on the hazard lights and got out of the car. April did the same.

"Stay here," shouted Jo to the children.

April and Jo walked around to the front of the vehicle; the driver was slumped forward with his head on his chest.

Jo knocked on the driver's window but the man didn't move. She tried the door and it swung open. She climbed up to the cab and checked him.

"He's unconscious," she shouted to April. "We need to call an ambulance."

April was looking around; the fog was still enveloping them. She took a mirror from her handbag, walked around the other side of the vehicle, out of sight, and held it up towards the trees.

"Be gone thou restless spirits," she exclaimed.

April replaced her mirror to her handbag.

"It looks like it's starting to clear," said Jo as April returned to the driver's side.

"How is he?" asked April.

"Well, he's breathing, but still unconscious; he needs medical attention. If we can't move the van, I'll need to reverse to the main road and see if I can get a signal on my phone."

The hazy sun was now visible through the trees and the road ahead clear. The fog had completely disappeared.

April did a quick assessment of the driver's condition. "Let's try and move him onto the passenger seat. I'll get in that side."

So, April went around the other side of the van and climbed in. Between them, they managed to unbuckle his seat belt and manoeuvre him away from the driver's seat. The engine was still running. Jo took over the steering wheel, and gently inched the van forward at no more than walking pace. April was holding onto the stricken driver.

"We can park it next to Mrs Wilkins' cottage," said Jo.

A short time later, Jo managed to get the van onto the waste ground next to the first cottage and parked.

"I'll pop over the road and call an ambulance from Mrs Forbes' cottage while you get back to the children."

They left the man propped up in the front of the van as April ran over the road. Jo hurried back up the road to the Volvo.

As she approached the car, there was no sign of the children. Panic set in.

"Zack! Far!"

She grabbed the driver's door and opened it. Zach suddenly emerged from the rear footwell; Farrah was next to him.

"Oh, you gave me such a fright. What were you doing down there?"

"We could hear strange noises," said Zack.

"Lily said the fog was evil and we should hide."

"Oh, thank goodness. Well, it's gone now; there's nothing to worry about. Sit up and buckle up; we need to move the car."

The children complied. Jo moved the Volvo forward in the direction of the village and turned off the road to park next to the van. April was back in the front with the driver who was starting to come around, but seemed delirious.

"Stay in the car," said Jo to the children, and she left the Volvo to join April.

"How is he?" Jo looked at him. He was probably in his late forties and wearing an earring in his right ear with tattoos down both arms.

"He's starting to come round I think, but he's mumbling."

"What's your name?" asked Jo.

"Des," wheezed the man.

"We've called an ambulance; it should be here in half an hour," said April.

April turned to Jo. "Gladys Forbes was in; she let me borrow her phone. They'll be coming over from St Austell; shouldn't be too long. There's no reason for you to stay. I can look after him until the ambulance gets here."

"How will you get home?"

"I'll walk; it's not far. I'm used to it."

"Well, if you're sure. I think the kids have found it all a bit stressful. They were hiding when I got back to the car."

"Hiding? Why?"

"Farrah said that Lily kept warning them about the fog, so they decided to hide."

"As long as they are ok," said April.

"Yes, they seem to be. Well, if you're sure... Why don't you call up to the cottage when you've finished here? You can join us for dinner if you've got nothing planned."

"No, I haven't but I don't want to keep imposing on your hospitality."

"Don't be silly, you're always welcome."

"Ok, I'll call back later once we've sorted the driver out."

There was a distant sound of an emergency vehicle.

"Sounds like they're nearly here," said Jo. "We'll see you later. Hope everything'll be ok."

Jo and the children returned to the cottage. Liam was still at the table making notes from the newspaper cuttings when they walked in. Jo was laden with supermarket carrier bags.

Farrah ran straight over to him. "The fog came again. Lily says the fog's evil."

"Hello, Far... Really?" He looked at Jo with some concern.

Jo put down her carrier bags of groceries by the table where Liam was working. "I don't know what's happening, but it's really weird. We were coming through the trees when suddenly that fog came down again and we nearly ran into the back of a delivery van."

Liam stood up. "What!? What happened? Are you ok?" He put a consoling arm around her.

"Yes, luckily I managed to stop in time. The driver was unconscious, looks like a heart attack. April went over to one of the cottages and phoned the ambulance. She's staying with the driver till they arrive." She looked at him. "What's going on, Liam?"

"I don't know, I really don't. Maybe April will have some answers," said Liam, with an expression of concern.

"She's calling over later. I've invited her for dinner."

"Oh, great, we can ask her; see if she can shed any light on things."

Jo picked up one the carrier bags and started walking into the kitchen. Liam picked up the other and followed. The two children ran upstairs to their bedrooms.

"Why do you think she'll be able to help?" said Jo as she started to unpack the provisions.

"It's something she told me," said Liam. "She's a white witch."

"A white witch? What does that mean?"

"According to her, she's sensitive to the spirit world."

"That's good to know," said Jo, sarcastically. She stopped her unpacking. "Mind you, she did say that the fog was nothing to worry about, but I have to say, it scares me. Think about it; it started with the car breaking down, then that poor breakdown truck driver, and we mustn't forget Mrs Wilkins. It can't be a coincidence. There was something else; April said there was a blanket of fog on the village on the day when the Waltons were murdered."

Liam looked at Jo. "Hmm, that's something I didn't know."

"Do you think we're in danger?"

"Goodness no," said Liam.

"Well, I'm worried about the children. Far's continually referring to this Lily person."

"Well, if you want to go home, we can. Let's see what the children say. We have only been here a few days; we're still getting used to the place."

"Yes, that's true. Funny, though, it seems like we've been here forever."

"I'll make us a cup of tea," said Liam.

"Great. Oh, I managed to get some more change for the electricity. I'll put it on the kitchen table."

Chapter Ten

April arrived at the cottage around six o'clock. Liam went to the door and let her in.

"Hi, how are you?" asked Liam as she reached the door.

She was wearing jeans, a white blouse, and trainers. She smiled warmly. "Oh, ok, thanks," she said rather wearily.

"Come in. Jo tells me you had another incident."

April followed Liam into the cottage. "Ha, you could say that."

Jo came out of the kitchen. "Hi, how did you get on?"

Liam invited April to sit down. "Would you like a cup of tea?"

"I'd murder a gin and tonic, if I'm honest."

"Will red wine do?" asked Jo.

"Oh, definitely."

April took off her jacket while Jo went to pour the wine.

"Here, this will hit the spot," said Jo presenting April with a glass of red wine.

"Thanks, oh, I forgot to ask; how's your arm?" asked April.

"Oh, it's much better thanks, just a bit red but the soreness has gone. Just a sec, I'll just get my glass and you can tell us what happened."

Jo brought in two more glasses of wine and handed one to Liam. They both sat down and waited for April.

"Well, the ambulance turned up about five minutes after you left. Des, the driver, was more awake by the time they arrived and they took him off to the Community Hospital in St Austell."

"Did he say what happened?" asked Jo.

"He just said that he was on his way to the village store

to make a delivery. As he was coming through the forest, he was suddenly hit by the fog." Jo cast a look at Liam. "Then he started getting pains in his chest, and passed out. Luckily, the van stalled when his foot slipped off the accelerator otherwise he could have been careering down the hill."

"Will he be ok?" asked Jo.

"Yes, he should be. The paramedics were great. They put him on oxygen and he seemed to be recovering when they left."

"What about the van?" asked Liam.

"It's still parked next to Mrs Wilkins' place. I expect someone will come and collect it sometime."

Jo looked at April. "But what does it all mean? Liam and I were talking about it earlier before you arrived. This is the third or fourth incident that's happened since we arrived; it can't be a coincidence, surely?"

"I really don't know," said April.

"Liam says you have a sensitivity to spirits. Is it something we should be worried about? We were wondering if we should just cut our losses and head home."

"Oh, that would be such a pity; I really hope you'll stay. But, to answer your question, yes, I do have a sensitivity to sprits. However, I have no control over them, or communication with them. I just occasionally get a feeling of their presence. Sometimes it's stronger than others."

"But, these spirits, are they dangerous?"

"No, not in my experience." She took a sip of wine and made eye-contact with Jo and Liam. "Look, it's easy to interpret unexplained circumstances into something they're not. Most of the time they are just that - unexplained circumstances, or coincidences. It doesn't mean they're somehow the work of the devil or evil spirits, just that we haven't been able to rationalise them within our own levels of experience."

"But what about this Lily? I'm worried about Far. The warnings about going in the sea, the fog; so far they've been proved right."

"Yes, and some people do have the gift of being able to communicate with the spirit world. Farrah is probably one of them. Have you talked to her how she contacts Lily or vice-versa?"

Jo looked at Liam. "No, not really, we took your advice and played it down."

"Yes, and that still stands. As long as she's not getting distressed."

"She doesn't seem to be," said Jo. "In fact, she seems quite settled now; she was all for going home when we first arrived."

"I would just keep an eye on the situation and not make a big deal of it," said April.

April took another sip of her wine then turned to Liam. "Did you find anything of interest in the newspaper cuttings?"

Jo intervened before Liam could answer. "I'll make a start on the dinner while you two catch up," she said and left the room.

Liam looked at April. "I've been through all the cuttings. There's nothing that jumps out. Do you know if they had any suspects?"

"There was nothing in the newspapers. I spoke to the police when they completed their forensic tests, an Inspector Travis. He said it was a mystery. I heard later they had scaled back the investigation, costs apparently. There's been no police round for a couple of months now."

"Hmm." Liam was deep in thought. "Can I ask you a question? What do you know about Christopher Deakin?"

"In what respect?"

"I don't know, business interests, that sort of thing?"

"Only what I told you. He told me he was a crypto-trader; the same as he told you."

"Do you think he's legit? I mean, have you noticed anything unusual?"

"Hmm, no, not really, why do you ask?"

"It's just, well, he seems so out of place. He's clearly got a lot of money. Why on earth has he based himself in a remote corner of Cornwall?"

"I don't know; I've never given it much thought. Maybe he likes the peace and quiet here."

"Yes, that's possible. What about his time before he arrived in the village? Do you know anything about that?"

"Hmm, no, not really, he was here before we were. He was based in London, I know that. We never socialised as such, just met him at village meetings and when I popped in to use his internet. He would call me occasionally if he was unable to see Mrs Wilkins."

"Why did he take an interest in her, do you know?"

"That's a good question, I don't. They weren't related as far as I know, but he does help a lot of people in the village; although I'm not sure his motives are entirely altruistic. He gives them advice on their finances. I think several have invested with him, including Mrs Wilkins. Rumour has it, he's the sole beneficiary to her will, but that's just gossip. He did ask me if I was interested in investing with him, but I told him I'd stick with what I understand. Mind you, he can be very persuasive."

"Hmm, yes, although he doesn't strike me as the kind of person that does empathy."

"I know what you mean. He does come across rather cold, and he certainly likes to be in control. He set up the monthly villagers' meetings. He calls it the village council;

he chairs it. It's like a parish council, although it's got no legal status. He has, though, managed to get several planning applications from outsiders overturned, including a mobile phone mast. I occasionally help with the administration, not that there's much to do. I think I'm the only other person in the village that can type."

"Why would he oppose a mobile phone mast? Surely that would be of significant benefit to the community."

"That's a good point. I don't know, but he told the residents that they give off harmful x-rays. Stuart and I were there at the meeting. I have to say it would make my life easier; that, and the internet."

"It does give him a great deal of power."

"Hmm, I suppose it does."

"Are any of the cottages second homes?"

"No, not now, but that directive comes from local government, nothing to do with Christopher. Same with buy-to-let, they inflate local house prices. It's why all the young people are gone; they just can't afford to buy a house in the village."

"Well, I can't fault that logic. So every cottage in the village is occupied?"

"Apart from this one, yes. Oh, and Ashley Morgan's place, although I'm sure she'll come back when she's ready."

Jo returned from the kitchen. "I could do with some more potatoes, Liam. Are there any more in the garden?"

"Yes, I'm sure there's another row. I won't be a moment." He turned to April.

"Actually, there's something in the garden I want to show you, if you don't mind joining me."

April put her glass of wine down on the table. "Sure, lead the way."

They walked through the kitchen where Jo was preparing dinner. "You can get a cabbage too if there is one. The trug's in the pantry."

Liam tugged on the back door. "If you know someone who has a plane, I'll fix that for you," said Liam as he left the kitchen holding the trug.

April noticed the struggle with the back door. "Thanks, that's good of you; I'm sure I can get one from somewhere."

Liam started walking up the path towards the sycamore tree.

He turned to April. "I would like you to check the outbuilding with me, see if you can sense anything, you know, after my experience."

"You mean the old outside toilet?"

"Yes."

"So, tell me, what exactly happened?"

"Things flying about, the floor moving, strange noises; I thought I was going crazy."

"And you want me to take a look?"

"Yes, please, I was wondering if you would be able to detect anything there."

"Of course. I have to say, Stuart and I didn't pay much attention to the outbuildings, and of course, we never used them for their intended purpose."

"I assume the police would have examined it?"

"I presume so; it's as they left it."

"There's some police tape in the pigsty, so they were obviously looking around. Probably looking for the murder weapon."

"Yes, that would make sense."

They reached the door to the old privy. Liam hesitated before he went to lift the latch.

"Wait, let me," said April, sensing Liam's anxiety.

She lifted the latch and pulled open the door. They were immediately hit by a strange smell. April walked inside. "Urgh, it smells like someone's been using the facilities."

Liam looked at the garden implements. They were neat and tidy, where they should be, except for the spade and fork which were still in the garden by the potatoes.

"Can you feel anything?" asked Liam.

"No, not really. Tell me what happened."

"Well, for a start, those tools started moving and eventually fell on the floor. That axe almost hit me, and there was this icy blast. It scared the hell out of me if I'm honest."

"Hmm, well, I can't detect anything." April looked around and peered down the holes with her hand held over her mouth and nose. She examined the hooks holding the garden implements.

"Let's go outside; I can't stand much more of this stench."

They left the privy; April took a deep breath of fresh air.

"What do you think it was?" said Liam. They stood for a moment.

"Well, what you have described would appear to be poltergeist activity."

"Poltergeist?"

"Mmm, although I have to admit I'm a sceptic on the phenomena. Very few reports of poltergeist activity remain unexplained." She turned and looked at him. "Most reports don't stand up to scrutiny. Often they turn out to be caused by some natural occurrence - a sudden gust of wind for instance, weak building foundations, or wood warping in the heat, that kind of thing. Then there're the pranksters... that's very common. Just trying to frighten people for various motives. There was a case where a landlord was trying to evict some tenants so he could sell the property and was sneaking in at night, removing pictures from the wall, and turning furniture around, that kind of thing."

"Yes, but I wasn't imagining it, and I would certainly put myself in the sceptic camp."

"Hmm, yes, I believe you, but it doesn't mean it's a supernatural event. I think you should keep an open mind for the moment and see what happens. It might be worth videoing it on your phone it if you experience any more instances."

"Yes, that's an idea. Let me show you something else." He walked across the garden to the herb patch. The ground was dry and hard, with no rain since the thunderstorm.

"According to Far, this was Lily's patch. That's her spade there."

"Oh, that's so sad."

"Far had a message from Lily saying she was happy for us to use the herbs. That was quite worrying. I mean, how did Far know we were going to use the herbs?"

"I really don't know, Liam, but I do sense a presence. I think Lily spent a lot of time in the garden, probably with her father."

"I don't know what to make of it all, I really don't," said Liam. "It goes way beyond anything I've experienced before."

"Yes, I understand, but I don't think you or your family are in any danger. The messages that Farrah have received from Lily have not been threatening, just warnings. It seems she wants to look after you, or Farrah, at least."

"Yes, I get that." Liam stopped and pondered the conversation. "Right, let's get some potatoes."

The spade and fork were still in the ground where Liam had left it. He retrieved the fork and started to dig up some roots while April watched.

Having unearthed sufficient potatoes, Liam cut a cabbage

and placed the vegetables in the trug. The pair returned to the cottage.

Later that evening Liam and Jo were relaxing, All the chores were done, the children were in bed and April had returned home.

Liam was studying the newspaper cuttings and making more notes. Jo looked up from her book.

"Are you still on that?" asked Jo. "You're supposed to be on holiday, you know, as in 'switch off'."

"I *am* finding this relaxing," he reposted. "So many questions, so few answers."

"Why don't you leave it to the police?"

"I don't know; I just have this deep feeling of injustice. April thinks they've given up. There's something else too. Hmm, I know you'll think I'm going crazy but, you know all this business with Lily and everything? I think they are trying to communicate with us."

Jo put her book down on her lap.

"Er, Earth calling Liam Drake, are you receiving me!?"

Liam looked at Jo with a frown. "Ha, you may mock, but there are some things that can't be explained. April was telling me things about the spirit world."

"Hmm, I'm not sure how much notice you should take of her."

"She does seem very knowledgeable on the subject."

"Really? Well, the jury's out as far as I'm concerned; she's good company, but I don't buy all this white witch nonsense."

"You're entitled to your view, but I'm keeping an open mind."

Liam picked up another newspaper cutting and started reading. Jo went back to her book.

The following day, Liam wanted to call in at Jack's cottage and see how he was; Zack agreed to accompany him. Jo and Farrah decided to look for more shells along the seashore in the harbour. They would meet at the pub for a coffee. The question of returning home to London wasn't raised.

Liam parked the car in the pub car park; the landlord hadn't voiced any objections, and the family went their separate ways.

Liam and Zack walked past the Harbourmaster's office and noticed Jack was outside his cottage on the sea wall attending to his crab pots. He looked up as the pair approached.

"Hello, Jack, I just thought we'd pop by and see how you were."

"Wasson m'dears, aye, thanks, that's very good of you; the Squire bought me 'ome yesterday afternoon."

Liam looked at the mariner; he had a black eye and there was a plaster on his forehead.

"Yes, he said he was going to. How are you feeling?"

"Aye, can't complain; it'll take more than a Bucca to see me off."

"A Bucca? Why do you think a Bucca was responsible?"

"When you've been at sea as long as I have, you find out things. I can sense a change of wind, when a Bucca is playing with us, having their fun."

"And you think that was what caused you to fall?"

"Aye, course, what else could it be?"

"Just a slip?" proffered Liam.

"Nay, it were a Bucca, right enough; though I don't knows why he were upset. We were doing no 'arm. They don't mind us fishing as long as we're respectful. It's why we always throw one back; it's a tradition goes back years."

Jack looked at Zack. "And 'ow are you, me ansom?"

"I'm fine thank you, Jack. I'm glad you're feeling better."

"So, what are you up to today, then?" asked Jack, looking at Liam.

"Not made any arrangements yet, Jo and Farrah are collecting shells."

"Aye, there's no shortage of them 'round 'ere. Just watch the tide if you go t'other side of the Hawn. It can catch ya out if you're not careful."

"Thanks, Jack, good advice. Well, we'll leave you to your work. Glad you're ok."

Liam and Zack turned and walked back towards the pub. "Come on let's see if we can find your Mum."

They crossed over the road and passed the store, which enabled them to see the shoreline from the sea wall. The tide was out and the small boats that were in the harbour were aground. It was a pleasant morning; white fluffy clouds skittered across the blue sky, the wind a moderate breeze, the type you could fly a kite by. The seagulls were again out in force; their constant shrieking adding to the ambience of the village.

Liam was feeling relaxed and despite the incidents that had happened since their arrival, was beginning to feel at home in the village; he was starting to 'get it', the beautiful scenery and the total tranquillity.

"There they are," shouted Zack, pointing in the distance. The rest of the beach was deserted.

As they reached the 'nip' where April's cottage was situated, Liam noticed April's car coming towards the junction, She flashed her lights.

"Wait a sec, Zack."

Liam left him and crossed the road. He reached April's car; the window was wound down.

"Hi April, how are you?"

"I'm fine, thanks, that was a stroke of luck, I was on my way to see you."

"We've just been to see Jack, see how he was."

"Oh, that's sweet of you. The reason I was coming to see you, that student's on her way. I'm meeting her at midday outside the pub. She wants to go to the graveyard; I wondered if you wanted to come."

"Oh, yes, definitely. Jo and Farrah are on the beach collecting shells; we're going for a coffee at the pub. Do you want to join us?"

"Yes, ok, I'll just park up."

April reversed the car back up the nip to her parking spot. Liam waited for her to walk back. Zack had been waving to Jo and Farrah, and they were now on their way.

A few minutes later, the family and April were in the pub catching up on the day. The adults were enjoying a coffee while the children were drinking Cola."

"How was Jack?" asked Jo.

"Well, he seems right enough; he was messing about with his crab pots outside his cottage when we got there. Still insists his mishap was caused by a Bucca."

"Yes, that sounds like Jack," said April. "Full of stories about sea spirits. He can talk for hours once he gets going."

They continued chatting until just before midday; the drinks had been finished.

"I think I better wait outside in case she comes," said April, checking her watch.

"Yes, I'll call in at the store to get a few bits, then head back to the cottage," said Jo.

"You better take the car keys; I can climb over the garden

wall when we've finished," said Liam and handed Jo the keys.

Jo looked at the children. "You ok with that, kids? We can get some ice cream."

"Yes, please," said Zack. Farrah nodded.

"How long will you be?" asked Jo.

"Not long I wouldn't think; she said she wants to take some photos of the headstone," said April.

"That's a pity; I could have sent the ones I took, save her a journey," said Liam.

"I think she wanted to take in the atmosphere and have a look around," said April.

Then suddenly Farrah looked at April. "Lily says the Spanish man is angry."

April didn't react but looked at Farrah in an understanding way.

"Did she say why he's angry?"

"No, she doesn't know," said Farrah.

"Tell her we don't want to cause him any distress; we just want to know more about him," said April.

Jo looked at Liam.

Farrah just stood up. "Can we go Mom?"

Liam and April waited outside the pub and watched as Jo and the children headed towards the village store. The cloud cover had increased and there was a threat of rain. There were very few people about.

Liam turned to April. "Why would Far say that?"

"I really don't know; I've not come across it before, but it does seem she has contact with a spirit," replied April.

"But what does it mean, the Spanish man is angry? It seems like a warning, bearing in mind what Far has said before," replied Liam.

"Yes, you're right, but I don't know what we can do about it."

Just then Liam spotted a blue Fiat Punto turning into the promenade from the steep hill and heading towards them.

"This must be her," said April and waved at the on-coming vehicle.

It slowed and pulled up outside the pub. The driver lowered the window and April approached the car.

"Hello, I'm April. Are you Yolanda?"

"Si, yes, Yolanda Calviño." She spoke with a strong Spanish accent.

"Do you want to park in the pub car park and I'll take you up to the graveyard?" April pointed to the entrance. The car moved forward and turned right; Liam and April followed on foot.

Yolanda parked next to Liam's Volvo and got out just as Liam and April arrived alongside. She was strikingly good-looking, the Mediterranean heritage reflected in her skin tone. She was slim with shoulder-length dark hair, and was wearing a fashionable pair of sunglasses, a black tee shirt, and white shorts and trainers. There was a bag on the back seat which she extracted, locked up, and joined Liam and April.

"This is Liam; he has an interest in your sailor. I hope you don't mind him joining us."

"No, no, *por supuesto,* sure." Liam offered a handshake.

They were still in the shade of the pub and she pushed her sunglasses up to her forehead. They talked as they walked.

"Nice to meet you, Liam. What interest is it you have?"

"We've rented a cottage, my family, that is, next to the graveyard and I found his grave. I'm fascinated to find out more about him."

This was not the time to mention restless spirits, Liam

decided.

"How was your journey?" asked April.

"Si, it was ok, nearly er, two hours. The road to here, it was not so easy to see. The er, navigation, it does not work."

"Yes, I know what you mean. I had the same problem when I arrived," said Liam.

"You're studying at Exeter University, you said?" asked April.

"Si, yes, er, a Masters in Spanish Studies. Professor Oscar Sanchez, he is my tutor; he was the person who translated the papers."

"What part of Spain are you from?" asked Liam.

"Madrid, it is my home, but I have been in the UK for five years."

They walked up the nip and reached April's car. Liam opened the back door for the student to get in. Liam got in the passenger seat, and buckled up.

"It's not far, five minutes," said April.

April drove down the nip and turned right, past the store, and turned right as if heading towards Pendle Cottage. Instead of turning left in the direction of the church, she kept straight on up another hill. There were more cottages left and right; the dark forest loomed ahead of them.

At the end of the cottages, there was a dry-stone boundary wall on the left-hand side, which encased the graveyard. It was surrounded by trees. April pulled up outside the stone archway which marked the entrance.

The three exited the car. Liam could see the roof of Pendle Cottage; the garden was just over the left hand wall, as they walked into the cemetery.

"It's just along here," said Liam, They were approaching the canopy of the sycamore tree.

They stopped and Liam pointed. "That's it."

Yolanda approached with almost reverence and put her hand on the headstone, taking in the rough contours of the stone, rolling her hand around the skull carvings. She scraped off a patch of lichen, the small yellow algae dropped onto the grass.

"Do you know what all the markings mean?" asked Liam. "I guessed the sextant was about the sea?"

"Si, si, the others are to warn, er, the, how you say? Er, evil spirits, to keep them away."

She took out an expensive pocket-sized camera and took several photographs of the headstone from different angles, with close ups of the inscriptions.

"This is very exciting," she said, with increasing enthusiasm. "Actually, we know quite a lot about this sailor; he wrote many accounts of his life which have survived and are in a museum in Bilbao. I've been doing some research, but there's nothing after 1588. The records say he was, er, drowned when his ship sank trying to return to Spain. When we got the papers you sent, it caused much, er, excitement, not just at the University here but in Español. The University of Castile has been sent copies of them."

She stood back for a moment and bowed her head to the grave before continuing her dialogue, reciting from memory.

"The sailor's name is Francisco Cortes. He was born in 1552 in the Castilian region, we don't know where exactly. He was raised as a devout Catholic."

Liam and April were listening intently.

"He actually joined the Spanish army in 1568 and, er, served in Portugal before moving to the navy. We don't know why he changed careers; it's not documented." She smiled. "He served under Diego Flores Valdés. Have you heard of him?" she asked.

There were blank looks from Liam and April.

"He was a famous naval commander and explorer at the time. Actually, he was the, er, how you say? Squadron Commander of Castile, in the Armada. Cortes sailed with him to South America and we know from records that he reached the Straits of, er, Magellan. Then he spent some time in Brazil before serving under the Marquis de Santa Cruz in the Azores. After that he was given his own ship, the *Tobago Valencera*. We know that this ship, er, like many others, sank in a storm on the way back from the Armada. The wreck is close to here. You will know that, I think. We had no idea he had survived."

April put her head in her hands and Liam placed an arm around her shoulders. Yolanda looked at April with concern. "Are you alright, April?"

"April's husband was killed, diving on that wreck," said Liam.

"Oh, I am so sorry," said Yolanda.

"It's ok," said April. "For a moment it brought it all back."

Liam noticed a drop in temperature. "Is it me, or has it gone cold?"

April having composed herself, started rubbing her bare arms. "Yes, you're right."

"Oh, no," said Liam.

"What is it?" said April.

"Look, through the trees, in the distance."

"Fog," said April. She turned and looked at Yolanda. "Have you got everything you need?"

"Si, si, I will take your pictures too. Stand together please."

"We should really get going," said Liam, anxiously.

"One moment." There was a flash as Yolanda took the picture. The fog seemed to retreat.

"I'm going this way and climb over into the garden," said

Liam, pointing to the step in the wall. "Do you want to call round later?"

"Yes, I'll let you know how we get on," replied April.

Yolanda took one last look at the headstone and bowed her head again, before turning and heading back to the cemetery entrance with April.

Liam walked in the opposite direction and made short work of climbing over the wall. He jumped down into the garden, turned and looked back at the graveyard; the fog appeared to have gone. He walked past the old privy and looked at the door. The latch seemed to be moving; the cold air returned. He hurried on past the sycamore tree and along the path to the kitchen door.

He could see Jo at the sink. He pushed open the door sharply making her jump.

"Oh, Liam you scared the shit out of me!"

Liam checked he wasn't being followed and closed the door, forcing it shut firmly with his shoulder.

"Sorry, I've been in the graveyard. I came back over the wall."

Liam took a deep breath and related the conversation with the student and the background of their sailor.

"It was weird; he was the captain of the ship that went down in the bay. The one where April's husband was killed, the *Tobago Valencera*."

Jo looked at Liam. "Really? What a coincidence."

April returned to the pub car park and they both got out.

Yolanda walked up to April.

"Thank you, April, very much for everything. Er, I want to ask you a question. Have you decided what you want to do with the papers?"

"Hmm, I hadn't thought really."

"As I said, they are very important documents, but more so I think to, er, Spain. I know the Museum in Bilbao would be very happy to receive them."

"Yes, I'll give it some thought," said April. They shared phone numbers and shook hands. "Good luck with your studies," said April.

April watched as Yolanda put the bag on the back seat and got into the Punto. She waved as Yolanda backed out.

April got into the Kia and headed back to the parking space at the top of the nip. As she was locking up, something distracted her. She looked across at the cliff and the cottages above them; there was a blanket of fog stretching from the forest to the end cottage which belonged to the late Mrs Wilkins.

She couldn't believe her eyes. From nowhere, a blue car suddenly shot out from the fog and over the cliff. It was like something out of a movie; the kind of shot that film producers love. The car appeared to be flying until gravity took over and it plummeted to the ground. There was no huge explosion or fireball, just an awful crunch as it hit the ground below the cliff face a hundred feet below.

April put her hand over her mouth. "Oh, my God."

Chapter Eleven

April was momentarily stunned and just watched the scene play out. She could see the shattered vehicle below the cliff; it seemed to be embedded into the ground on its bonnet. There was no sign of movement.

Getting to the wreckage would not be straightforward. There was no route across the ground between the top of the nip and the cliff. It would mean going along to the end of the promenade and, before the hill, cutting through a gap between the cottages.

She ran/walked down the nip and turned left, then had an idea. She came to the pub and went inside. There was no-one about and the bar was unoccupied.

"Clem! Clem! Are you there?" she shouted.

The landlord came out of the back room.

"Wasson, April m'dear, whatever's the matter?"

"Quick, Clem, there's a car gone over the cliff, call an ambulance. Tell them to get here as soon as they can."

The landlord looked at April. "Gone over the cliff! 'ow on earth did that 'appen?"

"I've no idea; I just saw it from the nip."

"I don't knows 'ow they'll get an ambulance up there; there's not much of a track."

"No, they'll have to walk from the road. Please hurry."

"Aye, I'll get on to it right away."

"Oh, and do you think you could drive up to Pendle Cottage and tell Liam? He'll know what to do."

"Aye right you are, m'dear." He went to the door to the backroom and shouted. "Aswen! Can you look after the bar?"

April left the pub and hurried along the line of seafront

cottages until she reached the gap where there was access to the waste ground below the cliff. She turned and ran up the narrow, weed-ridden footpath.

The area at the bottom of the cliff face was a mix of scrub and boulders, the result of previous cliff falls. Covered with groundsel, goosegrass, milk thistle, and several clumps of Himalayan Balsam, the floor was a wasteland and rarely frequented, even by dog owners. It was considered too dangerous.

April picked her way carefully across the rocks and thistles; it was at least two hundred yards to the stricken car. As she got closer, her worst fears were realised; it was a blue Fiat Punto, but unrecognisable as a motor vehicle.

It had landed on its bonnet which had crumpled to an arm's length; it had come to rest against a large boulder which was keeping the car upright. The front wheels were lay on the ground. The driver's door had been forced open by the impact and was hanging by its hinges. There was glass and bits of metal and plastic everywhere, and a distinct smell of petrol. The windscreen had been smashed and was hanging out of its frame. April could see the deflated airbag and the young student, her seatbelt holding her; she was suspended in mid-air, parallel to the ground. Then movement.

April rushed to the driver's side. "Yolanda, don't move; it's April. Let me try and get you out."

Yolanda groaned as April tried to work out a way of extracting her from the car without causing more injury. She did a quick assessment. There were bruises on Yolanda's face but luckily the front of the car had collapsed and absorbed a great deal of the impact. The airbag had done the rest. She checked her arms and legs; her right ankle was pointing in a strange direction, so that was an obvious issue, but otherwise, there seemed no other visible injury.

April could see the seatbelt fully extended and held in its clasp. She thought for a moment. As soon as the connector was released, Yolanda would fall forward. April made a decision.

"Yolanda, it's April, can you hear me?"

There was a groan and a feeble. "Si."

"Help is on the way; try to keep still. I'm going to try to get you out of the car."

April slowly crawled underneath the student. "Ok, can you still hear me?"

"Si."

"I'm going to release the seat belt; hold onto my back. You will fall forward but I will catch you."

Yolanda placed her arms around April's neck and shoulders while April found the seatbelt clasp. She pressed the red release button and Yolanda immediately fell on top of April. The student screamed in pain. "I'm going to rest you on the dashboard; you'll be more comfortable," said April.

Slowly, April eased Yolanda onto the dashboard. She was still groaning, the words, in Spanish. April completed the manoeuvre and the student was now lay on the deflated airbag. She did another check.

"I think you've broken your ankle. Does it hurt anywhere else?"

"Si, my neck... and, er... chest," she managed to wheeze.

"That's probably the whiplash. Try to stay still, the ambulance will be here soon."

April left the car for the moment and looked towards the cottages and the access footpath. Then, she spotted a figure. He was running towards her. "Liam," she shouted and waved. Liam waved back.

He was out of breath when he reached the car.

"Sweet Jeezus. What happened?"

"I don't know. I'd just parked my car and was about to walk back to the cottage, when I saw it come over the cliff."

"Yolanda's I take it. How is she?"

"Well, from what I can see, she's been very lucky. The car's landed on its front and the bonnet's taken the impact. She's got a broken ankle and whiplash, maybe some broken ribs."

Liam walked to the driver's side and looked at Yolanda lay across the dashboard. It was covered with glass from the windscreen.

"I think we should get her out of the car; I don't like the petrol smell."

"Yes, I agree; what's the best way?"

Liam looked at the wreck. "We could try moving her through the windscreen; let me shift it out of the way."

Liam pulled the broken windshield off and dropped it onto the ground, leaving the front of the car open with Yolanda lying on the airbag.

"Ok, I'll take the weight, try pushing," said Liam.

Liam gently eased Yolanda through the windscreen space while April held her steady.

They managed to slowly lower her to the ground.

Yolanda opened her eyes.

"It's Liam, you're going to be ok. What happened?"

She turned her head slowly and winced at the effort; she looked at Liam. "I do not know. It was the er... *las niebla*. I could not see, then the wheel; I could not hold it. I could not stop."

"Las niebla?" asked April.

"Fog?" suggested Liam.

"Si, si... yes, fog," said Yolanda.

April looked at Liam. He scanned the cliff top, towering above them, and the forest to the left. The fog had gone.

Liam looked around at the barren wasteland. There was evidence of previous encounters with the cliff, a broken windscreen wiper, an old tyre.

"How long before the ambulance gets here?" asked Liam.

"I don't know. Clem from the pub said he'd call it in. I'm concerned about Yolanda's ankle? We need to straighten it or she could lose her foot."

"Do you know what to do?" asked Liam with concern.

She looked at him. "Yes, I spent two years at medical school after college. We'll need something to bind it." April thought for a moment; then reached under her tee shirt behind her back and undid her bra.

"We can use this."

April carefully held Yolanda's right foot, the white trainer still in place. It was almost at right angles to her leg. She manipulated it into the correct position with a sudden twist. Yolanda screamed.

"Sorry about that; I'll just bind it." April wrapped her bra around the swollen ankle and pulled it tight. "There, that should hold it."

Liam turned to April. "Will you be ok with Yolanda? I think I'll head back to the promenade and wait for the ambulance; they'll never find us here."

"Yes, good idea."

It was another forty minutes before the ambulance arrived. Liam waved with both hands as it turned the sharp corner from the hill towards him. The driver slowed and parked the vehicle on the pavement next to the Volvo.

The medics got out. "Ok, what have we got?" asked the first medic.

"There's a car gone over the cliff. The driver's alive and conscious and we've managed to get her out of the car. You won't be able to get the ambulance down there."

"Right, you better show us the way," said the medic.

His assistant went into the back of the ambulance and returned with a collapsible stretcher and their equipment.

Liam and the two paramedics picked their way over the scrub to the wreck. April was talking to Yolanda.

The medics did a quick assessment, then lifted the student onto the stretcher and started administering oxygen. They were about to carry her away.

"My bag," Yolanda rasped and waved her arm. Liam went into the wreckage and found it. He handed it to one of the paramedics.

"Is there anyone you need us to call?" asked April.

"It is ok; I can call the University, thank you. I have my phone," she managed to say.

"We'll try and get over to see you tomorrow and see how you are," said April.

Liam and April followed the stretcher-bearers back to the ambulance. They watched Yolanda being driven away with the blue lights flashing.

"Come on, I'll give you a lift," said Liam.

As they drove the short distance back to April's cottage, Liam turned to April. "So what's going on?"

"I don't know, Liam, and that's the truth, but there does seem to be some significant activity."

"Activity?"

"Yes, para-normal activity."

"Really?" said Liam sarcastically. He glanced at April; his expression indicated scepticism.

"It feels like a vengeful spirt."

"You're kidding, right, a vengeful spirit? Come on, that's nonsense."

"Hmm, let me explain something." She looked at Liam.

"Some people believe that a vengeful spirit is that of a dead person that returns from the afterlife, seeking revenge for a cruel, or unjust death."

Liam screwed his nose in an expression of cynicism.

"Yes, I know it sounds ridiculous, but there's so much about the spirit world and afterlife we still don't know, despite all our wonderful science."

"And you think there's some vengeful ghost here creating mayhem to get his own back?"

April looked at him and smiled. "Let's just say, I'm keeping an open mind. Would you like to come in for a drink? I don't know about you, but I could do with one."

"Yes, ok, I can't stay long, mind; Jo's been complaining I'm neglecting the family."

Liam parked next to April's Kia and looked across to the cliff. The Fiat was still in the same position. "I don't know how she survived that; she's been extremely lucky. Just had a thought; the insurance company's going to have a job on their hands."

They walked back to the cottage and April led Liam inside. "What would you like? I've got a beer or a gin and tonic."

"Just a beer please," replied Liam.

He sat down on the settee as April went into the kitchen. She returned with a bottle of beer and glass.

"I just can't get my head around all this," said Liam, as April poured her drink. "There must be some logical answer."

"There probably is, but not within our present understanding."

"But Lily's message, the angry sea captain, another warning."

"Yes, but there was little we could do."

"So you believe that some angry spirit dressed up as fog is causing havoc here?"

"It's not quite that simple. Certainly, spirits have long been associated with fog."

"But surely this would entail logical thought. If it *is* Cortes, he's been dead for almost five hundred years. I mean why would they target Yolanda?"

"I don't know, they clearly sense something. whoever 'they' are."

"So, you're saying spirits have sensory perception?"

"No-one knows for sure but it's an interesting hypothesis."

Liam was trying to work this through. "So, you're suggesting that certain events are stimulating para-normal activity?"

"Or people. I've not come across this level of activity before."

"You mean before we came?"

"Frankly, yes. All the incidents appear to have involved you or your family, even that breakdown truck driver."

"Hmm, and Mrs Wilkins. But if that's the case, why?" said Liam, who was struggling with this inference.

"I don't know, not yet anyway. It just seems as though your family has become some sort of catalyst."

"What if we were to leave? Would it go away?"

"It's difficult to say. It depends what their goal is."

"So, you're attributing rational thought again; that there's some reasoning behind all this."

"I'm just speculating, Liam. As I said, I've not come across this before."

Liam finished his beer and was deep in thought.

April got up and put a caring arm around him. "I might be completely wrong, Liam."

"But if that's true, then that puts you in danger."

"Possibly, but I do feel connections with the spirit world. Maybe they don't see me as a threat."

"But we're not a threat... to anyone. We just came on holiday, a bit of rest and recouperation. That's why we chose the cottage, somewhere peaceful." His voice was raised.

Liam calmed down and looked at April. "Look, I'm used to being in charge; I don't do ambiguity. I'm finding this difficult to get my head 'round."

"Yes I understand. Anyway, you better get back to the cottage before you get into real trouble."

Liam looked at his watch.

"Hmm, yes you're right."

Liam returned to the cottage.

"Hi, I'm in the kitchen," shouted Jo, as he walked in.

Liam walked through the lounge. Jo was at the sink doing some washing.

"How did you get on? The landlord was very animated when he called.

"Yes, it was that student that came to take pictures of the gravestone of the Spanish sailor. She drove over the cliff. You know, the one by Mrs Wilkins' cottage."

"What? How is she?" replied Jo, scrubbing away at a couple of tee shirts.

"She was extremely lucky, a broken ankle and some internal injuries but the paramedics seem to think she'll be ok."

"Oh, that's a relief. But what was she doing driving off the cliff?"

"It was the fog, she said. Got disorientated, I guess."

"Well, thank goodness she's ok."

"What have you been doing?" asked Liam.

"Cursing the fact we don't have a washing machine,

mostly," she replied and laughed.

"I'm sure April will let you borrow hers."

Jo looked at Liam. "Yes, but I don't like to ask. It's a bit cheeky."

"I'm sure she wouldn't mind in the slightest."

She sniffed the air. "Have you been drinking?"

"April invited me for a beer. After the afternoon we'd had, I couldn't really refuse."

Jo threw a pair of pants into the sink causing water to splash everywhere. "Well, it seems you've got your feet under the table there."

"What do you mean by that?"

"Oh, nothing..."

"Maybe we should just leave and go back home," said Liam, his voice raised.

Just then, Farrah came into the kitchen having heard the arguing.

"I don't want to go home, Mom. Lily says we mustn't go home."

Jo got up and wiped her hands on a towel, then put her arm around Farrah.

"It's alright Poppet; your Dad didn't mean it."

Liam stooped to Farrah's eye level. "Why does Lily say we shouldn't go home, Far?"

"She says we haven't finished."

"No, that's true, we're not halfway through," said Liam.

Jo rinsed out the tee shirts and squeezed them dry. She turned to Liam. "If you're not doing anything, do you think you can rig up a clothes line? I did bring some pegs, just in case; they're in the bag in the pantry."

"Yes, ok, if I can get this blessed door open." He tugged again and managed to gain access to the back garden, then scanned for a suitable spot to extend a washing line.

By eight o'clock, the evening meal had been consumed and Jo and Liam were finishing the dishes; the children were in their rooms. The earlier washing had been completed and Liam's make-shift clothesline put to good used. Most of the clothes were now in the airing cupboard ready for wearing again. Just a couple of tee shirts remained outside to dry overnight.

The atmosphere was better; stress levels much lower.

Jo collected the bottle of tomato ketchup from the table in the lounge and took it to the pantry. As she walked inside, she stopped in her tracks. She dropped the plastic bottle of ketchup, which bounced on the stone floor, and put her hands to her face. She was paralysed momentarily, unable to take in what she was seeing.

The top shelf containing jars of jam and tins of beans and soup suddenly started to move. Jo's eyes were wide with fright. It was like something from a disaster movie when an earthquake had hit town. The vibration was causing the jars and tins to move in time with the shaking. Up and down, up and down, rattle, rattle; rattle, rattle.

First one jar of jam fell to the floor smashing in pieces, its sticky contents spreading across the stone tiles in a gooey mess. Then another, then the cans of beans, dropping like stones, making a dull clomping noise.

The shelf was fixed to the wall by brackets. The screws, loosened by the vibration, popped out, falling to the floor. "Liam!!!" she screamed. The single lightbulb flickered, went off, then back on.

Liam walked into the pantry. "Whatever's the..." He couldn't complete the sentence.

The whole of the back wall seemed to be in motion. A low roaring sound echoed around the small pantry. The light was still flickering.

Suddenly, the top shelf seemed to jump from its bracket. The remaining tins of beans and jars of jam crashed to the ground. The stone floor was covered with sticky jam. Then it stopped.

"What the fuck was that?" said Jo, holding her hands to her face. She was shaking like a leaf.

Liam tentatively approached the shelf bracket. The bottom two shelves were untouched but the top shelf was lying on the ground among the broken jam jars.

"Wait, what's this?"

There was a white mark where the shelf had been, where daylight had not been able to penetrate the emulsion paint. The top screw holding the bracket to the wall had dropped out, but just above the screw hole, Liam could see a rusting screw-head embedded in the wall.

"Mind the mess," shouted Jo.

Liam shuffled his feet and walked nearer to avoid the sticky goo on the floor, and started examining the wall more closely. His fingers traced around the rusty screw.

Liam gave it a sharp tug and a small piece of wood, about two inches in height and an inch wide came away in his fingers. It had been blended in the wall and totally obscured by the shelf. Liam peered closer; there was a small recess with something inside. He was able to get two fingers into the small hole and could feel the item. He slowly teased it out, then replaced the piece of wood.

"What is it?" asked Jo.

Liam had it in the palm of his hand and was examining it. "It's a memory stick."

"What's it doing there?"

"I have no idea. I'll get my laptop and see if we can open it."

"Can you give me a hand with this shelf first?"

The shelf was just a piece of painted plywood. Liam went to the drawer in the kitchen, took out one of the knives and put the bracket back in position using the knife as a screwdriver. Jo started handing Liam the cans of beans. The hidden recess was not visible unless you were looking for it.

Jo left the pantry still shaking from what she had witnessed.

"Tell me I dreamt that, Liam. I need a drink."

She grabbed a bottle from the kitchen worktop and poured a large glass of red wine. Her hands were shaking so much she was hardly able to lift the glass.

"No, you didn't dream it. Let's go into the other room and I'll tell you what I know." He was fingering the memory stick.

He related the discussion with April and the angry spirit theory.

"So, you're saying this house *is* haunted?"

"Let's just say there are things which can't be explained."

"You mean like fucking shelves falling off the wall."

Jo rarely swore but it was an indication of the shock she felt. Liam knew.

"Among other things." He explained about the fog.

"Well, the sooner we get out of here the better. How are we going to be able to sleep knowing we could get murdered in our beds? Look what happened to the Waltons. I don't want to stay here tonight. I know, we could drive over to St Austell and grab a B & B; I'm sure there'll be a vacancy somewhere."

Suddenly, the pit-pat sound of feet descending the stairs. Jo looked at Liam. Then Farrah came into the lounge rubbing her eyes. She spoke in a trance-like state as if she was sleep-walking.

"Lily says we can't leave. We have to stay."

Liam went up to her. "Why does she say that, Far?"

"She says they will stop you. It's not finished."

"What's not finished? Who are they?"

She opened her eyes. "Can I have a drink of water?"

"Yes, Poppet." Jo went into the kitchen. She ran some water into a glass and looked around. Everything seemed normal.

She returned to the lounge and gave Farrah the water. She took a large gulp.

"I don't want to go home. I like it here. Lily's my friend," said Farrah.

"Yes, but we can't stay here forever; we're only here for three weeks," said Jo.

"Yes, I know, but we can't go home yet."

Jo looked at Liam. "I'll take Far to bed. We need to talk about this."

Jo tucked Farrah in; her bedside light was on; her soft toy, Jumbo, the elephant, beside her. The collection of shells was in a jar next to the light.

"Do you want the light off, Poppet."

"Yes please, I don't think Lily will be back tonight."

Jo returned to the lounge where Liam was opening his laptop on the table.

"What are we going to do, Liam? I'm worried about the children."

Liam looked up. "Yes, I know, me too, but I think we should take notice of what Far's saying. April thinks she's able to communicate with sprits, a connector."

"And you believe all this nonsense."

"Well, it's not all nonsense. You saw what happened in the pantry."

"Yes, and that bothers me. What's next?"

Liam looked at her. "I don't know, I really don't."

"Hmm, I better clear up in the pantry. I think all the jam jars have broken."

"Do you want me to help?"

"No, I'll manage."

Liam opened up his laptop. Although there was no internet, he hoped he would be able to read what was on the memory stick.

Jo felt anxious as she went back into the pantry wearing her yellow rubber gloves. She had a bowl of soapy water, the wastebin, and a roll of kitchen tissue.

Liam, meanwhile, inserted the memory stick into one of the USB ports of his laptop and accessed the data.

There were several files and he opened each one. They had all been encrypted and were unreadable.

But then on the last file, there was a logo which headed the encrypted narrative that he recognised. – a dragonfish with a portcullis and crown above, surrounded by cinquefoil plants... MI5.

Straightaway, Liam's mind was racing. Someone had obviously secreted the memory stick in the recess in the wall. Until the information had been decrypted, he had no way of knowing what it contained or why it had been put there. He thought it through. The device was of recent design and a high capacity, two terabytes. There could only be one person to have put it there, George Walton.

Liam was thinking; he did know a man who might be able to help.

He cursed at the lack of internet. He could ping off a text message in a nano second, but it would have to wait until tomorrow; he had an idea.

The pair were in bed by ten-thirty, both reading for a few minutes before turning out the bedside lamp.

It had been a restless night. Jo found it hard to settle and tossed and turned, which kept Liam awake. The illuminous dial said quarter to midnight.

Liam turned over to Jo. "Do you want a cup of tea?"

"Well, I'm not sleeping; that's for sure. When I close my eyes, I keep seeing that shelf," she replied wearily.

Liam rolled over and kissed Jo on the cheek. "Won't be a moment."

It was a warm night; Liam turned on the bedside light and checked the time. He left the bedroom dressed in just his boxer shorts and went downstairs. He hadn't put the light on in case he disturbed the children. He could see moonbeams streaming through the lounge window.

He went over to the window and looked outside; it was like daylight. At about forty degrees in the sky there was the biggest, brightest moon he had ever seen. He walked into the kitchen and turned on the light, then filled the kettle and prepared the mugs with tea bags and milk from the fridge. He had a quick glance in the pantry; there were no signs of any further disturbance.

Suddenly a noise, a rustling, scratching noise at the kitchen door; he was on high alert. There it was again.

He turned the key in the lock and yanked on the door. It wouldn't move. He tried again, giving it a sharp tug and nearly fell backwards as it finally opened. He went to the doorway and poked his head around the frame looking left and right. He could make out dark shapes, scurrying away up the garden towards the graveyard. Curiosity got the better of him. He tentatively put one foot on the paving outside the kitchen door. His heart rate increased.

His bare feet made a crunching sound in the gravel as he

slowly inched up the path. He winced as the sharp stones cut into the soles of his feet.

Suddenly, he felt something wrap itself around his head and face.

"Jeezus," he exclaimed; it made him jump. Adrenaline coursed through his veins.

Instinctively, he made a grab at it. It felt cold and clammy as he pulled it from his face. Then realised he had walked into the remaining tee shirts that were still hanging on the clothes line. He saw the funny side of it.

Out of the lee of the cottage, he looked up; the moon had risen higher. A host of stars, like diamond fragments, twinkled in its shadow. He could make out the swallow's nest in the eaves. It was deathly silent. Not a sound, not the trees whispering, nor the roosting birds; the moon lit up the garden like the beams of a search light. He edged forward, carefully ensuring he didn't stub his toe on a protruding piece of stone. Common sense said he should go back and put on some shoes, but the momentum was with him. Common sense said he should not be there at all.

He reached the canopy of the sycamore tree. A tawny owl gave a warning hoot, and flew from its resting place. The flapping wings seemed to echo around the graveyard. Something was telling him he should head back.

Then the noise. It started as a low rumble as if a large piece of stone was being moved against another, and then, the sound of a ship's bell... ting, ting; ting, ting; ting, ting; ting, ting. Then silence. Four bells.

Liam was frozen to the spot. Suddenly a cold chill made him shiver. He remembered April's story of the old seadog Captain Dewar.

"Liam, are you there?"

Jo was stood at the doorway. The chill had gone; Liam

was sweating.

He turned and slowly walked back to the kitchen, remembering to duck under the washing.

"What on earth were you doing outside?" asked Jo. "You've got nothing on."

Liam closed the door and brushed the grit from the soles of his feet onto the floor. He was trying not to show the anxiety he was feeling; he didn't want to worry Jo any more.

"There was a rustling noise outside and I went to see what it was. I thought it might be badgers."

"Badgers?"

"Well, they do come up to houses, looking for food. Some people actually feed them."

"Hmm, I think we have enough problems without worrying about badgers. Did you see them?"

"No, whatever it was had gone. Have you seen the moon? It's amazing."

"Yes, I had a look through the window. Are we having this cup of tea or not?"

The next cup of tea was delivered at seven-thirty. Jo was sound asleep as Liam brought in the two mugs. He put hers down on the bedside table without waking her. Liam sat up in bed sipping his tea. Unsurprisingly, he had not slept well following the late night experience. He needed to speak to April.

He had the folder of newspaper cuttings in front of him and was reading them again in case he had missed anything. The memory stick was on the bedside table; he was dying to know what was on it. He would be going out after breakfast.

Jo stirred. "Good morning, there's a cup of tea; I didn't want to wake you."

"What time is it? I don't think I slept a wink."

"You were dead to the world when I got up to make the tea."

Jo gradually raised herself and took a sip of tea. "Urgh, it's cold."

"I'll go and make you a fresh one."

"You're not still messing around with those cuttings are you?"

"Just going through them again."

"Well after last night, I think we should get back to London. Leave that to the police." She nodded at the folder.

"I'm not convinced they've been particularly thorough," said Liam as he got out of bed.

"Well, it's not your problem, Liam, is it?" continued Jo.

An hour later, the family were at the table eating breakfast.

"What are we doing today?" asked Zack.

"Well, I've got some things to do this morning," said Liam. He looked at Jo. "Why don't you take the kids to St Austell, get them a Big Mac."

"Oh, yeah, can we?" asked Zack.

"What about you Poppet?" asked Jo.

"Sure, Lily says it's ok." Jo looked at Liam.

"Right, you guys go and tidy your rooms; I want a word with your Dad."

Zack and Farrah, left the lounge and went upstairs.

"I can't take this anymore, Liam. I'm worried about Far; she seems fixated by this Lily. It can't be good for her and what about last night? We need to go home."

"Not just yet, let's give it till the weekend and see how things go."

"Hmm, we might be dead by then."

"No, no, I really don't think we're in any danger, but I do need to speak to April."

"So, you'll be spending the morning with her, not going out with your family. Is that it? Fuck! A fine holiday this is turning out to be."

"No, I won't be spending all morning with her. I need to make some phone calls first, and I think I know a way of doing it."

"What do you mean?"

"I think the memory stick is the key. We were meant to find it."

"Oh, I see and some venging poltergeist rattles around in the pantry, is that it?"

"You saw the same as me. But I do know someone who might be able to help access the data."

"Who?"

"Do you remember Frank Hamilton?"

"The barrister?"

"Yes, he does all the Secret Service cases. If he doesn't know; he'll know someone who does. I want to contact him this morning."

"So, why don't you come to St Austell? There's a good signal there, 5G, I think you said."

"I want to speak to April to let her know about last night. I think if I can get close enough to the Deakin place I should be able to log into his Wi-Fi; I have his password."

"Is that legal?" asked Jo with a frown.

"He won't know," said Liam.

"Ok, till lunchtime, then we go out as a family, but if things don't improve, I'm taking the kids back. I'll take the train if need be."

"Yes, ok, you're right, it's a deal," said Liam. "Don't say anything to anyone about the memory stick for the moment; it's possible someone was murdered for it."

"That's a bit dramatic."

"Yes, I know, but to be on the safe side, eh?"

"Sure, ok."

"And can you bring me back a burger?"

"It won't be fit to eat."

"I'll pop it in the oven, it'll be fine."

"Rather you than me."

Chapter Twelve

By nine-thirty, Liam was walking along the cinder path past the church and the rectory. Jo had taken the children off to St Austell. It was another warm summer's day and he was dressed accordingly in a pair of jeans, a tee shirt, and a pair of trainers. Seagulls were out in force; their urgent calls providing the soundtrack to the day.

He felt nervous for some reason. He could see the boundary wall of the Squire's 'Palace' and, keeping close to the hedge that bordered the rectory to avoid the CCTV cameras, approached it. He soon realised that it was not going to be as straightforward as he'd hoped.

He would need to get closer to the house to get any sort of signal; the front entrance would be too far away. The area between the rectory's boundary hedge and the wall was scrub, mostly blackberry bushes, ferns, grasses of various kinds, and small trees, forming an impenetrable barrier; there was no defined footpath.

He reached the wall and leant against it. He looked left towards the scrub. On closer inspection, there was a gap between the wall and the brambles which, with careful manoeuvring, he thought he could squeeze through.

Keeping his back to the wall he slowly edged his way along. Brambles picked at his jeans, but after a few minutes, he'd made progress. He couldn't see the house itself, but given the distance from the cinder path, estimated he was close enough for his requirements. He took his phone from his pocket and opened it. He checked the Wi-Fi connection. Liam had the latest smart-phone and it automatically picked up the connection from his recent visit. Sure enough there was a signal.

He checked that the 'Wi-Fi call' option was enabled, then accessed his contacts, found the one he wanted and pressed 'call'.

It rang out. It hadn't occurred to him that his contact might not be available, then, the pickup.

"Liam? Is that you? I thought you were on holiday."

"Hi Frank, I am." He spoke in a shout/whisper, not knowing if anyone was on the other side of the wall. "Look, I hope I'm not interrupting anything, but I need your help."

"No, it's fine, I was just going through some pre-trial notes; fire away, what's the problem?"

"To be honest, I don't know where to start. But have you come across the name George Walton and his family?"

There was a pause. "The name rings a bell."

"Right, well, we're staying in a village in Cornwall called Polgissy and the Walton family were murdered here in January... actually, in the cottage where we're staying."

"Polgissy, ah, yes, I remember it now. That's a bit weird. What on earth are you doing staying in a crime scene?"

"Ha, good question, we didn't know about the murder before we got here. We might have made a different choice had we had known the circumstances. The point is, the police have not found the perpetrator and, according to one or two people I've talked to, they've pretty much closed the file."

"I see."

"Well, the reason I've phoned is, I've found a memory stick hidden in a secret panel in the pantry, and I'm pretty sure it belongs to George Walton, the man who was murdered. It's encrypted and I can't read it."

"Ok, so why not hand it in to the police?"

"Yes, I considered that, but, the thing is, there's a logo on one of the files... It's MI5."

"Hmm, I see."

"Now, I could be completely wrong, but it's possible that George Walton was working under cover. He was an illustrator, moved over to the village from Plymouth, that's what I was told."

"What do you want me to do?"

"Well, you have contacts at MI5; I wondered if you could make some enquiries."

"Yes, ok, so how do you want to do this?"

"Hmm, well, I do have a problem; there's no internet or phone signal here. Would you believe. I'm actually standing outside someone's house, using their Wi-Fi to call you?"

"So, how can I contact you?"

"There's someone in the village who's been helping me. I can give you her phone number. She'll contact me and I can call you or whoever. Her name's April."

"Sure, ok. What's her number?"

Liam provided the information. "Oh, while I'm on, can you also mention the name Christopher Deakin. He's like the boss around here and I'm not certain that he's completely legit. It's possible that the two are connected, but it's only a theory."

"Right, I've written that down. I'll be in touch."

"Thanks Frank. How're Susan and the kids?"

"They're fine, thanks, and Jo?"

"Yes, thanks, she's taken the kids into St Austell to do some shopping."

"Well, enjoy your holiday."

"Cheers Frank."

Liam dropped the call and edged his way back down the wall to the cinder track. There was little more he could do for the moment. He stopped and picked broken bramble thorns from his jeans, then walked along the unmade road, past the rectory and church, to the junction. He turned right, down the hill to the village.

The cinder track to the Squire's house flanked the back gardens of the cottages of the adjacent street, appropriately named Harbour View. The last cottage overlooks the Deakin mansion and is the home of Walter Rawlinson and his wife Ethel. From the back bedroom it was possible to see into the grounds of the house.

Earlier, Ethel was in the back bedroom, opening the curtains, and spotted someone in the shrubbery leaning against the boundary wall. She called her husband.

"What's that chap doing?" she asked, as Walter joined her at the window.

"I don't know, but he looks a bit suspicious to me. I better let the Squire know."

Walter went downstairs, picked up the phone, and started dialling.

"Christopher Deakin," came the voice as the call was picked up.

"Wasson, sir. It's Walter Rawlinson from Dori Cottage... Harbour View."

"Ah, yes, hello Walter, how are you?"

"Aye, mustn't grumble, got a spot of gout which is giving me a bit of gip but otherwise alright."

"What can I do for you?"

"Well, I thought you should know that there's someone next to your wall, in the bushes; seems he's acting a bit strange if you ask me, like. Looks like he's on the phone."

"Oh, now that's very good of you to let me know; I won't forget it."

Deakin dropped the call and went into the kitchen where Nathan, the odd-job man, was clearing a blocked drain.

"Ah, there you are, Nathan, can you go outside and check the external perimeter? Walter Rawlinson ˙ from Harbour View's been on the phone, says he saw someone acting suspiciously the other side of the boundary wall."

Nathan wiped his hands on a towel. "Aye, sir, right away."

Access to the back garden from the kitchen was by way of a pair of French windows. He left the kitchen and walked around to the front of the house and down the drive.

He reached the gate, pressed the security button, and walked through the pedestrian entrance onto the cinder path. Then checked the frontage left and right, before walking towards the rectory to the end of the boundary wall. He checked left and walked into the shrubbery. Nothing; it was clear.

He could see someone in the distance close to the church walking away from him towards the junction, but it was too far away to recognise them.

Satisfied the perimeter was clear he returned to the house to report back.

Back in London, Frank Hamilton was considering Liam's call. He had just the contact. He closed the door to his Chamber's office and made the call.

"Good morning, Thames House."

"Can you put me through to Andy Tennant?"

Moments later. "Tennant."

"Andy... it's Frank Hamilton, how're things?"

"Oh, hi Frank, you know, plenty of challenges."

"Well, I'm sorry to add to them, but I've just had a call from Liam Drake."

"Liam Drake?"

"Yes, prosecuting barrister in the recent Rainsford Case... Old Bailey."

"Ah, yes, I remember... great result."

"Yes, it was."

"What can I do for Mr Drake?"

"Well, it seems he's on holiday in Cornwall," Frank consulted his notes. "Some village called Polgissy."

"Polgissy? You did say Polgissy?"

"Yes."

"Look, do you mind if I record this call?" said Tennant.

"No, that's fine."

"Ok, it's recording. Right, from the beginning."

"As I was saying, they're staying in a cottage where apparently a murder took place earlier in the year, a family called Walton."

"George Walton?"

"Yes, how did you know?"

"Let's say Five have an interest."

"Really? Well that's curious, because the reason he contacted me is he's found a memory stick hidden in the wall or somewhere. He's opened it on his laptop and it's encrypted, but on one of the files he says there's the MI5 logo. It's why he contacted me because he knows about my connection with the Secret Service."

"A memory stick?"

"Yes."

"Right, how can I get hold of him?"

"He's given me a contact number; one of the villagers, who can pass on a message."

"Can you let me have it?"

"Sure." Hamilton gave him the information.

"Ok, I'll get in touch with him. Was there anything else?

"No, I don't think so... Wait, yes, he mentioned someone called; wait a moment, I wrote it down... Yes, Christopher Deakin."

"Deakin? What about Deakin?"

"He just said to mention him. Thought there might be a connection."

"Ok, leave it with us; we'll take it from here."

They dropped the call.

Tennant got up from his desk and walked to an adjacent office.

"Barry, there's been a development, Operation Blaggard."

Assistant Director General Barry Howard-Young looked up from his desk.

"You have my attention, Andy."

Tennant outlined the conversation with the barrister.

"Hmm, we need that memory stick, Andy; it could contain vital information."

"Yes, my thoughts entirely. If I can get hold of Drake, I'll get down there today."

"What's the latest on Deakin?"

"Still very active on the trading websites, but nothing out of the ordinary."

"Hmm, I'd love to know what he's up to," said the ADG.

Back in Polgissy, Liam had reached April's cottage. He knocked on the door; there was movement from inside, then the door opened.

"Hi Liam, lovely to see you. That's good timing, I was just about to make a coffee, come in. We can go out onto the patio; it's a beautiful morning."

April led Liam though the lounge and kitchen; the back door was open. There was a small patio with a table with two chairs in the corner. Liam made himself comfortable. The whole of the back was bathed in warm sunshine, not a cloud in the sky. He looked around the neatly maintained garden, a small lawn surrounded by shrubs and plants in their full summer finery. In the near-distance, he could see the forest and the cliff; Yolanda's car was still at the bottom waiting recovery.

To the right, the sea shimmered in the sunshine. Seagulls were out in force swooping over the village. There was a line of them on the sea wall, preening themselves. The promenade was deserted.

April brought out the coffees; she was wearing a tee shirt, shorts, and flip-flops.

"Where's Jo?"

"She's gone into St Austell with the kids. I'm meeting her at lunchtime."

She handed out the coffees and a plate with four chocolate digestives. "There're a few biscuits to keep you going. I always get a bit peckish mid-morning."

"Thanks." Liam picked one up and took a bite.

"We had another visitation last night," he announced dramatically.

"Oh, what happened?"

Liam described the incident in the pantry but said nothing about the memory stick.

"Jo's talking about going home; it scared the life out of her."

"Yes, I can imagine. Did you manage to record it by any chance, the visitation?"

"Oh, shit, no, I didn't think at the time, but it was very strong. The shelves seemed to be bouncing up and down; it was just like the thing with the outside toilet."

"Yes, I have no idea why you and your family seem to have been targeted. It certainly appears to be a poltergeist."

"Should we be worried?"

"No, no, they are harmless enough, just restless spirits."

"But what about the vengeful spirits you talked about?"

"Hmm, that's different; but they tend to manipulate situations."

"You mean like Yolanda?"

"Yes, exactly, talking of which, I spoke to the hospital this morning. They said she was comfortable. She should be able to go home tomorrow. They're keeping her under observation. I'm going over to see her this afternoon. I've decided to donate the papers to the University; I want to let her know."

"Oh, I'm sure they'll be very grateful."

Just then, the telephone rang. April got up and went to answer it.

"Hello."

"Oh, hello I'm trying to contact Liam Drake. I understand you can pass on a message."

"Yes, actually, I can do better than that, he's here. Just a moment."

"Liam, it's for you." There was a hint of surprise in her voice.

Liam came in from the garden and took the receiver from April. She went back into the garden.

"Liam Drake."

"Ah, Mr Drake, it's Andy Tennant, Thames House. I've received a call from Frank Hamilton, I understand you've come into possession of a certain item which may be of interest to the department."

"Oh, hi, yes, Andy, I have. It's Liam by the way."

"Ok, Liam. Will you be available to meet me this afternoon?"

"Er, yes, what time?"

"There's a train gets into St Austell at five-ten; I can be on it."

"Yes, ok, I can do that."

"Excellent, excellent, I'll see you then."

"How will I recognise you?"

"I'll be carrying a copy of the Telegraph."

"Ha, a touch of the John Le Carré."

"Five-ten then," said the caller not rising to any attempt at humour.

Liam returned to the patio. April was lay back in her chair with her eyes closed. She opened them on his arrival.

"Oh, is everything ok?"

"Yes, fine thanks. I must apologise; I gave your number to my chambers. It was just a query."

"It's fine, no problem."

"It's such a nuisance not having a signal."

"Yes, it is. But we can always call in on Christopher if you have something urgent, or you need to email. I'm sure he won't mind, and you're welcome to use the phone here anytime."

"That's very good of you; I really appreciate it. So, how can I convince Jo that it's safe to stay?"

"Do you want me to have a word with her?"

"If you wouldn't mind. What time are you going over to the hospital?"

"Not sure, about two-ish I expect; they tend to be more relaxed on visiting these days. The hospital's easy enough to get to, about thirty/thirty-five minutes."

"Well, why not join us for lunch? Perhaps you can reassure Jo it's safe for us to stay."

Liam and April walked down to the pub around twelve-thirty to wait for Jo and the children. Liam was thinking about his liaison with the guy from MI5, and how to square his absence with Jo. There could be some resistance.

It was ten-to-one before Jo and the children appeared. As soon as she came through the door, Farrah ran up to Liam.

"Dad, Dad, look what I've got."

She was holding a small toy.

"They were giving them out in MacDonalds," said Jo.

Zach was looking less than impressed with his plastic dinosaur.

"They're for kids," he said, dismissively.

"Hello, April. How was your morning?" asked Jo.

"Hi, Jo," April replied.

"Let me get the drinks and I'll tell you all. Do you want anything to eat?" said Liam.

"No thanks, I'm stuffed; that Big Mac will keep me going for a while."

"Would you like a sandwich, April?" asked Liam.

"Yes, great, thanks; I'll have a cheese and pickle. Aswen does a mean sandwich."

"Right, I'll just go and order."

"What about your burger?" asked Jo, as she extracted a compressed Big Mac from her bag.

Liam looked at it; it didn't appear particularly appetising. "Hmm, I think the seagulls can have it."

The meals were duly ordered and Liam returned to the table with the drinks.

"So, go on then, how did it go?" asked Jo.

"It was fine thanks; but I do need to pop out later."

"Why? I thought we were going to do something this afternoon."

"Yes, of course, we will. I don't need to leave until later; I thought we could explore down by the cliffs. Check out the rock pools."

"So where do you have to be?"

"I need to pop into St Austell; I won't be long." Liam wasn't giving too much away.

Jo seemed less than happy, but with April seated just opposite her, she didn't want to create a scene.

Sensing an atmosphere, April attempted to lessen the tension.

"So, where else did you go?"

"We had a look around the shops and went to the supermarket to get a few bits," replied Jo. "Then MacDonalds."

"Was it busy?" asked April.

"It was heaving with kids," said Jo, with a disapproving expression.

Farrah was listening and from nowhere announced. "Lily says to be careful by the cliffs, it's very dangerous."

April looked at Jo and Liam. "Why does she think it's dangerous. Poppet?" asked Jo.

"She didn't say," replied Farrah. "Can we go now?"

"Soon, we're just waiting for our sandwiches," said Liam.

Half an hour later, they left the pub; Liam and the family headed to the car park.

"Do you want a lift, April?" asked Liam.

"No, it's fine, thanks. I need to go to the store and get some bits and pieces."

April continued walking along the promenade while Liam and the family headed to the cottage. There was a distinct atmosphere and the short journey made in silence. Both children were looking out of the window.

Jo collected the groceries and Liam opened up.

"There's that smell again," he said as he went into the lounge.

"I'll open some windows," said Jo. "Urgh, it's worse than

the fish."

Jo went into the kitchen with the carrier bags; Liam followed.

"Look, I didn't want to say anything in front of April, but I'm meeting someone about the memory stick. They're coming down from London."

"What, all that way? It must be important."

"Yes, I'm sure it is, given the lengths that someone's gone to in hiding it."

"And you still think it's connected with the Waltons?"

"I do. It's a fairly new memory stick, two terabytes. There's a lot of stuff on it. I can't see it being anyone else."

Twenty minutes later, the family were back in the Volvo driving down into the village. At the bottom they turned right and passed the Harbourmaster's Office, then Jack's cottage. They reached the end of the road where there was a turning circle. Judging by the weeds protruding from the broken tarmac, this was not a road widely in use.

To the left, there was no sea wall, just the weed-ridden pavement, then the beach, such as it was, a mix of stones and boulders, some over six feet tall.

They parked opposite the last cottage; the cliffs towered way above them, three hundred feet or more. Like the rest of those surrounding the village, they were predominantly granite, a shear cliff-face with grey outcrops dotted by occasional greenery. Close up they were quite foreboding.

The family exited the Volvo.

"What do you want to do?" asked Jo looking up at the imposing rock formation in front of them.

"Lily says it's dangerous here," said Farrah.

"Yes Poppet, we'll be very careful," said Jo.

"I thought we could look around the rockpools; they're

always interesting," said Liam.

"Cool," said Zack.

There was a general agreement, and the group left the road and ventured over the shingle. The tide was on the turn but was far out leaving numerous pools around the rocks and boulders that littered the foreshore.

Farrah seemed reluctant. "I want to stay in the car."

"Come on Poppet, it'll be fine; we won't go far," said Jo.

Liam took Farrah's hand. "Don't worry, let's look and see what we can find in the pools."

The cliff face seemed to shimmer with the rays of the sun creating shadows among the crevice's and outcrops. A large bird of prey was swooping and hovering among the thermals.

"Hey Dad, look at this."

Zack had wandered further out and found a rock pool teeming with life. The family joined him and watched the inhabitants of this watery community, trapped until the tide returned. Look there's a canker," shouted Zack excitedly.

"That's a word I don't think we'll ever forget," laughed Liam, as they watched a crab scurry across the bottom of the pool.

"Look, there's a fish," said Zack again.

"It's like looking into an aquarium," said Jo.

The family were enthralled at the diversity of the marine life and spent another hour exploring. It became quite competitive; who can find the most interesting rock pool.

Liam was looking at one when he noticed movement rings on the surface, As if someone had tapped the side of the pool and sent shock waves rippling across it... then another. Jo and the two children were at another pool only a few feet away.

"What's that?" called Zack, pointing at the cliff.

Liam looked up and watched in horror as a number of large boulders hurtled down the cliff top, then over the edge.

"Quick!" shouted Liam and grabbed Farrah. Jo had hold of Zack.

They hurried towards the car about two hundred yards away.

First one huge boulder, then another, followed by smaller rocks that had been dislodged. Then without warning the whole side of the cliff gave way and started to slide downwards. It seemed in slow motion as gravity sent the dislodged granite to the floor.`

"Come on we've got to get away from the cliff," shouted Liam.

It was impossible to run and the tide had started to come in. Many of the rock pools that the family had been exploring only a few minutes earlier were now underwater. Negotiating them was difficult. Their footwear was now soaked but barefoot was not an option.

The rumbling continued. Liam was concentrating on moving forward and couldn't look back. He was carrying Farrah.

"I'm scared, Dad," she cried.

Half paddling/half walking, the family made it to the shingle beach and looked back. It looked like someone had sliced a portion of the cliff-face allowing it to slide downwards to the beach. Several hundred tons of granite were now at the bottom of the cliff, covering a large area, including many of the rock pools that the family had been viewing only minutes earlier.

They looked in awe at the mighty power of nature, and at their fortunate escape.

Farrah was holding onto Liam's neck. "Lily said it was dangerous."

"Yes, she did," said Liam.

"Well, I'm not sure I want to go exploring rock pools anytime soon." said Jo. "Let's get out of here and get back."

They walked onto the road and looked back at the cliff again; it had changed shape.

There was a lamp post at the end of the road by the turning circle, the final one before the cliffs. A black crow was perched on top of it. It cawed, then flew off in the direction of the forest. Liam watched it fly away. His mind was transported back to the motorway incident.

Just then, a familiar figure was walking quickly towards them.

"Wasson, m'dear, are you alright?" he said as he got closer.

"Yes, Jack, thank you. That was quite dramatic."

"Aye, those cliffs are very unstable, though I ain't seen a slip as bad as that for a while."

"What caused it?" asked Liam as he unlocked the car. Farrah and Zack climbed into the back, Jo was standing next to Liam, keen to hear Jack's account.

"Who knows? Experts say it's summat to do with erosion and climate change or some such. But folk round here reckon it's the spirits at work trying to upset the village."

"I'm more inclined to believe the former," said Liam.

"Who knows?" said Jack. "Just wanted to make sure you was alright; I saw you was on the beach."

"That's kind of you, Jack. Yes, we're fine, thanks."

Jack wandered back to his pots while Liam started the car and headed back to the cottage.

There was little reaction to the cliff fall in the village, no council visit or immediate geological survey. One or two people had come out of their cottages to see what the noise was and were walking down Low Harbour towards the scene to take a look. In the car no one was speaking, no suggestion of being traumatised, just a question of contemplation.

As they pulled up outside the cottage, it was Farrah who broke the silence.

"Is it ok to play with Lily, Mom?" Jo looked at Liam.

"Yes, if you want, Poppet."

"I need to get going," said Liam.

"Do you think you should go after what's happened?"

"Yes, I really need to; I want to take this as far as I can."

"Lily says you can go," said Farrah.

"Oh, thank her for me," said Liam and looked at Jo with a frown.

A short time later, Liam left the cottage; his mind now focussed on his meeting. He checked his pocket to make sure he had the memory stick and got in the car.

He felt anxious as the Volvo climbed the steep incline out of the village but the road was clear and there was no sign of the fog. He reached the last cottage and glanced left to the waste ground next it. There was a large van parked, with several men wandering around in Hi-Viz jackets. It would be engineers assessing the removal of Yolanda's car, he thought. He slowed to take a closer look at the activity. Then accelerated away past the shrine.

As he drove through the forest he reached the spot where the breakdown truck had crashed; that too had been removed, just leaving flattened foliage and saplings. Soon there would be no trace of it but it would be some time before it would leave Liam.

Liam reached the outskirts of St Austell and followed the signs to the station. He drove down High Cross Street and reached the short-stay and drop off car park and checked his watch, ten-to-five. He decided he would chance the twenty-minute maximum stay.

He exited the car, stretched his legs, and took in his surroundings. The station overlooked the town and there were extensive views with rolling hills in the distance, made all the more appealing by the beautiful weather; a very different community from Polgissy. The area was also a transport hub and several green buses were parked in their respective bays adjacent to the station.

The complex itself was attractive. To the left was a new modern facility fronted by several palm trees in huge flower pots. There was a modern footbridge accessed by two box-like constructions on either side. Further along was part of the old station with its Victorian footbridge showing signs of neglect with flaking cream paint and streaks of rust.

He locked the Volvo and walked inside the station concourse. The arrivals and departure screens over the entrance to the platforms were flashing updates. He looked up and checked; the London train was running three minutes late.

There was an open communal area on the right-hand side which served as a waiting room. Liam walked through. To the left, there was a coffee shop selling hot drinks and snacks. There were grey metal bench seats positioned around the perimeter and three wooden and chrome tables with matching chairs in the middle, nothing elaborate, just functional. There were maybe twenty people dotted around drinking or listening to music through headphones.

Liam went to the service bar and ordered a coffee and a chocolate bar; he wasn't sure if he would be eating for a while.

He chose one of the table seats, made himself comfortable

and sipped his drink. The luxury of Wi-Fi was too good an opportunity to miss, and he spent a few minutes downloading his emails to his phone. There were several requiring his attention.

His browsing was interrupted by the station tannoy announcing the pending arrival of the London train. Liam put away his phone and finished his coffee, then walked to the entrance gates.

The express roared into the station shutting out the light. There was the sound of doors opening and probably thirty people getting off along the length of the train. Liam scanned the passengers as they approached the exit.

There were a few holiday-makers with excited children running about causing parental stress. Some business people mingled among them, the crush causing a bottle-neck at the gate as passengers waited to insert their tickets into the automated barriers.

Then Liam spotted a man in a grey sports jacket, slacks, and trendy white-soled loafers at the back of the melee. He looked out of place carrying a leather briefcase and a small, expensive-looking, overnight bag over his shoulder. There was a rolled up newspaper under his armpit. He waited while his fellow passengers filed through the gates, watched closely by a rail employee.

The crowd dispersed.

Outside the station entrance, several cars were waiting with their boots raised to accommodate suitcases. A line of taxis pulled forward slowly as they acquired a fare.

Liam was waiting by the gate and made eye-contact with the man. The passenger fed his ticket into slot, the gate opened, and he walked though.

"Andy?" enquired Liam.

"Liam, pleased to meet you."

Tennant put down his briefcase and the pair shook hands.

"I've got the car outside. Do you want to find somewhere to eat?"

"That sounds an excellent idea. I had a sandwich on the train and enough coffee to keep me awake for a fortnight, but yes, I'd welcome something a bit more substantial."

"How was the journey?"

"Not bad, it was quite comfortable, thank you, four and a quarter hours, just over."

"Ha yes, the joys of train journeys. I'll drive us into town; there are a few places we can go."

They reached the car and Liam stowed the agent's hand luggage in the boot.

They buckled up and headed down into the town. Liam had a thought. "There's a nice Asian restaurant, 'The Water Margin', if that suits."

"Yes, that's fine; I'm partial to the odd Thai."

"So, what're your plans? Are you travelling back tonight?"

"Fuck no, I've had enough of GWR for one day. I've booked into a hotel, The White Hart."

"Yes, I know where that is; I passed it on the way here, quite close."

Liam parked just off the shopping precinct and led the way to the restaurant.

They were greeted by an attractive girl in traditional Thai costume. The décor was customarily Thai/Chinese with the ubiquitous pagodas, dragons, completed by beautiful trelliswork, pleasing to the eye. There was no-one else in the establishment and they were offered a choice of seats.

Choosing a table in the corner, the pair made themselves comfortable. Liam was wearing a casual shirt and jeans. Tennant removed his sports jacket, placing it over the back of his chair.

Liam was weighing up his dinner guest. Early forties, fit, smart, with an eye for designer labels judging by the make of his shirt; possibly ex special-forces, Liam surmised.

Having received their drinks and ordered their food; it was down to business.

Chapter Thirteen

"Frank mentioned you're also a barrister?" said Tennant, taking his first sip of Thai beer. "Worked on the Rainsford case, he was telling me."

"Yes, I was the prosecuting QC for the Crown."

"Excellent, you did a great job getting those bastards sent down."

"Thanks," said Liam.

"How long have you known Frank Hamilton?"

"Years, we were at law school together. I knew he did a lot of work for the agency which is why I called him."

"So what's your interest in the Walton case?"

"Curiosity, basically. We came to Polgissy for a family holiday last Saturday, my wife and two kids. We've rented a cottage for three weeks. We knew nothing about the murders until after we arrived. I have to say, we did think about returning home when we found out."

"Yes, I'm not surprised."

"Hmm, frankly, it was too much of a hassle to find somewhere else at short notice and, after the court case, I needed a break, so did the family. I don't think I've been the easiest person to live with over the last few months."

Liam could feel Tennant weighing him up, but then, he was doing the same. Tennant took another sip of his lager. His movement seemed measured and assured.

"Go on."

Liam took a drink.

"Well, what was interesting was the reaction from the villagers. I met one or two and they refused outright to talk about it, would you believe? My take on village life is that it would be full of gossip. The biggest happening in the village since goodness knows when, and the response I was getting was, 'folk round 'ere don't like to tork about it'." Liam spoke in a mock local accent. Tennant smiled.

"Apart, that is, from the owner of the cottage where we're staying. She gave me some background, and some newspaper cuttings, so I have an idea about what went on. According to her, the police investigation has been scaled back without anyone being charged. I guess I'm keen to see justice is done."

"Hmm, I see. And you're actually staying in the Walton cottage?"

"Yes, I found the memory stick hidden in a secret compartment in the pantry, quite by accident. Someone had gone to great lengths to hide it. It occurred to me it was Walton that put it there."

Tennant looked around. "So, do you have the item?"

"Yes, it's here." He removed the memory stick from his pocket and handed it to the agent.

"You think that's why the family were killed?" asked Liam.

"No, I don't. I think they were killed because of the laptop."

"Laptop?"

"Yes, the one which George Walton would have used to record his investigations, including transcripts of conversations."

"Hmm. yes, I see what you mean. Transcripts?"

"Yes, I take it you've signed the O.S.A.?"

"Yes, I have. We handle a lot of sensitive information in my line of work."

"Ok, well what I'm about to tell you is classified, but as you've worked out much of it, I'll fill in with some, but not all, of the gaps."

"Have you met Christopher Deakin?"

"Yes, I have. I went to his house earlier this week to use his internet."

"Really? Hmm, now that's interesting. What do you know about him?"

"Only what he told me, a dealer, cryptocurrencies, he said."

"Hmm, it's slightly more than that. Have you heard of Kim Dokgo?

Liam looked blank. "I can't say I have."

"Well, he was the founder of two cryptocurrencies, one called Firma, and another called Saturn."

"I haven't a clue about cryptocurrencies. I prefer good old-fashioned money," replied Liam.

"Ha, I know what you mean. Well, the currencies collapsed in May, the price fell to near zero. The impact was huge, it even affected the wider crypto-market."

Liam was struggling. He picked up his lager giving the impression he was following.

"It was substantially a fraud and a lot of people lost a great deal of money - life savings, pensions, even houses. Kim Dokgo's disappeared, and the South Korean authorities have issued an international arrest warrant for him."

"So how does Deakin fit in?"

"He's been on our radar for a while. We were contacted by the Koreans as part of their investigation. Apparently, Deakin had had dealings with Dokgo's enterprise around the time of the pandemic. They thought he might be still in contact with Dokgo, but we've found no evidence that he has. It's one of the reasons why Five are keeping an eye on him."

"I see," said Liam, trying to keep up.

"We've been monitoring his internet activity. We

discovered that Deakin switched out of Firma Saturn just before they went belly up, into another platform called FCX."

"That was lucky."

"Yes, it certainly was, probably tipped off."

"By this Kim fellow?"

"Possibly, it's a hell of a coincidence."

"So, this FCX, what does it mean? It's all Dutch to me."

"Yes, it's fairly new into the market."

Liam was looking blank.

"The way it was explained to me is that it's like a brokerage that invests on behalf of clients. Millions of dollars are involved on a daily basis and, in FCX's case, being new to the market, there are, potentially, greater opportunities for profit. It's attracting a lot of investment."

"Is this legal?"

"Yes, of course, investing in cryptocurrency is big business, but it's also an ideal vehicle for money laundering and fraud. We believe Deakin's involved with organised crime syndicates, investing proceeds from drug dealing and people smuggling, which is the other reason why Five are interested. We know for a fact he's made several million pounds, maybe as much as ten."

"Ten million? Wow, by money laundering?"

"Sort of, but a bit more sophisticated. You've heard of the phrase, 'follow the money'?"

"Yes, of course, it's in all the best police dramas."

"Ha, yes, well once cryptocurrency is involved, it's like a glorious black hole. It's gone forever as far as law-enforcement agencies are concerned, and it's very lucrative. We believe Deakin is acting as a broker for a number of unsavoury organisations."

"Hmm, having seen his house, I can confirm that. Why

can't you just arrest him?"

"Hmm, evidence is the issue; we don't have any. Trading in cryptocurrencies is not a crime. The challenge has been establishing the origin of the money he's using to invest; that's the difficulty. George Walton had been working undercover for six months trying to get close to Deakin. He was also monitoring conversations from a listening device he was able to plant. It's why Walton's information is so valuable. I'm hoping that it may reveal the name of some of his clients."

"Yes, I can see that."

Tennant took a sip of beer. "We have, of course, been working in close contact with the local police down here since the murders. Deakin was actually questioned about them but there was nothing to link him with the killings and he has a watertight alibi. He also has very good solicitors." Tennant gave a wry smile.

Just then, the waitress appeared with their meals. There was a pause in the discussion while the meals were distributed. Liam was beginning to regret eating the earlier chocolate bar.

The pair started helping themselves to the food. Tennant looked up at the waitress. "Two more beers please."

Liam finished his lager and handed over his empty glass. The waitress left to dispense the drinks.

He continued. "But surely, even if they've got the laptop, it won't be of any use to them; they won't be able to read what's on it."

"Well, it doesn't really matter. Think about it for a minute; they don't have to. They'll probably just destroy it. From their point of view, the important thing is that *we* don't get hold of the information."

"Ah, yes, I see what you mean. What do you think's on

there?"

"Hmm, well as I said, George was able to plant a listening device inside Deakin's house on one of his visits. We supplied him with a portable Wi-Fi router so he could record what was going on. I'm hoping there'll be some transcripts of telephone calls, the ones GCHQ were not able to monitor, and maybe, if we're lucky, details of conversations with visitors."

"But they won't be able to be used in court; it would be inadmissible."

"No, of course, it's for information gathering only. We need to get a clearer picture of what's going on and, if we're lucky, know who the other players are."

"What about his recording equipment?"

"Good question. Whoever murdered the family must have taken it. The police didn't find anything. In fact, there was no forensic evidence at the crime scene at all; they were very professional."

"Out of interest, who found the bodies?"

"The police made a forced entry when one of the neighbours couldn't rouse them. She had agreed to take the daughter to school. She became concerned and called them. It wasn't pretty, I can tell you. The forensic team believe that they, whoever 'they' are, killed the little girl first, then his wife; George was last"

"Jeezus, no wonder the spirits are restless."

"Spirits? What do you mean?"

"Oh, nothing, just thinking allowed. Why do you think the Waltons were targeted?"

"We think that someone, presumably Deakin, discovered he was working for MI5. We may know more once we find out what's on the memory stick."

"Let's hope so. You said the local police are aware of

your interest in Deakin?"

"Yes, but not the fact we had surveillance on him, or the fact that Walton was one of ours."

The waitress brought the drinks as the men tucked into their meal.

"I say this is very good," said Tennant, taking in another mouthful of a chicken stir-fry.

"Yes, it is; I'll have to bring the family. Come to think of it, I'll need to think of a peace offering, I said I wasn't going to be long."

Tennant took a sip of lager and sat back in his chair.

"Tell me about the owner of the cottage. You mentioned it was a woman; 'she', I thought you said."

"Yes, what do you want to know?"

"I'm interested why she kept the newspaper cuttings."

"Hmm, I don't really know; she never said. Although she was a friend of the family; used to babysit the daughter when both parents were unable to pick her up from school."

"I see. Does she have any connection with Deakin?"

"Well, she uses his internet, she was saying. She's a freelance journalist and sends in her copy from his place once a week, but other than that, I'm not aware of any connection."

"Yes, I see."

Liam had exhausted his questions; there was not much more he could do.

"So, what happens next?"

"Well, I'm booked on the one o'clock from St Austell tomorrow, gets into Paddington about five-thirty."

"Oh, you have my sympathy, rush hour."

"It shouldn't be too bad at the weekend, as long as there're no idiots demonstrating."

Liam smiled. "I couldn't possibly comment," he said and

smiled.

"Ha, yes, of course, your lot have been manning the barricades."

"Well, a couple of my junior chamber staff were out with placards, but I was too busy with the Rainsford case, so I didn't get involved."

"Yes, I can understand that. Actually, I had hoped to have a look around the village while I'm here. Would you be about tomorrow morning?"

"Yes, I can be, although I don't know what Mrs Drake will say, but I'll handle that."

"Just a couple of hours, something like that."

"Yes, that's fine. There's a pub on the sea front, the only pub I should add. We could meet there. What time?"

"About ten? How does that sound?" said Tennant.

"Yes, that's fine."

"Don't worry about picking me up, I can get a cab. Although I would be grateful for a lift back to the station."

"Yes, I'm sure I can manage that."

The meal was finished and Tennant paid the bill, courtesy of 'HM Government'.

"I'll give you a lift to the hotel, it's not far," said Liam, and the pair left the restaurant and walked to the car.

As they reached the hotel, Tennant opened the car door and looked across to Liam.

"Thanks for getting in touch. I'll be emailing the data to Thames House as soon as I get in; the techies can have some fun with it. I'll see you tomorrow at ten o'clock."

"Yes, see you later," said Liam, and Tennant picked up his briefcase and overnight bag from the back seat.

Liam drove away, deep in thought. He was digesting the information he'd been given by the MI5 agent. He was keen to continue to contribute to the investigation, but had no idea what he could do. It seemed MI5 had it all under control.

At least he'd been able to download his emails onto his phone and could spend a few minutes catching up when he got back.

It was as though he was driving on autopilot as he headed back to the village. It was a warm, bright summer's evening, around seven-thirty, and his mind was mulling through the events of the past week.

As he turned left off the main road, his illuminated Sat-Nav map on the dashboard disappeared again. He was back in the dark, surrounded by the trees.

Then something distracted him, something in his peripheral vision. He glance right and, coming through the forest, he could detect some movement. The fog was back, and it seemed to be heading towards him.

"Shit!" he exclaimed, as his survival mechanism kicked in.

It was still some distance away, but Liam wasn't taking any chances and floored the Volvo. He needed to get away.

His speed increased – forty, fifty, sixty; it was a narrow lane. He could see brightness in the distance. The end of the forest was approaching; blue sky ahead, closer, closer. He checked his rear-view mirror, nothing.

He shot out of the canopy and breathed a sigh of relief. Suddenly, right in front of him, a woman was stood in the middle of the road.

Liam hit the brakes with everything he could muster; the anti-lock system immediately cut in. There seemed no way he would miss her. At the last minute he yanked his steering wheel to the right. Gravel, dirt, tyre-rubber, bits of glass were scattered everywhere. He was still doing twenty miles an hour as he hit the waste ground next to Mrs Wilkin's cottage.

Mercifully, the chain fence that he had knocked over previously, afforded some traction, and the Volvo came to a stop.

Liam put his head on the steering wheel and breathed in deeply.

Slowly, he opened the door and got out; he was shaking, his legs like jelly.

He looked back along the road towards the forest. He could see the woman sat on the grass verge next to the shrine. Blonde hair, casual top and jeans, she was sobbing bitterly.

As he approached, she stood up, much to his relief.

Without warning, she rushed towards him, her face contorted with anger, her eyes bloodshot from crying.

"You crazy bastard, you crazy bastard. That's how my daughters were killed. What on earth were you trying to do?"

"I'm very sorry, I really am. There was a problem with the car. Are you alright?"

She started hitting his chest with her fists. Liam grabbed the woman in a hug; she was still crying bitterly.

"I'm so sorry, I really am," he whispered.

She pushed his well-meaning comfort away. "Get off me, you bastard. You should be locked up."

"As long as you're alright. Can I give you a lift?"

"Are you mad? You think I would get in a car with you? You should be taken off the road."

"I can explain," said Liam trying to show appropriate remorse.

"Yes, that's what that journalist said when he knocked down my girls. Still he got his just deserts. Not that it's brought them back. Nothing will ever bring them back."

She burst into tears again, deep convulsive sobs.

"Are you Ashley?" said Liam.

She stopped crying for a moment and looked at Liam.

"Yes, how did you know? I don't know you."

"No, we've been staying in the village; we know April. She's mentioned you a few times. She said you were at your sister's in Reading."

"Yes, I got back this afternoon. I wanted to see my girls again."

"Look, I'm really sorry, I really am; it's not how I normally drive. There was a problem, er, with the car."

She looked at Liam; she was calmer now. "Let me drive you back, please."

There was a sign of acquiescence and the pair slowly walked down to the Volvo. Liam opened the passenger door and she got in.

Liam reversed the Volvo slowly out of the clutches of the chain fence back to the road, and headed down the hill. There was no attempt at conversation.

"Turn right here," she said as they passed the pub.

"Yes, I know where you live; April told me, the end cottage?"

"Yes, that's right."

They pulled up outside her cottage and Liam could see April's car was not in her usual parking spot.

"It looks like April's out."

"Yes, I called round this afternoon but there was no reply," said Ashley.

"Yes, she was going over to the hospital in St Austell to visit a patient. If I see her, I'll let her know you're back. My name's Liam by the way, and I'm really sorry for causing you so much anxiety on top of everything else."

"Thanks for the lift," she said and exited the car with a slam of the door. Liam watched her go into the cottage without a backward glance.

Liam turned the car around and headed back to Pendle Cottage. As he approached, he could see April's car parked outside.

He went to the door and knocked in a rhythmic way. Jo opened it.

"It's gone eight o'clock, we were getting worried," she said standing aside and letting Liam by.

"Yes, I'm sorry, Andy insisted on buying me dinner. There were a few things we needed to catch up on. I hope I haven't missed anything."

"Apart from dinner, I saved you a portion. I didn't know if you had eaten."

"Yes, sorry, there was no way of getting in touch with you to let you know. I knew April was out this afternoon." He looked at April. "How did you get on at the hospital?"

"Oh, fine thanks. Yolanda's getting out tomorrow, broken ankle and three broken ribs; she was incredibly lucky. One of her friends from the University is going to pick her up. I came to tell you, and Jo invited me to stay to dinner."

"Oh, that's a relief," said Liam.

"You can say that again," said April.

"You know, when I saw that car on its bonnet like that, I don't know how anyone could survive," said Liam.

Just then Farrah came down the stairs and ran up to Liam. She wrapped her arms around him.

"Lily says she's glad you're ok. She said some people were angry."

Liam looked at Jo and April.

"Did she say why they were angry, Poppet?" asked Jo.

"No... Can I have a drink of water? I'm so thirsty."

Jo went in to the kitchen and returned with a tumbler of water and handed it to Farrah.

"I'll just get her settled and you can tell me all about it," said Jo.

Jo and Farrah left the lounge and their footsteps echoed as they headed upstairs.

"I've just seen Ashley," said Liam looking at April.

"Really? I had no idea she was back."

"This afternoon, apparently."

"So, how did you meet up with her."

"Hmm, well I'm definitely not her favourite person." He explained about the fog.

"I was trying to escape from it. It was weird. It was as though I had no control over what I was doing. She was standing in the road by the shrine when I came out of the trees. I didn't see her till the last minute and had to swerve to miss her. Luckily, she's ok, but of course, after what happened to her girls, she was not very happy. I did give her a lift back to her cottage, though."

"Oh, that's good of you. In that case, I'll get back and call round see if she's ok. Can you say thanks to Jo for me?"

"Yes, of course."

Liam escorted April to the door and watched her go up the path.

"Oh, has April left?" said Jo, as she came back into the lounge from the bedrooms.

"Yes, she said thanks for dinner. She's going to call in on her neighbour, Ashley. You remember, the mother of the two girls who were knocked down. She returned to her cottage this afternoon. She was at the shrine as I was passing and I stopped and gave her a lift."

"That's very noble of you. What's she like?"

"Seems very pleasant," said Liam, not wanting to be reminded of his near-miss.

"So how was your meeting? Did you find anything?"

"Yes, it was very informative, and they were very

interested in the memory stick."

"So, what are they going to do with it?"

"It'll get analysed by their technical people."

"Does that mean we can get on with our holiday. I thought we could drive out to the Eden Project tomorrow."

"Ah, it'll need to be Sunday if that's ok. The agent wants to visit the village tomorrow morning; I said I would show him around."

"Hmm, and what are *we* supposed to do, Liam? We were supposed to be having a family holiday."

"It's just for tomorrow morning, promise. I know, why don't we go out for the afternoon, a tourist attraction or something. What about The Lost Gardens of Helegan, that's not far away?"

"Not much fun for kids, is it, Victorian Gardens? They want to be doing something, not roaming around exotic plants."

"Hmm, yes, you're right. We'll ask them in the morning, see what they want to do. We can always find a nice beach somewhere."

Jo was far from placated but let it drop.

The following morning, Liam and Jo were up early, the children still in bed. The atmosphere was still frosty between them but beginning to thaw. In an effort to put things right, Liam had persuaded Jo that the morning's meeting with the MI5 agent would be the last of his involvement in the investigation. Jo wasn't entirely convinced but went along with it.

Just then, Farrah came downstairs; she seemed very sleepy. She walked up to the table where Liam and Jo were having breakfast. Her face was trance-like; her voice, deeper than her normal timbre.

"The girls are with their Mom."

It was as though someone was using her body to speak.

Liam looked at Jo. "What does that mean Poppet? What girls?" asked Jo.

"Meli and Clemmie."

Jo cast a concerned look at Liam.

"Is your throat alright, Poppet?"

She suddenly snapped out of her state.

"Can I have a drink, Mom? I'm thirsty." Her voice had returned to normal.

"Of course, Poppet, come and sit up; I'll get you some breakfast. I better get your brother up."

Farrah sat on the chair opposite Liam.

"What did Lily say again, can you remember?" asked Liam.

Farrah looked at him. "I think their Mom is with the girls."

Liam thought for a moment.

Jo came downstairs. "Zack's awake; he'll be down in a minute."

Liam looked at Jo. "I've just been thinking about Lily's message; I'm worried."

"You think there's something in it?" asked Jo.

"Well, all the previous warnings have been right. Mind you, this was different. It was almost as if Lily was talking through Far."

"Yes, I noticed that. What should we do?"

"I really don't know. We can ask April."

"If you think that will help."

Liam got up. "I won't be long; I need to go round to see her."

Jo looked concerned. "Yes, ok, I think you're right. I'll just get breakfast, but we need to talk about this."

Liam picked up his car keys from the table and left the cottage.

He parked next to April's Kia on the waste ground at the top of the nip and, as he looked across to the cliff, he noticed Yolanda's car had gone. He locked up and walked down to April's cottage. As he passed Ashley's house, he noticed the curtains were drawn. It was still not nine o'clock, so it wasn't particularly remarkable.

He reached April's and knocked on the front door with his knuckles.

After a few moment's April opened the door in her dressing gown.

"Liam...? Are you ok?"

"Yes, sorry to call round so early but I'm concerned about Ashley."

He explained Lily's message.

"Oh dear, you better come in; I'll just go and change."

A few minutes later, April appeared in a tracksuit and trainers. "I've got a key," she said and showed it to Liam.

The pair left the house and walked the short distance to Ashley's cottage. April knocked, and again. After the third attempt, April inserted the key and opened the door.

"Ashley... Are you there? It's April." They walked through the downstairs but there was no sign.

"I'll check upstairs," said April.

She ascended the stairs and checked the bedroom. There were three empty bottles of pills on the dressing table. April put her hand to her mouth. "Oh no!"

She went into the bathroom and stopped dead.

"Liam!!!" she screamed.

Liam rushed up the staircase two at a time. "What is it?" he replied.

"In here."

Liam followed the voice to the bathroom.

Around the outside of the bath were five small candle jars, their wax-lights long since expired, just carbonised remnants of burned out wicks.

Ashley was lay in the bath, her skin bleached, her lips blue, a resemblance of John Everett Millais' painting of Ophelia.

April checked her vital signs. "She's dead, Liam."

"Jeezus," Liam just stared at the naked body looking serene and peaceful.

April looked up at Liam. "I think she came back to die, to be with her children. I hope they are all at peace now. We need to call an ambulance. I don't know if Ashley's phone's working, but if not we can use mine."

The pair went back downstairs and April picked up the telephone from the small bureau.

"There's a line," said April and dialled the emergency services.

April was in shock. "I just don't believe it. I called round after I left you last night, but the curtains were drawn. I thought she must be having an early night so I didn't disturb her. I was going to pop round after breakfast. If only I'd been here yesterday afternoon."

Liam went to her and put a consoling arm around her. "There was nothing you could have done; you can't blame yourself. Do you want me to wait with you?"

"No, it's ok, you better get back to your family."

"If you're sure. I'll call round later see how you are."

Liam left the cottage and headed back.

Zack and Farrah were at the table having breakfast when Liam walked in.

"Where's your mom?"

Jo heard his return and came out of the kitchen.

"Is everything ok?"

Liam walked towards Jo and ushered her back into the kitchen out of earshot of the children.

"Ashley's dead," he whispered.

"What!?"

"Yeah, looks like an overdose. April had a key so we called in to see if everything was ok. We found her in the bath. There were some empty pill bottles on the dressing table in the bedroom."

"Oh, that's awful."

"Yes, it is, such a waste of a life."

"But Lily's message."

"Yes, I was thinking that."

"I just can't get my head around it, Liam."

"Yes, mine too."

"The question is what are we going to do about it?" said Jo.

She went up to Liam and threw her arms around his shoulders. "I'm scared, Liam. I think we should go home. We don't know what's going to happen next."

"Let's give it till after the weekend; I think April will need some support. She was very close to Ashley."

Liam checked his watch. "Actually, I need to go. I'm meeting that guy from London in ten minutes. I'll be back as soon as I can. Will you be ok?"

"Yes, I'll be fine; I'll see to the kids. Might take them down to the harbour."

Liam walked back into the lounge. "Bye, kids, see you later."

"Bye, Dad," said Zack.

"Bye," said Farrah. She shovelled a spoonful of cereals

into her mouth, then looked at him "Lily says to be careful of the fog."

"Yes, I will," said Liam and he left the cottage.

Liam decided to park in the pub car park and wait for the MI5 agent. He locked up and walked to the front entrance.

The pub was still closed, in fact Liam had no idea of the opening hours; the landlord appeared to please himself.

Over the road, the promenade seemed to be populated with far more seagulls than people. Liam couldn't understand it; a Saturday in high-season and Polgissy was virtually deserted. There was a villager that Liam didn't recognise walking his dog, scattering the gulls as they passed. The man stopped while the dog deposited something nasty on the pavement. He waited for the canine to finish, then dutifully took out a plastic bag from his pocket and cleared the mess.

There was a street light opposite and perched on top was a large crow. Liam watched for a moment; the bird seemed to be staring at him. The vision of the motorway incident returned. Liam averted his gaze. The crow gave a 'caw' and flew off.

Five minutes later, a taxi came around the corner and pulled up outside the pub. Liam walked towards it and watched as Tennant got out and paid the driver.

He walked towards Liam and the pair shook hands. Tennant was dressed casually in a sports jacket, shirt, and jeans with a pair of smart trainers.

"Quaint place," said Tennant as he looked around. "I was expecting it to be heaving with holiday makers."

"Ha, yes, I don't think anyone's found it yet."

Just then, the front door of the pub opened and the landlord looked left and right up the street. He saw Liam.

"Wasson m'dear, were you wannin' a drink?"

Liam looked at Tennant. "Fancy a coffee, then I can show you round?"

"Cheers, good idea."

"Two coffees, Clem, thanks."

The pair followed the landlord inside and walked to the bar.

"Have a seat m'dears, will bring 'em along directly." The landlord left the bar and went into the back.

Tennant looked around. " Good grief, they could do with some lighting in here."

"Yes, it is a bit on the gloomy side."

The pair walked to the far end of the bar under one of the porthole windows. Tennant was carrying his briefcase and overnight bag. He popped them on a vacant seat next to him.

"How was your night?" asked Liam.

"Busy, very busy. I managed to get the data back to Thames House and they've been working on it all night. It's thrown up a couple of leads."

"Really?"

"Yes, they're still working through. We thought there might be more on this Dokgo individual, but nothing so far. Still, that's not really our problem; that's a Korean issue."

"What about the murders? Is there anything that might confirm who was responsible?"

"No, not so far, but there's a lot of data they're having to sift through. It's going to take a while."

"Yes, I can appreciate that. So that's it then?"

"What do you mean?"

"The investigation, the murder, how are you going to take it forward?"

"Hmm, well we need to see what's on the recordings, there may be something."

They were interrupted by the landlord bringing a tray with two coffees, cream, and some biscuits.

"I bought you some of Aswen's biscuits. She sells 'em up at the Sunday market; right poplar (sic) they are too."

"Thanks Clem, that's very good of you," said Liam. Tennant nodded his acknowledgement.

Clem went back to his landlord duties and the pair started on the refreshments. "Hey, these are pretty damn good," said Tennant taking his first bite.

"So, you were saying, about the investigation," said Liam.

"Yes, actually I was. Hmm," Tennant paused for a moment as though he was weighing something up.

"Are you still interested in helping?"

"Yes, of course," replied Liam, completely forgetting his promise to Jo.

Tennant rummaged in his jacket pocket. "Do you think you could find a way of planting this?"

Tennant put a small listening device on the table.

"Yes, I might be able to. He said I could call round and use his Wi-Fi if I wanted. I can use that as an excuse."

"Good, good. Talking of which, I got this for you."

Tennant went to his other pocket and placed another item next to the listening device. "It's a Wi-Fi dongle. It means you can use the internet. We may need to contact you. It's very straightforward. Just sick it in your USB port and follow the instructions. It was what George was using."

"That's great, thanks. But you won't want me to look after the recording?"

"No, no, it's fine. No, with this receiver we can monitor it from Thames House."

Liam picked up the listening device and rolled it in his fingers.

"Is there a best place for hiding this?"

"Somewhere central, it's pretty sensitive."

"But won't he have some sort of detection device monitoring the place, I mean, given the amount of resources he has available?"

"Yes, that's quite possible. It's probably how Walton was discovered. I don't think we will ever know."

"I can't put my family in danger."

"No, no, of course not, but you'll be going back to the rat-race in what, two weeks? Once the device is in place, we won't need to bother you any further."

"Yes, ok. I'll find a way. You better let me know how I can contact you."

"Yes, of course." He reached inside his jacket and pulled out a card from his wallet. "Here's my business card; my email address and mobile number are on it."

The pair continued chatting for another half an hour, finishing their mid-morning refreshments, before Liam offered to show Tennant around the village.

Chapter Fourteen

Liam and Tennent left the pub and walked back to Liam's car. Liam had a quick glance at the street light; the crow was nowhere to be seen.

"Was there anything specific you wanted me to show you?"

"I wouldn't mind seeing Deakin's house," said Tennant.

Liam turned on the ignition and reversed out of the parking bay.

"Yes, it's not far, although we'll need to be careful, it's bristling with security."

"Yes, ok."

Four minutes later, Liam was pulling up outside the church. There were no other cars parked and the church itself looked deserted; its stained-glass windows glinted in the bright morning sunlight. The pair exited the Volvo.

"I'll leave my stuff in the back," said Tennant, as he took off his jacket and threw it onto the rear seat.

They walked past the church along the cinder track that led to Deakin's house. Then Liam saw something. At the end of the church wall, there was a gap in the shrubbery before the rectory; he hadn't noticed it on his last visit.

"Look, that sign, there's a footpath."

Liam pointed to a faded, green wooden sign. 'Public footpath', it said, in flaking, white-painted writing, pointing right.

Liam walked towards the footpath. It was narrow, not wide enough for two people side-by-side; Tennant was behind him. He looked along the path; there was a steep incline into the trees.

"It looks like it leads into the forest. I remember

April saying that George Walton spent some time taking photographs there."

"April...?"

"Yes, she's the one who gave me the newspaper cuttings. I bet that this was his way in. If we climb to the top and walk around the back of the rectory, we should be able to get directly behind Deakin's house."

"Sounds good. Now you mention it, there were some photos of the rear of the house in the files."

To the right, the church wall and small graveyard, to the left, an impenetrable screen of bushes and brambles which separated the path from the rectory; the gradient quickly increased. Liam could see the trees above them getting closer. He was starting to breathe heavily as they reached the canopy.

"Fuck, this is steep," said Tennant as they went into the trees. Liam felt uneasy and was on high alert.

The forest was predominantly made up of deciduous trees of many varieties, beech, elm, oak, ash, tall and mature, many over a hundred years old. There was the resonance of birdlife, woodpeckers, tree-creepers, nuthatches, all active and looking for insects.

After about twenty yards or so into the trees, the footpath levelled off and they reached a T junction with a slightly wider footpath, running left and right. The Deakin residence would be left.

Liam checked around and made the turn with Tennant close behind.

"That's the vicar's place," said Liam, pointing down through the foliage to the large eighteenth century rectory.

"Wow, that's not a bad reward for a couple of sermons a week and the occasional Bible group," said Tennant.

"You can say that again," replied Liam.

They continued walking for another two hundred yards or so. Sunlight streamed through the branches like mini torch beams.

"Right, we should be able to see Deakin's place." Liam pointed left.

They walked slowly forward, the trees providing them with significant cover. They would not be easily visible. The magnificent house was below them.

"Fuck, that's some place. Can we get a bit closer?" said Tennant.

"Yes, but keep down."

The ground sloped away at this point, down to the valley and Deakin's boundary wall, maybe a hundred feet below. Tennant left the footpath and walked sideways down the bank to give himself grip. Underfoot was treacherous, covered in fungi and slimy leaves in various stages of decay, and he slid to the last tree, an enormous copper beech, using it as a brake to stop himself falling further.

He hid behind the trunk and took out a miniature camera from his pocket, then, with one hand on the beech to give him balance, he turned and took a few pictures.

Tennant had neglected to check the ground around him. Not realising it, he was on the edge of a precipice and, below, the roots of the tree were visible. His extra weight and the force of him using it to stop, had destabilised the ancient beech. Without warning, the mighty tree suddenly lurched forward like a giant crane, and slowly toppled down the escarpment in spectacular fashion, taking a large mass of earth with it.

Liam was following Tennant and had almost reached him when the tree started going over. He managed to grab the agent's arm just as the earth gave way from underneath him. In the chaos, Tennant had dropped his camera which was rolling down the hill with the rest of the debris.

Tennant was heavy and his legs were now dangling over the edge. Liam was sliding on the slippery ground but somehow managed to hold on, enabling the agent to grab a sapling.

Liam heaved, and slowly Tennant was able to pull himself onto firmer ground. He lay for a minute to catch his breath then slid forward on his stomach until he was almost at the footpath and able to stand.

"Jeezus, that was fucking close; thanks for getting me out," said Tennant with an expression of relief. He looked over the edge. "Looks like I'm going to need another camera."

"I think we better get out of here," said Liam. "We may well have alerted him."

Inside the house, Deakin was on the telephone when Nathan, the odd-job man, disturbed him.

"Sir, sorry to interrupt but something's tripped the rear motion sensors,"

"Sorry, I'll call you back, there's an emergency," said Deakin to the caller.

He rang off.

"What's happened?"

"I don't know, looks like a landslip, but I'm sure I saw someone moving in the woods."

"Fetch my binoculars and meet me upstairs."

Deakin walked up the stairs to his back-room office and peered through the window. Moments later, Nathan arrived and handed him the binoculars. Deakin scanned the edge of the forest where the landslip had originated. There was a huge scar gouged out of the earth running downwards to the house from the trees. Branches of the toppled beech were just visible over the boundary wall.

Deakin looked left and right into the forest. Then he detected movement, two figures walking quickly away in the distance, but too far to make out any recognition.

"You're right; it was a landslip," said Deakin. "It's going to take some clearing."

Liam led the way along the footpath, back towards the car. The vicar's property appeared somewhere below them to the right, beyond that, the church, its spire dwarfed by the hillside. Then something caught Liam's eye and he stopped dead.

Deep in the forest ahead of them to the left, there was movement. He couldn't make it out at first, and then it seemed to be moving closer. The fog was back.

"Quick, Andy, we need to move."

"What's the problem?"

"Trust me, we need to move... just here," said Liam, as they reached the path that led down to the cinder track.

Looking at it, it seemed even steeper going down, the slope resembling being at the top of a children's slide, the ones you see in a park. Liam led the way trying desperately not to break into a run which would possibly have fatal consequences with no means of stopping. They were soon out of the trees and into bright sunshine.

They reached the cinder track and Liam looked back, up into the forest. There was no sign of the fog.

"What was all that about?" said Tennant.

"Oh, nothing, just needed to get out of the forest."

He looked at the agent. He was covered in mud; his jeans, and shirt were in a terrible state and his trendy trainers caked with leaf mould and dirt.

"Did you bring a change of clothes? You're filthy."

"In my bag," he said, trying to brush down his jeans.

"Would you like to come back to the cottage and tidy up? We're just over there." Liam pointed.

"Yeah, sure, thanks."

"We'll take the car in case Deakin starts looking around."

The pair got into the Volvo, and Liam drove the short distance to the cottage and parked outside. Tennant got out and looked up at the house. "So this is Pendle Cottage?"

"Yes, it is." Liam unlocked the front door and walked into the lounge. "Come in, it looks like the family have gone out."

Tennant took off his muddy footwear and walked in carrying his overnight bag.

"The bathroom's upstairs, you'll see it. Would you like another coffee?"

"Thanks, please, I won't be long."

Liam went into the kitchen and fed some pound coins into the electricity meter and started boiling the kettle.

Upstairs, Tennant was in the bathroom washing himself down. His jeans and shirt would need changing. He went in to Farrah's bedroom and opened his overnight suitcase. He took out his trousers and shirt that he had worn the previous day and changed into them. He put the soiled clothing inside and closed it. He noticed a cool draft coming from somewhere, enough to make him rub his arms, then from nowhere he heard a child's voice.

"Hello, have you seen my daddy?"

Tennant looked around the room, opened the wardrobe door. He was starting to shiver. He left the bedroom and walked downstairs.

Liam walked out of the kitchen carrying two mugs. "Everything alright?" seeing Tennant in a distressed state.

"I don't know. I thought I heard voices."

"Voices?"

"Well, *a* voice. It sounded like a child, wanted to know if I had seen her father."

"Oh, you better sit down. It's probably shock... er, you know, in the forest."

"No, no, it was quite real. Well, I thought it was."

"Did you manage to clean up, ok?"

Liam changed the subject, deciding it was not the time to reveal their own experiences. It would just complicate things.

"Yes, yes, I'd got a spare shirt and pair of trousers, the shoes will dry soon enough." He picked up his coffee and took a sip, deep in thought.

"Before you go, I'll show where the memory stick was hidden."

They finished their drinks and Liam led Tennant to the kitchen and through to the pantry.

"It was just here." Liam moved the cans of beans from the top shelf and showed Tennant the hiding place.

"Yes, he certainly went to some lengths to secure it," said Tennant, examining the hiding place.

"That's for sure."

The pair returned to the lounge. "Well, if you're ready, I'll take you over to the station in St Austell. We should be in good time."

"Yes, cheers, and for the coffee,"

The pair left the cottage, and it was with some anxiety that Liam eased the car up the long hill out of the village.

He reached Mrs Wilkin's cottage and then went past the shrine. There was no sign of the fog.

They continued chatting for the rest of the journey, which helped take Liam's mind off any possible dangers, and after just half an hour, they were pulling into the station car park in St Austell.

"Now, you're sure you're ok about planting the listening device? I can get someone else down if necessary. We're not too worried about phone conversations, GCHQ are monitoring that, but we're particularly interested in any visitors."

"No, no it'll be fine. I'll email you when it's done. Thanks again for the Wi-Fi connection, though I don't think my wife will be as generous; I'm still in the dog house."

The pair shook hands and Tennant got out of the car carrying his briefcase and overnight bag; his jacket was in the crook of his arm. Liam watched him go into the station concourse.

The journey back was, thankfully, uneventful; there was no sign of the fog. He passed the pub and turned right up the nip; he needed to pay a call.

There was a police car outside Ashley's cottage and getting past proved problematical. But with the use of the grass verge, he managed to reach the waste ground and parked next to April's Kia.

He walked down to the cottage and knocked on the door. After a few moments, April opened it, her eyes red and puffy.

"Oh, hello Liam, it's lovely to see you, do come in."

"I thought I'd pop in and see how you were."

"That's good of you, would you like a drink?"

"If you're having one."

"Go on through to the patio; I won't be a minute."

Liam walked through into the garden and sat down on one of the patio chairs while April disappeared into the kitchen.

"There're some more biscuits," said April as she returned with the coffees and a plate containing four chocolate digestives.

"Thanks. How are you feeling now?"

"I don't know how I feel if I'm honest. Not brilliant, I have to say. It was a hell of a shock seeing Ashley like that. I only wish I could have talked to her; I'm sure I could have given her some hope."

"Yes, I'm sure you could, but it looks like she came back deliberately to die."

"Yes, it does. It's so sad, and such a waste. We had some really happy times together. She was my rock when Stuart died. I don't know how I would have coped if she hadn't been there for me."

"So, what's going to happen? Do you know?"

"Well, the ambulance has just left and taken her away. There will be a post mortem and inquest they were telling me. I think the police are still there."

"Yes, there was a police car outside when I went by."

"What about her things?"

"I gave them Debra's number. That's her sister in Reading. They said they were going to contact her."

"What about the children's father?"

"No, Robert's long gone; a right bastard he was. No idea where he is now; the twins were little when he left them. She never heard from him, not even a Christmas card for the kids."

April put her hands to her face and started crying again. Liam got up and put a consoling arm around her.

"Do you want me to stay for a while?"

"No, it's ok, thanks. Actually, I've just remembered, there's a barbeque at Christopher's place this afternoon at four o'clock. I ought to go; I said I would. He invites all the villagers. It's like an open house, and it's usually well-attended. Why don't you come, and Jo and the kids?"

"Without an invite?"

"Yes, I'm sure he won't mind, probably won't even notice. He gets caterers in from St Austell to look after all the food. There's always plenty."

Liam was thinking. This might be just the opportunity he was looking for.

"Well, I'll ask Jo when I see her, but if she hasn't anything planned, that would be great. As long as it's ok."

"I'm sure it'll be fine. I need to phone him anyway to tell him about Ashley. I'll mention it and if there's any problem I'll pop up and let you know."

Liam drank his coffee and looked at his watch.

"Hmm, I better get back. I said I would spend some time with them this afternoon."

Liam made his farewells and headed back to the Volvo. The police car had gone.

As he was about to pull out onto the promenade from the nip, he could see Jo and the children walking along the harbour wall in the distance. He drove down to the Harbourmaster's Office to meet them.

He waved as they reached the slipway. Zack came running up to the car and got in. Jo and Farrah took a more leisurely approach.

"Hi, how did you get on?" said Liam.

"Oh, we've had a nice walk; we've been all the way across to the Headland, then back to the harbour. How did you get on?" said Jo.

"Oh, there's lots to tell you about. Do you want to go to the pub and get something to eat?"

"I need to get back; there's some salad stuff needs eating. Actually, we could do with some more bread. Wait here, I'll pop to the shop and see if she has anything."

Zack and Farrah were chatting excitedly about their

morning. A few minutes later, Jo returned carrying a French loaf.

Liam turned the car around and headed back to the cottage.

"Have you got anything planned for this afternoon?" he asked as he turned into the drive.

"No, why? You're not buggering off again are you?" said Jo sharply.

"No, no, of course not, we've had an invite to a barbeque."

"Really? Where?"

"Deakin's place, it'll give you a chance to see it."

"What about the kids?"

"It's ok, they can come. It seems most of the village will be there."

Jo turned to the back seats. "What do you think, guys, do you want to go to a barbeque?"

"Sure," said Zack. "It's cool."

"What about you, Poppet?"

"Whatever." Farrah folded her arms passive/aggressively. There was some reluctance in her voice.

They pulled up outside the cottage and the kids unbuckled their seat belts.

"Dad...? Lily says, has your friend seen her daddy?" said Farrah as she opened the car door.

Liam turned briefly to reply. "No, Far, he hasn't."

He looked across at Jo. "I'll tell you later."

The family exited the Volvo and went into the cottage. Jo headed to the kitchen to start on the lunch while the kids went to their rooms.

"How's April?" asked Jo, as Liam followed her into the kitchen.

"Hmm, not good, she's in bits about Ashley; they were very good friends."

"So what was Lily talking about," said Jo.

"It was Andy, he wanted to see the cottage and he went into Far's room to look out of the window. He said he heard a child's voice asking if he'd seen her daddy."

"What did you say?"

"I said he was probably imagining it."

"And he believed you?"

"I think so; he didn't pursue it."

"You didn't tell him about all the other incidents?"

"I decided not to. I just think it would have opened a can of worms."

"Yes, you're probably right." She was cutting up the French loaf and paused. "You know, I can't believe we've been here a week already. I was thinking this morning; it's certainly been eventful."

"You can say that again. Do you still want to go home?"

"I'm ok at the moment; let's see how we go."

Liam returned to the lounge, removed his laptop from its case, and put it on the table. The Wi-Fi dongle was in his pocket along with the listening device.

He placed the dongle in one of the USB ports and turned on the computer.

"Yes!" he exclaimed as the Wi-Fi signal connected. He quickly downloaded his emails and started browsing.

Jo had finished preparing the lunch and walked into the lounge with a plate of sandwiches, She saw Liam on the laptop.

"What are you doing? You said you would leave work behind."

"Yes, sorry, just downloaded my emails."

"But I thought you couldn't get a signal."

"Ah, yes, Andy gave me a Wi-Fi connector so I could let him know if we had any more information."

"You promised you would leave it to the police."

"Yes, sorry, it's something I'm doing for Andy, then I'm done."

He removed the laptop from the table to allow Jo to bring in the sandwiches.

"Go and tell the kids lunch is ready," said Jo, clearly still not happy with Liam.

At just turned four o'clock, the Drake family were making the short journey to the Deakin residence.

"What a quaint church," said Jo, as they walked by and joined the cinder track.

"You wait till you see the rectory," said Liam.

They passed the footpath that led to the forest. Liam couldn't help but look up towards the trees There was no sign of the fog.

"Look at this place," said Liam as they reached the magnificent rectory gates.

"Wow, maybe you should have been a vicar," said Jo.

"Hmm, too late for me."

The children were a few paces behind and also looking at the house.

The boundary wall of Deakin's house came into view. Farrah walked up to Jo and grabbed her hand, pulling her arm.

"Mom, can we go back? I don't like it here; Lily says there are some bad people."

"We won't stay long, Poppet. Tell Lily we will be careful."

Farrah was less than happy and stamped her foot in frustration. "Mo-om."

"Come on, Poppet, you like barbeques."

"Come and hold my hand, Far. You'll love the house; you won't have seen anything like it," said Liam, trying to placate his daughter.

Liam took Farrah's hand as they reached the front gate.

The pedestrian entrance was open and there was a man with a weather-beaten face, wearing overalls, stood beside it, monitoring people coming in. Liam didn't recognise him but he looked like a gardener judging by his grass-stained boots. He could see several other guests walking up the drive ahead of them.

The rhythmic sound of a bass guitar, and the thump, thump, thump, of a bass drum, could be heard in the distance.

The gardener eyed up the family with suspicion as they went through the entrance. Liam noticed the look and sought to reassure him.

"April said it would be ok," said Liam.

"Right, m'dear," said the man and smiled warmly. "You go on and make yer ways up to the 'ouse; Mr Deakin will be there to greet yer."

The family walked through. "Wow, how cool is that?" said Zack, looking up at the house in front of them. There was a catering van and two other vehicles outside the front of the house. The Porsche was obviously locked away.

"Now that *is* impressive," said Jo.

"Can we go, Mom? Lily says there are bad people here."

"Tell her not to worry, Poppet; we're quite safe." Jo looked at Liam and frowned.

"Come on, let's see the house; it's amazing," said Liam, taking Farrah's hand.

The family reached the entrance area and Deakin was there greeting guests. Around thirty people were milling around the front of the house. An elderly couple were swimming up and down the pool.

"Oh, I see what you mean; this is amazing," said Jo. "I never thought about bringing swimming stuff."

Deakin saw the family approach. "Ah, Liam, isn't it? And this must be your family." He held out his hand in greeting.

He looked as though he had come off a yacht, complete with deck shoes.

"Hello, Christopher, and can I just say thank you for the invitation, or at least April's invitation."

"You're very welcome. I'm glad you could come. It will give us chance to get to know each other better. April's not here yet, I expect she's still in shock."

"Shock...? Oh, yes, Ashley."

"Yes, poor Ashley. April phoned to tell me she had died. They were good friends."

"Yes, I was with April when we found her."

"Oh, I'm sorry, I didn't know. Ashley was such a lovely girl. I was very upset when April told me. I guess she couldn't get over losing those beautiful girls, so sad, so sad. Anyway, enough melancholy, did you bring your swimming costumes?"

"Oh no, we didn't; we never thought," said Jo.

"That's a pity, another time maybe. If you want to make your way around the back, there's some music and food."

Deakin moved to some more guests, allowing the family to have a look around.

As they reached the back of the house, the music became louder, the smell of onions permeated the air.

Liam spotted a friendly face. "Hello Jack, how are you? How's your head?"

"Ah, wasson, m'dear, much better thank you." His forehead still bore the scars of his accident.

"This is my wife, I don't think you've met her, Prudence"

"Hello m'dears; it's Pru. No-one calls me Prudence except our Jack when he's cross about something. He were telling us all about the do on the boat. Thank you for getting him back safe."

"My pleasure; I'm just glad he's ok." Liam made the introductions.

"Have you been to many of these do's?" asked Jo.

"Oh yes, we always come, don't we Jack?"

"Aye," said Jack who was distracted by something.

Liam noticed him staring in the direction of the forest. The scar in the escarpment where the tree had come down was clearly visible as were the branches of the stricken beech above the boundary wall.

"Are you ok, Jack," said Liam.

"What? Oh yes, seems the spirits are restless."

"Probably the music; it's loud enough to wake the dead," replied Liam.

This was clearly no laughing matter and Jack frowned his disapproval.

"Sorry, Jack, I meant no offence," said Liam, noticing Jack's annoyance.

Jack made no reply. He turned with his wife and walked away towards another group of villagers.

Liam fiddled in his pocket and could feel the listening device. He looked at Jo. "Do you want to get some food? I'm just going to find the toilet."

"Yes, ok, come on kids, let's get a burger," said Jo, leading Farrah and Zack towards the buffet.

The rear of the house was as impressive as the entrance, with a large patio in front of the extensive lawn. A net had been erected in the middle of it and two people were playing badminton.

A four-piece band had set up stage in front of the French windows and were doing their best to entertain the guests with some easy listening songs.

Jo and the children walked past the group and made their way to the side boundary wall where the food was being served by three people in catering company uniforms. A commercial barbeque was sizzling with various items cooking. There was a smaller table next to the barbeque where a girl in a tee shirt with a similar logo was dispensing drinks.

Liam walked back to the front door; he could see Deakin still greeting guests. He was in a dilemma; he could ask the host for permission to use the facilities or take a chance. He decided on the latter.

Checking that Deakin was still occupied with a small group of guests, he quickly snook inside the open front door. Even with his cover story of needing the toilet, he was starting to feel anxious.

He walked through the lobby area and reached the spacious lounge. It made sense to plant it in this room somewhere as it would be the likely location for any entertaining.

Liam remembered it from his last visit and scanned the room for suitable places. He thought about dropping into one of the Chinese vases, but discounted that. Then he had an idea. There were two alcoves either side of the TV and inside each, matching ornamental table lamps with beautiful shades in the art deco style. He lifted up the nearest one. The words 'Tiffany's of London' were printed in the bottom of the metal base. There was also a small indent, large enough to house his microphone.

He activated the device as Tennant had showed him, then peeled off the plastic strip which protected the adhesive patch and stuck it to the underside of the table lamp. He quickly replaced it in its original position. Even with detection equipment, it would not be easy to spot.

He had one last check; he was happy. He exhaled in relief and headed back the way he came. He reached the front door just as April was arriving. She was being greeted warmly by Deakin.

"Shit, shit, shit," he said to himself.

If she saw him, she would give the game away and Deakin would be alert to his incursion.

He retraced his steps through the lounge along the corridor and past the room where he had used the internet on his last visit. The door was slightly ajar. In front of him was another door but had no idea what was beyond it. The music was louder and appeared to be coming from the other side.

Then he heard a voice coming from the lounge; it was Deakin's voice. "Nathan, are you there?"

Suddenly, he could hear movement coming from beyond the door in front of him. Liam dodged into the computer room and lay flat against the wall out of sight. He heard the other door open, and footsteps heading towards the lounge.

Liam quickly left his cover and went through into the room recently vacated by Nathan.

It was the kitchen. In keeping with the rest of the house, it was magnificent, with its own dining area, a cooking isle, and all manner of labour-saving devices,.

The French windows were open and on the opposite side of the room. The music was much louder, now. Liam could see the back of the band through the open doors. The drummer was seated on his stool in the doorway.

Luckily, interest in the music didn't appear to be a priority as most people appeared to be queueing for food. Then he heard raised voices coming from the corridor behind him.

Deakin appeared to be annoyed about something and was berating the odd-job man.

Liam rushed to the open French windows and squeezed past the drummer. The band were in the middle of a song and the man looked around in surprise. Liam put his hand up in apologies. The drummer just nodded as he continued his paradiddles.

Liam could see the family queueing for food and had been joined by April. He walked quickly down the patio steps and joined them.

"Hi, we thought you'd got lost," said Jo as he approached.

"Yes, sorry. Hello, April, how are you feeling, now?" he asked, in an attempt to avoid any further inquisition.

"Yes, feeling better, thanks. I'm glad I came; I think I needed company."

"That's good. Have you ordered yet?" asked Liam.

"We're next," said Jo,

April turned to Liam. "Does Christopher know you've been inside his house?"

"No, why? Is there a problem?"

"Hmm, he's very fussy about who goes in there. He's got all manner of security gadgets he was telling me. There are toilets over there," she pointed to some outbuildings at the side of the house.

"Oh, I didn't see them. Best not say anything; I don't want to get on the wrong side of him. I may need to borrow his internet again."

"But I thought you had a gadget," said Jo.

"Oh, yes, sorry, I forgot for a moment. Does anyone want a drink?" he said quickly.

Liam went to the free bar and returned with bottles of lager and Coke for the children.

Just then, Nathan also dodged the drummer, and came

down the patio stairs. He walked towards the catering team. He noticed the family in the queue and smiled.

It was Jo who noticed it first.

Farrah dropped her plastic cup of coke. She was as white as a sheet; her eyes started staring blankly, then rolling, round and round. They seem to disappear into her head; her eyelids fluttered wildly.

"Are you alright, Poppet?" said Jo. Zack looked on in horror.

Liam bent down. "What's the matter, Far?"

She started shaking uncontrollably, more a convulsion. She spoke in an unrecognisable voice.

"Go away, go away, don't hurt me again."

It was deep resonant voice, like the one they had heard before. April was watching with concern. She placed her hands on Farrah one on each shoulder.

"Let it go Lily, let it go, you're safe now. No-one can hurt you again."

Farrah fainted.

Liam caught her before she hit the grass.

"Quick, somebody get some water!" shouted April.

Jo went to the drink table and returned with a small bottle of still water.

"Tip her head forward," said April, who was now talking to Farrah and rubbing her brow.

"Here Farrah, have a drink."

Liam was holding her and Farrah seemed to come round. She sipped on the bottle of water.

She opened her eyes. Other villagers had come to see what the problem was.

"Is she alright?" asked Mrs Trevelyan, the owner of the village store.

"Yes, just fainted, probably the heat," said Jo.

"Can we go, Mom, Lily's frightened?" said Farrah in a sleepy voice.

"Yes, of course, Poppet."

"I'll come with you, Jo, if that's alright; Farrah's just suffered a major trauma and we need to keep an eye on her."

"Thanks, April, if you wouldn't mind," said Jo.

Chapter Fifteen

Liam was carrying Farrah over his shoulder, as the family and April walked around to the front of the house. There were still a couple of guests arriving, including the vicar who Liam acknowledged. Deakin was back on meet-and-greet duty.

"Is everything alright?" he said with some concern, as Liam approached.

"Yes, I think so, my daughter's just been taken ill. We need to get her back."

"Oh, I'm so sorry to hear, of course. If you need to use a phone or anything, please just say. I do have a doctor I can call if necessary."

"That's very kind, thanks, I appreciate that. I'll see how she goes."

Deakin noticed April. "*You're* not leaving are you?"

"Yes, I'm sorry Christopher, I want to keep an eye on her."

"Yes, well, let me know if I can be of any help."

"Thanks," said Liam and the group headed down the drive.

The group walked back to the cottage with Farrah holding Liam's neck, her head on his shoulder. She seemed asleep.

"Mom, what's wrong with Far?" said Zack, looking concerned.

"She's ok, it's probably the heat."

"But why was she speaking in that freaky voice?"

"We don't know, Zack."

"It's nothing to worry about, Zack," intervened April. "She'll be right as rain in no time."

Zack respected the opinion of someone outside the family and let it drop, but he did have another issue he needed to raise.

"Mom, I'm really bored here; can we go home? I miss my friends."

Liam heard the comment. "Well, I'll tell you what, Zack, I've managed to get a wi-fi connection. Why don't you get your phone and link it to the laptop. You should be able to message them?"

"Really!? Wow, that's cool, yeah."

Liam looked across at Jo and raised his eyebrows.

They reached the cottage and Jo led the family inside; Liam was still carrying Farrah.

"Urghhh, it stinks in here," said Zack, as they entered the lounge.

"Hmm, yes, it's that awful smell again," said Jo. "I'll open a few windows." She looked at April. "Sorry about that."

"It's ok. I know that smell." April stood for a moment and closed her eyes.

"There are spirits here. I can feel them, so strong."

Jo looked at Liam, then April. "What should we do?"

April opened her eyes. "Nothing, they are benevolent spirits; they won't harm you in any way. I detected a young girl;. she seems very anxious."

"Lily?" said Jo.

"Possibly."

"Dad, can I get on the internet? You said I could," pleaded Zack.

Jo looked at Liam and smiled.

"Yes, just give me a few minutes to sort out your sister."

Zack turned to Jo. "Mom, I'm hungry; when are we eating?"

"One moment, Zack." She turned to her husband. "Why

don't you take Far to bed, Liam. I think a lie down will do her good. I'll find us something to eat," said Jo.

"Yes, ok." Liam turned and headed for the stairs. "Come on Far, you can rest for a few minutes. It will make you feel better."

Farrah didn't reply but tightened her grip around Liam's neck.

"I'll give you a hand, Jo, in a minute. I just need to speak with Farrah," said April.

Zack followed his mother to the kitchen. "Are there any crisps? I'm starving."

Liam carried Farrah to her bedroom; she was still very drowsy. April followed.

April folded back the bedclothes. Liam lay Farrah down, covered her with a blanket, and placed her soft toy next to her.

"Can I speak to her?" asked April.

"Yes, of course, but I think she's asleep."

"Lily, are you there?"

Suddenly, Farrah's eyes opened wide, her face seemed to change shape. Her eyes rolled again as they had at the barbeque. She started to convulse again.

"We need to stop this," said Liam.

"No, don't worry, Farrah's in no danger. Lily's trying to communicate through her."

"Lily, don't worry, my darling, no one can hurt you. You remember me, don't you? It's April."

The voice was low and throaty. "I want my daddy. The man hurt me."

"What man, Lily? Who hurt you?" asked April.

"The man."

"But which man?"

"I've... seen... him," said the voice.

"Lily, please listen to me. No one can hurt you now. You're safe and in a better place."

"Why can't I find my daddy?"

"I think he's moved on, Lily. You need to move on too. You will soon find peace. I promise you, no one can hurt you."

"I saw him. He wants to hurt me again, and my daddy, and my mummy."

"No, darling, he can't. You must move on. You must find peace."

"But he is still there."

"Who is it, Lily? Can you tell me?"

"I need to find my daddy; he knows."

Farrah uttered a deep sigh, then opened her eyes.

"Can I have a drink of water, Dad. I'm so thirsty?"

"Yes, of course, just a minute."

Liam went downstairs. April was sat on the bed stroking Farrah's brow.

"Has Lily gone?" asked April.

"Yes. she's looking for her daddy; she's frightened."

"I know, Farrah, but it's good she has you as a friend. Tell her she mustn't worry."

"Yes, she's nice."

A few minutes later, Liam returned with a glass of water which Farrah drank down in one go.

"Can I get up now? I'm hungry."

Liam looked at April and smiled.

"Yes of course, if you're sure you're ok."

"Yes, I'm ok."

The three went downstairs; Farrah seemed much more

alert and none-the-worse for her experience.

Jo came in from the kitchen. "Hello, Poppet, how are you?"

She saw Zack eating his packet of crisps. "I'm ok. Can I have some crisps, I'm hungry?"

"Yes, help yourself, in the pantry."

"Dad, can I use the Internet, now? You promised," said Zack.

"Yes, just hold on a second."

The laptop was on the table and Liam opened it up. He placed the Wi-Fi dongle in one of the USB ports and fired it up.

"There, check now," said Liam.

Zack opened his phone and fiddled frantically with his thumbs. "Hey, Dad, that's great, thanks."

"That will be the last we see of him for a while," observed Jo.

Liam opened his emails; he had a message to send. *'To Andy Tennant, Thames House. Package delivered'*.

"What can I do to help?" said April.

"Well, if Liam can get some vegetables, I've got a couple of pies that need eating. There should be enough to go round."

Liam seemed hesitant.

"The trug's in the pantry," said Jo.

Liam tugged the back door and left the kitchen holding the wicker container. A swallow flew to the nest in the eaves and he stopped for a moment to watch.

His anxiety returned as he crossed the vegetable patch looking for more potatoes. It was still broad daylight and humid. He found the fork and dug up a couple of roots; he was beginning to perspire. Then he became aware of a presence. The temperature changed; Liam knew the signs.

He looked towards the graveyard and in the distance he could see the fog rolling among the trees.

Then something else. A large black crow flew down from the roof of the cottage and perched on the drystone wall. It ruffled its feathers for a moment, then stared at Liam and gave a loud 'caw'.

He quickly placed the potatoes in the trug, dug up a cabbage, and headed back to the kitchen without a backward glance.

"Are you ok?" said Jo as Liam walked through the door. "You're sweating."

"Yes, it's very humid. We could be in for a storm."

He placed the produce on the floor. "I'll just go and freshen up."

Later that evening, around eight o'clock, the children had gone to their bedrooms. Liam, Jo, and April were in the lounge drinking red wine. April was seated one side of the settee, Jo, the other. Liam was in the armchair.

"April, I know you know about spirits and things, but I have to say, I'm really worried. We can't continue to subject Far to these episodes, however benign they might be. We have no idea what it's doing to her mental health," said Jo.

"Yes, I quite understand," said April. "Are you thinking about leaving?"

"Well, frankly, yes, it's been one thing after another since we got here."

Liam was listening; he had unfinished business, despite his concern for his daughter.

"She doesn't seem to be bothered by it, Jo. Let's give it a couple more days, see how it goes."

Jo was less than happy. "But you said that a couple of days ago. Give it till the weekend, you said. Well, here we are, and things keep happening."

"Look, I've no intention of influencing you one way or the other; it has to be your decision, but from what I've seen, this phenomenon will not affect Farrah long term. She is sensitive to sprits, that's all, and because of the activity here, they've been using her as a conduit. It's not uncommon."

"I believe you, April, but we are unnecessarily exposing Far to something that is beyond my understanding, and it frightens me... and what about that cliff fall? That was no benign spirit."

"That was just coincidence," said Liam. "Come on, let's give it a couple more days. I know, let's go to the Eden Project; get away from here for a day. We've not really explored anywhere yet."

"And whose fault's that? You've been obsessed with this investigation. We came here to switch off, remember."

"Yes, you're right, but that's finished now. We can do something tomorrow."

Jo took a swig of her drink, clearly still far from happy.

"You'll enjoy the Eden Project, Jo, it's so interesting. There's so much to see and I think the kids will find it educational as well as fun," said April.

"Well, at least it will get us out of the house for a while," said Jo.

Liam looked at April. "Actually, there is something I wanted to mention. Something that's been bothering me since the barbeque."

"Go on," replied April.

"I was trying to work out what it was that caused this evening's episode with Far and Lily. Something must have triggered it. You know, I think it was that odd job man. It started when he came down the patio steps. I remember him looking in our direction. That's when Far had her turn."

"Hmm, now you come you mention it, I think you're right," said April.

"So, what are you saying?" asked Jo.

"Well, what if it was him that killed the family?"

"Ha, I can just see that at the Old Bailey," said Jo sarcastically. "Calling our next witness... Oh, by the way, she's a ghost!"

"No, I think Liam's right," said April. "Although, I don't know how you're going to prove it."

"But it's in the police hands now. Why don't you just tell them?" said Jo.

"It would certainly make legal history, victim rises from the dead to identify her killer. I don't think the Crown Prosecution Service is going to buy that," said Liam.

Back at the Squire's house, the band had packed their gear and left, and the catering crew were taking boxes of left-over food and drink back to their van. The barbeque belonged to Deakin and would stay for future use.

Deakin was in the front saying goodbye to the last of his guests. He felt a vibration in his pocket.

"Excuse me a moment," he said to the departing visitor and took out a mobile phone from his pocket. It was a cheap Nokia, a 'burner phone', completely anonymous and untraceable. He walked to the side of the house and took the call.

"Oh, hello Aaron, how are you?"

"Fine thanks, what about you?" said the familiar voice.

"Oh, you know. just been entertaining the locals to a barbeque."

"Oh ok, I won't keep you. Are you free tomorrow? I've got some more business for you and I'd prefer not to discuss it over the video in light of recent events."

"Yeah, I can understand. It was disappointing to hear the verdict. I was certain your Marty would walk."

"Well, there's always the appeal."

"Yeah, fingers crossed, eh? As it happens, I am free tomorrow. What time?"

"There's a train gets into St Austell around six-thirty tomorrow night."

"No problem. I can pick you up at the station. I assume you'd like a bed for the night."

"Yes, if you don't mind. I can get a hotel, if its inconvenient."

"No it's fine; I'll see you tomorrow."

He dropped the call and went to find Nathan and spotted him sweeping the patio with a besom.

"Ah, there you are. Can you prepare one of the guest bedrooms for tomorrow? We have a visitor."

"Yes, sir, who is it?"

"Aaron... Rainsford, says he's got some more business."

"It's a long way to come; you usually video call him." replied Nathan.

"Hmm, yes, it's security. Since Marty's trial, he's being especially vigilant. At least the court case doesn't appear to have affected the enterprise."

In Thames House, Andy Tennant was reacting to Liam's email, providing details to Nan Murcty. She headed a small team engaged in monitoring listening devices; Tennant was providing her with background information. All conversations would be automatically digitally recorded, with key words used to trigger listening activity.

She activated the device and checked the signal. There were rustlings and the sound of muffled footsteps, someone pacing on carpet.

"Coming through loud and clear. Would you like to listen?" said Nan.

She passed him a set of earphones.

"Thank you, Liam," said Tennant, to no one in particular.

His ears pricked up as someone entered the room.

"What time will Mr Rainsford be here tomorrow, sir?" said the new arrival.

"He'll be on the two o'clock from Paddington, gets into St Austell at six-thirty. I'll meet him at the station."

Tennant was scribbling down the names and details.

"Thanks, Nan, let me know if there's anything else significant; I need to speak to the A.D.G."

He reached the office of the Assistant Director General.

Barry Howard-Young was at his desk; Tennant knocked on the open door.

"Barry, I've got an update on Operation Blaggard."

"Go on."

"The listening device I left with Liam Drake has been activated."

"That's excellent."

"Yes, we were able to eavesdrop a conversation, and it seems Christopher Deakin is entertaining tomorrow."

"Really? Anyone of interest?"

"Oh yes, definitely. The name Rainsford was mentioned. He'll be on the two o'clock from Paddington, arriving in St Austell at six-thirty."

"Rainsford?"

"Yes, this is new. We had no idea Deakin was involved with the Rainsford syndicate. I think it's Aaron Rainsford, Marty's cousin."

"Cousin?"

"Yes, with Marty in prison, we think he's taken charge. He was never arrested as part of Rainsford enquiry."

"So, you think there's a link between Operation Blaggard and the Rainsford syndicate?"

"It looks like it. My guess is Deakin's laundering for the Rainsfords."

"Bitcoin you mean?"

"Crypto-currencies of some sort, almost certainly. We've been monitoring his internet traffic and he's regularly on crypto investment websites."

"Hmm, you better keep the local police in the loop; I don't want to be falling out with them."

"Yes, I'll get on to them. I think we need to have a surveillance team in place. I'll get it set it up."

The following morning, the sound of the church bell echoed around the village. It was a bright, sunny day, not a cloud in the sky.

"Urgh, what time is it?" asked Jo, rubbing her eyes.

Liam looked at the alarm clock on the adjacent bedside cabinet. "Eight-O-five"

"There must be a law against that noise at this time of day."

"It probably wouldn't apply here. They're a law unto themselves," said Liam.

"Ha, yes, you're right there. Do you want a cup of tea?"

"Yes, please."

Jo got out of bed and put on her dressing gown just as Farrah came into the bedroom.

"Mom, what are we doing today?"

"Your Dad's suggested we visit the Eden Project; it's not far."

"What is it?"

Liam intervened. "There's all kinds of things there. When I open my laptop, I'll show you; there's lots to do."

"But I want to stay here with Lily; she's lonely."

"I'm sure she won't mind; it's only for the day. We'll be back this afternoon."

"But we're not going home yet?"

Liam looked at Jo.

"No, Far, we need to have our holiday," said Liam.

Jo raised her eyes. "I'm going to make the tea. Do you want a cup, Poppet?"

"Yes please. I wish I could give Lily a drink; she must be very thirsty."

"I'm sure she manages, Poppet. Go back to bed, I'll bring you a cup."

Suddenly, there was a silence. "Oh, thank goodness for that," said Jo, hearing the bells stop.

Liam and Jo were in the kitchen preparing breakfast.

"You were very restless last night, " said Liam.

"Hmm, yes, I kept thinking about Far. I still think we should head back. I don't think she should be exposed to what's going on." She looked down. "Of course there is an alternative solution. We could find another place in Cornwall; there must be loads of vacancies. I know, you could search on your laptop now you've got it working."

Liam was in a dilemma. He was also concerned about Farrah but was keen to help the Deakin investigation.

"Yes, I understand but we're not going to get in anywhere now, are we? Everywhere's going to be booked up."

"But you don't know that. What about that Last Minute website? It's worth having a look, surely; there are always cancellations."

Just then, Farrah came into the kitchen, having heard the conversation. "I don't want to go anywhere else. I want to stay here. I like it here."

"It's alright, Far, your Mom was just concerned about everything that's been going on."

"It seems I'm outvoted," said Jo, still not happy with the situation.

"Let's just see how it goes over the next couple of days, yeah? I think we'll enjoy seeing the Eden Project."

"Hmm, well, at least we'll be away from this place," said Jo, and took her frustration out on a plate in the washing up bowl.

By ten o'clock, the family were heading up the hill out of the village for their excursion to the visitor attraction. Zack and Farrah had been convinced by Liam that they would enjoy the experience but there was not a great deal of enthusiasm.

As they approached the end of the cottages, there was a furniture van outside Mrs Wilkin's cottage with two removal men carrying furniture. There was a 'For Sale' sign outside.

"Goodness," said Jo. "That didn't take long. I find it so sad that's all there is to mark a whole lifetime."

The atmosphere was distinctly downbeat as they made their way into the trees to the main road. Liam was feeling anxious as they passed the place where the van driver was killed.

Visibility was good. He could see the main road in the distance at the end of the canopy, about three hundred yards away. Cars were passing by at regular intervals. Liam exhaled.

Then something distracted him; a shape was it? He couldn't make it out, just a shadow; then it disappeared behind a large sycamore tree about fifty yards in front of them.

The verge on that side was raised, about four feet from

the road and the roots of the tree exposed to the elements. It was very old with lichen and moss covering the trunk. Without warning it seemed to move; first a shake, and then it toppled and crashed to the ground.

"Watch out, Liam!" shouted Jo.

Liam hit the brakes. Everyone lurched forward, activating the seat-belt mechanism. They came to a halt with the front of the Volvo, inches away from the trunk of the giant tree. Whether it would have crushed the car was difficult to say, but it was certainly big enough to cause serious damage. It stretched right across the road.

"Is everyone ok?" asked Liam.

He checked in the back; Farrah was crying.

Zack was looking anxiously at the blockage. "We can't get by that, Dad. What are we going to do?"

"I'll call the emergency services. We need to warn others."

Liam got out of the car to examine the situation then took his phone out of his pocket. There was a 'one bar' signal. He punched in the three nines. "Fire brigade please."

He went back to the Volvo and got in.

Jo looked anxious. "How long are we going to be stuck here?"

"Hmm, your guess is as good as mine. I called the fire brigade; I assume they'll send someone. I told them there was a tree down."

Jo was looking through the trees. "Well, I can't see much point in sticking around; we might as well go back to the cottage."

"I think we should wait for the fire brigade. We can warn other drivers."

"What other drivers? No-one comes down here."

"Of course they do, the Post Office, delivery vans, there're lots."

"Well, they can hardly miss it can they?"

"I want to go back," sobbed Farrah. "Lily says they are angry."

"Who's angry, Poppet?" said Jo.

"She didn't say," replied Farrah.

Liam looked around; there was no sign of the fog, but the reality was, he had no desire to be stuck in the forest.

He reversed the car away from the tree and did a three-point turn.

"Why did that tree come down?" asked Jo, as they reached the end of the forest. "I mean, there's no wind. I can't understand why it would just come down like that."

"Who knows? It looked very old; I guess it was the vibration from the traffic," said Liam.

"What traffic?" retorted Jo.

"Well, over the years it must have become unstable. We were probably the last straw."

It wasn't very convincing but the only logical explanation Liam could come up with.

Farrah had stopped crying and suddenly called out from the back seat.

"Lily says we mustn't leave."

"But we weren't leaving, Far. Just going out for the day. Why would she say that?"

"I don't know," said Farrah.

Liam accelerated away and they headed back to the village. Just before they reached the cottage, there were several people milling outside the church. The Reverend Slaughter was there chatting to them. Liam noticed April among the gathering. She waved as they went by.

The family reached the cottage and went inside. The children immediately headed to their rooms.

"So, what are we supposed to do now?" asked Jo. "We're trapped here."

"No, no, I'm sure they'll soon clear the road," countered Liam.

"Hmm, I won't be so sure about that. That tree was enormous and I can't see them getting tree surgeons out on a Sunday."

"I'm sure the council will have people on call for emergencies."

"Oh, that's all right then. What a fucking holiday this is turning out to be," said Jo and stormed off into the kitchen.

Just then, there was a knock on the door. Liam answered.

"Oh, hi, April, come in."

April spoke as she entered the lounge. "I came to see if everything is alright; I thought you were going to the Eden Project."

"Hmm, that was the general idea, but we had a problem?"

"Oh," said April with a look of concern.

"Yes, we were going through the forest towards the main road and a tree came down right in front of us. Luckily, I was able to stop in time."

"Oh, that's terrible."

Liam checked to see if Jo was still in the kitchen.

"Actually, it was rather strange. It looked like someone, or something, actually pushed it over," he whispered.

"Really? But that's impossible; those trees are enormous, been there for hundreds of years some of them."

"Yes, I know, but I saw this strange, er, thing. Well, I say 'saw', it was more of a shadow, really. It was small, reminded me of the old pictures of hobgoblins, you know what I mean?"

"Yes, I do. But they are house spirits."

"Well, I could have imagined it, but whatever it was, it seemed to rush behind the tree and it started shaking. Then it just toppled in to the road right in front of us."

Just then Jo came out of the kitchen holding a towel and started wiping her hands.

"I thought I heard voices," said Jo.

"Yes, I hope I'm not intruding, I was concerned something might be wrong; you said you were going to the Eden Project. Liam's just told me about the tree."

"Yes, another unexplained event. They seem to be following us around. The sooner we can get out of this place the better, as far as I'm concerned."

"Oh, I hope not; it will be a shame if you have to leave," said April.

"Well, I don't know what's going to happen next. We've got our daughter talking to some dead person; there was Zack nearly getting drowned, the cliff fall, now we nearly get crushed to death by a tree, not to mention that business with the shelves in the pantry. The whole thing's bizarre. We need to leave before anything else happens to us."

"I really don't think you're in any danger; the spirits I've detected are benign."

"Yeah, so you keep saying, but I didn't come on holiday to be visited by spirits; I came to unwind. At this rate I'm going to need counselling when I get back."

"Well, we can't do anything today with the road blocked," said Liam.

"I might as well do the washing, then," said Jo, sarcastically.

"Do you want to use mine, only the nearest launderette is in St Austell?"

Jo sat down and put her head in her hands and started to

cry.

"I don't know what to do," she sobbed.

Liam went to her and put his arm around her.

"Look don't worry, as soon as the road is clear, we'll find somewhere else. We can check on the internet, yeah?"

"Can I do anything?" said April. "How about I make us some coffee while you decide."

Just then, Farrah came downstairs.

"Hello, Poppet, is everything ok?" said Jo, who had recovered her composure.

"Lily is upset, she said she thought we were going to leave."

"Well, we can't stay here for ever, Poppet."

"No, I told her, but she says we need to stay as it's not finished."

Liam looked at Jo.

"What's not finished Poppet?"

"I don't know; she didn't say."

"Are you speaking to her now?" asked April.

"No, she went away again. She's still looking for her daddy."

"We can't go on like this, Liam," said Jo.

"No, you're right. Let's give it till this afternoon; hopefully, the tree will be cleared by then, and we'll go. To be honest, I don't feel like a holiday anymore. I think we'll just head home. We could have the odd day out in town, visit some of the attractions we never get around to seeing."

Jo brightened up.

"Yes, that's a good idea."

"But I don't want to go," said Farrah. "I want to stay with Lily."

"I'm sorry, Poppet, but we can't stay here, not with everything that's going on; it's not safe, and I'm sure Lily will find another friend."

"What about the washing?" said April, somewhat incongruously.

"It's ok, I'll do it when we get home. I just want to get out of here."

"I'm so sorry you've been exposed to everything. I've no idea why you should've been targeted by spirits. It really is a nice village."

April left the cottage while the family started packing their things and within an hour their suitcases and provisions were piled in the back of the Volvo.

The family were in the car. Farrah was deeply upset and sobbing loudly.

"I don't want to go; I don't want to go. I want to stay here with Lily; she needs me," she cried bitterly. Jo was trying to placate her but without success.

"I'll just go and do a final check, make sure we've not left anything," said Liam.

He returned to the cottage and went into the lounge, opening drawers; through to the kitchen, pantry, then up the stairs. He checked Zack's bedroom, then the master suite, and, lastly, he walked into Farrah's bedroom. Despite it being a warm day, the room was remarkably cool, goosebump cool. He opened the wardrobe, then, without warning, the bedroom door slammed shut.

"What the...?"

He grabbed the handle and pulled. It was stuck. He pulled harder. There was a click. The door flew open, the momentum sending Liam backwards at speed. His head hit the brass bedstead with some considerable force.

He fell to the floor.

Outside in the car, Jo was getting impatient at the delay.

Farrah was still remonstrating and the temperature was climbing without the air-conditioning functioning.

Suddenly, Farrah stopped sobbing and stared blankly. "Lily says there's something wrong."

Jo was in the passenger seat and turned around, "What's wrong, Poppet?"

"Lily says there's something wrong."

Jo got out of the car and walked up to the front door of the cottage. The front door had been replaced with a five-lever mortice deadlock. It was shut; Liam had the keys.

Jo walked around the side of the cottage to the kitchen and tried the door; that was also locked.

She banged on the door with her fist. "Liam, are you alright? I can't get in."

Jo returned to the front of the cottage and looked up at the windows; they were all closed. She didn't know what to do. She banged on the front door again and listened. There was no movement. Jo was getting anxious.

Think, think. April would have a spare set; it would mean a walk. Liam had taken the car keys.

"Where's Dad?" said Zack.

"I don't know, the doors are locked and he's not answering," replied Jo.

"Lily says something's wrong," said Farrah.

"Yes, Poppet, I need to go round to April's and get a key. Will you be ok here for a few minutes?"

"It's hot in here," said Zack.

"Yes, yes, I know. Ok, well, you can get out of the car, but don't wander off."

Jo started running down the cul-de-sac, then turned left at the telephone kiosk and down the hill. It was over seven minutes, but seemed longer, by the time she reached the nip and April's cottage.

She walked up to the front door, panting, and knocked frantically. She put her hands on her knees; she was sweating profusely.

"April, are you there?" she shouted.

Moments later the door opened.

"Jo…? What on earth's the matter? Is everything alright?"

"I don't know but something's wrong. Liam went back inside the cottage to check whether we had left anything and hasn't come out, about twenty minutes ago. Apparently, Lily said something's wrong. The door's locked and I can't get in."

"Oh, goodness. Just hang on a minute; I'll get my spare keys."

April returned moments later and locked the door. "Come on, we can take the car; it'll be quicker."

They walked up the nip to the parking space and got into the Kia; it was stiflingly hot.

A few minutes later, they were outside the cottage and April parked next to the Volvo. Zack and Farrah were leant against the car.

Jo got out of the Kia and walked up to them. "Any sign of your Dad?"

"No," replied Zack. "Far keeps talking to Lily... I want to go home."

"Yes, ok, let's just see what's happened to your dad."

April walked up to the front door of the cottage and opened it.

"Urghhh," said Jo. "That smell's back again."

April stopped for a moment. "Yes, the spirits have been here."

They checked the downstairs calling out but there was no sign of Liam.

"I'll check upstairs," said Jo.

"I'm coming with you," said April.

They checked Zack's, then the main bedroom. Farrah's door was closed. Jo turned the handle.

"It won't open," said Jo, looking at April with an expression of concern.

"Let me try," said April.

She held the handle and said something that Jo couldn't make out. The handle gave way.

"Liam, Liam! Are you ok," said Jo, seeing him lay on the floor next to the bed. There was blood coming from the back of his head.

"It looks as though someone's hit him," said Jo.

"Let me have a look," said April.

Liam started to come round and began moaning incoherently.

"Liam, are you ok?" said April.

He opened his eyes. "Eh, oooh, my head. Yes, I think so," he whimpered.

He was trying to sit up.

"Just lay still for a moment; let me check you over," said April.

"What happened?" asked Jo.

Chapter Sixteen

"I don't really remember... Oooh." He tried to get up again. "I fell backwards. I must have hit my head."

April checked his eyes, then slowly helped Liam into a sitting position so she could examine the back of his head.

"Yes, you've given your head quite a crack. You should be going to hospital; you could have concussion." She looked closely at the wound. "We need to stop this bleeding, Jo. Can you get a flannel or something and some hot water?"

Jo went into the kitchen and boiled the kettle, then went outside to the car.

Jack and Farrah were in the back with their seat belts fastened.

"Ok, guys, you better go back inside; your dad's hurt his head. It doesn't look like we'll be leaving today."

"Oh Mom," said Zack. "I want to go home."

Farrah had already undone her seat belt.

The kids exited the Volvo and went inside while Jo searched for the medical kit among the luggage in the back.

Seeing Liam wasn't in the lounge, Zack and Farrah ran upstairs and immediately wanted to know how their father was. He was leaning against Farrah's bed with April still examining his head.

"What happened, Dad?" said Zack, with some concern.

"I just slipped and banged my head, not looking what I was doing. I'll be fine."

Farrah tried to put her arms around him but April intervened. "Let your dad recover for a few minutes; he's got a nasty bang on his head."

"So, we don't have to go home?" said Farrah.

"Not for the moment, Farrah. It's best your father rests

for a while. He certainly can't drive."

"Oh, Lily will be pleased; she said we mustn't go."

Jo returned with a bowl of water and a sterile cloth.

"Thanks," said April, taking the cloth from Jo, and soaking it in water. "This might sting a bit."

April started to part Liam's hair to reach the wound.

Back at Thames House, Nan Murcty was reviewing the overnight transcripts, triggered by the different key words. Andy Tennant had arrive to check on the latest.

"Nothing of interest, Andy, but the meet with Aaron Rainsford is still on; there was a call about nine o'clock."

"Thanks, Nan, it's a good job we had ears on the inside, GCHQ are having difficulty in monitoring these calls. They're using burner phones."

"Are you going down to Cornwall again?"

"I'm not planning to. We do have a surveillance team lined up from the local force; that should be sufficient. They're going to send the photos through."

In the Deakin residence, the Squire and Nathan, were in the back garden discussing what to do about the fallen beech tree over the back wall.

"It's going to need a crane, I reckon," said the handyman. "Although how it'll get access I don't know."

"They'll have to clear the gap between here and the rectory. Actually, that's no bad thing. I was thinking the other day about what old Walter Rawlinson was saying, you remember, someone was hanging around outside the side wall. If we get it cleared it will definitely improve security, Can I leave that to you to make enquiries?"

"Sure thing. Will you need anything else for Mr

Rainsford's visit?"

"I don't think so; we're well stocked with drink."

"Yes. I had a thought; we can eat out here. I'll prepare the barbeque; there's plenty left over from Saturday."

"That's an excellent idea, Nathan. I'll leave that up to you to arrange. I'll need the car for five-thirty to be on the safe side."

"Are you taking the Porsche?"

"Yes, why not? It could do with an outing."

"I'll make sure it's ready, sir."

At Pendle Cottage, April had stemmed the bleeding to the back of Liam's head and applied a plaster. It had required cutting his hair around the crown with a pair of nail scissors.

"You're going to have a bald patch for a couple of weeks," joked Jo, showing Liam the removed hair in her hand.

"Hmm, maybe we can stick it back later; I might need it," he managed to reply.

"Can you stand up?" asked April.

Slowly, with Jo supporting him, Liam got to his feet. He felt giddy and staggered for a moment.

"We should really get him to the hospital, Jo, just to be on the safe side. If he's fractured his skull it could be dangerous."

"What about the tree?" said Jo.

"Well, we can go and check. They may have been able to clear a path," said April.

Liam was very unsteady on his feet and was hanging on to Jo's arm.

"But they can't leave the village cut off, can they?" said Jo.

"Hmm, I wouldn't be so sure. Sometimes I wonder whether the council forget we're here," said April.

"What do you suggest?" asked Jo.

"Well, I'm happy to drive Liam to the hospital," said April.

"We'll have to take the kids. I can't take leave them on their own."

"Oh, Mom," said Farrah. "I want to stay here."

"Look, let me take Liam; it's pointless all of us hanging about. It's likely to be a long wait, given it's Sunday."

Jo looked at Liam. He was still very groggy.

"Yes, ok, I'll need to unpack some of the suitcases. The kids can give me a hand."

It was gone midday before April set off in the Kia with Liam.

They drove up the hill out of the village. The removal van was still parked outside Mrs Wilkins, and as they approached, the driver got out of the cab and waved the Kia down. He approached April's window.

"You can't get through," said the man. "There's a tree down. I've just been up there. They've got a digger trying to shift it. Reckon it's going to be mid-afternoon before it's clear."

"Oh, damn, I need to get this man to hospital."

The driver looked across to Liam who appeared to be dozing. "What's he done?"

"Banged his head; he's concussed."

"Well, I don't know what to suggest. I suppose you could take him up there and get an ambulance to meet you on the other side. Although god knows how long they'll take; you know what it's like."

"No, it's ok, thanks. I'll get him back and see how we get on. I can always try later."

April turned the car around and headed back to the

cottage.

Meanwhile, Jo had lugged the suitcases back inside and was considering what to do next. Zack was complaining bitterly that he wanted to go home, while Farrah was overjoyed at being reunited with Lily. Jo was stuck in the middle. Her main concern was Liam.

The room felt cold and musty despite the summer temperatures outside. Jo started to open the suitcases and take out some bits and pieces they were going to need. She would have to go to the store and stock up with a few provision. She had binned what was left of the bread and other items that wouldn't travel.

Just then, she heard April's Kia pull up outside and went to the front door to see what was happening. Liam staggered uneasily out of the passenger side and waited while April helped him walk back to the front door.

As they approached, something distracted Liam. He looked up at the cottage and tried to focus his groggy eyes. The crow was perched on the apex of the thatch looking down at the pair. It let out a large 'caw', turned its head to one side, then flew off into the forest.

"What's happened?" asked Jo as the pair approached.

"The road's still blocked. Should be cleared later this afternoon, apparently. We were stopped by one of the removal men at Mrs Wilkins."

"So, what are we going to do?" said Jo as she led them inside. Liam immediately went to the settee and sat down.

"I don't think Liam's in any danger; his wound's stopped bleeding. I think he'll feel better after some rest."

"Yes, I think I'll go and have a lie down," said Liam.

Liam slowly tried to stand up, but fell back down again. Jo helped him to his feet.

"So, does that mean we're going to have to spend another night here?" There was an expression of concern on Jo's face.

"Well, I wouldn't advise a long journey at the moment and certainly not with Liam driving," said April.

Slowly, Jo and April helped Liam up the stairs.

"I can't believe what's happening; it's as though someone's deliberately trying to stop us from leaving," said Jo as they reached the bedroom.

"No, Jo, it's just a coincidence," said April.

Jo helped Liam take off his shoes and he climbed into bed. He had said nothing to Jo about what he had seen prior to the tree falling.

"Thanks," said Liam. "I'll try and get some sleep; I feel really tired."

They left the main bedroom and closed the door.

"I just want to check on Far," said Jo, and opened Farrah's bedroom door opposite. She was sat on the floor with her seashells scattered around her. She looked up at the intrusion.

"Just checking you're ok, Poppet," said Jo.

"Lily says she's happy we're not going home. She likes to play with my seashells."

Suddenly, the shells started to move of their own accord. Jo gasped. April was standing behind Jo and had seen what had happened.

"It's alright, Jo, nothing to be concerned about. It's well-documented that spirits can move objects. Leave them to it."

Jo's instinct was to intervene but accepted April's council. Farrah seemed to be happy.

She closed Farrah's bedroom door.

"I just had a thought," said Jo, as they reached the staircase to the lounge. "What about trees? Can spirits cause them to go down?"

"I don't know; I wouldn't think so. I've not heard of any evidence of that."

Jo was deep in thought but let it go. "What time does the store close? I'll need to get some food in; I threw out the bread that was left over for the birds."

"Come on, I'll run you down; we should just make it."

The cryptocurrency market is a twenty-four hour operation. Speculators are buying and selling all the time. Deakin was in his office on one of his computers in the middle of a deal when Nathan walked in.

"Sir, is it worth doing another security sweep before Mr Rainsford arrives?"

"I can't see the point; no-one's been in the house since the last security check."

"What about the barbeque?"

"Everyone was outside."

"Nevertheless sir, we can't be too careful; remember Walton."

"Hmm, yes, you're right. You know, I liked him, and his wife and daughter, such a polite girl. I was quite devastated when I discovered he was a spook. It was sad how things turned out."

"But you had no option, sir. It could have brought down the whole operation."

Deakin looked pensive. "Hmm, that's true. But with hindsight, we could have spared the family. Just dealt with Walton."

"Well, what's done's, done. At least we got the laptop and the recording equipment," said Nathan incongruously.

"Yes, we did. I hope it found a good home."

"I'm sure it will; the Exchange Shop is very popular."

"Very well, you can do the sweep while I'm going to collect Aaron."

"I'll see to it, sir."

Meanwhile, work on clearing the stricken sycamore was continuing on the forest road. The local council's Highways Department had engaged a firm of tree surgeons to complete the work and they were unloading the equipment they would need to complete the job. The priority was to open the road as soon as possible and a mechanical digger had been utilised to push the trunk off the carriageway. There were no footpaths on the road and the giant tree just lay forlorn in the margin; its enormous root complex at its base, the size of a man.

The tree surgeons had arrived in a lorry containing their tools of trade - goggles, boots and three impressive Stihl chain saws. The truck, emblazoned with their company name, 'Enys Rowe and Sons, Tree Surgeons', was parked on the verge.

Enys Rowe had been a tree surgeon all his working life and had a good reputation locally. His two sons, Jethro and Sam, both in their twenties, had also acquired a great deal of experience. On the face of it, this was a routine job; one they had done on numerous occasions following storms. Enys donned his hard hat and goggles and set about the task.

The tree was in full leaf and the green 'helicopter' seeds hung down in bunches. Large branches were still stretched across the road which was preventing vehicles from passing. Fortunately, there was only a delivery van and a private car waiting patiently for the clearance to be completed.

The team had assessed the situation and it was Enys, himself, that fired up the first chainsaw with an almighty roar that echoed through the forest.

He moved to the trunk and started on the first branch. Being close to the base of the tree, it was also the thickest and as he cut away, sap started to ooze from the incision.

Enys stopped for a moment and examined his handiwork. "Well, I'll be blowed, Jethro; have a look at that."

"It's red. I've not seen nothing like that before," said Jethro. "Hey, Sam, have a look at this."

His brother joined him. "It's bleedin', looks like," said Sam.

"I'll telly what, must be summat in the soil," said Enys. "Right, best get on, folks need to get past."

The three continued to work on the large bough with the two sons taking off the smaller branches. After a few minutes, they managed to clear it from the road and move it the other side of the trunk.

"When're they collecting the tree and taking it to the sawmill?" asked Jethro.

"Tomorrow, Johnson's haulage are doing it. They're gonna need a crane up 'ere to shift this lot, I reckon," said Enys.

Jethro was distracted by movement in the forest.

"What's that?" said Jethro.

"What's what?" said Enys.

"Look... there... It looks like fog." Jethro pointed into the forest.

"Aye, so it is, 'ow strange. It were bright sunshine when we got 'ere."

"It's coming this way, look see. Hey Sam, have you seen this?"

Sam was starting on the next branch and looked up; his chainsaw was in his hand. He peered over the trunk. "What's that? It looks like a shape or summat."

Without warning, an unseen force appeared to wrench the chainsaw from his hands. The motor immediately cut out but not before the blade had hit his thigh. He screamed in pain as it ripped into his jeans.

Enys and Jethro immediately ran to him. Blood oozed from the top of Sam's leg.

"We need to get him to 'ospital, right away," said Enys.

Enys took off his belt and wrapped it around Sam's thigh above the wound.

"That should help stop the bleeding."

There was movement in the car that was waiting the other side of the 'road closed' sign. The driver got out and walked quickly to the men.

"Are you ok?" he called as he got closer.

Enys rushed up to him. "No, it's my lad; he's cut his leg; it looks bad. We need to get him to the 'ospital quick."

"Aye, I saw what 'appened. I couldn't believe it; looked like the saw jumped onto his leg. Not seen anythin' like it afore." The driver looked at the stricken tree surgeon. Sam had gone into shock and his face was now white. "Right, I can run you there; it'll be quicker than your truck."

"Aye, that it will, thank you."

Enys and Jethro carried Sam under each shoulder to the car and helped him into the back seat. The driver went and grabbed a blanket from the boot.

"Here, wrap this 'round him," said the driver.

Blood was dripping down Sam's leg into the footwell.

"Jethro, you stay here and finish clearing the road. Then come over the 'ospital."

Enys got in next to Sam and the car pulled away.

Jethro watched as the car turned and headed back up to the main road and turn right.

The van, seeing the main branch had been cleared,

started moving forward, avoiding the 'Road Closed' sign. The driver wound down the window.

"Can I get through? I've got a delivery in the village."

Jethro waved him by, and the van bounced up the verge on the opposite side of the road and over some end branches before returning to the carriageway. The driver looked into the forest to his right. Beams of sunshine were gleaming through the canopy.

Meanwhile, April and Jo had arrived at the store; it was just five minutes before it was due to close.

The elderly proprietor looked up as the clang of the bell alerted her to a customer. "Wasson, Mrs Thornton."

"Hello, Mrs Trevelyan, sorry to call late, we need a few bits and pieces. The road's closed so we can't get out."

"Aye, I heard as such. Summat to do with a tree down."

"Yes, the road's blocked."

"Well, I'm blowed. That'll be why my delivery's not turned up. Been expecting 'im since ten a smornin'"

"Yes, that'll be it."

"Not know trees go down afore. Mind you, there's been some strange goings on of late." The old woman leaned forward. "Since them visitors arrived, I reckon," she whispered, and nodded towards Jo who was on the other side of the store and hadn't heard the remark.

"No, no, just coincidence," said April.

"Aye? Not what folk round 'ere 'ave bin sayin'."

"It's just tittle-tattle, Mrs Trevelyan; people should know better."

"Aye, if you say so."

Jo went to the counter and handed over a box of cereals, six eggs, and two tins of beef stew. "Can I have a loaf of bread and four pints of milk too, please."

"Aye, just one moment."

The proprietor disappeared into the back and returned after a couple of minutes with the said items.

"Anything else?" asked the woman.

"No that's all, thanks. I only have a card, is that ok?" asked Jo.

Mrs Trevelyan look disapprovingly at the piece of plastic and shuffled into the back room again.

"Why everyone 'as to use these cards I'll never know. What's wrong with cash like us always 'ad?" she exclaimed and put the card machine on the counter.

"Sorry, I've not had chance to get to a cash machine," said Jo.

"I've got some change if you prefer," said April.

"It's alright; it'll save me cashing up again," said the woman. "Put your card in and press your numbers." Jo complied.

She gave Jo the paper receipt and placed the shopping in a paper carrier bag.

"So, 'ow long're you expecting to stay 'ere?" asked Mrs Trevelyan as she handed over the bag.

"Not sure yet, my husband's had an accident and can't travel at the moment."

"Accident? Sorry to 'ear that. Mind you, you 'ear all sorts, don't you. I told you the place was cursed, din I?"

"Yes, you did," replied Jo.

"That's nonsense, Mrs. Trevelyan, with respect; you shouldn't be saying things like that. There's nothing wrong with the cottage."

"Aye, if you says so, Mrs Thornton; if you say so. Was there anything else cos I need to close up?"

"No thank you," said Jo and the pair left the shop.

There was a click of a lock turning as soon as the door

was closed. The sign quickly change from 'open' to 'closed'. Jo looked at April who shrugged her shoulders.

April had parked on the pavement on the opposite side of the road and as they walked towards it, Jo had a question.

"What do you think about places being cursed? Is there any truth in it?"

"Goodness, no, not at all, old wives' tales. The villagers here are terribly superstitious; they blame everything on evil spirits and the like. It's part of the DNA of the place. There are one or two who haven't moved out of the eighteenth century, never mind the twentieth. It is a bit quaint and endearing, really; they don't mean any harm, just making up answers to things they can't understand."

"Hmm," said Jo, still deep in thought as they got into the car.

"What about this Lily thing?" said Jo, as she buckled up her seat belt.

"Well, that's different; that's not a curse." April looked across at Jo.

April started up the car. "Look there's a van," said Jo, as a vehicle came around the corner and headed towards them. "They must have opened the road."

"Hmm, he'll be lucky. The shop's closed; I doubt Mrs Trevelyan will open up for him."

Five minutes later they were back at the cottage. Jo deposited the provisions in the kitchen and then went to check on Liam.

"How is he?" asked April, as Jo returned to the lounge.

"He's sleeping; I didn't disturb him. Would you like a spot of lunch? I don't know about you but I'm feeling a bit peckish."

"Yes, thanks, I would like to check Liam again before I leave."

"Well, I'm so grateful, I don't know what we'd have done."

Just then Zack came into the lounge. "Mom, I'm starving, when're we having lunch?"

Later, around five-thirty, Deakin was ready to collect Aaron Rainsford from the station. Outside, the Porsche was waiting for him. Nathan was there to see him off.

"I'll have a final check round while you're gone, sir; just to make sure we're secure."

"Yes, ok. Let's hope that GWR are on time for once. Hopefully, be back within the hour."

The throaty-sounds of the Porsche's engine echoed around the forest as Deakin headed out of the village towards the main road. The way had been cleared of branches, although twigs and pieces of wood were still strewn across the road from the clearing operation. On the left-hand side, the tree was lay on its side covered in the branches that had been removed. Deakin took little interest. At almost fifty-miles-an-hour as he passed the scene; it was no more than a blur. The throaty roar of the Porsche echoed around the forest but there was no sign of any fog. He cursed as the car bounced over the obstructions.

He arrived at the station around ten-past six and decided to wait in the small cafeteria for the train, which was mercifully on time.

The car park was fairly empty with only three or four cars parked. An innocuous-looking van was parked in the 'disabled' bay. Inside the van there had been a lot of activity since the Porsche's arrival.

Back at the house, Nathan had started sweeping the rooms for listening devices using a radio frequency detector. It was a high-end spec and extremely sensitive.

He had completed the office area and the kitchen and moved to the lounge. Suddenly, there was a reaction from the detector. He followed the signal strength and, after a few minutes, he was lifting the Tiffany lamp and discovered the device. He examined it with an expert's eye. The question was how did it get there and, more importantly, who had put it there. He went into the kitchen and placed the bug in a glass of water.

The train pulled into St Austell station less than five minutes late, and Deakin was waiting at the barrier for Aaron to arrive. It was his first face-to-face meeting but he recognised Aaron straightaway, alighting one of the carriages carrying an over-night bag. He was walking smartly along the platform, dressed casually, jeans, shirt, and a light-weight jacket.

"Aaron, how are you, my friend? How was the journey?" said Deakin, as Aaron fed his ticket into the automatic barrier.

"Yes, fine thanks, Christopher."

They walked to the Porsche. In the van, an officer with a long-range lens was taking pictures one after the other.

In Thames House, there were looks of concern as the feed from Deakin's house suddenly stopped. Nan Murcty made a call.

"Andy...? It's Nan. The signal from Deakin's place has stopped responding. I think it may have been found."

Andy thought for a moment.

"Hmm, I better warn Drake."

"You think Deakin will work out who planted it?"

"I don't know; it depends on what other security he's got. If he's got internal CCTV, we could be fucked."

"There's something else you need to hear, when you've got a minute."

"Right, I'll be up shortly."

A few minutes later, Andy Tennant was in Nan's department ready to listen to the last of the transmissions from the Deakin house before it was cut off.

"Who is it speaking?" asked Tennant.

"It's Deakin and someone he calls Nathan."

Tennant picked up a set of headphones and listened.

"Oh, fuck, we were right. 'Could have spared the family'; what's that all about?"

"Yes, I thought you would be interested in that."

"And they found the laptop."

"It seems so, and we know what happened to it and the recording equipment. Would it be worth checking that exchange place they mentioned? It might still be there."

"Yes, I'll mention it to Travis when I speak to him. When was this conversation?"

Nan checked the time-log. "Seventeen twenty-four."

"Hmm, ok, there's not much more we can do for the time being. I'll email Drake straightaway."

"What about the local Police?"

"Yes, I'll give them a call and update them after I've emailed Drake."

"But surely they could arrest Deakin on suspicion and search his place for new evidence."

"Hmm, unlikely, no one would sanction it without more evidence. Actually, I've just had a thought, if Deakin has a solid alibi, it's possible that his sidekick could have murdered the Waltons. What's his name?"

"Nathan, Deakin calls him."

"Hmm. I'll get on to Travis and let him know what we've found. I don't recall that name being mentioned in the investigation."

Liam was feeling much better by late afternoon. Having taken a couple of paracetamol, his headache and dizziness had gone, just a lump, and a bald patch, on the back of his head.

April had returned to her cottage, but had been invited back for dinner as appreciation for her help. She arrived back around six o'clock, dressed in a white top and jeans. It was another warm evening.

Liam was at the table in the lounge with his laptop open. Despite protestations from Jo, he had downloaded his emails and was working through them.

On her arrival, April immediately checked Liam over and was satisfied that a hospital visit was not necessary.

"Where are the children?" asked April as she was presented with a glass of red wine by Jo.

"Both in their bedrooms. Zack keeps complaining he's bored and I don't blame him. He's been on his computer games most of the time, although at least he can communicate with his friends now."

"What about Far?"

"Hmm, that's more difficult; she seems obsessed with this Lily. I don't know what we can do about it, but if Liam's fit to travel, we do intend to leave in the morning."

"I see. Oh dear, it's such a shame, but I do understand. I'm sorry it hasn't been much of a holiday."

"Well, it's been an experience, I will say that," said Jo.

"Can I give you a hand with anything?"

"Well, I could do with some more potatoes." She turned to her husband. "Liam, are you feeling up to collecting a few more potatoes. A couple of roots should be enough."

Liam looked up from his laptop. "What? Sorry, potatoes?"

"Yes, are there any more left in the garden?"

"Yes, I think so."

"Do you feel up to digging a couple of roots for dinner?"

"Yes, ok. I'll be fine." He closed his laptop and walked towards the kitchen.

"I'll give you a hand," said April.

Liam walked to the kitchen door as Jo gave April the trug. Liam felt less anxious with April with him; she seemed to have a way of dealing with the spirits.

He pulled on the kitchen door; it was still troublesome to open. "I was meaning to plane that door for you. Is there a handyman in the village? It's not a big job."

"I'm sure I can find someone," said April and they walked out into the garden.

It was a beautiful summer's day; the late afternoon warm, but not oppressive. For some reason, the garden felt different. The swallows were still busy ferrying insects to their chicks, quite audible from the footpath.

"I'm going to need a gardener," said April as they walked towards the vegetable patch. "Actually, I do have someone in mind."

"Oh?" replied Liam.

"Yes, Jack, I'm sure he'll do it. The last time I spoke to him, the fishing seemed to be down to just a couple of days a week."

"Is that all?"

"Quotas, he was telling me. He's talking about retiring, but that would be a shame. There's very little fishing left now. Thirty years ago the place was thriving."

They reached the last row of potatoes. April looked around. "The spirits have gone," she announced.

"Really, where? Do you know?"

"No, no-one knows. Spirits come and go as they please."

Liam looked around; there was definitely a different atmosphere. He was beginning to wonder if he too could actually detect supernatural presence. Then a black shape flew out of the trees and perched on top of the thatched roof.

April noticed his anxiety. "What's the matter, Liam, you're shaking?"

"Nothing, I'm ok, that bird spooked me."

"The crow?"

"Yes."

April watched the crow as it strutted up and down the thatch on the roof's apex. It gave a loud 'caw'.

"Sounds like a warning," said April.

"It's just a crow. Sorry, I was being stupid."

April stared at the crow.

"No, you're not. Crows do have mystical powers. In Welsh mythology they believed that witches and sorcerers could transform themselves into crows to avoid detection. They're also seen as harbingers of death."

"I'll stick with the carrion description, I think," said Liam. He picked up the fork and completed the potato gathering.

April was holding the trug but still looking at the crow.

"You know, we don't see many crows around here, certainly not singularly. They don't get on with the seagulls, so they tend to be in groups."

"Yes, 'murders', I believe," said Liam, looking up at the bird. "Crops up in crossword puzzles occasionally. Quite appropriate given the circumstances."

"Ha, yes," said April.

The crow flew back into the trees overhanging the graveyard and disappeared into the branches.

Liam and April retuned to the kitchen. April was carrying the trug.

Liam left April and Jo in the kitchen and returned to his laptop. He accessed his emails again; there was a new one.

"Oh, shit," he exclaimed.

With Jo and April in the kitchen, no one heard his expletive.

He read it again, from Andy Tennant. *'Package inoperative, possible detection.'*

He considered the implications. If Deakin was ruthless enough to kill the Walton family; then there was a real possibility that he and the family were in danger. The sooner they were away from Pendle Cottage, the better.

The Porsche returned to the house where Nathan was waiting for the guest.

Aaron got out of the car and looked at the house. "What a magnificent place you have here, Christopher."

"Thanks, we like it."

"Who designed it?"

"I did. Well, I say I did; it was built to my specifications. Let me introduce you to Nathan; he's sort of my, er, assistant. Actually, he has many strings to his bow, don't you Nathan?"

"That's true, sir, although you do flatter me somewhat. I've set out the food on the patio as you suggested." He leaned towards Deakin and whispered. "If I might have a word."

They walked inside. "Nathan will show you up to your room; I'm sure you'll want to freshen up and then you can join us on the patio. It's just through there," said Deakin, indicating the way with his hand.

Nathan escorted the visitor to the guest room, then returned to the patio where Deakin was waiting with a glass of beer.

Nathan walked out of the kitchen and joined Deakin; he was carrying a glass of water.

"I found this while I was sweeping the house, sir."

Deakin took the glass and peered at the listening device.

"Is that what I think it is?"

"Yes, sir, Special Services by my reckoning."

"But who could have planted it?"

"Well, it must have been recently; I only swept the house last week."

"Before the barbeque?" asked Deakin.

"Yes. It must have been planted then, at the barbeque. We've had no visitors since... except..."

"Except?" repeated Deakin.

"Mrs Thornton."

"April?"

"Yes, sir, she's the only visitor since the last sweep and she does enjoy a certain amount of freedom while she's here."

"Yes, that's true, but she's been using the internet here for ages. No, I can't believe she would do such a thing. She's never made any enquiries about my work, not in detail anyway."

"Nor did Mr Walton, as I recall."

"Hmm, yes that's true."

"Well, if it wasn't Mrs Thornton, it must have been someone at the barbeque."

"But we know all the guests from the village."

"Well, there was that family from Pendle Cottage."

"Yes, that's true. Mind you, they didn't stay very long."

"Long enough," countered Nathan.

"Hmm." Deakin was in deep thought as their guest arrived to join them.

"Ah, Aaron. Everything ok?" asked Deakin.

"Yes, Christopher, thank you, very comfortable."

Chapter Seventeen

Deakin, Nathan, and their guest were seated on the garden furniture on the patio enjoying Nathan's culinary labours from the barbeque. All three were drinking bottles of beer.

"It's a nice spot here, Christopher. I have to say I couldn't see the attraction of living cut-off from civilisation, but now, I can understand completely."

Aaron was in his forties, dressed in a casual shirt, chino's and smart trainers. He looked like he could handle himself in a fight with a slim waist and sculptured chest, probably through a great deal of gym work. He wore an earring in his left ear and spoke in an understated London accent; not the harsh East End brogue, but a more refined version, as if he'd schooled himself out of his heritage.

"Yes, indeed, we're very fortunate," said Deakin.

"So, shall we get down to business?" said Rainsford, confident and forthright.

"Yes, why not."

"Like I mentioned, we've got a further investment we want to make."

"Yes, you did. What've you got in mind?"

"I know Marty's been pleased with the business he's been doing with you. We've got another two hundred and fifty k in the Cayman Islands we want to transfer."

"Excellent... And when he gets out, he'll be able to enjoy the fruits of his labours to the full."

"Yeah, he's very much looking forward to doing just that, sooner rather than later, an'all. Can you handle that amount?"

"Sure, of course, and more besides."

"I trust the cryptocurrency market is still doing well."

"Yes, very well. I made forty thousand in ten minutes earlier today."

"Bitcoin?"

"No, I'm using one of the newer platforms, FCX, and investing in altcoin. There's more room for profit growth. There's a suggestion that Bitcoin might have plateaued."

"Altcoin?"

"Yes, there are newer currencies in the market; they call them altcoins. FCX acts as a broker and finds the best performing one and make the investment, a bit like a stockbroker."

Rainsford was lost. "I'll leave it in your hands, as long as it's safe."

"Of course," confirmed Deakin.

Nathan returned from the barbeque with two plates of food; steak, sausages, chicken wings, with coleslaw and salad. Deakin and Rainsford started eating while Nathan returned for his own meal.

"Oh, I know what I meant to mention; I assume you were at the trial," said Deakin, looking at his guest.

"Yeah, course."

Rainsford stopped eating and took a long sip of his beer; his expression one of annoyance, not aimed at his host but the painful memory of the occasion.

"Do you remember the prosecuting brief?"

"Liam Drake QC? Oh yeah, course, how could I forget?"

"Would you believe, he's actually staying in the village."

"Yeah? Really? I know a few people who would willingly put an end to his career and that's a fact."

"Yes, I'm sure."

"Just a thought," said Deakin. He took a sip of his beer. "Do you think he would have any connection with the Secret Services? Just asking hypothetically."

"Nah, how would I know? I can't see it, though, can you? I mean, you can't be a brief and work for that lot, surely."

"No, no, that's my thought, exactly."

"What did you want to know for?"

"Oh, no reason. I tell you what, when we've finished here, I'll show you my operation to put your mind at rest regarding security. In fact, if you wanted to complete your transaction, the Cayman Islands will still be open; they're five hours behind us."

"Yeah? Ok... Is there any more of that steak left?"

Nathan intervened. "Of course, I'll just put another couple on the barbeque."

Back at Pendle Cottage, Liam was on his laptop. April had gone home to do some writing and Jo was on the settee with her legs curled under her, reading a chick-lit novel.

Jo looked up from her book. "How much longer are you going to be on that laptop?"

"Only a couple of minutes, I just want to get rid of a couple of emails. I'm going to be up to my eyes in it when I get back if not."

"Hmm, ok. How's your head?"

"It's fine, thanks. Those pills got rid of the headache."

"I think I'll just go and check on the children," said Jo.

She left the settee and went upstairs. Zack was in bed playing on his computer games.

"Just came to say goodnight. Put that console away now."

"Just a couple of minutes; I'll finish this game." His thumbs were moving at incredible speed.

He stopped, switched off his game, then looked at his mom.

"Are we definitely going home tomorrow?"

"If your dad's well enough, yes."

"That's great, I don't want to stay here another day."

"No, I know, Zack, but we all have to do things we don't want to do sometimes. It's part of life."

He folded his arms. "Whatever... Goodnight."

Before Jo could answer, he had moved down into bed and turned over with his back to her. Jo sighed.

"Goodnight, sleep tight," said Jo.

There was an indecipherable grunt. Jo turned out the light and closed the door.

She walked across to Farrah's room. There was a small bedside light which was still switched on. Jo looked at Farrah as she lay fast asleep clutching her pet elephant. Jo bent down to kiss her when suddenly Farrah's eyes opened wide. It made Jo jump.

"Are you ok, Poppet?"

She slowly raised herself, back straight, the sheet dropped from her shoulders. She sat for a moment in her pyjamas then turned her head. It wasn't a natural turn, more like an owl. She stared at Jo.

"You... must... not... leave."

The voice was low and guttural, not from this world.

Jo put her hand to her mouth in shock. "Why can't we leave," she managed to stammer.

"It... is... not... finished."

Jo realised what was happening.

"What's not finished, Lily?"

"They... must... be... stopped."

"Who, Lily?"

"He hurt my Daddy and Mummy. I can't find them."

"I don't understand, Lily. Who?"

Farrah leaned slowly back onto her pillow and clutched her elephant. Jo started to cry.

She checked again. Lily had gone; Farrah was in a deep

sleep.

Jo left the room and went back downstairs, tears falling down her cheeks.

Liam looked up. "What's the matter?"

Jo sat down on the settee with her head in her hands.

"It's Far." Liam went over to her and put his arm around her shoulder.

"What's happened?"

Jo described the metamorphosis. "It was terrifying, as though someone had taken over Far's body. I don't know what to do, Liam. I just want to go home."

"We will, first thing tomorrow; I promise."

"But, I don't know if we will be able to. She kept saying 'it's not finished' again."

"Yes, I know but I still can't understand what she means. What's not finished?"

"I asked that, but she just said they must be stopped."

"But who is it she's referring to?"

"The ones who hurt her and the family, I think."

"Hmm, well I have an idea who that might be."

"Who?"

"It's that Deakin fellow; it's what I've been helping MI5 with."

"Really? You didn't say."

"I didn't want to worry you."

"But we need to contact the police," said Jo.

"Don't worry, MI5 are dealing with it. It's just a question of evidence."

"But what'll happen if we do try to leave? Look at what's happened before. It seems someone, or something, is trying to stop us."

"Hmm, I know." Liam put his head in his hands in frustration, then looked at Jo. "We need to speak to April, she seems to understand how these things work. Maybe she can get us away."

With the meal finished, Deakin took his guest upstairs to the office suite and opened up one of his computers. Rainsford looked around in amazement. "I have to say, you have an impressive set-up Christopher."

"Thank you Aaron, and totally secure through a VPN, all totally untraceable."

"Good to know."

"Do you want to go ahead with that transfer? Then I'll buy the equivalent cryptocurrency. The sooner it's invested, the sooner it's making money for you."

"For Marty," corrected Aaron.

"Yes, of course."

With the transactions completed, Rainsford excused himself; he had messages to deliver. "I assume I can use your Wi-Fi connection." It was more a statement than a question.

"Yes, of course, I'll let you have the password. Would you like me to take you to the station tomorrow?"

"Oh, yeah, thanks. Train leaves at nine-thirty."

Deakin returned to the patio, where Nathan was finishing tidying up. He had collected a can of beer from the fridge and poured himself a glass and invited Nathan to join him.

"Nathan, I need to find out who planted that listening device; it could threaten everything. Have you checked the CCTV footage for Saturday yet?"

"No, not yet, there's quite a lot to look at," replied Nathan with an air of reluctance.

"Well, I'm pretty certain we can narrow it down to the barbeque."

"Or Mrs Thornton," interrupted Nathan.

"Yes, ok, or April, but we need to check the CCTV before we start passing judgment?"

"Yes, of course, but I think it <u>has</u> to be Mrs Thornton," responded Nathan.

"Why do you think so?"

"Well, she was a close friend of the Waltons. They could have been in it together. Maybe Walton was using her, I mean, knowing she had access to you."

"Hmm, I guess that's possible."

"She's been using your facilities for ages, and she's been left on her own when she's here. Who knows what damage she could have caused. She'd certainly have had the opportunity."

"Hmm, yes that's true. I'm just glad I had a good alibi, I'll say that; and it was a good idea of yours to disappear for a couple of months after the murder." Deakin was in deep thought. "For the moment, let's see if the CCTV throws up anything."

"But I still don't understand why the Secret Services are interested in you," said Nathan, with a quizzical look.

"It can only be the Korean," said Deakin.

"Who... Kim?" replied Nathan.

"Yes, I was reading he's disappeared; the Koreans are looking for him. I'm glad we got out of there when we did. They probably want to see if I'm still in touch with him. Well, they'll be disappointed."

"Yes, that's true. But what about your clients?" said Nathan.

"There's nothing illegal in what we're doing, and they have no access to my clients; they're completely anonymous. I think they'll eventually give up out of boredom. We just need to stay vigilant."

"And hope there are no more bugs."

April was back in her cottage; seated at her dinner table on her laptop, writing her latest piece for her newspaper; she entitled it, *'Spirits'*.

She started her narrative. *'A friend of mine has been troubled by spirits. Not the drinking kind for a change, but the spooky ones. This is not a unique experience. Spirits have lived among us for centuries, sparking superstitions and folklore. Even the great Winston Churchill who was visiting the White House just after the war is said to have had an unexplained experience. Having had a long bath with a Scotch and cigar, he reportedly walked into the adjoining bedroom – only to be confronted by the ghost of Abraham Lincoln. Unflappable, even while completely naked, Churchill apparently announced: "Good evening, Mr President. You seem to have me at a disadvantage". The spirit is supposed to have turned around and disappeared.*

Arthur Conan Doyle spoke to ghosts through mediums, while Alan Turing believed in telepathy. So clearly it's not the rantings of the uneducated or mentally unstable.

The idea that the dead remain with us in spirit is an ancient one, appearing in countless stories, from the Bible to "Macbeth". The belief that somehow our deceased relatives are looking out for us brings a great comfort to many.'

She continued the piece with more examples of unexplained events asking readers for their experiences, then saved the document. She would pay a call to 'the Squire' in the morning to use his internet connection to send it to the newspaper.

Just before midnight, it was a warm, stifling evening, one of those nights when the heat made sleeping difficult. Liam lay in bed; he could feel his head throbbing but not a real 'headache', just the reaction to the healing wound. He was just wearing a pair of boxers and his chest was drenched with sweat.

There was just a sheet covering the pair of them.

Jo, too, was uncomfortable. The anxiety of Farrah's experiences and the desire to get away were at the forefront of her mind. She kept replaying the recent event in her mind, over and over. It was beyond her comprehension.

She opened her eyes and sensed Liam was awake.

"Are you awake?"

"Yes, it's this heat, I'm thinking of getting a shower; I'm burning up," replied Liam.

"I think I'll join you, save the water. The meter will be running low."

Jo had already dispensed with clothes; she got out of bed and headed to the bathroom. Liam joined her and started running the water.

It was no more than tepid but would be refreshing.

"How's your head?" asked Jo as she applied soap to Liam's back.

"Much better now, thanks."

Any romantic thoughts were suddenly dispelled by an enormous clap of thunder.

Jo looked up towards the window. "Jesus, that made me jump. I better check on the kids."

She got out of the shower and wrapped a towel around herself. Liam did the same. He looked out of the bedroom window just as a flash of lightning lit up the village. It was quickly followed by an equally loud retort. The cottage seemed to shake to its foundations.

Jo went into Farrah's bedroom just as Zack opened his door rubbing his eyes.

"I don't like this thunder," he exclaimed.

Liam went to him and put his arm around his shoulder.

"Don't worry son, it's only a storm. It'll soon pass."

Jo went to the bedside. Farrah was fast asleep. She heard a noise behind her and stifled a low scream.

Liam ushered Zack back into his room then went to see what was happening.

Jo could hardly speak. "The... wardrobe..." She pointed.

Liam slowly opened the door.

The coat-hangers were bouncing up and down creating a discordant rattling sound. Liam slammed the door shut.

Suddenly, Farrah opened her eyes and sat up.

Before she could speak, Jo grabbed her and lifted her out of bed. An enormous crack of thunder rocked the cottage.

"I'm not having any more of this. She can sleep with us. I don't want her in this room again. Can you bring Jumbo?"

Liam picked up the cuddly elephant and went back to their bedroom. Jo put Farrah into bed and covered her with a sheet, then got in beside her.

"What about Zack?" said Liam.

"Hmm, why don't you sleep with him? I'm sure he'll soon settle."

"Good idea. Will you be alright?"

"I feel better now Far's out of there and I can keep an eye on her. I just hope there won't be any repercussions."

Another flash of lightening illuminated the bedroom, followed almost immediately by the crack of thunder. Liam went to the window and stared out; the rain was now torrential.

It took another hour before the storm subsided. For Jo, sleep had been elusive, continually disturbed by strange eerie noises, coming from beyond the bedroom door. A distant cockerel heralded the dawn of a new day. Jo checked the bedside clock, ten-to-five. She sighed, nature called. She slipped slowly out of bed. Farrah was still sound asleep facing the other way.

Jo put her ear to the bedroom door; it seemed quiet.

She turned the ball-handle, and slowly pulled it towards her. There was a creaking sound. She peered out along the landing, left, then right. Zack's bedroom door was slightly ajar. She turned left and headed for the bathroom, closing the door behind her.

The first light of daybreak streamed through the frosted glass of the bathroom, negating the need for the light switch. Jo wiped her face with a wet flannel then completed her toilet.

She left the bathroom and walked the short distance to the master bedroom. The door was open; she was sure she had closed it. She pushed it open and gasped. Her hand went to her mouth. The scream wouldn't come.

Farrah was sat up in bed. Hearing the door open her head swivelled towards Jo.

Farrah's lips moved; it was the voice again.

"It... is... not... finished. Danger... is... near."

"Please leave us alone, Lily. We just want to go home," said Jo.

Liam had heard the voices and left Zack's bedroom. Jo was stood looking into the master bedroom.

"What is it?"

Jo turned to Liam with her hand over her mouth. "Lily's back."

"What!?"

He looked into the room. Farrah was lying down.

"She's gone now, I think," said Jo.

"What did she want?"

"She just said it wasn't finished and danger was near."

"I wonder what she meant."

"That's all she said."

"Would you like a cup of tea?"

"Yes, I'd love one. You'll need some money for the meter

I think."

"Ok, I'll see to it; I've got some change. You stay here and keep an eye on Far."

It was seven o'clock before Liam decided he'd give up on trying to sleep and make the use of the day. He did have a major worry. Tennant's message that the bug had been discovered was on his mind. He tried to rationalise the situation. He was sure he hadn't been spotted planting the device and therefore there was nothing to link him to the intrusion. If they could get away this morning as planned, he was sure they would be safe.

Andy Tennant was also up early and at his desk in Thames House being briefed by Nan Murcty who had been in since four a.m.

"I've had a message from GCHQ, they picked up some internet traffic last night from Deakin's computer which is of interest."

Tennant looked at her with a degree of expectation.

"We think he was moving money into cryptocurrency again, but we're waiting for confirmation from the bank."

"Rainsford?"

"Can't rule it out; he was with Deakin. It's probably why he went."

"I'll contact the SIO in Truro and let them know."

"Do we have enough to go after Deakin?"

"Hmm, I'm not sure; everything we have so far is inadmissible. It's possible the local police will apply to a judge for entry but I don't think we're there yet. We do have an idea what's going on, though, which is useful."

A few minutes later, Tennant's mobile phone rang.

"Andy, it's Liam Drake. Have you anymore news?"

"Hi Liam, how's the holiday going?"

"Oh, don't ask. It's been a nightmare."

"Oh, sorry to hear. In answer to your question, no, nothing definite; still waiting for more information."

"Hmm, I see. Well, I'm ringing to let you know we're leaving today; we need to get back."

"Yes, I can understand that. It probably makes sense in the circumstances."

Liam signed off and keyed in another number.

"April, it's Liam."

"Hi Liam, how are things? I hope the storm didn't cause you any problems last night."

"Well, sleeping wasn't easy, that's for sure, and we did have another visit from Lily."

"Oh dear. How's Farrah?"

"She seems to be ok; she's still asleep."

"What did she say, Lily?"

"Said something about it not being finished, which she's said before, but she also said that danger was close. Something like that, it was Jo that heard it. I've no idea what she means."

"Hmm, I see, and are you still thinking of leaving today?"

"Yes, which is the reason I've called. Do you think you can accompany us? Just to the main road."

"Yes, of course. Was there a reason?"

"I think the spirits might leave us alone if you are with us, that's all. I can't believe I'm saying this."

"It's ok, Liam, of course I will."

"Just follow us to the main road. I'll feel happier once we're out of the forest."

"Yes, I understand. When are you thinking of leaving?"

"As soon as possible after breakfast and we can get

packed up."

"No problem. I want to pop over to see Christopher and send a piece for my column, get it out of the way, so I'll call in on the way back, how's that sound?"

"Sounds good. What time are you thinking?"

"I'm going to get a shower and something to eat, then I'll go; so I'll be leaving here, I don't know, about quarter-to-nine, something like that. I shan't be long."

"Great, I'll make sure we're ready, and thanks."

"No problem. See you later."

In the Deakin house, Nathan was serving breakfast.

"So, did you sleep well, Aaron?" said Deakin as they tucked into their 'full English'.

"Like a top, Christopher, like a top; it must be the sea air."

"Yes. I've heard it said."

"What time will you be needing the car?" interrupted Nathan as he poured more tea from a China teapot.

"What time did you say your train was, Aaron?"

"Nine-thirty."

"Hmm, we need to leave about eight-thirty to be on the safe side. It's always busy at that time in town, especially in the holidays. Tourists are a nightmare, clogging up the roads, not knowing where they're going."

"Yes, I can imagine," said Rainsford, as he pasted a layer of marmalade onto a slice of toast.

April parked her Kia next to the church and walked along the cinder track to Deakin's house. She was carrying her laptop and handbag. The clock on the church tower was showing ten-to-nine. It was a cloudy morning, much cooler, but the rain had gone; a stiff breeze blew from the south-west. There were puddles and debris from the storm everywhere. Small branches littered the path.

She reached the gate and pressed the intercom button; Nathan answered.

"Oh hi, Nathan, it's April, I've an article I need to send to my editor. Can I use the internet please?"

There was a delay, then a click as the lock was disengaged. April pushed open the gate and made her way to the house. Nathan was waiting at the entrance.

"I'm afraid Christopher's not in at present. He's gone over to St Austell; he won't be too long. You're welcome to wait."

"Is it ok just to log in? I have my laptop with me. I don't want to stay long; I've an errand to run."

"I don't see why not; you can use the office. You know where it is."

"Yes, thanks," said April and Nathan followed her to the second floor.

He was in a quandary. He was certain she was the one who had planted the bug. Who else could it have been? Why was she here on a Monday morning? She didn't normally use the internet until later in the week. Perhaps she had come to replace the bug that he had found. It would make sense.

He watched from the office door as she retrieved her laptop from its case and opened it. She saw Nathan stood there. Something about his demeanour disturbed her. She looked at him nervously as she entered her password and logged in.

She downloaded her emails, including many passed on by the newspaper from readers with comments on her previous articles to which she would reply. She had a quick scan at the list of correspondence; it would keep her busy for a while. Then she uploaded her 'Spirits' piece with a suitable introduction for the editor to provide some context.

A final check that it had been sent, then she logged off.

"There, that didn't take long, thanks very much," said April, as she started to put her laptop away. "Can you thank Christopher for me? Tell him I'll see him again on Thursday."

"I think he would want to see you. He shouldn't be long."

April picked up her handbag and laptop and walked to the doorway. Nathan was blocking her path.

"I'm sorry, I really have to go. I have a call to make," she snapped, anxiously.

"I insist," replied Nathan.

"Insist? What do you mean? Please let me pass, I'm in a rather hurry. I need to leave."

"Christopher wants to talk to you."

"Well, tell him I'll call back later."

Nathan's eyes widened menacingly, bloodshot red. His face contorted into a snarl. Beads of sweat appeared on his brow; his nostrils wide. April backed away; she was staring at the devil itself.

"Please, let me pass; you're scaring me."

Without warning his two hands wrapped themselves around her throat, gripping tightly. His stubby thumbs pressed into her larynx. There were clicking noises; her eyes bulged, then closed. She tried to scream but only a guttural noise emerged. Her body went limp and Nathan let her drop to the floor.

He stood staring at April's lifeless body, his shoulders heaving. He snarled, more as a wild animal.

Deakin arrived thirty minutes later. The throaty exhaust echoed around the front atrium. Nathan was stood there, calmness personified.

Deakin got out of the car and looked at Nathan.

"Everything alright?"

"You've had a visitor."

"Oh... who?"

They walked inside.

"Mrs Thornton."

"April...? Why didn't you ask her to stay?"

"I did, but she, ahem, refused." Deakin looked at Nathan; he recognised the signs.

"Oh dear Lord, you haven't."

"It was necessary; she was a problem."

"A problem?"

"Yes, I think she came here to plant another bug. She doesn't normally come on Monday."

"But we don't know it was her for certain. Have you checked the CCTV as I asked?"

Nathan looked down. "No, not yet."

"What about her handbag? Have you checked that?"

"No." He looked down sheepishly.

"Dear God, you've really done it this time. How are we going to explain this away?"

"I've been giving it some thought, while you were out. I have an idea."

"I need a drink," said Deakin, and walked over to the drinks cabinet and poured himself a large brandy.

"Did Mr Rainsford get away alright?" said Nathan, incongruously.

"What?" Deakin didn't process the question.

"Mr Rainsford... the train?"

"Oh, oh, yes." He took a large gulp of his Remi Martin.

"Don't worry; leave it to me. I know what to do," said Nathan.

Deakin was seated on the settee staring into space.

Nathan went upstairs and took April's car keys from her

handbag. She was still lay on the floor where she dropped.

He went back downstairs and opened the front gate from the internal console, then left the house.

It was still relatively early as Nathan walked along the cinder track to the church. Sure enough, April's car was still parked by the church wall.

He aimed the fob at the Kia and got in, then slowly drove back along the track to the front gate and up to the house.

"Looks like the Squire's got a visitor," said Walter Rawlinson as he looked out from his bedroom window.

"Oh, aye. It'll be that journalist women, Mrs Thornton," said Ethel.

"Seems strange, she don't usually take her car up to the 'ouse. The Squire don't like oil on his drive he were saying... Are you still wantin' to go shoppin' asmorning, m'dear?"

"Aye, if you don't mind."

Back at the house, Nathan went upstairs and carried April over his shoulder down to the car which he had parked directly outside. Deakin was watching the charade.

"What are you doing?"

"Resolving the problem," said Nathan cryptically.

Nathan opened the passenger door and manoeuvred April onto the front seat. He fastened the seatbelt to keep her upright, then placed her laptop and handbag on the back seat. He went across to the garage and returned with a five litre can of petrol, which they always kept in emergencies, and splashed petrol around the inside of the car. He returned the remainder back to the garage.

"I won't be long," said Nathan.

"Where are you going? It's broad daylight. Someone will see you."

"No they won't, and if they do, they won't say anything, will they?"

He drove down the drive and turned left along the cinder path. The bouncing caused April's body to lean to one side but Nathan decided to continue. There was no one about.

He headed down the road from the church and along the promenade road. A couple of dog walkers were strolling along the pavement; otherwise the place was deserted.

He drove up the long hill out of the village and slowed as he reached Mrs Wilkin's empty house.

He turned onto the patch of wasteland then over the flattened chain-link fence to the top of the cliff and got out. He unclipped the seatbelt around April's body and moved her behind the steering wheel, then buckled up the seatbelt. He took out a cigarette lighter and opened the back door. He lit the lighter and held it beneath the driver's seat until there was a whoosh of flame as the petrol ignited.

Nathan disengaged the handbrake and gave the Kia a push. It needed little encouragement and quickly gathered enough speed to take it over the cliff and crash to the bottom in a fireball.

There was a short cut across the top of the cliff through the forest. A footpath ran all the way through the trees from the top of the hill to the headland on the other side of Deakin's house. It was the one Liam and the MI5 agent joined. Nathan broke into a jog, his feet splashing through the puddles caused by the previous night's storm. He was soon passing the graveyard, then the back of the rectory, and on to the site of the landslip. The Squire's house was below him. Nathan stooped on his haunches. The slope was slippery from the rain and acted like a slide as Nathan slalomed down the slope on his backside.

He was able to use one of the branches from the stricken beech as a ladder and climbed the wall into the Squire's back garden. Then made his way up to the house where Deakin was waiting.

"I heard the explosion; I just hope no one saw you," said Deakin as Nathan approached. "Get yourself cleaned up and we'll go through the CCTV footage together."

"But why? I've dealt with it."

"I just want to be sure. It won't take long, the two of us."

Nathan went upstairs to shower and change, muttering about wasting of time.

Back at Pendle Cottage, Liam was getting concerned. He kept looking at his watch. "I don't know what's happened to April."

"Maybe she's overslept. Why don't you give her a call?" said Jo, as she put some bits and pieces into one of the holdalls. The three suitcases where shut and waiting for transportation.

"I already have, just a couple of minutes ago. It just went to answer phone. I'll just check the car. Then we can load up," said Liam.

He left the cottage, Five minutes later, he returned to the lounge; his face showing concern.

"The car won't start; I think the electrics are wet from all that rain."

"Oh, no, not again," said Jo. "What are you going to do?"

"I'll pop down and see Jack and see if there's a mechanic in the village."

Just then there was a rumbling noise in the distance.

"Did you hear that? It sounded like an explosion."

Jo looked at Liam with concern. "Yes, it came from the other side of the village."

Chapter Eighteen

After another abortive attempt to start the car, Liam made the trek down to the quayside. Ten minutes later he was walking past the Harbourmaster's office. The road was littered with debris and, where the drains had been unable to cope, lines of sand stretched downwards in geometrical patterns carried by the torrent.

He could see Jack on the sea wall working on his crab pots.

"Wasson, m'dear," he said, as Liam approached.

"Hello Jack, I wonder if you can help."

"I'll try. What appears to be the problem?"

"My car won't start. I think the plugs or something have got damp from all that rain. Is there anyone in the village who could take a look at it?"

"Aye, you'll not be alone an'all, I spect. Hmm, well there's young Peter Melgrove, now he's a mechanic. Works on the boats mainly but I'm sure he knows about cars."

"That's great. Where can I find him?"

"I don't know. He'll be working most likely. I'll give him a call. Wait here, I won't be long."

Jack walked over the road into his cottage. A few minutes later, he returned to Liam with a grin across his face.

"I got through to him all right. He said he'll get over at lunchtime. Working on one of the boats over at Par docks asmorning."

"Oh, that's very good of you, I'm very grateful."

"So, you going out are you?"

"Actually, we're going home, Jack; we need to get back."

"Oh, that's a pity, though folks round 'ere reckons you wouldn't have lasted this long."

"Really?"

Just then the sound of sirens echoed across the valley. Jack looked along the promenade.

"That'll be for that car, I spect, although it'll be too late by now to do any good."

"Car? What car?"

"Another car gone over the cliff apparently; that's all I knows."

"I heard an explosion."

"Aye, that'll be it, about half an hour since. One of the lads said he saw it. Gone to see what's happened, he has. He called the fire brigade but it takes 'em a while to get 'ere; that's the problem."

"Do we know who it is?"

"No, that's all I knows."

"Well, thanks again, Jack and we'll see Peter later, you said?"

"Aye, Peter Melgrove. He'll be over lunchtime."

Liam left the fisherman and started to walk back to the cottage, deep in thought. For some reason he had a strange, uneasy feeling; he could sense his headache returning. The village store was open and he crossed the road.

His entrance was announced by the customary 'clang' of the bell above the door.

"Wasson, m'dear," said Mrs Trevelyan.

"Good morning, I need some paracetamol, do you sell them?"

"Aye, but I can only let you have one packet. It's the law."

"That's ok; it's all I need," replied Liam.

She went into the back toom and returned moments later with a small box.

"There you go m'dear. Was there anything else?"

"No, that's all thanks," said Liam and handed over a five

pound note.

The shopkeeper handed Liam the change. "It's terrible news about Mrs Thornton?"

"Mrs Thornton? April?"

"Aye, it were her car that went over the cliff."

Liam was stunned. He just looked at the woman. "Are you sure?"

"Aye, well, I think so. One of the lads called in and said a car had gone over the cliff, a Kia, he said. She's the only one in the village who owns a Kia as far as I knows."

"Oh no!"

Liam turned and left the shop, his mind racing. "No, no, no," he said to no one in particular.

He stood for a moment and could hear more sirens coming from the other side of the village. He broke into a run, passing the pub, just as a second fire engine turned the corner and stopped at the entrance to the undercliff next to an earlier arrival. Hoses snaked from the connections on the side of the vehicle along the footpath all the way to the stricken Kia. His mind went back to the Spanish student; maybe there was still a chance.

He reached the pathway and looked across towards the wreckage. He could see fire officers hosing down what was left of an unrecognisable mangle of metal.

He ran along the path towards the fire crews but was stopped before he could get too close.

"Sorry, sir, you can't go any further," said a burley firefighter in full kit.

"But, I think it's a friend of mine, a Kia SUV?"

"Aye, that's right. There's nothing to be done, I'm sorry. We're waiting for the police. It's a possible crime scene."

Liam just stood for a moment trying to take it in. He could see the smouldering wreck; there would be no chance of anyone getting out alive.

"A crime scene?"

"Aye, sir, if you don't mind, can you let us get on with our jobs?"

"Yes, yes, sorry, of course."

Liam would never remember the twenty minutes or so it took to walk back to the cottage.

The Volvo was still parked with its bonnet up in an attempt to dry out the interior, although the sun was yet to make its presence felt. Dark clouds hovered above the village as the threatened low pressure system rolled in from the south west. The possibility of more rain remained.

Liam walked along the path to the front door. From nowhere a black shape appeared on the cottage roof. It perched itself on the top of the thatch and looked down at Liam. Then let out a loud 'caw, caw'. Liam ignored it and knocked on the front door with his knuckles. Jo opened it.

"Oh, there you are; I was beginning to get worried."

Liam couldn't speak. He walked to the settee and sat down with his head in his hands.

"Liam? Are you alright? What's happened?"

He looked up. "It's April... she's dead."

"Dead? No she can't be. How?"

Jo was trying to take it in.

"That explosion we heard? It was her car going over the cliff. I've just been to check. There's a couple of fire engines there. They're talking about a crime scene."

"Crime scene...? You mean someone has deliberately tried to kill her?"

"It looks like they've succeeded."

Deakin and Nathan were huddled together in front of

a laptop watching footage of the CCTV cameras from the weekend's barbeque.

They had been viewing the entrance door for about half an hour.

"There... look. Someone's gone in the house," said Deakin.

They paused the screen, reversed the footage, and ran it through again frame-by-frame.

"Can't make out who it is. It was too quick. It looked like someone in a green shirt."

"Can you remember anyone wearing a green shirt?"

Nathan thought for a moment. "Not off hand."

"Hmm, me neither, but it does suggest whoever it was, wanted to get in without being seen."

"Yes, true enough," said Nathan.

They continued running the video.

"Well, that's an hour," said Deakin after a while. "There's no sign of anyone leaving by the front door. Let's check the kitchen."

Nathan had been sent to make some more coffee while Deakin continued the laborious job of watching the comings and goings of the guests.

Suddenly, he spotted something. He stopped the recording and rewound it.

The camera above the kitchen door pointed down but slightly forward so it was difficult to tell for certain if anyone had actually used the kitchen door. It was the rear of the band that dominated the screen with people milling about in the background out of focus.

Nathan returned with two mugs and placed one down on the desk next to the laptop.

"Here, have a look at this. What do you see?" said Deakin excitedly.

Deakin re-ran the footage. "It's that barrister. Look, he's dodging around the drummer. He must have come out of the kitchen," said Nathan.

"Yes, that's what I think," said Deakin. "And he's wearing a green shirt."

"Hmm, you're right," replied Nathan uneasily.

"I think it must have been him that planted the bug. Why else would he be going into the house?"

"Use the toilet?"

Deakin looked at Nathan.

"No, there are toilets by the barbeque. It seems you were wrong, and I was right, and now April's dead. You're beginning to become a liability I can't afford, Nathan."

"But she must have been in on it. I mean, she was a friend of the Waltons and now this Drake fellow and his family; that's not a coincidence."

"Hmm," replied Deakin, unconvincingly.

"What do you want to do? I can deal with it if you like. I'm sure that Rainsford fellow would be more than happy if something unforeseen happened to the barrister."

Deakin was thinking. "Well, yes that's true."

"The other thing is, they could've known Mrs Thornton was calling here this morning; they're bound to say something."

"Hmm, yes, you could be right."

"I know what to do," said Nathan. "Leave it to me."

"Oh, I will; I want nothing to do with it."

At Pendle Cottage, the family were trying to come to terms with April's demise. There was an overwhelming feeling of sadness.

"I need to speak to someone; I won't be long," said Liam. He opened up his laptop and inserted the Wi-Fi dongle to enable him to use his phone. He decided to go outside to make the call. He pressed the keys.

"Hi Andy, it's Liam Drake. There's been a development."

"Hi Liam, a development? Tell me more."

"You remember the woman who was helping me here, April?"

"Yes, of course, I spoke to her."

"Well, this morning her car was driven over the cliff, apparently with her in it. I went round there and spoke to the fire chief and they're treating it as a crime scene."

"Oh, I'm sorry to hear, Liam."

"The thing is, she was due to call in on Deakin this morning to file some copy for her newspaper column."

"Why couldn't she do that at her place?"

"No internet. Deakin's house is the only place in the village with a connection. It was a regular arrangement. It's possible she was murdered while she was there."

"But why? I mean if she was doing this regularly."

"I don't know... unless they thought she had something to do with the bug. You said it had been discovered."

"Hmm, yes, I guess that is a possibility."

"It's the only explanation. She's hardly going to drive over the cliff, is she?"

"No, I suppose not, unless she had mental health issues."

"No, no, no... no way, I can't see that. Look, can you mention this to your contact with the local police? The ones who were working on the Walton case."

"Yes, I will... I thought you were leaving today."

"Ha, yes, we were, but the car wouldn't start. Looks like water's got inside the electrics; we had torrential rain last night. I've got someone coming to have a look at it shortly."

"Well, look, I wonder if you can hang around for another day? I'm sure the local police will want to talk to you."

"Hmm, that's not going to go down too well. Jo's desperate to get back."

"Ok, hold fire for the moment, I'll get onto my contact in Truro and see what he says. Actually, thinking about it, this might just give us the excuse we need to seize his computers. In any event, with what you've just told me, they will certainly have cause to interview Deakin. I'll call you back when I've spoken to them."

Liam dropped the call and went back into the cottage.

Jo was in the kitchen washing some dishes.

"I've just spoken to my contact in MI5 and told him about April. He says the local police will want to interview us and we need to stick around."

"Jeezus, no! They can talk to us in London." Jo's frustration was boiling over.

"Well, at the moment the car won't start so it's academic."

"I thought you said someone was coming to fix it."

"Yes, but by the time it's fixed, it's going to be mid-afternoon and I'm not keen on doing the journey in the rush hour; the M25 will be a nightmare."

"Fuck!" said Jo.

"Yes, I know, but one more night's not going to make too much difference."

"What, after last night!? And now April's dead! The sooner we get out of here, the better, who knows what'll happen next?"

"Look, I understand; I'm not enamoured with the idea either, but there's nothing much we can do until we get the car fixed. Let's wait till Andy rings back and see what he says."

The children were restless. Farrah hadn't heard from Lily since yesterday and Zack was just being annoying due to the sheer boredom.

"I'll take the kids down to the harbour for a walk. We can call in the store and get them some chocolate or something; they're bored silly," said Jo.

Liam had left his phone connected and half an hour later, the ring tone sounded.

"Hello, is that Liam... Liam Drake?"

"Yes, that's correct."

"This is Inspector Tom Travis, Devon and Cornwall Constabulary, I believe you may have some information regarding April Thornton."

"Yes, that's correct."

"Can you just tell me over the phone for the moment? We can take a statement from you later."

Liam explained the arrangement made with April and their concern when she didn't show.

"She said she was going to see Christopher Deakin; she uses his internet connection. It's a fairly regular arrangement. She was due to meet us after that, but she didn't arrive. Then of course, we heard the explosion."

"I see. Do you know of any reason why Mr Deakin would want to harm Mrs Thornton?"

"Well, I do have a theory. I take it you've spoken to Andy Tennant at Thames House."

"Yes, we have been in touch."

"Then you are aware that they have been monitoring Deakin?"

"Yes, he has shared that information."

"I think Deakin believed that April was connected with the Secret Service. I'm pretty sure that was why the Walton's were murdered."

"Yes, that is a line of enquiry."

"Out of interest, Tennant mentioned Deakin was interviewed regarding the Walton murder? What was the outcome? If you can tell me."

"Yes, he was a person of interest, but we had no evidence to charge him. He had a solid alibi for the night of the murder. He was in a meeting with some of the fishermen and they vouched for him. Putting together some petition or other about crab quotas, apparently."

"What about his assistant, Nathan?"

"Nathan?"

"Yes, I don't know his surname, but he seems to be hanging out at the house on a regular basis. April said he was his assistant."

"Really? Now that's very helpful. I don't think we were aware of this individual. He's not come to our attention."

"Hmm, well, I reckon Deakin would have covered his tracks. It's more than possible he has someone else to do his dirty work."

"Yes, that is a possibility. Thanks, Liam. I've made a note."

"Is there anything else you need from me?"

"No, not for the moment. How long are you staying in Cornwall for?" asked the Inspector.

"We were due to leave today, but I've had an issue with the car so it looks like it will be tomorrow now."

"Ok, well, I know how to contact you if I need you. I'll ring you on this number."

"Yes, no problem."

It was gone one-thirty by the time Jo returned with the children.

"I've spoken to the police," said Liam as Jo walked in. The children ran upstairs.

"What did they say?"

"Well, I told them about April going to see Deakin and not returning as she planned."

"What's happening?"

"He's what they call 'a person of interest', so they'll be looking to find more evidence that might connect him to April. I also mentioned that Nathan fellow. They weren't aware of him, apparently."

"So, does that mean we can go?"

"He said he would call me again if he needs us."

"That's good. We can leave as soon as the car's fixed. Has he been yet, the mechanic?"

"No, he hasn't." Liam checked his watch. "He said lunchtime."

"Hmm, ok, I'll get some lunch. I got some bread and a few bits from the store. Oh, and I got some change for the meter."

"That's great. I don't know what's happened to the mechanic. I don't have his number, so I've no way of contacting him."

As time ticked by, Jo was getting more and more frustrated at not being able to leave. She was continually up and down, looking out of the window, unable to settle.

It was nearer four o'clock before there was a knock on the door. Liam looked out and could see the top of a van.

"It looks like the mechanic," he said, as Jo came out from the kitchen.

Liam opened the door.

A twenty-something, fresh-faced young man in dark blue overalls stood in front of him.

"Hello... Is it Liam?"

"Yes."

"Pete Melgrove, I understand you've got a problem with your car."

"Oh, yes, thanks for coming. It wouldn't start this morning. I think water's got inside from the storm last night."

"Aye, ok, let's go and have a look. I'm sorry for being late only they closed the top road. There'd been an incident it said. There was a sign up, so I went onto another job. I didn't have your number to let you know. It's open now, but there's a police wagon up on the top."

"Well, I'm very grateful you made it. Let me get my keys."

Liam retrieved the fob and accompanied the mechanic to the Volvo which was still parked with its bonnet up.

"Hey, the XC90... great car. I've not known any problems with these." Pete looked into the engine and started checking for possible causes.

"Would you like a drink?" said Liam.

"Aye, if it's no bother, a tea would be nice, white, two sugars."

Liam left the mechanic and walked back inside.

"How long is he going to be?" asked Jo, anxiously.

"I have no idea; he's only just arrived. It depends on what's wrong. Can you make him a cup of tea, white, two sugars? I'll go and check how he's getting on."

Jo was not happy and her demeanour reflected it as she stormed into the kitchen.

Back at the car, Pete, the mechanic, was checking the various connections.

"I think I've found the problem for you. Your central electronic module's become waterlogged. That's the kit responsible for communication between all other electronics, including the ignition," he explained. "Probably caused by the storm."

Liam was lost.

"Can you fix it?"

"Well, I certainly can't replace the central electronic module. That's a big job an'll need to be a Volvo garage with the right tools, but I'll try and dry it off and see if that works, but my worry is, it may cut out again."

Jo walked up the path holding two mugs.

"Hi," said Jo. "Here's your tea. How is it? Can it be fixed?"

Pete looked up from the car's innards and accepted the mug from Jo.

"Ta. I was just telling your husband; it's water got into the electrics. I'm going to try and dry it out."

"How long will it take?"

"Hmm, difficult to say. Depends on if I can get it dry enough. I've got some spray which may sort it."

"Oh, ok, we better let you get on," said Jo.

She indicated with a nod of her head to Liam to return to the cottage. Liam took the mug and followed Jo.

Half an hour later, there was the sound of an engine running from outside. Liam looked at Jo.

"Sounds like he's got it going," said Liam and got up and went outside.

"That's a great sound, Pete," said Liam, hearing the gentle purr of the Volvo.

"Aye, it should be alright. You might want to give it a short run just to make sure it doesn't cut out. All the systems are working properly; they seem ok."

"Oh, I can't thank you enough. How much do I owe you?"

"Let's call it a hundred; that should cover it."

"Yes, ok, give me a minute. I'll see if we've got the cash."

"Aye, that'll be best," said the mechanic.

Liam went back to the cottage and returned a few minutes later holding six twenty-pound notes.

The car was still running.

"Thanks so much. There's a bit extra for a drink."

"That's very kind of you, much appreciated."

The mechanic cleaned off his hands with a rag and passed the empty mug to Liam. There was oil around the handle.

"Thanks for the tea. I'll let you have my mobile number. Call me if you have any more problems." He handed Liam a business card.

"Thanks Pete, much appreciated."

Liam watched as the mechanic got into his van and drove away.

Liam walked back inside. "The car seems to be working, but he suggested I give it a short run to make sure it's ok."

"Does that mean we can leave?" asked Jo.

"Look, it's gone five o'clock; I don't want to run the risk of breaking down on the motorway at night. Let's leave first thing in the morning. We can pack the bags tonight and put them in the car ready. We can sleep with the kids again if you prefer."

Jo was still not pleased but reluctantly accepted the logic.

"First thing, then, no excuses."

"No excuses, as soon as we're ready, we're out of here," replied Liam.

"And I shan't be sorry about that. Ok, go and do what you need to do; I'll see to the kids and get some dinner on."

Liam left the cottage and took the Volvo around the village and back again. He went as far as the headland and turned. All the instruments on the car seemed to be functioning fine and the engine was running as normal. He stopped for a moment at the entrance to the undercliff. He could see the shell of April's car at the foot of the precipice.

There was still a forensic police van parked at the entrance to the footpath and in the distance, three officers in white overalls and masks, continuing their investigations. Liam was filled with sadness; he had grown very fond of April.

It was gone midnight when Nathan left Deakin's house carrying the remainder of the petrol in the plastic can. It was pitch dark. The approaching low pressure system was hammering the village with strong winds. Light debris was being blown around as he walked down the cinder track.

He was dressed for the job in a dark hoody and kept to the margins of the path in the remote chance that anyone was awake. All the houses were in darkness, his eyes now in night-vision mode. He reached the church and skirted the wall before crossing the road to Pendle Cottage.

He reached the front door and set about his task. Given the construction of the property, which was primarily wood and clay, he was confident that with just a little encouragement, the cottage would readily ignite.

The front door was old and latch-opening, but a more substantial lock had been added later. Breaking in through the door was not going to be an option. Another addition had been a letter-box, in the middle about halfway down.

He thought for a moment; he had an idea. He lifted the plastic can and shook it, pushed open the letter-box flap, inserted the nozzle, and started pouring the petrol through. He could hear it splashing on the floor the other side of the door. He emptied the petrol container.

Nathan took out a box of matches from his pocket and struck one, waited for it to take hold, then dropped it through the letterbox. There was the familiar whooshing sound as the petrol caught fire. Flames started lapping under the door. He had a quick glance through the window, the curtains were now ablaze. The rest would soon follow.

Pleased with his work, Nathan walked around the side of the house. He recalled his earlier visit to the cottage and would use the same escape route. He passed the kitchen and headed up the garden path towards the sycamore tree, turned left past the old privy, and reached the wall of the graveyard.

He leapt over with ease, then stopped; something was wrong. He dropped the petrol can.

From nowhere, he was surrounded by fog, thick, penetrative fog; visibility was down to almost nothing. The temperature had dropped noticeably.

He could hear strange noises coming from beyond the mist. A voice in an unfamiliar tongue, a shriek of a banshee, it's death warning rising above the host of garbled whispers.

"Who's there?" said Nathan, backing slowly from the cacophony. The spirits were united in force.

He could make out the gravel under his feet and inched slowly along the track around the graveyard towards the style which would take him to the footpath and the route back to the Squire's house.

He was under the large oak which dominated the corner of the cemetery. The fog was even thicker. Without warning, Nathan was blown off his feet by an unseen force. He was not one to be frightened, but this was something beyond his comprehension and it did scare him.

He was lay on the dark earth surrounded by a scattering of old decaying acorns. He tried to get up but was pinned to the ground as if weighted by a heavy object. He wrestled with the invisible power, but it was hopeless; he was lay prostrate with his arms and legs spread out in the sign of the cross.

He might have heard the crack of a heavy branch, its rustling through the canopy as gravity propelled it downwards.

The broken end of the branch was sharp and pointed; shards

of broken wood and bark showered down on Nathan before the impact. The weight of the broken bower, penetrated his clothes, then his flesh, then his stomach. His intestines spilled out like spaghetti before the branch impaled him to the earth. His legs writhed in pain.

He looked down and could see the tree limb protruding from his stomach. Then shock took over.

The waling continued.

A Spanish voice penetrated the caterwauling. Francisco López de Grijalva Cortes announced his presence. A mark appeared on the trunk of the oak tree. It looked as if it had been made with a Spanish rapier... the letter 'C'.

Then it was gone. The fog seemed to just evaporate in a second. The graveyard was deathly quiet. Deakin's odd job man was still moving; his hand tried to reach the branch but was well short. The pool of blood soaked into the earth and would provide nutrients for the acorns. Seeds would turn into fledgling trees.

There was a long scream, and then the silence returned.

Back in the cottage the front of the house was now well-alight and the flames were heading upwards towards the ceiling. The settee had caught fire and was giving off black putrid smoke.

In the master bedroom, Farrah stirred, then sat up. "You must get out. You must get out."

Jo turned over and could see Farrah sat up. Farrah turned her head and repeated the warning. "You must leave; you are in danger." It was Lily's voice.

Jo could smell smoke. Then she realised.

"Liam we're on fire!" she shouted at the top of her voice.

She leapt out of bed, slipped on her jeans and a tee shirt and walked to the landing. She could see thick black smoke coming from the lounge. The flickering of flames cast shadows on the stairs.

At that moment, Liam came out from Zack's bedroom and immediately coughed as the smoke penetrated his airways. Instinctively, he put his hands to his mouth. He rushed back into the room and quickly dressed.

"Ok, get the kids up; I'll go and check and see what's happening."

He walked halfway down the stairs and stopped. The whole of the front of the lounge was on fire.

He rushed back upstairs.

"Quick, grab some towels; we only have seconds."

Jo rushed to the bathroom and collected the towels from the side of the bath.

Jo picked up Farrah. Zack was holding Jo's hand but he was very drowsy.

"Right, everyone, I'm going to put a towel over your head. You need to hold your breath; we're going to head for the kitchen," instructed Liam.

Liam threw a towel over Jo and Farrah. He picked up Zack and covered himself and his son.

"Right, hold your breath and don't look."

Liam led the way and reached the lounge. The settee was now well-ablaze and flames were starting to move along the ceiling. Liam edged along the wall opposite the front door until he reached the kitchen door; it was closed. He quickly grabbed the handle and pulled it open, then stood to one side to allow Jo and Farrah to pass through. He was about to join them when he spotted his laptop on the table. He lowered Zack to the floor and ushered him in to the kitchen, then leaned forward with his hands protecting his face and made a grab for his computer. He managed to hang onto it and was about to enter the kitchen when part of the ceiling collapsed.

He jumped forward just in time and closed the door, joining Jo and the children.

Liam looked at Jo. "Right, the door will keep out the smoke for a while; let's get out of here. He turned the handle on the kitchen door and pulled. Nothing; it was jammed solid.

Flames were now licking around the side of the cottage, clearly visible from the kitchen window. Smoke was beginning to pour under the lounge door into the kitchen. Zack was coughing; Jo was bent forward, staying low.

Liam pulled the external door again. "I can't move it; it's stuck."

He was beginning to panic, frantically tugging at the handle.

Farrah looked at the door. It was Lily's voice again. The words were indecipherable; it sounded like a short chant.

The door suddenly flew open and a cold wind blew into the kitchen. The family ran out into the garden.

Liam looked up. The thatch at the front of the cottage was now on fire with flames shooting twenty feet or more into the air. All you could hear was the crackle of burning.

"I hope the swallows will be alright," said Farrah sleepily, looking up at the nest.

Jo was holding her as they walked up the garden path, well away from the cottage. They stopped for a moment to recover their breath. Liam was coughing from smoke inhalation, bent over clutching his knees.

From the back of the house, the conflagration looked frightening as the cottage finally gave in to the flames. Burning embers were rising thirty or forty feet into the night air, fanned by the strong winds.

"How are we going to get to the car? We can't go around the side path?" said Jo.

"It will have to be the graveyard. We can go through the main entrance. Can you look after Far? I'll see to Zack."

Jo was now carrying Farrah who seemed have gone back to sleep, clutching her elephant.

Liam held Zack's hand. He was still in his pyjamas and very sleepy; he coughed again. The temperature had dropped in the evening air and Liam wrapped the towel around him to keep him warm.

Jo and Farrah followed Liam until they reached the wall where they could access the graveyard. Liam climbed over, still holding his laptop. He placed it on the ground.

"Pass Far." Jo handed her to Liam. "Now you, Zack." Jo went to pick him up.

"I can do it; I can do it," he remonstrated, and climbed up onto the wall. Liam helped him down and then Jo joined them.

He picked up Zack, wrapped the towel around him, then bent down and retrieved his laptop.

"This way," said Liam.

The wind rustled through the trees making weird whistling noises; branches swayed in the gale, groaning at the pressures being placed on them. It seemed the whole canopy was in motion.

The family walked along the rows of headstones towards the front entrance of the cemetery. Any fear Liam felt had been overtaken by the need to survive.

Liam stopped for a moment. He thought he could hear a shout; actually, it was more a cry for help. It was coming from the far end, by the old oak tree. He was not about to investigate it.

The family made their way through the entrance of the graveyard and walked down Cemetery Road, then back up Forest Lane towards the cottage.

The inferno could be seen for miles and, as they approached the cul-de-sac, they could see someone outside the cottage gate, next to the Volvo. Other villagers were making their way to see what was happening.

"Oh, thank Jesus you're safe," said the man as the family approached.

"Oh, hello, vicar. Yes, we managed to get out just in time."

"I've sent the verger to call for the fire brigade, although I think it will be sometime before they get here. We saw the flames from our window and came to investigate."

"Oh, thank you, I don't think I'll get a phone signal."

There was now a small gathering, ten or fifteen people watching, as the roof gave way dropping burning thatch into the heart of the fire, and sending more flames and embers high into the night's sky, blown by the wind.

"How did it start?" said Reverend Slaughter.

"I have no idea. I expect the fire brigade will investigate. Luckily, my wife woke up, and we were able to escape."

"I am so pleased, but you know." He paused for a moment. "I'm not unhappy to see the end of the cottage. It's been an unhappy dwelling for so long. Maybe it can have a new start."

Just then, strange wailing noises could be heard from the flames then slowly disappeared.

The reverend turned to Liam. "The spirits are leaving."

Jo was still carrying Farrah; Zack was holding her hand.

"What are we going to do?" asked Jo.

"Well, I guess we could head back home. I'll say this, I'm glad we decided to pack the car at least we didn't lose much."

"No, no, no, you don't want to be driving all that way this

time of night. You can stay with me; I have the room," said the Vicar.

Liam looked at Jo, there was some reluctance, but it did make sense.

"Yes, thank you; that's very kind of you," said Jo, just as the verger arrived.

"I've called the fire brigade, Reverend, about half an hour, they reckon."

"Oh, thank you, verger. I wonder if you could show Mr Drake and his family back to the rectory. I've said they could stop with us this evening?"

"Why of course."

"Actually, I think I'd better stay until the fire brigade arrive," said Liam. He turned to Jo. "You go with the verger and take the children. I'll bring the suitcases as soon as things are done here."

"I'll stay with you," said the vicar.

Jo followed the verger, still carrying Farrah, with Zack holding her hand.

"Lovely family, Mr Drake, lovely family," said the vicar.

It was nearer forty minutes before the fire engine arrived. There was little left of the cottage, just the frame of the front door and a pile of burning ashes and rubble.

The lead fire officer approached Liam who described what had happened. Minutes later the crews were dowsing down what remained of Pendle Cottage.

Chapter Nineteen

Eight-thirty, and the Drake family were finishing their breakfast at the rectory. The atmosphere was down and gloomy; the shock of last night's narrow escape still raw. Reverend Slaughter was dressed in a smoking jacket over white shirt and trousers. Mrs Darwin, his housekeeper, had arrived early to help with the catering.

"Would you like any more toast?" asked the vicar.

"Not for me," said Liam.

"Yes, please," said Zack. It had been a while since they had enjoyed a 'full-English'.

Farrah was quiet and had left most of her scrambled egg.

"Come on Poppet, you must eat something, we've got a long journey," said Jo, putting her hand on Farrah's forehead as if checking her temperature.

"I want to play with Lily."

"I know you do, Poppet, but I think she'll be with her family now."

"Yes, I know, Mom, but I miss her."

"When we get home, you'll be able to see your friends again."

"Most of them will be away."

"I'm sure, you'll be fine, Poppet."

"Is there any news about April, Reverend?" asked Liam as he sipped his tea.

"I understand the police are treating it as murder. I've been in touch with Mrs Thornton's brother in Lichfield and he's coming down tomorrow."

"I didn't know she had a brother."

"I don't think they were close."

"Do you know when the funeral will be?"

"No, not yet, they're still carrying out their forensic investigations, but I just hope they find the perpetrator."

"Are there any suspects?"

"The police haven't said anything. There were one or two journalists late yesterday in the pub asking questions, according to Clemmo. It'll be all over the news this morning. He rang me last night to let me know."

"What about the cottage? What will happen?"

"Well, from what the fire officers were saying last night, there will be further investigations today to try and find out what started it."

Liam decided not to reveal his thoughts. He was certain it had been deliberate; there was no other explanation, but he had no desire to become embroiled in anything that would delay their departure.

Six a.m. at the Squire's house, Christopher Deakin got up from the breakfast bar in the kitchen and looked out across the back garden to the boundary wall. It was not the first time. The branches of the stricken beech tree were still visible. His assistant had not returned and he was concerned for his safety.

Earlier, he had seen the glow of the fire from his bedroom window and knew straightaway that it was Nathan's handiwork.

He decided to return to his office and check the overnight markets.

He logged into the FCX Platform and stared at the screen; he couldn't believe his eyes. 'Dealing suspended'.

Deakin began to panic. He searched for the financial news on CNN, and there it was, in banner headlines, 'Cryptocurrency giant collapses'. He read the narrative.

'*It was confirmed last night that FCX, one of the newest*

of the cryptocurrency platforms, has gone into receivership leaving millions of investors out of pocket.

As global investigators and regulators prepare to delve deeper into the collapse of this now-defunct crypto empire, others in the digital-asset industry are keen to show that they have everything in order. But once authorities are done with the most immediate problem that FCX presents — including possible criminal behavior — their next action will likely be to crack down on bad habits that are rife throughout the sector.

Lacklustre risk management, slippery governance and incomplete disclosures can be found across crypto, a direct result of it still being a young industry with a lot of freedom and not enough scrutiny.

While not always illegal, these things would be frowned upon in more traditional sectors that have been subject to longstanding oversight by regulators. They also include opaque financial disclosures, a complex web of offshore entities, or suspiciously close relationships with sister companies — all things found in yesterday's FCX bankruptcy filing.'

Deakin sat there, not moving, considering the implications. As well as a significant amount of his own money and the Rainsford investments, there were other less-scrupulous clients who would be asking questions. Then there were the villagers to whom he had been providing financial advice; most of them, including the fishermen, Ada Wilkins, Mrs Trevelyan at the store, and the pub landlord, entrusting their life savings to his investment plans. But they were the least of his worries.

Time was on his side, at least; he couldn't imagine any of his investors reading the financial papers.

Thoughts of his missing assistant had gone from his head.

His immediate concern was one of his own survival.

He went to his desk drawer and took out his passport, then into the bedroom and started packing a few clothes. One of his overseas investments, a property in Cyprus, would be his first destination.

He was sure that there were direct flights from Bristol or Exeter. He logged onto one of the budget airline's website and checked. There were none from Exeter but a nine-thirty flight from Bristol. He had missed today's but he would head out that way and stay in a nearby hotel.

He made a coffee and was in the process of booking a flight when the buzzer to the front-gate intercom sounded.

He went to the monitor and froze. A uniformed police officer, accompanied by two others with dogs. There was a van behind them.

He pressed the intercom button. "Hello."

"Christopher Deakin?"

"Yes."

"Open the gate, Inspector Travis, Devon and Cornwall Constabulary."

The gate slowly swung open and the police officers walked through followed by the van.

Nine-thirty, Mrs Trevelyan walked through the gates of the cemetery carrying a small wreath of posies. It was another half an hour before she would open the store; just enough time to complete her task. She walked along the line of old gravestones until she reached the final resting place of her beloved husband. She cleared away the dead flowers, left on her previous visit. She would drop them in the green recycling bin by the entrance on the way back.

She placed the fresh posies in front of the gravestone and said a quiet prayer. Today would have been their wedding anniversary, fifty-five years; it seemed like only yesterday.

She picked up the dead flowers and was about to walk back to the entrance when she saw what looked like a pile of old rags under the large oak tree with a branch sticking out of it. Out of curiosity she walked towards it; then stopped in her tracks. "Oh dear Lord," she said, and put her hand to her mouth. She dropped the dead blooms.

She turned and quickly walked back towards the entrance. She hurried up to the front door of the first cottage and knocked frantically.

The door was opened by an elderly gentleman. "Mrs Trevelyan? What on earth's the matter?"

Liam and the family walked out of the rectory carrying their suitcases, having said a grateful farewell to their host.

"I've got your number; I'll call you when I have the date for Mrs Thornton's funeral," said Reverend Slaughter as they shook hands.

It was a bright morning, cloudy with a stiff breeze. There was little conversation as they walked past the church. Liam noticed a crow perched on the top of the lynchgate in the boundary wall. It gave a haunting 'caw' as they walked past, then flew off into the forest.

The Volvo was parked at the end of the garden path which until a few hours ago led to the front door of a fairy-tale cottage; one that could have blessed the cover of any biscuit tin.

The family stood and looked at the pile of ashes and charred beams that was all that was left of the sixteenth century dwelling. What tales could it tell? Only the spirits knew.

There was police tape surrounding the debris although

Liam had no intention of venturing beyond the boundaries.

"Do you have the car keys?" asked Jo, anxiously.

"Yes, in my pocket. Come on guys, let's get on board and go home," said Liam.

He pulled his key fob out of the pocket of his jeans and aimed it at the Volvo. There was a click and flash of indicators. Liam opened the boot and started loading the suitcases.

Farrah was still clutching her cuddly elephant. She looked up at Jo.

"I miss Lily."

"I know you do, Poppet, but it's time to say goodbye."

"Bye, Lily. I love you," said Farrah towards the ashes, and climbed into the back. Zack did the same.

Jo got in the passenger side and turned to Liam. "I'm so glad we loaded the car last night; we would have lost everything."

"Yes, we were very lucky, although I'll need to get some more toiletries when we get back; I wasn't able to shave." He stroked his chin.

She turned to the children in the back. "Make sure you're belted in. Do you have your game consoles?"

"Yes," said Zack.

Liam pressed the starter and held his breath; the Volvo burst into life. The dashboard came alive with its various instruments and warning lights. There was still no Sat-Nav. He took a moment to check.

"Looks like we're good to go."

He took one last look at the remains of the cottage and pulled away, along the cul-de-sac, then down to the promenade. Despite everything, there was a sadness as they passed the pub and the entrance to the undercliff. The remains of April's car was still there.

Liam started to feel anxious as they drove up the steep hill out of the village. The 'For Sale' notice was still in place outside Mrs Wilkins' cottage.

"I wonder if anyone will buy it," said Jo as they went by.

"A second home, you watch," said Liam.

"Yes, you could be right. It's such a shame; it's a lovely part of the world."

He glanced at the shrine on the right-hand side. It was looking overgrown.

"Do you think anyone will look after the shrine," said Jo.

"Hmm, I wouldn't think so," said Liam.

"The girls are with their Mom," said Farrah, looking up from her game. Jo Looked at Liam.

The Volvo entered the forest, just another mile or so to the main road. There was no sign of fog.

A few minutes later, they were through. Liam indicated right and waited for a gap in the busy holiday traffic.

A few minutes later, as they made their way towards the dual carriageway trunk road, Zack looked up from his phone. "Are we nearly there yet?"

Jo looked at Liam and for the first time in a while, laughed.

Two days later, the family had settled back into their London home. Jo was up to her eyes in housework and washing. Liam was 'working from home'. Since the Rainsford trial, he was in big demand. Zack was glad to be back with his friends. Farrah, though, was withdrawn and morose. Jo was concerned that the trauma of the previous two weeks had affected her mental health and was considering counselling. Liam was less worried. "She's missing Lily; she'll soon get over it."

A call came through to his mobile.

"Liam? It's Andy... Thames House, just wanted to give you an update. Did you get back ok?"

"Hi, Andy. Yes thanks, long journey but safe, thanks. So what's the latest?"

"Some good news; Deakin's been taken into custody, arrested for possible money laundering and accessory to murder; they've got his computer equipment."

"That is good news. What about the murders?"

"Well, there is some news here too. They found the body of his assistant."

"What, that Nathan chap?"

"Yeah, he was found in the graveyard. Apparently he'd been impaled by a falling branch. A million to one chance, they were saying. They did find a petrol can a short distance away from his body. He's being linked with the Walton murders and April Thornton, as well as the fire at the cottage."

"I see, so what will happen now?"

"Well, Deakin's been remanded in custody for three weeks. Five have closed the file; it will be a police matter now."

"Oh, well thanks for keeping me updated. Let me know if you get any more news."

"Sure thing, and thanks again for your help. Glad you're all ok."

A few days later, Liam received another call.

"Hello, is that Mr Drake? It's the Reverend Slaughter from Polgissy."

The mention of the name unnerved Liam.

"Oh, hello Reverend, how is everything?"

"Oh, you know, slowly getting back to some kind of normality. We've had more journalists asking questions about the Squire. The police have finished at the cottage, but I'm not sure what will happen. It looks very strange, just a large space where it used to be."

"Yes, I expect it does."

"Look, I won't keep you; I know you're probably busy. I just wanted to let you know about Mrs Thornton's funeral; I said I would."

"Ah yes, of course, thank you."

"It's a week on Friday at two o'clock. I'm sure I can find you some accommodation if you wanted to attend."

"Oh, thank you for letting me know; that's good of you. I'll need to speak to my wife. I'll phone you back in the next couple of days and let you know if we intend to come."

Jo had taken some physio appointments and was out at her surgery.

Liam was considering the Reverend Slaughter's message. He had reservations whether to go to the funeral. Polgissy conjured up some bad memories. The very mention of the name had him feeling uneasy.

On her return from work, Liam confronted Jo with the news.

"I had a call from Reverend Slaughter earlier; April's funeral's a week on Friday."

She looked at him with an expression of concern. "What are you going to do?"

"I'm not sure. I'm torn if I'm honest."

"Well, I'm certainly not exposing Far to that place again."

"No, no, of course not." Liam looked down, deep in thought. "Actually, you're right; I don't think I could face another drive down there anytime soon."

"You could always go on the train."

Liam wrestled with this option; part of him felt an

obligation. "No, to be honest, I'm up to my eyes in it at the moment. I'll ring the vicar in the morning and let him know."

Later that evening, Liam was in Farrah's room reading a story before she went to sleep. He noticed her eyes slowly closing as he finished the story. He shut the book and went to switch off the bedside light.

Suddenly, he became aware of a drop in temperature. He rubbed his arms which were covered in goosebumps.

Then a child's voice.

"Hello, have you seen my daddy?"

Epilogue

Three weeks later, Christopher Deakin was back in his house. With the help of a top lawyer, he had been released on conditional bail after lengthy questioning. The police could find no conclusive evidence to link him with any of the murders. The investigation into possible money laundering was ongoing. All his computer equipment had been impounded. He was tagged and restricted to his residence. This left him with a problem. He'd heard in prison that there was a contract out on him. The Rainsfords had lost all the money they had invested through Deakin and were bent on retribution. They weren't the only investor after him.

It was midnight. Deakin had set the various alarms and retired to bed. His own bed, a welcome change from the prison bunk he had endured since his arrest.

He was trying to sleep when he thought he heard strange noises from outside. It sounded like whispers. He couldn't make it out; the voices didn't sound human.

His worst fears... a hit squad, it had to be.

He got out of bed and crawled across the bedroom to the wardrobe. He opened the door and the automatic light illuminated the inside.

Despite the extensive search by police and their forensic colleagues, they had not found Deakin's secret panel. He pulled back the skirting board and reached inside. The Glock pistol was still in its usual place. It was there for this very eventuality. He checked it was loaded.

He slipped on a pair of jeans, put the gun in his back pocket, and made his way downstairs. He couldn't see anyone, but the sounds were definitely coming from the back of the house.

He cowered down and crept into the kitchen, then slowly moved forward to the French windows that led to the garden. The whispers were louder. There was more than one person. He crawled across the kitchen floor and peered outside. He couldn't see anyone, just a white mist. He slowly turned the key in the door and unlocked it, then removed the pistol from his jeans.

He gently pulled the door open a couple of inches, then wider. There was no-one there; the voices were lost in the fog.

He edged along the patio with his back to the kitchen wall; his gun primed ready for use. He could still hear it. His eyes became accustomed to the lack of light; he squinted into the gloom, but could not make out anything, just strange, unrecognisable sounds.

Then another noise, a louder noise that turned into a long piercing scream. No, not a scream exactly, more a manic laugh. It was followed by a deep rumble, almost like an express train.

He stooped down and looked behind him, then swept the area, just the mist. Then without warning, he could make out a shape. A black morass was rushing towards him, rolling through the fog, blocking out the night.

He could see it, but do nothing, as a huge wall of earth, boulders, mud, and water, was on him, crushing everything in its path. Deakin tried to cover his face but it was hopeless as the dark slime enveloped him. The house crumbled behind him like a pack of cards; his beloved Porsche flattened in its garage out of all recognition.

Newspapers the next day were comparing the Polgissy landslip with that of Aberfan, all those years earlier, except in this case there was only one fatality. It appeared Deakin's house had miraculously saved the rest of the village by acting as a barrier. The avalanche had come to rest against the front boundary wall; it was almost as if it had been singled out. Even the old rectory next door had escaped damage.

There was something else. Among the debris, investigators found numerous human bones.

Polgissy was again the centre of attention as journalists and archaeologists flocked to the village. Clem at the pub had never been so busy.

"It was a disaster waiting to happen," said an 'expert' on the morning news broadcast as drone cameras captured the scene of devastation. It appeared the whole of the hill above the house had fallen away and slid towards the village. The expert continued his assessment in grave tones. "Saturated, porous, clay ground, and unstable rock formations, all contributed. Global warming can't be ruled out."

There was speculation about the origin of the bones and skeletons that had been recovered from the site. Carbon dating suggested they were from the Middle Ages; a plague pit was the conclusion.

The villagers knew the true cause of the tragedy.

"It was a Bucca," claimed Jack in the pub that evening.

THE END

Alan Reynolds

Following a successful career in Banking, award winning author Alan Reynolds established his own training company in 2002 and has successfully managed projects across a wide range of businesses. This experience has led to an interest in psychology and human behaviour through watching interactions, studying responses and research. Leadership has also featured strongly in his training portfolios and the knowledge gained has helped build the strong characters in his books.

Alan's interest in writing started as a hobby but after completing his first novel in just three weeks, the favourable reviews he received encouraged him to take up a new career. The inspiration for this award-winning author come from real life facts which he weaves seamlessly into fast-paced, page-turning works of fiction.

Milton Keynes UK
Ingram Content Group UK Ltd.
UKHW040944281123
433414UK00004B/187

9 781914 560804